Affliction

RIVER SAVAGE

©2014

Affliction is a work of fiction. All characters, organizations and events portrayed in this novel are either products of the author's imagination or used fictitiously.

All rights reserved. In accordance with the U.S. Copyright Act of 1976, the scanning, uploading and sharing of any part of this book without the permission of the publisher is unlawful piracy and theft of the author's intellectual property. Thank you for your support of the author's rights.

First edition: November 2014

Edited by Becky Johnson, Hot Tree Editing
Cover design ©: Louisa Maggio at LM Creations
Image: Mofatt Photography
Model: Nick Potato
Formatting by Max Henry at Max Effect
Information address: riversavageauthor@gmail.com

Prologue

Sy

"Chemotherapy was unsuccessful." His words echo around the small, stuffy office.

Three words.

I never thought three words would once again have the power to destroy me. The room is silent as we take in the devastating news. The clock ticks obnoxiously above us as I force myself not to break down in front of him, in front of Katie.

"What's our next option?" I ask, swallowing past the lump forming in my throat. I reach out to grab Katie's hand. Her cold grip holds onto mine, our fingers intertwining, and in that one moment I feel like the connection of our fingers, our mere touch alone, could get us through anything. Even this.

"The high-dose chemotherapy has destroyed the bone marrow.

With both aggressive treatments now unsuccessful we need to prepare ourselves that a stem cell transplant is our last hope," he explains as Katie's first sob tears from her throat. "My concern is finding a match in our time frame. Ideally, with a stem cell transplant, the best chance is a sibling donor. Since we don't have that option, we broaden the search. I want to discuss the possibility of contacting Keira's biological father before we move to anonymous donors. The chances of him matching are small, but as you both came back negative, we should try every avenue."

"What?" The question gets stuck in my throat as my world spins out of control. "You must be confused." I look from the doctor to my wife, thinking it's some kind of sick joke.

"Oh God." Katie draws in a sharp breath and something in me clicks.

"Katie?" I ask, pulling on her now lax hand.

"I'm sorry," Dr. Parks cuts me off, looking between both of us, his eyes growing wide as he puts something together. "I was under the assumption that you knew Keira isn't your child." He shifts awkwardly, looking between us.

"Sylas, I'm so sorry. This is not how I meant to tell you." Katie pulls out of my grasp, moving away from me.

"What the fuck is going on, Katie?"

"Oh, God, don't hate me," she cries, rocking back and forth, holding herself.

Protecting herself.

"Hate you?" I search her face, still not sure my brain has caught up. "What are you saying?" I ask again, frantic as realization slowly creeps in.

"Keira isn't yours," she says, barely above a whisper, but the words blare into my ears like someone just announced it over the PA system. "Sy." She reaches out, but my body jerks away, her words running through me, breaking through the hardness I've erected since our daughter became ill.

"No," I argue, not believing what's coming out of her mouth. It's not true. I've been there every step of the way. From the first sonogram, to holding her hand as doctors figured out what was wrong with her.

This can't be real.

"I'm sorry, Sy. You have to believe me. I never meant to lie to you. I just couldn't bring myself to tell you." She frantically tries to reach for me. I move to the door, the stuffy oncologist's office closing in on me. I look at the woman who has had my heart from the moment she became mine. I want to scream and shake it out of her to admit she is lying, but I don't. I feel lost. Broken. My daughter lies dying in this hospital and my wife just told me she isn't even mine.

Three words.

What is it with three words?

Acute Myelogenous Leukemia.

Chemotherapy wasn't successful.

Keira isn't yours.

1

Sy

seven years later

HAVE YOU EVER LOOKED AT A STRANGER AND FELT YOURself going back to another time in your life? A time you just want to completely forget. It was her laugh that grabbed my attention. The moment she walked through the door, I was shot back to the first time I met Katie. It was like déjà vu. Not an 'I've done this or been here before' type, but my reaction as I look at the smoking hot blonde who just came in, is something I have only ever felt one other time in my life. A time I try every day to keep blocked from my memory. It was as if God was playing some sick, twisted joke on me.

"What a ball of fucking sunshine." Her sultry voice is projected to me instead of her friend. I've already turned her down for a tattoo, but she just won't give up. If it wasn't for the fact the woman she walked in with was the same woman who's had my Prez's head messed up since last week, I would have told them to leave ten minutes ago. Looking at her now, I remember seeing her the first night at Fireside Bar when Nix was working double time to get some tail, but I didn't take much notice of her then. I never take much notice anymore—not since Katie. But this fiery blonde has been running her mouth since the moment she stepped in to my store, and for some reason, my mind and my dick won't let it go.

Checking the clock, I count the minutes until my Prez gets his ass down here. I called him as soon as I realized who had walked in, letting him know to get down to Ink Me if he wanted to catch the woman who's been messing with his head for the last couple of weeks. Ever since he was called in for a meeting at his son, Z's, school he's been chasing his tail following the woman around. I know she's been messing with him, and when I made the phone call, I thought I was helping him out, but I'm regretting getting involved. I don't know what the fuck I'm going to do if I have to hear her friend's voice for much longer.

"What crawled up your ass?" The blonde asks when her friend moves away to fill out the release form for body piercing. She leans over the counter, her tits pushed up for all to see. My eyes are drawn to her creamy white skin, so clean, so fucking pure. I want to tell her to shut the fuck up before I find a better use for her mouth, but I can't seem to form a sentence.

"You really are a ball of sunshine. I think I should just call you 'Sunshine' from this point on," she continues, unfazed by my lack of reaction. The more her mouth keeps running, the harder my dick gets.

I keep my expression blank, trying so fucking hard not to respond. I don't want to engage with her, but something tells me this woman isn't about to give up.

"Okay, let's do it." The brunette hands me the form just as Nix walks in.

"Where the fuck are the rest of your clothes?" he barks out, and I now know the asshole is a goner. He's been sulking all week and the boys have been giving him shit every chance they've had. I step back, not really interested in watching Nix hand the woman his balls. I look over and watch the blonde taking in the whole scene. While she's lost in the drama, I'm lost in watching her. *What the fuck?*

"That was so hot," she announces to the shop at some shit Nix just spewed and I can't help the scoff that falls from my lips. She turns and gives me a look of challenge, and then takes up a spot next to her friend.

"Don't be a pig," I hear her say, but I'm not paying attention. I'm too busy checking out her ass. Jesus, there is something about her, some sort of fucked up pull that I don't like one fucking bit. Shaking off the attraction, I force myself to forget it. This woman is not what I need. I need less drama and a woman who isn't going to con me into falling for her just from a few sassy words.

I never used to be this way. Never used to be afraid to open up. But when the woman you love betrays you—leaving you broken and mourning the loss of a child who was never yours—it changes a man. The anger flowing through my veins never leaves. The hurt seeping from my pores never stops, and the pain of losing a child will never leave me, even if the child I loved with everything I had was never mine to begin with.

2

Holly

"WHAT DO YOU MEAN, DESK?" I ASK, LOOKING BETWEEN MY best friend, Kadence, and her new man, Nix. He winks, smirking while she death stares him. I'm not normally a jealous person, but standing and watching the way the man looks at her would make any grown woman jealous. The man is sexy, mixed with a sprinkle of bad news. If I knew the Knights Rebels were this hot up close, I would have crashed one of their parties sooner.

"He doesn't mean anything." Kadence tries to recover, but I can see it in her eyes. Sexy biker daddy and the naughty school teacher played freaky in class.

"You had sex on your desk?" I ask, putting two and two together, wondering how she failed to fill me in on that bit of information. We are best friends, have been since our first day of college. When she walked into orientation looking all serious inocent, I knew we would be the perfect match. She's always been the serious one and I've been the crazy one, but as we stand out the front of Ink Me, ten minutes after Kadence just got her belly pierced, I'm beginning to think Kadence just took serious to a whole new level. I'm actually shocked she went through with it.

We were heading home after a girls' night when I dragged her through the doors of the newest ink shop in Rushford. My only play was to check out the eye candy sitting behind the counter. His dark looks and inked skin were what drew me in, his bad boy attitude was what made me stay. We had no idea the Rebels owned the place or that the bad boy who lured me in is a patched member.

"We didn't have sex," Kadence argues, but I know she's not telling the truth. If she didn't have sex, she did something else nasty.

"Kadence," Nix warns again and I can see it in his eyes, he's losing patience. I've only met Nix Knight one other time and patience is not his strong suit.

"Go," I tell her, giving her the extra push she clearly needs. She might be the bravest and strongest woman I know, but she sure can be clueless with men. If I had a man as sexy as Nix there would be no begging involved.

"Fine," she huffs, walking forward to get on his bike. Nix doesn't waste time. He takes her hand and drags her the rest of the way.

"Sy, make sure Holly gets home," Nix calls out his final command to the man who lured me into the shop in the first place. Sy. The badass biker with a bad attitude has a name. The minute I walked through the doors I thought *this is going to be fun*. Little did I know the ray of sunshine is everything but fun. I try not to look back at him while Kadence fiddles with the strap on her helmet, but I can't control my eyes when they move to him. His stern stare tells me he isn't impressed with his job of getting me safely home, but I don't focus on that. His tattooed arms and neck have my attention, teasing me with what could possibly be hiding under the dark Henley he's wearing tonight. Even if he doesn't seem interested, I can't help myself. I've run over every scenario of how I can get him into my bed.

"I'm sorry, Holly," Kadence calls out, breaking my obvious staring.

"You don't look sorry." I turn back and watch as Nix taps the top of her helmet and picks her up to place her on the back of his bike. She yelps, and then accepts his kiss when he leans forward for one. Their connection is almost sickening. She waves one more time before Nix starts his bike and pulls out, leaving me alone with the cranky biker.

"So, Sunshine." I turn to watch him, using the name I now dedicate to him, "I'm curious. Do you treat everyone like this, or am I just special?" Not answering, his dark grey eyes glare at me, but I'm expecting it. The man hasn't spoken one word to me, ignoring every question I've asked. He blinks once, then twice before he turns and stalks to his bike. Man, this guy is one broody, sexy asshole. It's a crying shame he hasn't taken to my advances. I don't often find myself in these sorts of predicaments, but I have to admit, the thrill of the chase makes for pretty hot foreplay.

"Let's do this," I say, following him and feeling like a fool talking to myself. Maybe he doesn't know anything but asshole talk? He continues to ignore me as he hands me the helmet, and then starts his bike. The ground under my feet shakes as he pulls the throttle back. The loud, deep rumble moves through my body and I can't help the excitement I feel knowing I'm about to get on the back of this sexy man's bike.

Putting the helmet on my head, I fiddle with the strap, but he doesn't turn back to help like Nix did for Kadence. He simply sits, waiting for me to climb on.

"Okay, I'm ready," I say, trying not to let his silence bother me. He is intimidating; I'll give him that, but the tattoos, the darkness, and the mystery…who wouldn't put up a decent fight? Ready to get on the back, I move forward and put my hand on one shoulder, ready to mount. I lift my leg, but my dress stops me from getting on. "Don't turn around," I tell him, hiking my skirt up to get on behind him. He still doesn't say anything, just stares ahead while I fix my skirt, making sure I don't flash anyone. *Jesus, Kadence made this look easy.*

"Where do I put my feet?" I ask, a little unsure of myself when I finally settle in behind him. He leans to one side, bends from the waist and reaches down. His large, callused hand slides down my naked leg. I don't respond, but the intimate touch feels so good I have to force myself not to purr. His touch is firm, but still has a softness about it as he positions my foot on a small peg. He holds it there for a moment, and for a brief second, I feel his thumb slowly sweep along my skin in a small caress. It's so subtle I second-guess what I felt until he releases my ankle and then does the same for the other side. I don't react, unsure of what it means, or if it means anything. What I do know is this man seems like a list of contradictions. So hard and filled with so much anger, while in the next breath he's gentle and even a little lost. I lean forward when he sits back up and wrap my hands around him. His body feels hard underneath them, the leather of his cut cool on my fingertips.

"Second right off Main, then first left," I tell him, my fingers flexing instinctively at our closeness. He nods, still not speaking, and after a few revs of the throttle we take off. My grip on his cut deepens as the forward motion catches me off guard. I've never been on a bike, and after hearing Kadence's rendition of her ride with Nix, I can now say the woman did not lie. Even if we only go slow, the air blowing my hair back is exhilarating. I don't know if I want to get off.

"You can go faster," I encourage, hoping he takes the hint, but something tells me he's not the type of man to take any sort of hint. He continues to stay mute, so instead of wasting my breath, I hold on tighter and memorize his hard body under my hands.

The short ride to my apartment is over before I know it, and when he pulls into the lot, disappointment fills me. I shouldn't be feeling like this; the man is all wrong. He doesn't even seem interested. *Why do I always go for the ones not interested?* He idles in the drive while I manage to untangle myself without flashing my neighbors.

"Well, thanks for the ride, Sunshine," I say once I've handed back his helmet. He takes it without speaking a word and places it on his head before looking back at me. *Jeez, he really is a man of few words.*

"Okay then," I say awkwardly, even giving him a small wave and goofy smile. *Holly, the guy isn't interested. Don't be cute.* I inwardly groan at my discomfort.

His eyes narrow as he watches me and I realize I'm better off hitting my head against a wall. The man clearly has his own issues and is not interested in me being cute. I know rejection can happen—I'm just not familiar with it. I try to ignore the sting of his dismissal. I turn before I make a bigger fool of myself and start walking up the front path.

"See ya," he finally acknowledges while revving his bike and pulls out before I can even reply. *What the fuck? Now he talks?*

Hitting the button for the elevator, I go through the events of tonight. The whole situation was weird. Between his instant snarky attitude at me being in his shop, to his obvious annoyance, I'm pretty certain cranky sexy biker doesn't like me at all.

The doors open and I walk through ready to put this whole night behind me.

I don't need some sexy tattooed biker to warm my bed. I push the button to take me to my floor. Shit, I might not need him, but

I sure as hell want him—even if it's just to say I've had him. Or at least, that's what I'm telling myself.

"So, let me just get this right for a moment. You went to visit your asshole ex-fiancé without telling me. He is a part of some huge drug ring and the men after him—the men who started the fire at your house—are friends of Nix's?" I tick off everything that just went down as Kadence sits back down on the sofa the following morning.

"Yes," she admits, crying into her hands.

I knew something was up when I received a text message from her. I had only just spoken to her about her first sleepover at the clubhouse and filled her in on my non-eventful ride home with Sy. She told me she was hanging out for the day, when not twenty minutes later, she needed a lift. I didn't ask questions, just jumped in my car and drove to get her. I should have pushed her, demanded she tell me what had happened, but she brushed it off as nothing. I didn't even second-guess her when she was home for five minutes and then raced out the door. When she came through the door an hour later, white as a ghost, I knew something serious had gone down. Next thing I knew, sexy, badass Nix was banging the door down telling her that her ex-fiancé was second in charge of one of the county's biggest drug rings. I wasn't expecting the blow up, but hearing Zane's name alone has my skin crawling. I'm not surprised he's come back to start some shit. I never liked the douche. Even back when things were good between him and Kadence he always rubbed me the wrong way, but being the good friend I am I kept my mouth shut and helped her plan her dream wedding.

"Why would you go and see Zane?" I ask first, shocked she would want to see the man who destroyed her only a few years ago.

"He threatened you, Holly. Threatened our place." She motions to our small apartment to add emphasis.

"I don't care if that asshole threatened me, Kadence. I'm not scared of Zane, besides, what's the point in having a badass biker daddy if you're not going to use him to your advantage?" I ask, still not understanding her. The man tried to kill her for Christ's sake.

"This isn't funny, Holly. You heard what Nix just said to me." She cries into her tissue again, feeling sorry for herself. She's right. I did hear what Nix said to her. I also heard what he didn't say, and going by the look on his face when he realized how they were connected, he didn't look too happy.

"I'm not laughing. I'm serious. Zane tried to kill you. Did you hear what Nix said? Yes, sexy biker daddy was a douche talking about your oral abilities, but you have to give it to him, he held back for a while, and you were kinda bitchy," I admit, trying to get her to see it from his side.

"He was the one who was out of line. Don't side with him," she snaps, but I can see her mind ticking over what just happened.

"You both were out of line," I correct her.

"I don't want to talk about it anymore," she huffs when there's nothing left to say. She knows I'm right and in time she'll admit it.

"So what do you want to do?" I ask, moving over to sit next to her on our comfy sofa. I know she's upset. The best course of action would be to fill her with junk food and let her cry it out.

"I want movies, ice cream, and chocolate," she orders, and like any good best friend, I leave her sitting there to search for supplies.

"Cookies and cream or peppermint," I call out, checking our stash from the freezer.

"Both," she cries and I hold in my laugh.

"You know you owe me for this," I say, throwing the spoon at her. "I want all the juicy details on your first night in the clubhouse," I demand before handing over the tub.

"Holly, don't make me relive it," she complains, thinking her pout will sway me.

"Girl, you have a real-life sexy-ass biker. Let me live vicariously through you," I beg, watching her roll her eyes. If only she knew just how lucky she is.

"Fine, but I want details about what Sy said to you when he dropped you off last night," she replies, taking the peppermint tub out of my hands

"Ha, I told you, the man said two words—'see ya'." I repeat what I told her on the phone this morning.

"You weren't kidding?"

"No. Total asshole too, but seriously, did you see the ink on him?" I ask, remembering how sexy he looked in his dark jeans, Henley, and cut.

"I've seen him. I wonder what his deal is?" she asks, heaping a large spoonful of ice cream into her mouth.

"Don't you know?" I ask, shocked she has no inside scoop for me.

"Nope, he's a mystery. He doesn't talk much and if he did, it wouldn't be gossip, that's for sure." She reaches for the cookies and cream. *Mystery, hey?* I can handle mystery. I can't help but hope I see the mysterious Sy again. I know I didn't have a good first shot at him, but I know if I get another chance, I'll have him eating out of my hand.

"What are you smiling at?" Kadence asks, watching me closely.

"Nothing, just remembering something from earlier." I don't want her to know I'm thinking about one sexy, broody biker. We already have one of us messed up with the Knights Rebels.

"Well, let's stop talking about Nix, or any of the men associated with the Knights Rebels. I'm done with them." She swallows down another heaped spoon of cookies and cream.

"Calm down woman. You can't dump him until I get inside their club. You hear me?" I ask, only half joking. I'm more concerned for her. She's only just coming back to herself and I won't let one fight bring her down.

"I'm serious. I'm done with him," she says, crying again, but I don't correct her. She will work her shit out with Nix, and by the end of the week, she'll be back at the clubhouse in his bed while I'm stuck thinking about a cranky, sexy Sy.

Ain't that the truth.

Fuck my life.

3

Sy

"FUCK ME," I WHISPER TO MYSELF AS I WATCH HER MOVE her ass up against yet another guy for the night. *God has to be playing some kind of cruel joke on me.* Her blonde hair hangs loose, wavier than last week, and the short dress and heels she's wearing tonight are even sexier—if that's even possible. I haven't been able to get the fiery blonde out of my head since I dropped her off at her place last week. Of course I was an asshole, not even helping her on the bike. I was pissed Nix left me with her. I knew having her close would be too much. I tried not to give in to the temptation of having her behind me, but as soon as she asked where her feet should go, I just had to touch. I knew the move was stupid and dangerous as my hand ran down her silky smooth leg, but it didn't stop me from repeating the action on the other leg. It was reckless, and now I can't stop thinking about the feel of her skin under my fingers.

Shifting in my booth along the far wall of Liquid, I watch as she smiles up at the asshole who hasn't taken his eyes off her. The motherfucker is pissing me off with his smug look. *Hell, everyone is pissing me off.* I never wanted to come tonight, but with Nix and Kadence having some bullshit fight over her ex and his connection with Gunner Jamieson, we've been watching Kadence at a distance. And everywhere Kadence goes, Holly goes.

"Be careful, brother," Brooks warns, sitting back in his chair, while he scopes out the club. Liquid is one of the four businesses the Knights Rebels MC own in town. With an average size club and legitimate business dealings, we do well enough to live comfortably and then some. Hence this overdone club Jesse runs. "She looks more like trouble than fun," he continues, taking the words right out of my mouth. He's right, but as I sit here watching her, it just makes me want her more. I don't say anything, just watch as she looks up at the guy and smiles before turning her back to him, rubbing her ass against him again. "I can see it all coming down around you," he laughs, shaking his head. "First Nix and now you."

"Me? Fuck that. No way am I going there," I tell him, forcing myself not to search for her again. He's wrong. There is no way I'm turning into our Prez.

"No? You haven't fucking stopped looking at her since we walked in," he accuses, letting me know just how perceptive he is. Brooks is one of the old boys, and the only Rebel married with a daughter. He's a good, family man, but most of all, he lives and breathes the brother-hood.

"Kind of our fucking job, Brooks," I say, looking at him. He just smirks. "Do you think I want to be watching her?" I ask him, pissed that one, I'm even here tonight when I have more important things to do and two, he's gonna give me a hard time about it.

So much has happened in the last week. The front of Ink Me was destroyed in a fire right after I had taken Holly home, and the Rebels had to call in the help of our rival club, the Warriors. Things have been tense. The shop was a mess, and we've all been on high alert.

"I think you're having a hard time watching her about to go home with that asshole," he adds, pointing over to the fucker who just had his hands all over her. He's right. I don't know why it's bothering me so much. I have no claim over her, but sitting here, watching her about to pick up when I'm about to go home alone—it's just too fucking much.

"Whatever, Brooks. I'm out," I'm done with watching her and pissed he's seeing what I'm only just realizing now. *Jesus, I am a jealous fucker.*

"Aww, don't be like that," he laughs, watching me throw a twenty down.

"I gotta go. Ink Me re-opens tomorrow and I have a shitload to work through."

"You need any help?" he asks, but the boys have all worked their asses off this week to get it back up and running. It was only the front of the shop that was damaged, thank fuck, but still a pain when it had to be gutted and repainted.

"No, go home to your wife and girl, Brooks. I know that's where I would rather be if I were you." I flick my hand goodbye as I turn away before he asks me what that was about. I don't talk about my past with my brothers. I don't let them in on the shit that lives in my head. That's not to say the fuckers haven't clued in on it, but sharing? No. That shit is not for me.

I walk through the crowd, hoping to see her one last time before I head out. Neither she nor Kadence have noticed they've been followed and I'm glad for that. After the shit that's been going down with T and his boys, who knows what Gunner could be planning. Kadence really has no clue who she was once engaged to. The man is dangerous, and knowing he has a pull over us now only puts me on edge.

After looking around the club and not finding Holly, I give up and head down the back hall to leave. Not ten seconds after admitting defeat, I run into her.

"Oh, sorry," she stumbles as my hands come up to steady her. Looking up, it takes her a second to register before she smiles her sexy smile. "Why hello, Sunshine," she acknowledges me, not missing a beat and I can't help the scowl that forms at the stupid name she called me last week at the shop. *Why does her happiness make me angry?* "Aww, nice to see you're so happy to bump into me," she jokes, pulling back from me, but I don't let her out of my grasp. Watching her dance up against some asshole all night had me wanting to rip her off the dance floor, yet now when she's teasing me, making a joke of everything, I want to unleash my anger on her.

"Jesus, do you even talk?" she snaps when I don't reply. I fight the pull she has on me. "Nothing? Really? Okay, well good chat," she says, stepping out of my hold. "See you later." She waves, making her way around me, ready to meet back up with that fucker I bet.

"What the hell do you think you're doing?" My voice stops her, and she spins on her heel to face me. I should let her walk away, not let myself get caught up in this game, but for reasons beyond me, I can't.

"Sunshine, you talk!" She lights up like she just received the greatest news.

Yeah, I fucking talk.

"You pick up all your fucks from clubs?" I ask, like the fucker I am.

She's unfazed by my harshness. "No, not always. I like variety." She smiles up at me. "You should try it sometime, Sunshine.

Maybe you just need a good fuck." She winks, and if I wasn't such an angry fuck, I'd give her a lip twitch.

"Do you know that guy?" I ask, ignoring her jab. She's right. I need a good fuck, but she doesn't need to know that.

"No, but I do know I'm going to get laid," she laughs, pissing me off again. "Why? What's the issue here?"

"You ready?" the asshole who thinks he is getting his dick wet tonight asks Holly as he comes up behind her, enveloping her in his arms.

"No, she's not" I step up, grab Holly's hand and pull her out of his hold. "She's with me, so fuck off," I order as I level my stare at him. He looks shocked for a second, not expecting to come up against an angry-looking fucker. I can see him assessing his chances. Not a moment passes by before he leaves.

"What did you do that for?" Holly turns, pulling her arm from my grasp. *Fuck, why did I do that?* I don't know why, but watching the fucker touch her pushed me over the edge.

"Sorry," I shrug, not feeling one bit apologetic.

"Sorry? Jesus, Sy. What the hell?" she asks, just as shocked as I am. "You so did not just do that." She pushes past me to leave.

"Where the hell are you going?" I call out to her, but she doesn't respond. I follow her, catching Brooks' smirk on the way, but I'm more interested to see if she follows the fucker than to worry that he called it right.

"Holly!" I call out when she leaves through the front and walks in the direction of her apartment.

"Go away, Sy. You're really annoying!" she shouts back, but I don't stop.

"You didn't even know the asshole, Holly. You could have found yourself in trouble." I ignore the fact that it's the first time I've called her by her name, or how good it feels rolling off my tongue.

"Maybe I wanted to be in trouble," she snaps as she walks past my bike.

"Stop right there," I demand, watching as she pauses, turning to me at my command. Why it stirs something in me, I don't know, but watching her obey when she doesn't want to is bad news for me.

"I'll take you home," I say in the same commanding voice, pointing to the bike.

"I'm not going anywhere with you." She crosses her arms over her chest. Sexy, funny Holly is hot. Pissed off Holly is a bigger temptation.

"Well, you're not fucking walking, so get on," I demand, passing her the helmet. She doesn't take it.

"I'm not getting on a bike with you again." She makes her stand, taking a step back.

"Listen, I don't wanna fucking fight. Just get on the bike so I can get this shit done," I snap, pushing the helmet toward her and not giving a fuck if I sound like an asshole.

"You're a real asshole, Sunshine, you know that. Now I'm going to have to find less desirable ways to satisfy myself tonight," she teases.

I don't know if she's joking or just trying to get a reaction from me, but hearing her talk about satisfying herself makes me angrier. "Holly," I warn, knowing I'm starting to slip. I get on first, waiting for her to do as she's told.

"Fine." She caves and finally climbs on the back of my bike. She leans forward and whispers into my ear, "but I'm only getting on because I don't want to walk." I try not to react, but the blood rushing to my cock is involuntary. She reaches around me and I look down at her small hands holding on to my cut. I feel her legs tighten as she rubs up against me. I can handle her hands on me, but her body rubbing against my back is too much. My palm goes to her leg, stopping her with a squeeze.

"Don't," I warn, shutting her down. She huffs her annoyance, but I don't respond. Instead, I take off out of the lot, ready to be done with this night, knowing I should never have played with fire.

Three minutes later after a silent ride, I pull up in front of her building and I cut the engine. She lives in one of those secured apartments, but it doesn't stop me from checking out the surroundings.

"No need to stop. I'll be fine," she says, passing me my helmet back.

"I'll walk you up," I tell her, ignoring her eye roll. I really shouldn't. I need to turn around, walk back to my bike and get the hell away from her and her tempting ways, but my brain is telling my body I just need to get her up to her door.

"Oh, a real Prince Charming tonight," she snorts, walking up ahead of me. The elevator ride up to the top floor is silent and I wonder if being this close to her alone is such a good idea. I regret my play just as the doors open. Following her out and down the hall, I watch as she approaches the second apartment and takes her keys from her purse.

"Well, thanks for ruining my night, Sunshine. I was guaranteed hot, sweaty sex tonight, and now I'm left with my hand or trusty vibrator." She smirks like it's a game we're playing and she's about to score. It takes everything in me not to push her up against the door right there and punish her for thinking she can play with me.

She huffs when I keep quiet, and turns to open the door when she doesn't get the reaction she's looking for. The lock clicks and she pushes the door open. I want to follow her in, fuck the attitude out of her, but I stand still in my resolve.

She pauses and I can see the uncertainty in her eyes as she turns and lays her cards out for me to see. "You don't even want to have sex?"

"No," I tell her, hating the word as it comes out of my mouth. I don't want to have sex. I want to fuck her so hard she wishes she never tempted me.

"You know that just made me wet," she jokes, and I see her trying to cover the shock of my rejection with her humor, but it doesn't make me laugh. Nothing about this woman teasing me makes me laugh.

"Holly," I warn and watch her smirk slowly as she closes the door. Relief fills me as I hear the lock click closed, followed by frustration that I'm left craving more of her. Tempted to knock on her door, I force myself to turn and leave before I do something stupid. Two steps into my retreat the door opens and her voice calling my name stops me.

"If you weren't going to fuck me tonight, then what was your play?" she asks. Her question has me hating myself more. What was I doing in the first place? I'm not gonna lie. Seeing her pick up the asshole was not a fucking easy pill to swallow, but it's not like I have a claim on her. I'm not even sure I want to claim her, but my body reacted differently. It was as though it was on autopilot. Before I knew it, she was on the back of my bike and I was taking her home—again. I turn to face her, ready to lie and tell her it's club business and I had to bring her home, but when I see her standing there, all sex and sass, and the biggest fucking temptation ever, something changes. I see something I haven't seen in such a long time. A small glimmer of light.

The air around us becomes thick with tension and anger, lust and sexual need, but we're both stuck in a stare-off.

"What happened to you?" she asks so gently it nearly breaks me. I don't know how to respond. I'm lost in the question, and the silence of the moment as something passes between us. I don't want her to know what I hide. I don't want to talk about it, but I still take a step forward, my body disobeying my brain. This is going to be a mistake. I can already feel it, but if this woman wants to play, I'll fucking play.

4

Holly

"SY?" I ASK, CONFUSED BY HIS SUDDEN CHANGE. I STEP back again as he takes another step closer. "What are you doing?" My voice shakes as he steps past the threshold of my small apartment, kicking the door shut with a booted foot.

The tension in the room is building as we face one another. I'm confused. One minute, he's looking so torn I had to ask the question, and the next, something snapped in him. My chest rises and falls as the anticipation of having him builds every second he stands inside my home. I don't know if he's teasing me, or what this is, but the look in his eyes is telling me he's just as turned on as I am. Ever since the night at the shop last week I knew he was bad news, with an equally bad attitude; but as he stood in front of me in the hallway, fighting whatever he was fighting, I knew no matter how hard I tried to condemn him for it, I couldn't. Now that I'm about to get what I want, what I've craved since I walked into Ink Me, I'm not so sure of myself.

He takes yet another step towards me.

"Wait," I say, holding my hands up for no reason other than to get my breathing under control. The man is dangerous. He has me wanting him with just one look and he'll probably have me coming apart with his touch. He steps closer as I step back, his eyes narrow at each one of my retreats. One step forward, one step back. Him the predator, me his prey.

"Sunshine," I warn, feeling like I've bitten off more than I can chew. It was fun teasing him. Now as I retreat, I second-guess my play. My back reaches the wall, halting me in my escape. His grave face drops for a moment when he sees I have nowhere else to run, and then his hard, warm body presses up against me, pushing me further into the wall.

Getting on his bike tonight, I knew this was going to happen, but when he let me close the door, I was shocked. In one moment he looks at me like he could eat me, and the next it's like he can't get away quick enough.

"I'm going to ask this once, and once only." His gravelly voice whispers precariously, and I'm beginning to worry I've messed with the wrong person. "You want this?" he asks, running his nose along my jaw, breathing me in. His short stubble rubs along my skin—the sensation mixing the right amount of pleasure with roughness. I nod as a tremor runs through me. I know I crave him. I know I need to have him more than anything.

"Fuck, I can smell how much you want it," he declares, and then his mouth is on me in a brutal attack. I latch on while his hands come to my hair, snapping my head back in a sharp pull. I don't know how far he's going to let this go, but that doesn't stop my leg from coming up and anchoring him to me, or grinding against him. The growl rolling from his mouth tells me he's just as desperate as I am and for a brief second I think about pulling back, putting an end to what can only spell trouble for me. But his tongue dominates my mouth, connecting us on a level which unravels me. *Holy shit, the angry man can kiss.*

His hands loosen their grip from my hair and move slowly down my body to the hem of my dress. I know he's about to break the kiss, know he has to if he wants me out of my dress, but even though I know it's about to happen, I can't stop the sigh of frustration when our connection is broken.

"Fuck, Holly," he pants, pulling back from me. My lips feel bruised, but before I get a chance to touch them, he rips my dress up over my head, exposing me completely to him. My hands go to his cut, ready to strip him of his clothes, but his command stops me.

"No," he says, shaking his head.

"What do you mean, no?" I question him, suddenly feeling vulnerable standing in my white matching panties and bra while he stands fully clothed.

"No, means no," he repeats, taking my panties and ripping them between his fingers.

Fuck me. I don't even care if he has destroyed my favorite panties with his bare hands. My need to have him inside me grows at his total act of dominance.

My hands go to my bra, unhooking the back and letting it fall from me. He steps back, shaking his head and taking in my naked body.

"It would help if you undressed," I say, eager to know just how much of his body is tattooed. I want to feel it under my hands.

"No," he growls, rejecting my request.

"Sy," I argue, but don't get far before he steps back into my space and drops to his knees before me.

I can't even control the moan that erupts from within me when he spreads me open and licks me hard. *Fuck.* My hands go to his head. The short hair is not long enough to hold on to, so my fingers graze his scalp in a need to touch him as my shoulders lean against the wall supporting me. He feasts on me like a starved man.

"Fuck, Sy," I rasp as he builds me up with each flick of his rough tongue against my clit. He's vocal in his oral assault, surprising me since he's so annoyingly quiet. The hungry moans vibrate against me, pushing me further into a haze as he worships my most sensitive area. The pleasure becomes too much, his skillful tongue demanding I fall apart. "Fuck, fuck, fuck!" I scream as heat fills me in a short but powerful orgasm. My hips ride his face as his thick fingers find my entrance, filling and stretching me wide. He pumps them into me repeatedly, setting off another orgasm.

"Jesus!" I pant as pleasure rocks through me. My legs are jelly and my head is lost in its own bliss as I feel his tongue lazily sweep through my wetness. Small bursts of orgasm run through me and if it wasn't for Sy holding me up, I'd fall into a puddle in front of him, lost in the afterglow of two incredible orgasms.

"Sy?" I ask, looking down and watching his head rest against my stomach. "Sunshine, do you know what happens next?" I ask, trying to get his attention. He looks up. His eyes come to mine, and instead of seeing the dark anger that lives in them, now all I see is a lost, faraway look, like he doesn't understand what is happening. He stands, drops his jeans, lifts my leg, and enters me before I even have time to process what's happening.

"You have no idea what I know," he threatens, pinning me to the wall as he pushes into me again. My legs are still shaky from the first two orgasms. I hold onto his cut as he continues pumping into me. The loud slapping of his balls against me fills the room as his stare drills into me.

"Oh, God," I moan as he pulls my other leg up, suspending me against the wall.

"No," he snaps, pushing into me harder and planting himself

there before grinding against me. His length hits the right spot as his pubic bone hits my clit.

"What?" I croak, my throat scratchy from my shouts.

"Not God," he repeats, his breath coming out harsh, but I can't keep up. My head is lost in a haze focusing solely on my impending orgasm that's running full speed ahead.

"Ouch!" I shout as he leans forward and bites down on my shoulder.

"Did God just bite your shoulder, Holly?" he asks, pushing his hips harder into me.

"No," I pant, unsure how I'm still even breathing. Between the pleasure running through my core and the pain of his bite, I don't know how I feel.

"Didn't fucking think so," he growls, leaning back down and licking the bite mark.

"Sy," I breathe, feeling my body tense as he rolls his hips faster. Harder. That edge of pleasure and pain dangles in front of me again, and like a greedy woman, I want to snatch it.

"Hmm" He kisses the soft spot behind my ear; his hot breath sending goose bumps along my skin as his own groans grow louder. I don't want it to stop. I want to hold on to this feeling and never let go, but I can't control myself as I spiral out of control.

"Oh, God, yes," I moan out my intense rush of ecstasy.

"Fuck," he grunts, following me over the wall of our temporary bliss. I know this is nothing more than a screw, but something shifts in me as he draws a third orgasm out of me. My emotions run hay-wire, but even in the heat of the moment, I know if I don't get a hold of it now, it will only spell trouble.

"Holy shit," I say quietly, looking at the patch sewn into his leather cut. Our breathing syncs as we come down from our marathon wall sex. Sy drops one leg, still planted inside of me.

"Jesus," he whispers as he drops the other leg, slowly letting himself out of me. He steps back, pulling his pants back up without taking his eyes off me. I've never been taken up against a wall like that before, and now I have, I want it again.

"Fuck," he curses.

"What?" I ask as an ache runs through my body. My muscles, lax in my post-orgasm state, can barely hold me up. I then register his cum running down the inside of my leg.

"You didn't use a condom?" Annoyed doesn't even begin to cover how fucking stupid I am.

"Fuck," he repeats again, balling his fists at his side.

"Will you stop saying fuck," I snap, pissed at seeing him freak out. "Pass the tissues." I use my hand to capture his release before it makes it to the carpet. He walks over to the coffee table, retrieves the box, and hands me two tissues.

"Thanks, I'll just go clean up," I tell him, replacing my hand with a tissue.

"I need to go," he counters, turning and moving to the front door.

"Are you kidding me?" I ask, but he doesn't reply—just walks straight out without saying a word. I stand there not sure what just happened or how to respond. I knew it was some kind of heat of the moment, sexually-fuelled slip I had instigated, but to simply walk out while I'm standing here naked? *What an asshole.*

Jesus, how could I be so stupid?

"Asshole," I voice to the empty room realizing he played me when I was meant to play him. "Fucking moron, Holly," I whisper to myself as I lock the door behind him.

Fucking moron.

5
Sy

COULD I BE ANY MORE FUCKING STUPID? FUCKING HER AND then leaving her standing there naked and pissed. They both fall under the most-stupid-shit-I-did-last-night category. I was screwed when she came out of the bathroom and crashed into me. With her milky white hands coming to my arms, the look of them against my ink made me want her in that second. Her smart-ass mouth reminded me why she was bad news, but when that fucker walked up and smirked at me, I knew I had to do something. I fucked her because I didn't want anyone else to. *No, I cock blocked her, but then couldn't keep my own dick in my pants.* If I could beat my own ass, I would. I shouldn't have left her standing there, but the panic in her eyes when she realized I didn't use a condom had me itching to get out of there. What the fuck is wrong with me? This woman has me twisted inside out. Yet, I can't seem to get enough.

Setting up my station for our first day back in Ink Me, I try to push all thoughts of Holly out of my head.

"You all right, boss?" Rue asks, coming to stand in front of me. Rue is one of Ink Me's employees. Her dark purple hair, heavily pierced face, and sleeve-tattooed arms are a total fucking turn-on. But since I'm her boss, she's off limits. Not to mention, since I met one pure-skinned, sexy blonde, I haven't had eyes for anyone else. *Fuck me.*

"Yep," I answer, not giving her my attention. I'm not in the mood for her, or anyone this morning.

"Sweet, you have a nine a.m. first up, and then back-to-back all day." I nod in answer, knowing it's easier to be an asshole from the start of the day. Spinning on my stool, I dismiss her and continue to set up my station. She gets the hint, leaving me alone so I can get lost in my head. I need to work. I need to clear my head from everything that happened last night.

Finished setting up, I move to the employee lounge, and make myself my second coffee of the morning. When I first came back to Rushford, I never thought I would go back to tattooing again. I left that part of me back in Brighton with the family I left behind, but I knew a part of me was missing. It was something I didn't want to let go. When the club discussed another shop, I knew it was my chance to get that part of me back. The boys didn't dig into my shit when I told them my idea, and if they were shocked to learn about my tattooing background, they didn't say anything.

"Sy, there's someone to see you," Rue interrupts my thoughts of the past.

"Have them come through," I tell her, finishing the rest of my coffee.

"Not your appointment. Someone else."

Standing from my position, I make my way back out to the front of the shop and curse when I notice Holly sitting there. *Fuck*

"What are you doing here?" I bark out before I think. She flinches and then quickly hides it before standing and brushing her hands down her yellow dress. I follow the movement, holding myself together as I take her in. Fuck me. She calls me sunshine, but standing before me, she looks the picture of it today. The morning sun kisses the tops of her shoulders and her hair sits up on top of her head hiding its long length. Visions of her up against the wall, her rose-tipped nipples peeking out through the golden ends of her hair, flash in front of me as I remember just how perfect she is.

"Not that I want to be here, Sunshine, but we need to talk," she says, walking toward me. Her calling me Sunshine stirs my gut more than it should.

"I've got nothing to say," I tell her, feeling more like an asshole every time I give it to her. There's something about this woman that fucking gets to me.

"Yeah, I gathered that, when you left me with your cum still rolling down my legs," she snaps. I flinch but don't say anything. "Seeing as you left—" She raises her brow, "—I had to come and speak to you." She folds her arms across her chest, waiting for me to respond.

"Don't know what we have to talk about? We fucked. That's it," I say, annoyed she's turning into a hang on.

"Fuck, you're a piece of work. I thought you might like to know I'm clean," she says, waiting for me to respond, but I don't. I'm more pissed that just seeing her again has my dick wanting more and my mouth watering at remembering her taste. Fuck, I should never have caved.

"And?" she asks, prompting me.

"And..." I reply, being a bigger asshole.

"Well, how about you?"

"I think I'm fine," I tell her, shrugging like I don't really give a fuck, but I know I'm clean. I don't normally fuck without protection, so for me to even fuck her without a condom has my mind completely messed up.

"You really are something, you know that?" she huffs, pissed no doubt that I'm acting this way. If only she knew this way is better.

"Believe it, woman."

"Oh, I believe it, and you better believe if you give me some fucked-up disease, I'll let every asshole in this town know what a filthy, fucking small-cocked, douchebag you really are." She ends on a shout right as my first customer walks in. I don't say anything, so she turns and storms out of the shop without a backward glance.

"Shit, boss. That was totally a douchebag move," Rue comments from the front desk, obviously listening in instead of greeting the customer.

"Don't give a fuck," I tell her and head back to my station.

"I hope for your sake you don't give her anything. I wouldn't put it past her to follow through on her threat," she chuckles, turning to the customer. Fuck me. I knew she was gonna be trouble. I should go to her and explain everything; tell her just to leave me the fuck alone, but I don't. She's better off thinking I'm an ass. That way, she'll stay away. I can't tell her there are some wounds that can't be mended, yet we carry them with us, hoping for a chance that maybe someday, someone can fix them.

I can't be fixed.

"Yeah, I gathered that, asshole, when you left me with your cum still rolling down my legs." I replay Holly's words over and over in my head the next morning. After she left the shop yesterday, her words fucked with me all day. I fucked up when I took her against the wall. Even in my reasoning that one time would be enough to get

my fill, I knew I was kidding myself. I crossed the line and now I'm dealing with it.

"Hey, brother." Jesse knocks on my door, pulling me out of the pissed-off Holly rant running through my head. "Nix wants a meet, now," he says.

"Yep," I yell, rubbing my hands over my face. "Got it." I grab my cut and force myself to stop thinking about the past and more importantly, Holly.

Closing the door to my small apartment, I make my way back up to the clubhouse.

I need to get my head clear and stop fucking thinking of her. What is it about this woman? Since I walked out of her house two nights ago, leaving her without a goodbye, I haven't stopped thinking about her. It wasn't my intention to fuck her. But the question in her eyes as she stood in front of me, asking what happened to me, made me snap. Her whole attitude when she speaks to me snaps something inside me. Maybe it's the fact she's the first woman who isn't clingy, or hasn't seen me as a conquest to fix. She looks at me as a challenge on a different level; not one for her to play, but one for her to conquer. I tried to stay away, tried to force myself not to be tempted by her, but now I've had a taste, I can't seem to turn my need for her off.

"Don't look so excited to see me," Jesse says as I walk into church.

"Piss off," I grunt, hitting him over the head. Jesse is the joker of the group. Sometimes, he's a funny fucker—other times, he just pisses me off.

"What's crawled up your ass?" he asks as I sit down around the oak wood table. "Let me guess: that hot chick you got working in the shop is giving you blue balls?" He laughs at his own joke. *If fucking only.*

"Where's Beau?" Nix growls when he walks into the room, taking his seat at the head of the table.

"Careful, Nix. You're beginning to sound like Sy," Beau snickers, coming in behind him.

"We're all here. Let's get this shit sorted," he says, ignoring Beau's dig. "First up, we have fucking issues with Liquid." We don't normally run church like this, but the club is under pressure with shit going down around us. I don't blame Nix for his anger.

"What issues?" Jesse calls out, the name of his baby grabbing his attention. The man lives and breathes the place, while it only gives Nix a headache.

"I swear to fuckin' Christ, Jesse, the place is more trouble than it's worth."

"Nah, come on, boss man. You don't mean that."

"I fuckin' do. Especially when you're sleepin' your way through the fuckin' waitresses. Keep your dick in your pants from now on," he warns, and I can't help but smirk. Jesse keeping his dick in his pants? Yeah, right.

"Who's bitching now?" He shakes his head, not looking at all surprised.

"Fuckin' Tammy. You need to sort that shit out, brother. She has a daughter who needs feeding. Don't be a cockhead. She needs this job," he warns. Jesse might be a player, but he knows when he needs to step up.

"Right," Jesse agrees, ending it there and moving on.

"We still have no word on Gunner. T and his boys are keeping an eye out, but I don't doubt this shit with Kadence was a play, one he will pull again. Until we sort shit out, I want all hands on deck until the fucker is found. Any problems?" Nix asks.

"So, we're still on babysitting duty?" Beau grumbles, saying what I'm thinking. I don't have a problem with Kadence, but I need to stay away from Holly. The woman is too dangerous for me.

"You have a problem with it?" Nix asks.

"No problem. Just want to know where we stand here? We've

worked so hard to keep out of T's shit. Now some pussy comes along and we're on meet-ups, taking phone calls with the Warriors. Don't have to remind you what you've lost to get the club to where it is," he states, and he's right; we have worked hard to get the club to where it is today, but Nix has claimed Kadence as his, therefore, he will do anything to protect her. Beau knows this.

"You got your feelings hurt 'cause your boyfriend went and found a woman, Beau?" Jesse calls out.

"Fuck you, Jesse."

"What is wrong with everyone today?" Jesse asks, looking around the table, but everyone ignores him.

"You call Kadence pussy again, we're gonna have problems, brother." Nix slams his fist down on the table.

"I'm just telling it how it is," Beau says, not ready to step down.

"I don't give a fuck how it is to you. It is what it is. End of story," Nix warns and Beau nods, leaving it be, but I know the asshole won't be easily swayed. He keeps his cards close to his chest and doesn't trust easily.

"Where are you with the shop?" he asks me, moving on from Beau.

"First day back was busy; closing for a week has put us behind, but we've had a few inquiries for the job ad we put out."

"Any good ones?"

"Yeah, couple came in with some good portfolios. Gonna have them come work a day next week." The truth is with the success of the shop so far, we could put on two more artists and still be holding our own.

"Let me know how you go." I nod, knowing whoever I choose, the boys will trust my decision. "Anyone have anything else?" Nix moves on, asking the table.

"Received a call from Tiny yesterday." Beau taps the table as he speaks. Last month, the club owed a marker to an old friend of

Red's. We transported a mother and child to a safe house, kept her guarded until they could arrange her documents, and then escorted her on to the next point. Seeing her so severely beaten and her kid so fucking scared messed with most of us. Fucker got away with it, but at least we were able to get the woman and her son out.

"What's he want?" Nix asks, his attention grabbed.

"Wants us on board to help out with this underground gig."

"You know we're juggling a full plate right now?" Brooks asks, always the voice of reason.

"I know what we have on our plate right now, but when shit calms down, I want in," Beau says, his voice absolute.

"What we looking at?" I ask, wondering how we could work it.

"We start off small; pickups, drop offs, and if there are any recoveries. Tiny wants to hang his hat up so if we vote on it, I want to do it with the intention of taking over."

"Jesus, Beau. You go from not wanting to do this shit, to wanting to run it?" Jesse asks, shaking his head.

"I want it if I can have the control, run it the way I see it. We help these women where we can. We got Jackson helping us where he can, and then we have a smooth run." Jackson is Jesse's brother who works for the county sheriff's department in the next town over. In the past, he's helped us out on a few things; walking the fine line of the law by turning the other way, but I didn't know he was in on this shit.

"Okay, you can have it, but only after this shit with Gunner is sorted," Nix agrees.

"We're voting on this then?" Beau replies, shocked at his answer.

"You all want in?" Nix asks the table, making it legit. I know this is something Beau wants, and coming from a family whose father beat his mother, I'd vote anyway. The table echoes with "yeahs" as Nix calls it as agreed.

"This is on you, Beau. We'll help where we can, but we go in clean and come out clean, got it?" Nix warns.

"Only way to do it," Beau replies, a small smile on his face.

"Right, well that's about it. Anyone else?" Nix asks one last time, but just like me, everyone seems ready to call it and be done. "Remember, keep our eyes open and any news of fuckin' Gunner or Edwards, we move." We all nod, agreeing with what needs to be done. Standing, I follow my brothers back out to the main room of the clubhouse.

"Sy, I'm heading to the gym, ten minutes. You in?" Jesse asks, walking past me to his room.

"Not today," I say, not in the mood for his fucking chirpy mood.

"Your loss," he shrugs, turning and leaving.

"You all right, Sy?" Nix asks, coming up once everyone has cleared out.

"Perfect," I tell him and regret the choice of word. He smirks, shaking his head.

"Brace, brother, it's only gonna get worse," he says, slapping on my back and chuckling to himself.

I don't know what the fuck he's talking about, and I don't want to know how he knows about the shit I'm dealing with. All I need to do is get this fucking woman out of my head and all will be back to normal. Right?

I fucking hope so.

6

Holly

"WHO IS THAT MAN?" SARAH ASKS FROM BEHIND ME AS I turn to lock up for the day.

"What man?" I ask, looking over my shoulder.

"That one." She points over the parking lot to a man waiting on his bike. *Shit, Sy.* His head comes up at our voices, but his eyes are hidden behind his glasses so I can't see his reaction. I scan his body and zone in on his tattooed arms. They're crossed at his chest. Anyone walking past would double take at the dark, and broody man sitting there, but not me. No, I'm forcing myself to not look back.

"Not sure," I reply, checking the lock one last time before turning away. I don't need to see him tonight—not after working all day.

"Damn, he is fine," she continues, checking him out. "I wonder what he looks like under all *that leather*." She runs her eyes down his covered body. Yeah, if only I knew. I've had the man inside of me and I have no idea what's under *that*. How depressing. Especially when the man is on my shit list. I don't even know what he is doing here. Last time I saw him was when I was threatening him with bodily harm and stormed out of his shop.

"He's all right, if you like the biker type." I push our hot sex out of my head and brush off his hotness. "I have to run. See you tomorrow." I wave and start the short walk home.

"You want a lift?" she asks, but I decline; the fresh air is great after working long hours.

"No, I'm good," I smile, and wave her off. I don't look back and don't make eye contact with Sy as I pass him.

"You aren't going to say hi?" he calls out, his voice sending a shiver down my spine. I can't react. I'm still pissed about last week. Instead, I pick up my pace and hope he gives up. His bike starts up; the rumble of the pipes vibrating in the still, early evening. He roars past me and I ignore the feeling of frustration that he's gone. I don't know why it bothers me. He's done nothing but be a dick since the first day I met him at the tattoo shop. I'm not everyone's cup of tea, but I'm not that bad. Turning the corner to my street, I regret the disappointment from a few moments ago when I see his bike parked out the front of my apartment building. *Great.*

"What do you want, Sy?" I snap when I get to my drive and see him resting against my car. There's no point ignoring him when he's gone to all this effort.

"I'm clean," he assures me, putting his hands in his pockets and looking slightly guilty.

"Yeah, like I'm gonna trust you," I tell him, not the slightest bit interested in his bullshit. I made an appointment to get tested next month. Fucker.

"I get checked every six months."

"Great, thanks for letting me know." I nod and turn, leaving him standing there.

"Wait," he calls out, but I don't. What I should do is cut his big, fat cock off and make him eat it.

I don't know what it is about this man. He has this pull that I can't fight, even if he is a mess of contradictions. His attitude yesterday should have been enough to douse the fire building in me, but even after the way he acted, all I can think about are his tattooed arms holding me up against the wall. *Jesus.*

I make it to the elevator before he catches up. "Go away," I groan as he steps in behind me, not giving up.

"No. We're going to talk," he calmly replies. His tone surprises me.

"What do you want to talk about?"

"We'll talk when we get inside."

"Umm, no, we'll talk now," I protest. No way is he getting back into my apartment.

"No," he merely states.

"Yes," I reply, not giving in. The doors open, and in one fast motion, Sy has my hand and is dragging me to my door.

"Let me go, Sy." I try to pull away, but his hold is too strong.

"Open the door," he demands in his powerful voice.

"Fine," I huff, opening the door and turning to stop his advance.

"You are not welcome, Sy. Say what you have to say and leave."

"I'm sorry," he blurts out.

Once again his response surprises me. "No problem," I say, accepting his apology, hoping he'll take that as leave to go. I need to be away from him.

"Don't do that," he growls.

"Do what?"

"Brush me off."

"Sorry, I don't want to chat, Sy. You're kind of an asshole. Excuse me for not playing into your bullshit."

"I'm sorry. I am an asshole."

"Yes, I already know this," I agree, almost laughing at how ridiculous we might seem.

"Holly, just stop," he growls. The sound of my name and the pleading in his voice has me retreating. "I fucked up. I don't know what I'm doing," he admits, and for the first time since I've known him, I feel his honesty.

I don't know what he expects from me, so I don't say anything.

"I don't know what the fuck to do with you, Holly," he says, taking a step toward me.

"Sy," I warn him, watching his jaw tick and his fists flex. "You should go." The tension between us builds again. *Jesus, this is ridiculous.*

"What if I don't want to go?" Taking another step inside my home, he kicks the door shut.

"I need you to go." I put my hand up, stepping back to stop him coming closer. The anticipation as he closes in has my heart picking up speed and my breath coming in short, shallow bursts. "Sy," I all but whisper as his mouth descends on mine. My early declaration of never letting this man near me is over with just one touch of our lips. But it's not just a simple kiss that has me coming undone. The hungry kiss is rough and raw. Nothing like the other day as our teeth smash, our tongues duel, my lips bruise, and my stomach drops—all from the touch of our mouths.

Every thought I had of the man in front of me has gone out the window with just one kiss. Breaking the connection, he brings my dress up over my head exposing my naked breasts to him in the middle of the living room. My hands find his pants, eager to feel him under my fingers, but he stops me again, holding my wrist in his large grip.

"Fuck you, Sy," I growl. Once again, he won't let me touch him.

"Don't," he warns, before taking my mouth hard, silencing me with his tongue. I want to stop this, tell him it's bullshit that I can't touch him, but his hands find my breasts and all thoughts of putting him in his place disappear as his hands work their magic.

"Turn around and get down on your hands and knees," he commands. I don't even hesitate for one second. Sliding my panties down my legs, I turn and do as he says. *What is it with this man that has me disregarding all my rules?*

"Condom?" I ask when I hear him drop his pants behind me, without looking back.

"Fuck that, I want you bare again," he states, running his shaft between my ass cheeks.

"No, Sy." My words leave me on a heavy breath when he finds my slick entrance. My brain is screaming at me to stop this, to not let it go on, but my body has taken over. Even though I know how ridiculously stupid this is, I can't stop it.

"Yes," he growls, leaning against my back. "I haven't been with anyone since you," he admits before leaning forward and biting down on my shoulder.

"Jesus, you're a biter," I accuse as he licks at the spot he just chomped on.

"Mmmhhm," he slowly enters in soft, gentle strokes.

"This is wrong," I say breathlessly, but not putting up much of a fight anymore because feeling him inside me, skin to skin, feels way better than it should.

What is wrong with me?

"So wrong." He repeats my sentiments, and then bites down on the opposite shoulder as he picks up speed.

"Stop biting me," I complain half-heartedly, too lost in the feeling, too lost in the moment.

"No," he grunts, pulling my hair back and biting down on the side of my neck, hard. The pain and the sting send me over the edge as he pumps into me harder. The thrill of how he causes me to react this way vibrates through me. My body moves in time with each hard thrust, building with the frantic need to feel more.

"Oh, fuck," he groans, his hands coming to my waist, his fingers digging into my soft flesh. A mixture of pleasure and pain that only Sy can give me erupts inside of me as his release takes over, pushing me into the bliss I crave.

"Don't move," he warns as he comes down off his high. Still planted inside of me, his movements slowly start back up. The sensation of gentle strokes while his fingers dig painfully into my skin have me building back up again.

"Did I hurt you?" he asks, kissing my shoulder.

"No," I answer, shaking my head.

"Good," he says, pulling out of me slowly. He then presses his body weight on top of me. *Oh, my God, what is wrong with us?*

"What was that?" I can't look at him, too pissed off with myself to make eye contact.

"That's what seems to happen when we're alone," he answers, rolling off me to the side. "Didn't come back here to do that. Wasn't expecting that, but fuck, every time I'm around you and you open your mouth, I can't help but want to rip your clothes off," he admits, both of us still lying on the floor.

"Well, what are we going to do about it?" I ask, reaching over to the coffee table for a tissue.

"Nothing to do about it. It is what it is, Holly. A fuck." He sits up, scowling at me.

"Jeez, Sy. Calm down. I'm not some fucking crazy bitch who wants to have your babies now that you've given me a couple of orgasms," I say, reaching for my dress, feeling exposed while he's fully clothed. "I'm asking because you can't just walk into my house, strip me naked and fuck me when you decide *you* have a taste for it." I stand, stepping into my panties, ready to lay down the law.

"Well, it's not like I forced myself on you," he replies, standing to do his pants back up.

"No, but you didn't make it easy for me, just taking me how you want me."

"Well, when you throw your fucking anger at me, I can't help it," he says, taking a step toward me.

"Is this what you like, Sy? Do you have an appetite for an angry fuck?" I ask, not trying to figure him out; that shit would take a lot more than one question, but I want to know what makes this man think he has any right over me.

"Lived with it for such a long time, I don't know if the anger is doing anything for me anymore, but you, you're a different kind of anger." His voice is low and filled with the same honesty from earlier. He's also now completely in my space.

"And what type would that be?" I force myself to stand strong, not wavering under his dark stare.

"A type I've never known before: dangerous. A type I need to stay away from," he admits, his stare now softening somewhat.

"Well then, by all means, stay away." I cross my arms, ready for the brush off. At least this time, he has the balls to say how it is.

"See, right there with your anger again. You're making it hard for me to stay away," he whispers.

"You're the one who needs to walk away, Sy." I hold his stare.

"I'm leaving now."

"Great," I reply, giving him my fake smile.

"This can't happen again," he reminds me, like I'm going to find it hard to keep my clothes on around him.

"Really?" I ask on an eye roll. "I was thinking about calling my parents, letting them know I was in a committed relationship."

"Holly..."

"Sy," I reply, enjoying this more than I should.

45

"Fuck me," he curses under his breath.

"Would it be simpler for you if I stripped naked again? That seemed to work for you last time you had to leave," I remind him, trying to keep the sting out of my voice.

"I think I can manage," he retorts.

"Great."

"Great," he repeats. The air of electricity we seem to create stirs again, building momentum as we stand staring at each other. It's like a force dragging me in. With no control over my own reflexes, I step forward as he leans into my space, and just as our lips touch, his phone rings from his pocket, the intrusion breaking our connection.

"Yeah?" he asks into his phone after the third ring. I take a moment to move away from the vortex he sucked me into.

"Okay, give me five minutes."

Turning my back, I walk to the kitchen, wondering if he will follow me. After a moment of silence, I hear the door open. The slow creak of the hinge sounds so harsh in the quietness of the apartment. I don't call out, or turn from where I stand. The heaviness of rejection hits me strangely, and with the release of the door handle, and the click of the lock, I get my answer. Sy doesn't follow anyone.

You can't get shitty, Holly. You knew this going in, I remind myself as I walk to my room and clean myself up.

So why does it hurt a little?

Past

Sy

"Do you believe in God?" Her small hand grips onto my larger one.

"Yeah, baby girl," I say, looking down and watching her smile at my answer.

"Do you think God will let me see you again?" She continues to ask questions that keep breaking me.

"I know he will," I say, believing it more than anything. My faith has now been shaken, but I can't lose hope that where she is going will be somewhere beautiful and amazing.

"When I go to God, will I see Charlie the goldfish?" She yawns, almost drifting off as the hospital machines beep around us. I nearly smile at her question, but I can't, because at the end of the day we're talking about death, and the inevitable end that's fast approaching.

"I don't know, baby girl," I tell her, wishing I had the right answers for *her. We've had hospital staff come in and talk with Katie and me about how to approach the subject of death. I try to take everything they suggest on board, but sometimes, Keira will hit me with a question that floors me and I can't lie to her.*

"I want to go home," she says, nestling further into the stark white hospital pillow. It's the same thing she's said every day for the last three weeks we've been stuck here.

"I know you do, baby." I reach out and brush the soft skin of her cheekbone.

"I love you, Daddy," she says, slowly drifting off to sleep. I wonder how many more days I have with her. Will she die in this hospital, the one place she doesn't want to be?

"I love you too, baby girl."

Z

Holly

"COME ON, WOMAN. SUCK IT UP." I TAKE KADENCE'S HAND and drag her inside the Rebels' Clubhouse. I'm trying to keep my fake bravado up as we walk through the darkened hall, but as leather and smoke fill my nose, I'm reminded of the last time I saw Sy and how it felt when he walked out. I knew coming here would be dangerous. I was happily settling in for a quiet afternoon of sappy movies and junk food when Kadence came rushing through the door telling me I had to get up and get ready as I was going to my first ever clubhouse barbecue. At first, I was against it. The last thing I need is to see Sy in his territory, but when Kadence told me Z, Nix's son was going to be here, I knew I had to come for support. She has been freaking out about letting Z know about her relationship with his father since the moment she started seeing Nix. I personally don't think she has anything to worry about, but nonetheless I'm here, questioning my sanity and wishing I was still on my sofa.

Loud music beats out of the surround speakers, making the framed pictures of club members hanging on the walls next to us shake slightly.

"We need to go straight to the bar," Kadence orders next to me as we turn the corner to a large open area. I nod, following behind her, needing the same liquid courage as she does.

"Two Coronas, please," I ask the younger guy as we sit down. He nods, turning and getting our drinks.

"This place is cool," I say, looking around. My eyes take everything in. Even if I'm nervous about seeing Sy, I still love that I finally have the chance to come here after everything Kadence has told me.

"Yeah," Kadence mumbles, turning to greet someone, but I don't hear her as my eyes connect with *his*. His body stiffens at my presence and I try not to let it affect me, but how do you do that when the man can get me out of my clothes in less than two minutes. *Jesus, what was I thinking, letting him fuck me?* I thought it would have made it easier not to want him as much after the second time he left me, but even after he was the biggest asshole, I can't help the want flowing through me.

I don't know how long he holds my gaze, but after what feels like a ridiculous time, I force my eyes away and focus on the man who just picked up my hand to kiss it. He's blond, built, and has the biggest smile I've ever seen.

"I don't think we've formally met," he drawls, releasing my hand.

"Holly, this is Jesse. Jesse, this is my best friend, Holly." Kadence introduces us before turning back around to scan the bar.

"Hello, sweetheart." He moves in close.

"Hi," I reply, not affected by his flirting. But he doesn't give up, reaching out and pushing a loose strand of hair from my face.

"Jeez, you're a pretty little thing, aren't ya?" he says and I roll my eyes at Kadence. Men like this look good, but I'm not a sucker for it.

"You done?" Sy's voice comes up behind the modern day Casanova, and I lock eyes with Kadence. Her expression is shocked for a small moment before her eyes widen, waiting for my reaction.

"Sorry, brother. Am I stepping on some toes here?" Jesse pulls back from me to turn and face Sy. What the hell? He fucks me and leaves me, yet now he's going to give me attitude. I don't think so.

"No toes," I say, reaching out and taking Jesse's arm. I smile sweetly at Sy before he can respond. I have no attraction to Jesse, but if it means pushing Sy into an angry state, then I'm all for it.

"Fuck me," Sy grumbles, but I pretend not to hear it. I can't be swayed by his moody ass. Yes, something is happening between us, but he can't expect me to be okay with the way he keeps treating me.

"Want to show me around?" I ask Jesse as I climb down off the stool and flash my 'fuck you asshole' look to Sy. His eyes narrow, but I'm not going to be intimidated by him. Jesse nods and we move past them heading out to the backyard. I half expect him to reach out, but then I remember it's not his style. Clearly, he doesn't want me, and more importantly, doesn't want anyone else to have me.

"What was that about?" Jesse asks when we walk out through the back doors.

"Don't know what you're talking about." I act indifferent, taking in everything around us. Today is my first time in the clubhouse and everything is exactly how I expected.

"I'm not blind, sweetheart, and I've never seen Sy act that way. I'm not about to let any lady come between me and my brothers," he tells me.

I can respect that. "Look, just keep him away from me and I promise you that won't happen."

"I can do that." He nods, walking me over to introduce me to some people in the club. I smile and greet everyone, but my mind is still stuck on Sy and his outburst at the bar. After the way things ended the last time I saw him, I would have never expected that kind of reaction to me.

As the day goes on—with me pretending to ignore Sy, and Sy standing back following my every move—I'm ready to confront him. Excusing myself from the table, I make my way inside to use the bathroom. Knowing he will follow, with the way his eyes haven't left me all day, I take my time in the bathroom, mentally preparing myself to see him standing on the other side of the door. Opening the door, I'm surprised to find him not there. Frustrated and deflated, I decide to give up this cat-and-mouse game we keep playing and call it a night. Halfway down the hall, I'm grabbed and pulled back against the wall. I let out a scream and Sy's hand comes to my mouth to silence me.

"What the fuck are you doing here?" His warm breath hits my stunned face. My heart beats heavily, as his formidable frame towers over me. Part of me doesn't know how to react, his stare alone paralyzes me, but caught in the low light of the hall, my panic turns into something else. Something I felt the last time he had me against the wall.

I start talking, but my words come out muffled by his hand.

"What do you mean, what am I doing here?" I snap when he moves it from my mouth.

"What the fuck are you doing in my club?" he asks again, moving his body closer.

"Your club?" I ask, raising my brow. "Last time I checked, I came here with my best friend, not to see you, so if you'll excuse me," I say, trying to push off the wall, but he steps right in, his knee coming between my legs.

"You gonna fuck him?" he growls, his eyes growing angrier by the second.

"Maybe," I tell him, knowing he's talking about Jesse. "I wonder if he will leave me standing naked after a quick fuck up against the wall," I continue. His hold on me gets tighter. I know I shouldn't tease him with my words, but he's seriously delusional if he thinks he has any claim over me.

"I knew you were a tease, but I didn't know you wanted to be a club whore," he replies, and I try not to let his words sting.

"Are you done?"

"Are you?" he counters.

"You left me standing there. I didn't fucking do anything. What are you so angry about?"

"You coming into my club, throwing yourself at one of my brothers."

"Jeez, get over yourself, Sy. Jesse was just showing me around the place. And if I decide I want to have sex with him, or anyone else for that matter, I'll do what I want. You don't fucking own me. You had me, fine, but it was mediocre at best, so keep your hands off me," I snap, trying to get out of his hold.

"Mediocre?" he repeats back to me. I'm so pissed at his attitude I don't falter in repeating it.

"At best."

"Didn't feel like that when your cunt was gripping my cock like a vice," he throws back, his words causing my pussy to throb.

"That's called pelvic floor muscle exercises," I say, ignoring my body's response to having him so close.

"Right," he whispers, leaning further into me, "and what about when I dragged my tongue through that sweet pussy of yours, and lapped up your juices dripping from you?" he questions. It takes everything in me not to respond. "Now that I think about it, when you walked into my shop, all pissed off, you were walking like you had been fucked so hard. Did you feel me for days, sweetheart?" he continues, pushing into me further. "I bet your pussy is aching for me now, isn't it, Holly?" he asks, his lips so dangerously close to my neck.

Fuck me. Two seconds ago I hated the man, and now I'm trying to squeeze my thighs together to stop the ache coming from my lady parts.

"Too bad you won't find out," I counter, staying strong. I might want him more than anything, but he is still an ass.

"I don't even need to touch you to find out. It's written all over your face, Holly."

"Whatever, Sy. Let me go."

"You know I'm right. You're so fucking turned on right now and so frustrated you're not going to get any relief," he teases, telling me what I already know.

"There's always Jesse," I threaten, trying to get a reaction from him.

"Like fuck," he spits out, pushing his hard cock against me. "You're not gonna let that fucker touch you. Do you understand me? None of my brothers will taste your pussy. Do you hear me?" His hand runs up my leg, running along my short denim skirt and finding the outside of my panties. A small gasp leaves my lips at his feather-light touch. "This sweet pussy belongs to me. I fucking had it first. Now, it's mine."

"No, it's not," I fight back, but my mind is too busy memorizing each lazy stroke of his finger over my lace panties.

"It will be again," he warns before taking my mouth hard, suppressing me with his tongue. His fingers pull my panties aside, slipping in and dancing over my aching heat.

"Shit," I breathe against his lips, forgetting where I am for a moment. Forgetting we can't stand each other.

"You want relief, Holly?" he asks as my hips start to ride the rhythm of his talented fingers.

"Yes, give it to me, Sy," I plead, feeling myself build with each flick of his finger.

"Say please," he demands, slipping his thick finger inside of me.

"Please, Sy," I cry out as he pumps me harder.

"That's it, girl. Fuck my finger," he growls. The heat of his voice causes goose bumps to break out on my skin. A wave of impending bliss washes over me, and then my orgasm hits, hard and fast.

"Sy," I hiss, but don't get anything else out as his tongue is dancing with mine again, muffling my shouts of ecstasy. His taste reminds me of beer, mint, and all things Sy. He latches onto my tongue, sucking it hard into his mouth, sending pleasure and pain rolling through my body.

Fuck, this man is dangerous with his bad-boy attitude, his sexy as hell dirty mouth and his ability to take me on the highest of highs in less than a minute. He slows the kiss, lingering for a moment before resting his forehead on mine. This right here is why this man is dangerous: bringing me apart in the middle of the club, and making me forget I hate him. Removing his fingers, he brings them to his mouth and sucks them clean.

"Mmm," he murmurs.

I'm not surprised by the drop in my stomach watching him get lost in the taste of my orgasm.

"Now, tell me that was mediocre." He smirks after licking his fingers.

"Get off me." I push at him, jolted back into reality.

"Not until you admit it."

"Fuck you."

"No, fuck you, Holly. Don't come into my club and think you can play me. You won't win," he says, turning, leaving me again after a mind-blowing orgasm. I don't know what's worse, watching him leave while I stood naked in my house, or now, fully dressed and feeling like a whore in his club.

Fucker.

Pregnant...

"How can I be pregnant?" I ask the doctor two weeks later.

"Sometimes the contraceptive pill isn't one hundred percent foolproof. Anything as simple as taking your pill a few hours late can mess with the accuracy of it," he repeats for the second time this morning. I made him retest me twice before I believed him and now I'm freaking out.

Well, shit, I'm going to be a mom. I race to the small sink in the doctor's room and throw up my breakfast for the fifth morning this week. I knew something was off last week when I started feeling nauseous. I didn't think this was what he would be telling me though. I expected something more along the lines of a virus.

"I can't believe this," I say to myself, shaking my head. How the hell am I going to be a mom?

"We can look at your options, but I'd like to give you all the information and give you a few days to think on it," he says, seemingly reading my mind.

Shit, how am I going to tell Sy? After our two times together a few weeks ago, we've kept our distance. The way we left things should be enough to prove to me there is no way he will ever be okay with this when he can't stand to be around me. *Oh, God.*

"Speak to Carla out front and ask her to book you an appointment a week from today. We can then discuss your options," he says, standing from behind his desk and handing me some pamphlets.

"Thank you." I nod numbly, leaving the room before I break down. I need to call my mom.

Racing out with my mounting anxiety, I make it to my car and ring my mom before I have a full-on panic attack. I don't even bother making an appointment. My head is too foggy. She picks up on the third ring.

"Hey, sweetheart," she answers, her normal happy self.

"Hey, Mom." I begin to cry, knowing she'll be supportive but still be worried.

"What's wrong, doll?" she asks.

"I've messed up, Mom," I say, sniffing into the phone.

"Okay," she says calmly, not freaking out.

"I'm pregnant," I croak out, knowing I just have to get it out there. The line goes quiet and for a moment I think I've lost her.

"Mom?"

"I'm here. I just had to sit down a moment."

"I'm so sorry, Mom, for calling you like this," I cry into the phone, clearly not thinking this through. What kind of daughter just calls their mom and dumps this shit on them?

"Oh, baby, it's okay," she says, trying to calm me down as I sob into the phone. This is not meant to happen.

"I don't know how this happened. I'm on the pill. The doctor said it can happen, but shit, Mom, two times with a guy and I'm pregnant. I was just so stupid."

"Does he know?" she asks, talking about the baby's father. *Sy, the man who doesn't even want me.*

"God, no," I respond, drawing in a breath at the thought of telling him. "It wasn't anything serious," I cringe at admitting it, but it's the truth. Even if I wanted more, Sy isn't the type of man to go there.

"It's going to be okay, Holly," she tries to comfort me, but there's nothing she can say that will take away my unease and fear.

"I don't know what to do, Mom," I say, not listening to her reasoning.

"What do you mean, what to do?" she questions carefully.

"You know what I mean, Mom."

"No, I don't, Holly."

"Well, if I'm going to keep it or not," I explain and hear her suck in a breath at my confession.

"Holly, you know I love you and I'll support you through anything you decide, but I really think you need to take a breather first. I want you to think this through. You need to discuss this with him."

"I know. I'm just so confused."

"And I get that, I do, but don't make any decisions just yet, okay?" she pleads.

"Okay, I won't," I tell her, knowing I need more time.

"Have you told Kadence?" she asks and I cringe. *Oh, shit, how am I going to tell her?*

"Not yet. I pretty much just threw up in the doctor's office and flew out of there. I don't know how I'm going to tell her," I admit, knowing that's a copout. She will ask questions I'm not ready to answer.

"Let's do lunch, tomorrow."

"That would be good, Mom."

"Okay, darling. I'll call you in the morning to see how you're feeling. I remember when I was pregnant with you. You made me bring up my breakfast for twelve weeks," she laughs and her voice gets that soft wispy sound it always does when she talks about my brother and me as children. Instantly, my hand goes to my stomach.

"I love you, Mom," I whisper, wondering if I could ever be as good a mom as her.

"I love you, too," she says before hanging up.

Taking a deep breath, I rest my head on the steering wheel as the pamphlets the doctor gave me sit heavily on my lap.

What am I going to do? I need to tell Sy before making my decision. I could never keep this from him. The thought alone has my head out the door of the car, heaving up the rest of my stomach's contents.

He might not be okay with it, but I can't make this decision alone.

8

Sy

"Hey, Sy." Tina walks up to me, her tits falling out of her top. I don't know what her game is, but I've shot her down already tonight. The bitch is clutching at straws. Yeah, I've fucked her once in the past, but since Holly walked into my shop, I haven't been able to sort my shit out. "What are you doing all the way over here?" she asks, sitting her ass down on my bent knee.

"Tina, fuck off," I say, not in the mood for club pussy. I'm pissed. I can't get my head around a certain blonde woman. Tina pouts, but knows I'm serious when I nudge her off my knee. *Bitch should know not to fucking touch me.* She rises in a huff, pissed she's not getting what she wants and stalks back inside.

"That wasn't nice," Jesse says from behind me.

"Don't give a fuck."

"Yeah, we all know that," he laughs, finding the whole thing funny.

"What do you want, Jesse?"

"Just checking in with you, brother," he says, taking a seat.

"I thought you were on Kadence watch tonight?" I ask, trying to keep up with everything going on in the club. After the club barbecue two weeks ago, shit went down between Nix and his ex-wife, Addison. The blowout happened right after I finger fucked Holly in the hallway. I knew I fucked up when I saw the look of disgust on her face after what I said to her, but I couldn't go to her. Nix needed me more as Addison went at Kadence and Z. Everyone left soon after the drama, and by the time I was able to talk, she had gone.

"Nah, Brooks is on," he says, kicking back, stretching his legs out in front of him. "I'm on tomorrow. You?"

"Tomorrow night," I tell him, hoping like fuck Nix gets his ass home soon. If I could avoid this shit, I would.

"So, Holly," Jesse smiles and my body tenses at her name. He laughs when he gets a reaction out of me. "What's the deal?"

"No fucking deal." I act indifferent while inside my body is humming at the sound of her name.

"Didn't look like no deal when you were finger fucking her last time she was here," he jokes and I move fast, bringing him up by the scruff of his shirt, and banging him back up against the wall.

"You didn't see anything, asshole," I threaten, feeling a fierce protectiveness over Holly and what the fucker is saying.

"Okay, okay. Calm down," he says, still smiling. "Jesus, Sy. You're a fucking goner." He shakes his head watching me come down from my freak-out.

I stand for a few minutes taking in his words. I don't want to admit it, but he's right. I'm fucked. The woman has had my head messed up for the good part of a month and a half now. I'm completely lost and have no fucking clue how to react to it.

"Shut up," I finally respond, sitting back down.

"You're not going to get very far with that attitude," he puts in, giving me his opinion.

"I don't need to get very far, Jesse. I'm not fucking interested," I lie. I've been lost in the same lie for the last few weeks. I am interested and fuck me if that ain't the worst truth ever.

"Keep telling yourself that. When you need help, come see me."

"I won't be coming to you for advice," I scoff.

"Why not?" he asks, sounding offended. I simply look at him. The man is a player. I can never see him settling down. Besides, I'm not looking to settle down, but he's right. Holly does have me twisted, but that's all there is to it. Right?

"What? I'm serious," he pushes me as my phone rings from beside me. I ignore him and answer on the second ring.

"Sy," her voice whispers down the line and instantly I'm on alert. *Why would Holly be calling me and why does she sound scared?*

"Holly?" I ask, coming out of my chair.

"Help us," she says over the sound of a moving car. My blood runs cold and my heart rate picks up.

"Where are you?" I ask, snapping my fingers to get Jesse's attention. He stands, reading my body language.

"Zane grabbed us coming out of the theater in town. Brooks is hurt I think," she adds.

"Are you hurt?" I question, not wanting to know the answer.

"I'm okay, but Kadence isn't. He knocked her out and I can't get her to stay awake."

"Do you know where you are?"

"No, I only know we turned left out of the back entrance of the parking lot." She takes a shaky breath.

"Fuck, okay. I need you to hang on for a minute while we get the boys on this, okay?" I ask, walking inside the clubhouse, ready to round up all our available men.

"Okay, Sy," she says quietly. I have to give it to her, she sounds scared, but she has her shit sorted.

"Hold on. I'm still here," I reassure her, trying to keep her calm while my body hums with adrenalin.

"Jesse, try to get Brooks on the phone. Hunter, get to the theater." I start barking orders out as the clubhouse comes to life with the stress of it all.

"Holly?" I ask when I hear a shout in the background.

"Yeah?" she says quietly.

"What's happening?"

"I don't know. We're still driving."

"Can you see anything out the windows? Know which way you could be going?"

"No, I lost count of how many turns we did. Kadence keeps coming in and out of it. I've been trying to keep her calm."

"Okay, sweetheart, we got everyone on this. Hang tight. We're on our way," I assure her, even though I have no fucking idea where she is.

"Hurry, Sy," she whispers, her fear coming down the phone and hitting me like a punch to the face.

"I'm coming and that motherfucking asshole is dead," I promise her, meaning every word of it.

She doesn't say anything, her silence telling me enough.

"Are we sure they're in here?" I ask Chip, one of T's men, when we pull up at the front of the old barn about thirty miles outside of town. With no idea how to find the girls, we called in a marker with our rival club, Warriors of Mayhem. Where the Knights Rebels run a clean club, the Warriors run it dirty. I don't like the fuckers, but with Nix still thirty minutes out and both Holly and Kadence in danger, I have to trust them. T set us up with all the information we needed to get to the girls. Information that's led us to here.

"Yeah, we have guys around the perimeter," he says, walking around the van to get to the side. We follow quietly, keeping ourselves hidden. "We'll go in, see what we're up against and sort it out. T wants Gunner."

"We don't even know if Gunner is in there," Jesse says, coming up behind me.

"We're taking that chance," Chip cuts him off.

"I don't want fucking chances. He has two of our women in there, about to do who knows what. I fucking want him," I growl, my control slipping. I just need to get to her and worry about Gunner later.

"It's our recon and we'll run it the way we want to," he repeats, not stepping down. I look him over, sizing him up, seeing if I can take him. He has about two inches on me, but what I lack in height, I make up for in size. I could take the fucker. He holds my stare, but I don't give a fuck. If I have to walk in and kill Zane with my own hands, I will.

"Sy, step back," Jesse insists stepping between us. "You're too close." I know he's right, but I don't give a fuck what anyone says. I'm going in with or without them.

"I'm in. End of story," I say, leaving no room for argument.

"Just let us secure the perimeter, and then we can move," Chip says finally, agreeing to my play. I don't have a moment to agree before a gunshot rings throughout the quiet night. Racing forward, I don't care about the consequences. When I hear Kadence scream Holly's name, I know I have to get in there.

"Sy," Jesse calls quietly after me, but all I see is red. The asshole is dead. I'm gonna fucking kill him.

Kicking the door open, my eyes search the small area and go straight to Holly. Sitting against the wall, her hands cover her stomach. My gut tightens and something I haven't felt in a long time ignites in me. Rushing forward, my gun goes straight to the asshole leaning over her. The bullet goes straight through his skull, but I don't have a minute to register I just killed a man. I fall at her side and watch as she struggles for air.

"Holly," I shout and shake her to make her open her eyes. My mind is running all over the place. *I can't lose her, not when I only just figured out I want her.*

"Lay her flat and put pressure on the gunshot wound," Jesse instructs while holding Kadence's body over his lap. Fuck, when did he get here? Everything runs in slow motion. The commotion around us ceases to exist as I sit here watching all life leave her body.

"Holly!" I shout, pressing into the wound. "She's not breathing," I choke out, as panic seeps through me.

"Start compressions," he says calmly. How the hell he can he be so calm while I'm freaking out?

"Holly," I plead, pumping her chest eight counts before blowing my breath into her body. "Don't you die," I yell between breaths, remembering the feeling of loss and never wanting to have to live through it again.

"Don't you dare die." The words repeat over, and over as I pump her heart, begging it to start. "Don't you dare die…"

9

Holly

"DON'T YOU DARE DIE," SY'S PANIC-LACED WORDS PLAY over in my head. *Die?* What does it mean to die? Would the pain and the emptiness growing inside of me cease to exist? Would death be better? I wished the darkness that had crept behind my eyes in that old barn would come back to me and blanket me. I want to cry, to scream, but my throat is numb, my heart heavy and belly vacant.

"Holly, Sy's here to see you." My mom's voice breaks through my distant stare.

"I don't want to see anyone." I look up and realize silent tears are falling from her tired eyes and I know I've caused them. My mom has always been beautiful. Her flawless skin and perfectly sitting hair was one of the things I admired when growing up.

Standing before me now, I realize that woman is long gone. Worry lines that were never there fill her forehead and run down around her sad eyes. I know she hasn't left me for more than a few hours in the last two weeks and she's no doubt exhausted, but it hasn't stopped me from being difficult.

"Holly," she says again, breaking through the haze surrounding me.

"What?" I snap, over talking about Sy.

"He has sat outside your room every day for the last two weeks," she informs me; her tone speaks of disapproval. She thinks I'm rude. Maybe I am, but I can't bear to see him right now.

"Just don't push it," I whisper, hating myself for putting her through this.

"Do you really mean what you just said, about death?" she whispers, throwing me off for a moment. We were talking about Sy and now death? "You were mumbling while you were sitting there," she explains when she sees the confused look on my face.

"No, Mom," I lie, not knowing what I mean anymore. "I was just thinking aloud," I tell her, hoping she believes me.

"Have you been talking to the grief counselor when they've stopped by?"

"Mom, I promise I'm fine."

"Okay, good. Then tell Sy yourself. Tell him you don't want to see him, and maybe he will listen to you." I hold in the initial panic, hoping the steps the doctor taught me last week will help me through this moment.

"I'm not telling him anything, Mom."

"You will be," Sy's voice interrupts mine, and instantly I'm taken back to the place I'm trying desperately to forget.

"No," I manage to get out before my chest tightens as confusion clouds my mind. It's like a sudden and terrible awareness of the world around me—like I'm watching myself from a distance.

I struggle to catch my breath; each pull of air stretches out my heart.

"Holly?" I hear my mom's faint voice, but I'm too taken in the moment. My hand goes to my chest; the overwhelming feeling to run burns through me. If I could just get out of this room, maybe I could breathe.

"Holly," Sy's deep murmur anchors me to the bed. The man that tailspins me into a panic, now has the calming effect I need.

"Deep breaths." The timbre of his voice is soft and controlled. "Focus on me," he instructs as I clutch hard at my hospital gown. "You're safe. Nothing is going to hurt you." His words slowly chase the intense pain away. "Close your eyes." He continues to take control of the situation and my body listens. Closing my eyes, I continue with my breathing exercises and soon the sensation of my world spinning slows as the numbness separates me from reality. I stay in it, not caring if I ignore the world.

"Good girl," my mom finally says, reminding me she too just witnessed another of my panic attacks. I block it out. Worrying about it will probably set me off again. Instead, I focus on the slow rhythm of my deep breathing. To the room, I look as though I've returned, coming back calmly after what just transpired, but to me, I return with a piece of my sanity missing. My body feels heavy and my head foggy. After five minutes of silence, I build up enough courage to open my eyes.

"Welcome back," Sy says first, and I can't bring myself to look his way.

"Please go," I plead, feeling the tears start to fall.

"Don't make me go," he replies and the anguish in his voice makes me want to cave, to let him stay, but I can't even look at him.

"Please," I repeat, turning away from him and protecting myself under the itchy hospital blanket.

"Holly—" my mom pleads, but I cut her off.

"I can't do this with him here," I tell her honestly. Just knowing he witnessed my meltdown has my chest tightening again.

"I don't want to go, but I will," he finally replies after moments of silence. "I'll come back tomorrow."

"Don't," I say, knowing I won't want to see him tomorrow.

"I will and I will wait outside this door until you see me, Holly," he warns, his tone telling me he means every word of his threat, but I don't reply. There's no point. The room is quiet, but I don't chance a look. I need him gone. After a few more minutes, I hear the door click shut, but at his exit, I realize the heaviness in my heart doesn't leave, the gunshot wound to my stomach doesn't stop throbbing, and the darkness I crave never takes me.

"You know you have to tell him," my mom finally speaks after a few beats of silence.

"I know, Mom," I snap, regretting it instantly. I don't know what's wrong with me. One minute I'm having a breakdown and the next I'm angry. "I will," I say gentler this time. "I just need to get through these panic attacks."

She knows without me telling her that Sy was the father of my baby. She asked me the first day I was awake. I didn't deny it. What was the point? I did make her promise she would never tell anyone. I decided when the doctor told me I had lost the baby that it wasn't meant to be. Getting into that side of things with Sy would only spell trouble, and somehow in my messed-up head, I thought it would be better. But as the days go on, it doesn't make me feel better. I mean, how do you deal with the loss of someone who didn't have a chance to live?

No matter how hard I try, the memory of waking up in this room and asking about my baby has the darkest of clouds descending over me. The doctor's silence told me everything I needed to know. I didn't know until that very moment that the thought of not having my child nestled inside of my womb would be the most heartbreaking thing I would ever have to endure. To know the baby you were carrying is no more, where only a week earlier, its heart was thumping with life, fills me with a pain so deep I don't think it will ever fade. I feel alone, lost to the emptiness that settles within me and I don't understand.

"The doctors said it's normal, Holly." She comes to sit on my bed, her warm hand taking my own. I know they've said it's normal to experience all these feelings after a trauma, but it doesn't make me feel better.

"Darling girl, you know I'll support anything you decide, but that man out there is fighting the darkness just as you are. I see it in his face. You shouldn't be pushing him away." I don't say anything, just keep staring ahead, my eyes growing heavy. "No man sits outside a hospital room fighting his demons for no reason. Give him a chance." I agree with what she is saying, I see it in Sy's eyes, but I can't do it. I can't push past it yet.

"I'm not ready," I simply say, knowing she won't understand. No one understands.

"Okay, darling." Her hands go to my cheeks, wiping away my silent tears. "I love you, Holly Bear," she says as my eyes close.

"Holly Bear," I whisper my childhood name back to her. "I love you, Mom," I say just as sleep takes me.

My exhaustion blankets me. I love my mom; her love is beyond comparable. I'm so thankful for her trying to dissipate the clouds of darkness surrounding me, even if it doesn't work. As my mind drifts into slumber, I wonder if I would have been a mother like her, sitting by my daughter's side while she tries to push everyone away?

And just like that, I'm back in my nightmare.

10
Sy

"Holly," I plead, pumping her chest eight beats before blowing my breath into her body. Fuck, I never thought I would ever have to do this again.

"Don't you die," I yell between breaths, remembering the feeling of loss and never wanting to have to live through it again.

"Don't you dare die." The words repeat over, and over as I pump her heart, begging it to start.

"Don't you dare die…"

MY PLEADING PULLS ME FROM MY SLEEP. SWEAT COVERS MY brows as memories from that night flash through my mind. Fuck, another nightmare to add to the fucking reel.

"Are you all right, Sy?" Holly's mom asks, sitting next to me in the waiting room of the hospital.

"How is she?" I ignore her concern for me. I'm only worried about her daughter.

"I calmed her until she fell asleep." I nod as a sense of relief fills me. I've been coming to the hospital every day for the last two weeks. Every day, Melinda fills me in when Holly refuses to see me, but today I just had to push. I don't know what it is. Every day since that night in the clubhouse, I knew the connection between us was something different; something more than just a one-time deal. I was just too scared to see it for what it was. You would think watching my child take her last breath would teach me to love without attachments and fears. Instead, I held back from her, afraid of what hurt someone else could inflict on me, and look where that got me.

I should have never gone there with her, never let a part of me open up again, but I did and now I'm stuck between wanting to walk away and knowing I can't.

"Are you sure you're okay?" she asks again, pulling me out of my head.

"How many is that now?" I reference the panic attack. I know she told me she's been having them. I didn't realize how bad they were. I don't think I can handle seeing that look of fear on her face again.

"She's been having at least one a day, sometimes two. The doctors said to expect it. She's seeing someone and has been prescribed something to help."

"Any news on when they're releasing her?" I ask the one question I've asked every day for the last two weeks. I hate hospitals. The sooner she's out of here, the sooner I can relax.

"A couple more nights. They want to make sure she doesn't have another bleed." I nod, understanding how touch and go it was last week. After the second surgery to stop the bleed from the gunshot wound, no one knew if she was going to make it. I wish I could take it all back, get there in time. If only I didn't fuck around arguing with one of T's boys, I could have beaten the bullet. "You should go home," she whispers, pulling me out of my self-loathing,

"I can't leave her," I tell her truthfully. I don't even know why, but something is keeping me here. Holding me in the hospital when I can't fucking stand to be here.

"Even though you're struggling?" she observes, trying to figure me out.

I solemnly nod. There's no point in denying it. "This isn't about me. It's about her, and I need to be here."

"You need to give her some space. She can't deal with everything she is going through, Sy," she says, letting me know in her sweet motherly-way what I already know deep down inside. I might be feeling these feelings, but Holly is dealing with shit and I can't push her.

"Go home. I promise I'll call you when she's released, and I'll keep you updated," she says, resting her hand over mine. "But please, give my girl some time," she says, patting it softly. I haven't had the nurturing touch of a mother in such a long time, I'm stuck in the sensation of it. I don't move, don't respond—just sit, lost in it.

Knowing I can't help Holly when she is only twenty feet away from me is going to kill me, but I know if I force her, I'll only end up pushing her further away. If I ever want her light to help me out of my darkness, then I need to wait. So I'm going to do just that. I will sit in the darkness waiting—waiting for her to come and guide me back out. And while I wait, hoping the light comes soon, I will thank God I'm not afraid of the dark.

11

Holly

three months later

"YOU CAN DO THIS," I SAY, LOOKING AT MYSELF IN THE rear-view mirror. "You have to do this," I repeat, forcing myself to just get it over with. Still outside the Knights Rebels' clubhouse, I'm so tempted to turn around and not come back. But I can't. I can't keep running away.

Swallowing past the lump in my throat, I push my new bangs off my face and steal a breath as I exit the car. I can do this. I just need to remember my breathing exercises and pray I make it through the night. The last thing I need tonight is to lose it.

The gravel under my feet crunches as I walk to the front of the clubhouse. I don't want to be here, but I know if I don't pull my shit together I'm going to have Kadence and Nix on my back. It's Kadence's birthday party, and as much as I love my best friend,

I'm struggling to even make it through the front door.

My stomach rolls as I walk past the first row of bikes lined up.

"Hey, Holly," someone calls as I walk down the hall to the main room.

"Hi." I fake smile and keep walking, too chicken-shit to stop and make small talk. *Just get this over with*, I remind myself before turning the corner to face the people I've been hiding from for the last few months. My eyes scan the clubhouse, and I feel lost, like everything and everyone has a purpose but me. In a daze, everything around me becomes misty, but like a beacon in the night, my eyes instantly connect with his. *Oh, God.* He watches me across the club and his stare alone has me wanting to turn and walk straight back out. I have not seen him since that day in the hospital when I completely flipped out. I thought for sure I would have seen him the next day. He seemed so adamant that we would be talking, but he never showed. At first, I was relieved that I didn't have to see him and thought the panic of what he represented wouldn't follow me. But as the days went by and he didn't return, I realized I was wrong. The panic still came, and what he represented was still in my mind. For every day he ignored me, I became more lost. He walked away, when I asked him to, yet I needed him.

I divert my eyes finding Kadence and Nix, but before I know it, I'm back to watching Sy. His eyes narrow when they meet mine. Before I can make a move, I see him stalk toward me. I falter in my step not sure what to do. I can't leave. I've made it this far. Instead, I try to find an escape, somewhere to detour away from him. But before I can come up with anything, his hand is around my wrist and he's growling in my ear.

"What the fuck did you do to your hair?" *What the fuck?* The man doesn't speak to me for weeks and that's what he asks?

"Get your hands off me." I jerk, trying to release myself from his hold.

"I'm not even kidding, Holly. What the fuck did you do to

your hair?" he asks again. I've pictured this scene play out so many times in the last few weeks, and never in any of the scenarios did I think that's what he would be asking.

"Sy, what the hell do you think you're doing?" Kadence races over to where we stand before I can answer him.

"Stay out of it, Kadence. This is between Holly and me." Sy's eyes rest on me, not releasing his grip.

"Like hell, Sy. Let her go," she snaps back, moving in to break the connection he has on me. His grip softens, but still stays firm. I narrow my eyes when he smiles and my heart rate spikes up. *Keep it together, Holly.*

I see Nix pull Kadence back to the side, but I don't take my eyes off the arrogant man holding me.

"You're keeping your shit together. I'll give you that," he whispers, his breath warm and inviting over my ear. "But we will be talking tonight. You can guarantee that," he promises before pulling back. I don't move, but focus on my breathing. He's right. I am keeping my shit together, but if I don't get away from him, I'll fucking lose it.

"If you'll excuse me, I need a drink," I say, turning my back and heading for the bar.

"Holly," he calls before I get too far away. "I'm serious. I'll give you that play, but after that," he points at Nix dropping down to one knee, "we will talk." I don't reply. I just stare as my best friend stands awkwardly while Nix proposes marriage in the middle of the clubhouse.

"You okay, girly?" Mr. Turner asks when I walk over to where Kadence's parents watch on.

"Shouldn't I be asking you?" I ask, nodding as Nix drags Kadence, his new fiancée, through the crowd.

"He's good people. He wouldn't ask her if he didn't have every intention of making my girl happy," he says, reaching over, hooking Kadence's mom around the waist, and pulling her close to him.

"He is good people," I agree. "The whole club is." Hell, if it weren't for them, Kadence nor I would be here right now. Even if I have pushed these people away, I know they saved me and I have them to thank.

"Come on. Let's go congratulate our girl." He pulls me out of my thoughts.

"You go. I'll wait," I say, pointing to the bar, eager to have a drink. The line to congratulate the couple is already ten-people deep. I'd rather try to relax myself before trying to fake happiness.

"Okay, save a drink for me. You and me have got some catching up to do," he says, turning back to see his daughter. I walk back a few steps watching them go and when my back meets with the bar, I turn, ready for a distraction.

"Hey, Hunter. I need you to get me drunk," I say, pointing to the bottle of whiskey, catching the young prospect off guard. "Start me off at two and keep them coming," I boss him. He smiles and places a glass in front of me. I watch as he fills it with an amber-colored liquid, and when he's done, I pick it up, tip my head and throw it back. Slamming the glass down to the bar, I take a second and repeat the action.

"Whoa there," he says, watching me carefully.

"Another," I demand, ignoring his concern. He raises his brows, but I raise mine back, letting him know I mean business. He shrugs and fills my glass back up.

"Good, now keep them coming," I say, watching him shake his head in laughter.

"You got a broken heart, Holly?" he asks, leaning over the bar.

"What?" I'm thrown by his question.

"People only drink like that if they have a broken heart." He shrugs, thinking he has me worked out.

"What do you know about a broken heart? Do you even have a girlfriend?" I rudely ask.

"No, why? You offering?" he jokes and I laugh, the noise sounding foreign to me. I haven't laughed in such a long time I forgot how great it felt.

"You wish." I shake my head at him. He might be cute with his dark features and great body, but he's just a kid. Besides, I wouldn't go there. One pissed-off biker is already enough to handle.

"Yeah, that's one wish you're not getting." Kelly, Brooks' wife, comes up and flicks Hunter's ear. "How are you, Holly?" she asks, smiling across at me.

"Good," I lie, because who wants the truth? No, I'm not fine. I'm a fucking mess and just pretending everything is fine.

"I love the new do," she compliments me and inside I cringe. I don't know why I cut it and changed the color. I blame it on one of my famous rash decisions.

"Thanks," I fake smile. "So, good news about Kadence and Nix." I move the conversation off me and onto something else that won't make me want to break down.

"It is. I can't believe the Prez is settling down." She shakes her head, looking over as Nix and Kadence talk with her mom and dad. "You'll be next." She winks and I laugh. Only this time it's forced. I turn to Hunter giving him the nod.

"Another one, Hunter," I say, ignoring the look passed between them. This is what I need; something to stop the pain and help me pretend. 'Cause I sure as hell need to tonight.

12

Sy

IT'S HER LAUGH THAT LETS ME KNOW SHE'S OUTSIDE. NOT that it's her usual happy laugh that I once remember. The one that no matter how many times I told myself I hated listening to, it would still bring me some kind of peace. Like for once in my fucked-up situation, I could see some light. No, this laugh was something else. A mask hiding her pain. She thinks no one can see it; see the hurt she hides behind, but to me it stands out, screaming for someone to take it all away. If only I weren't so fucked up, maybe I could help her.

"Hey brother, you sort out the front gate?" Brooks asks, coming to stand next to me on the threshold of the back door. I just did a check after seeing Nix and Kadence off. We might have had Gunner sorted out, but we're still keeping our eyes open. Since the girls have been home, we've had eyes on them every day. I've kept my distance from Holly at her mom's request, but that doesn't mean I haven't been watching.

"Yep, all good on my end," I reply, scanning for who's left tonight and how much trouble Holly can get herself into. Most of the party has broken up, and now the Friday night crowd's starting to settle in for a weekend of booze and pussy.

"You gonna go sort that out anytime soon?" he asks, and he doesn't have to say her name for me to know who and what he's talking about.

"Getting there," I tell him, turning back to watch her plant her ass down on the runt's lap. She started drinking after our little talk and I haven't had a chance to get her alone. Once everyone said their congratulations, she never left Kadence's side. But now that her bulldog-protector best friend has gone home, I've got an opening.

"She's so far in her own head, I don't think she realizes we can see past it all," I say, turning back to him. I know I have no claim to her, but at the same time, just the thought of her pert ass sitting on Hunter's lap has me grinding my teeth.

"She's still dealing. I get it. We've all been there, been watching you do it for the last few years," he says, taking a pull of beer.

I ignore his dig at me, but agree with him about her. Thinking back to the first time I met her, walking into the shop drunk and throwing her attitude around. She might think she has everyone fooled, but I know she's not the same person.

"Two different things, but I'll give you that," I tell him, not prepared to get into sharing.

"Might be, but her way of coping is no different than what you do," he says, telling me what I already know. I do know, fuck. I live with that shit every day, but seeing her live through the shit she's hiding is getting old. Fast.

"Sy, can you help me with her? She's completely off her face,"

Kelly asks, looking over at Holly as she throws back another shot.

"Yep," I say, ready to end this shit now.

"Sunshine," Holly cheers from Hunter's lap, jumping up and down as I stalk toward her. I ignore her name for me, pissed she would use it now, and even more pissed it stirs something in me.

"Keep those fucking hands to yourself, asshole," I tell the runt. My tone leaves no room for argument, but for extra measure, I level my stare at him. He nods, swallowing obviously and keeping his hands up.

"She just sat down," Hunter says in his defense, but I don't give a fuck.

"Sy, why have you got to be so cranky all the time?" she asks, looking up at me. Her glassy eyes shine with a playfulness I haven't seen in a long time.

"Come on. Let's go." Taking one of her wrists in my hand, I pull her off him.

"Ooh, where are we going?" she asks, leaning into me. "Are you going to take me back to your room?" she whispers into my ear, her warm voice spreads through me. I try not to let it affect me. She's so far gone; she would never act like this sober. Instead, I march her ass inside, away from all the fucks looking at her like they want a piece.

"Sy, take me to your room," she tries again, this time pulling out of my hold.

"What the fuck are you doing?" I ask, taking her arm back and pulling her into the kitchen.

"What do you mean? I'm having a drink, having fun. Seeing as though I'm at a party and all," she laughs her fake-ass laugh.

"How much have you had to drink?" I ask, wondering how much Hunter has been serving her.

"I don't know, but you're still annoying me, so I need more."

"Holly."

"What? You are," she says and if I weren't pissed that she was just rubbing her ass up along one of my brothers, I would be excited her attitude has returned.

"Are you meant to be drinking with your pills?"

"How do you know about my pills?" she snaps, my question almost giving away that I've kept tabs on her.

"Answer the question, Holly."

"I don't want to talk about it, Sy." She spins to leave, but I hook my arm around her waist and pull her back to me.

"Oh, I know, but what you want and what you're going to get are two different things," I tell her, picking her up and planting her ass on the counter. She doesn't fight it; instead, she pushes herself back and rests her head on the wall, pouting.

"Are you listening to me, Holly?" I ask and wait for her to answer.

"'I'm so tired, Sy," she says, barely above a whisper, and for a moment I don't know if she means tonight or in general. Then she looks at me, her eyes so fucking lost I don't even know how to help her find her way.

"I know, girl. Fuck, you work so hard; no wonder you're exhausted." I wait for her to respond, but what is there to say really. Moving away, I get a cup ready to sober her up.

"Do you take sugar?" I ask, coming back to her. "Holly?" I touch her when she doesn't respond, but she's already asleep. Her head falls to the side and her eyes are closed. Taking her in my arms, I walk her through the clubhouse to my room. There's no way I'm leaving her out here alone. Wrestling with the handle, I manage to open the door and get through without dropping her dead weight.

"Sy?" she mumbles from my arms.

"Shhh," I soothe her, not up for an argument.

"I think I'm going to be sick," she mumbles, forcing me to detour to the bathroom.

"Hold on," I say, flicking on the switch.

"I'm going to be—" She doesn't get to finish before vomit covers the front of both me and her dress.

"Oh, God," she moans, bringing her hands up to cover her face.

"Shit, Holly," I curse, placing her on her feet in front of the toilet.

"I'm so sorry," she apologizes, leaning over into the toilet bowl before throwing up again. "Oh. My. God," she repeats again as her body wracks with silent heaving while I get her a glass of water. Looking down the front of me, I quickly remove my fucked-up cut and shirt.

"Sy," she moans, "I don't feel too good." She shakes her head in the bowl.

"Get it all out. You'll feel better tomorrow," I tell her, cleaning myself off. I watch her for another ten minutes until she starts to fall asleep.

"Come on, girl," I say, pulling her up and sitting her on the toilet.

"But it's so comfortable," she argues, looking like complete shit.

"You'll be more comfortable without vomit down your tits." I point down the front of her.

"God, how embarrassing," she says, looking down the front of her. Her hands go to her straps, pushing them off her shoulders. I keep my gaze up high, knowing I can't handle seeing her naked and so close to me.

"Help me, Sy," she slurs, pushing the dress down her body and swaying on the spot.

"Here." I offer her my hand, and pull her up to standing. My hands go to the tops of her arms, holding her still as she steps out of the dress.

"Oh, does this remind you of something?" She giggles and I make a note to check her meds, and alcohol side effects.

"Give me a second," I tell her as I guide her back down to sit on the toilet lid while I grab a clean washcloth and an old T-shirt for her to throw on.

"You awake?" I ask when I come back in and see her slouched over herself, her head hanging low. "Holly?" I nudge her, but she's completely out of it. Who the fuck falls asleep sitting up? Wetting the cloth, I try to wipe her down as best as possible before I put her in one of my shirts. She doesn't stir once and I know my night is going to be rough making sure she's okay. Picking her up, I carry her back to my room, and place her on the left side of my bed. She rolls into the fetal position, curling into herself and nestling into the pillow. She looks so innocent, yet when I look at her, I see myself; a lost person who's trying to fight the darkness. Only I've had years to perfect it.

Taking the blanket, I cover her and pray she doesn't get sick again. The last thing I need to be doing is changing my sheets after the night we just had.

"Night, Holly." I brush a piece of hair off her face.

"Sy," she murmurs before she's out again, but the damage is done. My name coming from her lips as she finds sleep explodes into my heart.

I'm fucking screwed.

13

Holly

MY HUNG-OVER ASS ROLLS OUT OF BED AND LOOKS AROUND the room. *Where the hell am I?* The bare room rings no bells as I sit up and get my bearings. My legs are naked and I'm wearing a worn black tee and my panties. *What the hell?* The shower runs in the next room and for a moment I panic that I've ended up in some stranger's bed. *How did I get here?* My eyes search the room some more, only stopping when they land on the leather cut draped over a chair. *Shit.* The memories of Kadence getting engaged, Sy and his calling me out, and me getting drunk off my ass all comes back. *Oh, God, that all happened.* My stomach turns, and before I know it, I'm racing for the bathroom. I don't care if Sy's in the shower, naked, only a few feet away from me—or the fact I'm only wearing panties, and a T-shirt. My only concern is the toilet and hoping like hell I make it in time.

"What the hell?" Sy turns as I push the door open and run straight to the toilet. Dropping to my knees, I hug the bowl like it's my long lost friend.

"Holly, are you okay?"

"Yep," I croak into the bowl, hiding the crimson shade I'm sure to be wearing on my face. I dry heave some more, my embarrassment growing as the sounds being exorcised from my mouth echo around the small bathroom. The shower door opens, and I don't have it in me to turn and tell him to stay in there.

"Fuck," he curses, leaving me alone for a moment, before returning a few seconds later. "Here," he says, pulling me away from the bowl and holding out a cold glass of water. I look up, my eyes watering from the intense chuck-up session, but through the haze, I'm met with the image of pure fucking sex. Sy is wrapped in a towel, every inch of his body covered in tattoos, and dripping with water.

"Fuck me," I curse, taking him in.

"I already have," he says, smirking. If it weren't for the fact that I'm probably still drunk, a wet, naked Sy standing in front of me would totally mortify me. But it doesn't. I swallow past the lump forming in my throat and take the glass of water, swallowing the bitch down fast before I choke on my drool.

"Care to tell me how I ended up in your bed?" I ask after handing the glass back up to him.

"Well, I could have put you in the spare apartment, but I was worried you might have choked on your own vomit." He smirks again, resting his hip against the basin.

"I vomited already?" I wince, wondering how much I had to drink.

"Twice," he informs me as he folds his arms across his tatted-up chest. Jesus, the man is covered in ink. Every single inch of him.

"Is that why I'm not wearing my clothes?" I ask, putting two and two together.

"Yeah, you totally fucked them up," he tells me, shaking his head.

"Did you change me?"

"Yep, stripped you, washed you and dressed you." My face heats up again, embarrassment filling my cheeks.

"Not like I haven't seen it all before," he remarks, and at his comment I tense. The past comes crashing back, reminding me of my grief, but most shockingly, the regret. *I need to tell him.*

"Where did you just go?" he asks, his eyes narrowing, watching me carefully like he can read me every which way.

"Nowhere."

"You went somewhere. For a moment there, I thought I had you."

"Had me?" I ask, coming to a stand, but I'm shaky on my feet. He reaches out, steadying me.

"A small glimpse at the old Holly," he says.

"I'm still the same Holly," I defend myself, yet at the same time I know exactly what he means. *The old Holly wouldn't be hiding.*

"You keep pretending, and I worry I won't ever get her back."

"You say that like you had me in the first place," I snap, not liking where this is going.

"Oh, I've had you, Holly. Don't deny it. Had you with a snap of my fingers," he purrs, the mischievous grin breaking out over his face. *Oh, God, that shit works.*

"Please, keep telling yourself that," I say, still holding onto his arms. His strong, wet, naked arms. Releasing my hold, I step back out of his reach. I try to look anywhere but at him. My eyes have other ideas though as they keep drifting back to the towel wrapped low on his waist. They then zero in on the water droplets forming over his inked body. I wouldn't be surprised if my mind and tongue took over and started worshiping each drawing he has etched into his skin.

"Like what you see?" he asks, catching me checking him out.

"I've seen better." I go for the cool and collected vibe, failing miserably.

"You feeling okay now?" He ignores my blatant lie; it's for the best. I even feel embarrassed for myself.

"Yeah, I'm good. I'll just wait back in the room." I go to walk past him, but he stops me in my escape.

"Probably best to get that vomit out of your hair first," he says, pointing to my head. *Oh, my God, it just keeps getting worse.*

I turn fast, looking in the vanity mirror. Fuck. Chunks of spew sit on the ends of my hair. *Just kill me already.*

"Ewww," I say, turning the tap on and leaning forward to rinse out the mess.

"Just get in the shower, and shampoo it out," he says and I look up, catching his gaze through the mirror.

"Okay," I respond, thinking how perfect a hot shower would feel right now. I turn and face him, noticing the smirk on his face.

"Why did you change your hair?" He asks the same question as last night, the one I don't want to answer truthfully. I knew the drastic cut and color would shock everyone, and maybe that was my intention; get them to talk about something other than the fact that I'm fucked up from what happened.

"Wanted a change," I go for a simple version. Because really, telling someone you hated yourself so much you wanted to feel like someone else, isn't what they want to hear. "Why?"

"Just can't believe you cut your hair."

"What, you don't like it?" I strike back.

"Didn't say that."

"Oh, you're the type of guy who loves their woman long and blonde," I accuse.

"Didn't say that either. Just wanted to know why."

"Well, now you know," I say, feeling like I've just gone on the offensive for no reason whatsoever. "Are you done?" I ask, pointing to the empty shower, needing to get out of here.

"Yeah, all yours." He nods, still not moving from his space.

"Umm, a little privacy please?" I ask after a moment of him not moving. The man has lost his damn mind if he thinks I'm undressing in front of him.

"Don't worry, Holly, I've seen it all before," he teases, but I can't be sucked in by it.

"Well, I'm not going to undress in front of you."

"I'll turn around," he smirks, and if it weren't for the fact that the shower is completely glass, or that I would feel vulnerable standing naked in front of him again, I would do it. I never used to be like this. I never used to question everything I would normally do, but the thought of breaking down in front of this man has my hand going to my chest and forcing myself to steady my breaths.

"Are you okay?" he asks, taking a step forward.

"Yeah," I say, taking my eyes, and casting them past his shoulder to stop panic from clawing at me.

"You're not, but I'm not going to push. I'll meet you out there." He turns and leaves me standing there, giving me the moment I need.

"No, I'm not okay, but you can do this," I talk to myself in the mirror. I should never have drunk that much last night and left myself open like this. All I need to do is get in the shower, wash the vomit out of my hair, and leave. I nod before pulling Sy's shirt over my head and stepping out of my panties. Standing in the shower, I let the hot water wash away the vomit and alcohol seeping from my pores. If only it could wash away the grief and guilt. Wash away the lies I've told myself, my family, and my friends.

After ten minutes of hiding in the shower, I shut off the water and reach for a towel. I dry my now Sy-smelling hair, knowing I have to carry his smell around with me all day, and pull through the knots with a small comb I find in the vanity.

"Holly, are you almost done?" Sy calls through the door, startling me.

"Umm, almost," I reply, hoping he doesn't walk in here.

"I've got to go into the shop is all," he says and I'm not sure if he wants me to leave with him or he's saying goodbye. All I know is I'm not ready to leave this bathroom just yet.

"Okay you go," I say, hoping I can get out of seeing him this morning.

"I'll wait." *Fuck.*

"No, go. I'm not feeling good. I might get back into the shower," I lie, thinking fast. He's quiet for a moment not saying anything.

"I know what you're doing," his voice is so close to the door my heart rate picks up waiting to see how this will play out. I don't reply, just silently pray he doesn't push this morning. It was wrong of me to come last night, and getting drunk and ending up in his bed was the last thing I needed.

"Your clothes are on my bed," he finally breaks the silence.

"Okay, thank you, and sorry about last night," I apologize, feeling more like a fool as the minutes tick by in our silence.

"I wish you would open the door, but I get it. I'll see you soon and we'll talk then." I force myself to hold in my objection. I can't see him again. *I don't think I would survive.*

"Bye, Holly," he whispers, but it doesn't sound like a goodbye, more like a promise. After a few moments of quiet, I risk it and open the door. The room is empty, and my dress lies clean on the bed. Lost in the embarrassment, I quickly dress and try to hatch a plan to get out of here without being seen. The last thing I need is for everyone to think I'm doing the walk of shame. Even though Sy and I didn't do anything, other than him cleaning up my vomit, I feel like I'm sneaking out. I hold in the urge to vomit again. I take a breath, send up a prayer and get the hell out of there.

Past

54

"We want to take her home," I say, exhausted and defeated. He warned us of this in the beginning when the bone marrow transplant failed, but Katie still held on to the hope it wouldn't come to this. Today we're letting go of that hope.

"We can discuss your options," Dr. Parks says, looking up from his notes.

"As soon as possible," I insist, looking down at her sleeping body. My daughter's life slips away from me and I have to sit here, and watch it as it happens in this small fucking room. I can't take it any longer.

"We can arrange home hospice care. Let me talk with her team and we will go from there," he says, leaving us alone.

"Are you sure you want this?" Katie asks across from me.

"It's not about what I want; it's what she wants." I know this is the best *thing for her, for us.*

"She doesn't know what she wants," she protests, but I don't listen. Just looking down at her, I know this is the best thing. If she's not asleep, we're waking her up for treatment only to medicate her again. What sort of life is this for her?

"She knows what she wants. If this is it, we will give it to her." Leaning down, I kiss her pale skin.

"Are we giving up?" she asks. It's a question I've struggled with for the last few weeks.

"Katie, you know this is the best thing for her. We don't want her to be on the machine and have these tubes coming out of her when she goes," I declare, absolute.

"I know. I just feel like we're giving up," she sobs into our daughter's hair, stroking it away from her face.

"We aren't. We're giving her a chance at a peaceful passing. This part matters to her." I walk around the bed to comfort Katie. As much as I struggle to move past the hurt she has brought on us, I can't bear to see her break. "You know it's time, Katie. She's ready. We need to let her go," I tell her, hating every moment of it.

14

Holly

I FEEL LIKE I'M DROWNING, LIKE I'M GASPING TO GET MY old self back. Desperation claws at me as my soul craves a sense of peace, yet no matter how hard I try, how hard I pretend, I can't seem to push past the pain that suffocates me. I've tried everything to break through this darkness that keeps pulling me down. It controls me, threatens to take me, and I fight it. I do, but some days, it's too much.

"What the hell are you doing in there?" Sam, my older brother, yells from the other side of the bathroom door, sending the dark shadows away. *Jesus, I've been doing so well. What the hell is going on?*

"Getting ready," I yell back, still looking at myself in the mirror. I'd like to think no one sees the pain I hide, but some days, even I look at myself and see my reflection telling me I'm a fraud. Swallowing past the lump in my throat, I exhale and prepare to face him.

"Well, hurry up. I need a shower," he replies, like every other morning after he's stayed the night.

"Maybe if you stayed at your place, you wouldn't have to wait." I paste on my fake smile. The one I've perfected, the one I hide behind, and open the door to face him.

"Why would I want to do that?" he laughs, flicking my nose as he walks past me, slamming the door shut.

"Asshole," I yell, walking down the hall to start the coffee maker.

"Love you too, little sis," he calls back. Hearing those words today settles some of the uneasiness I've been feeling since seeing Sy again at Kadence's party. Today is a good day. Today is going to be *better*, I remind myself while setting the coffeepot up. If you had asked me three months ago where I saw myself this year, this would not be my answer. I never imagined my days would only get better with the help of anxiety pills. But grief isn't predictable; it can strike so hard that even the strongest fall. When you live your life in color, surrounded by happiness, yet your world is painted with grief, how do you find equilibrium?

"You doing okay, sis?" Sam grills me, pulling me from my thoughts.

"Yep," I answer, looking up at him from my spot in the kitchen.

"What are you doing just standing there?" Reaching over, he flicks the switch on the coffee machine. *Shit.*

"Oh gosh, still waking up," I fake a yawn and hope he doesn't push. "Want eggs?" I ask, walking past him to get breakfast started. *Shit, I don't have eggs.*

"Nah, I have to run, and I won't be in tonight," he reminds me; like I care he isn't dropping in to babysit. He hasn't been in a lot lately and the less time he spends here, the better. I love my brother, but having him around all the time is just painful. He showed up the first day I was released from the hospital, taking up Kadence's old room. I didn't protest in the beginning, it wouldn't have gotten me anywhere. My brother is a fierce protector and in his eyes this was something that would let him feel like he was fulfilling his brotherly duties. I gave him that, knowing I needed it too, but now, three months later, it's getting old.

"I know, dear brother. However will I survive?" I joke and watch his lips quirk at my attitude.

"I'm sure you'll manage, but if you need me, just call," he says, coming forward, and wrapping his arms around me.

"I'm not a child and you're not my parent, Sam. I'll be fine," I counter, pulling back to face him. I hate feeling like a burden to my family.

"No, Holly, you're my sister. You were shot. You're dealing with some serious shit, and I'm worried about you. We all are."

"Sam, that was three months ago. I'm fine," I protest, with only a small amount of lying laced in my words. *I am fine, aren't I? I was until I saw Sy last week.*

"I know how long ago it was, Hol, and the more you say you're fine, the less I believe you. I'm your big brother; I'm allowed to worry."

"You worry too much," I tell him, hating that I can't fool him.

"Do I?"

"You know you do. Quit it. You're turning into Mom," I tease.

"Take it back." He reaches for my arm and twists me, holding my arm behind my back. I try to out twist him, but he's too quick. I know his moves; he's been pulling them on me since I was five years old.

"Let me go. I thought you had to leave?" I try for a different tactic.

"Not 'til you take it back."

"Sam, you are so like Mom it's disgusting," I say as an insult. He reaches around and flicks my nose again. "Quit it. You're going to mess with my make-up."

"Take it back."

"Fine, okay. You're not turning into Mom," I lie. "Now, let me go," I demand. He holds on for one second longer, and then releases his grip.

"I miss this side of you," he quietly confesses, causing me to look up at him.

"I'm getting there," I tell him.

"Love you, little sis," he smiles, reaching out and scuffing my hair.

"Sam," I screech, smacking his hand away.

"I'll see you tomorrow," he laughs like he loves the fact that he has now pissed me off.

"See ya, asshole." I wave him off and walk back to the bathroom to fix up the teased mess that is now my hair.

"Make sure you lock up," he calls after me from the front door.

"Yes, *Mom*," I yell back, hearing him laugh. After fixing my hair, I walk back out and finish getting ready for work. A knock at the door stops me from reaching my coffee, and I curse, realizing I keep getting interrupted. Opening the door, I feel the color drain from my face when I see Sy standing there.

"Sy," I murmur, hiding my reaction. *Oh, God, what is he doing here?*

"Holly," he responds, the sound of his voice sending a rush of pain through me. It's the most beautiful pain in the world, one only I can feel.

"What's up?" I try for cool, but don't feel like I even pull it off. I haven't spoken to him since the morning after the party where I had made a fool of myself.

"Can I come in?" he asks and like a dumb fool, I step aside

and let him inside.

"Is everything okay?" I ask, surprised I'm less panicky to have him in my home.

"Yep, but you've got a tail today," he states without any further explanation.

"Umm, okay, why exactly do I have a tail today?" I ask, knowing this has to do with Kadence.

"Club business," he says, shrugging, his hands going to his pockets.

I cross my arms, waiting for him to tell the truth, because if he thinks for one second I'm in any danger, Kadence would have already called me.

"Well, considering I'm not part of your club, doesn't look like it concerns me," I say, walking back to the kitchen to try for the third time this morning to get my coffee.

"Well, you are a part of the club, so don't even start that shit," he says, following me into the kitchen.

"What do you want, Sy? 'Cause I'm certain you didn't come all this way to argue with me about if I'm a part of your club or not, which by the way, I'm not."

"I did come here for Holly watch. Got shit going down. Nix wanted eyes on you. There's been some talk circulating 'cause of the fallout from Zane."

"What talk?" I inquire, my panic spiking.

"Just some whispers; we're looking into it."

I try not to let my panic show, but just hearing Zane's name has my hand grasping my chest.

"Don't fucking touch her, asshole," I yell out to Zane.

"Don't worry, Holly. You can watch, then you'll be next," Zane taunts and the bile I had been holding down since being thrown in the van slowly starts to rise.

"Don't," Kadence pleads with him. "You can have me, but please don't

touch her," she says, giving herself over to him.

"Are you okay?" Sy's voice pulls me out of my memory as concern fills his eyes.

"Yeah, I'm good." I take a large breath and control my breathing. I haven't had a panic attack for a week; my first one over Zane in two.

"You're not," he accuses like he did back in his bathroom last week.

"I'm fine," I try again, this time letting my breathing relax me again.

"You do know you have a tell?" he smirks, folding his arms across his chest.

"Shut up, Sy. I'm not in the mood today," I tell him, not feeling up to faking it. "I have to get ready for work," I say, walking back out of the kitchen and down to my bedroom—ultimately ending our conversation and making me miss out on my coffee again. *Fuck.*

"Okay, I'll wait for you here," he yells down the hall, not giving up.

Sitting on my bed, I force myself to calm my racing heart. *Shit, shit, shit.* Every time I see the man, my heart aches. Why does he have to come here and shake my world upside down again?

Forcing myself to work through it, I grab my keys and handbag, and make my way out of the room past Sy who's now sitting in my favorite chair.

"You ready to go?" he asks, snapping his head up before running his eyes down my body and creating an awareness in me.

"I'm ready to go without you," I argue, ignoring the tingling sensations that prickle in me at watching him watch me.

"Babe, I already told you, club business."

"Well, I'm not going to the clubhouse. I'm working in the salon," I inform him, ignoring his babe comment.

"Didn't say you had to, but today, you have a tail. Sound good?"

"No, like I said, I'm in the salon today. I don't want a scary biker dude standing in the corner of my shop looking like a creep."

"You think I look like a creep?" he questions me, a small amount of amusement in his eyes.

"No, I don't, but I can't help but think a tattooed biker in my upmarket salon will look a little creepy."

"You could come back to the clubhouse, you know, less creepy and all."

"I have to work," I say again, not that it would make a difference if I didn't go in. I've been at the new hair salon for a couple of weeks now, and I'm still building a new clientele. I'd probably spend half a day cleaning up the other stylists' mess, or reading a trashy mag in the back room. Even though the environment is a massive change and I miss my old clients, I'm glad no one knows who I am and more importantly, no one knows my past.

"Looks like I'll be tagging along then."

"Great." I force my smile, feeling everything but.

"Don't look so put out," he mumbles, standing from the chair and walking forward.

"I didn't ask for this, remember," I sneer, watching him move.

"You got no clue what you asked for," he mutters under his breath, giving his head a quick shake which confuses me more. "You ready?" he asks, now acting pissed. *What the hell?*

"Yeah," I reply, still not sure what's going on. I don't understand why Sy has to be here, and now he seems annoyed about it.

"What's going on here, Sy?" I ask when we travel down the elevator in silence.

"You tell me, Holly."

Tell him? God, I wish I could just let it all come out, but I'm just so caught up in my darkness I don't know how to let anyone in. Not even the one person I should be letting in. And that shames me each day, knowing what I hide from him.

15

Sy

I WALK CLOSE BEHIND HER, HOPING LIKE FUCK I DON'T mess this up. I know pushing her right now is not wise, but I've sat back for the last three months and I can't do it anymore. I need to be the one to help her, to pull her out of this funk she's been living in.

I follow one step behind her as we make the ten-minute walk to the new salon she started working at a couple of weeks ago. It's only a few blocks further down than her last salon, but I hate that she walks alone. *Something we will be talking about later.* Her small frame shivers in the brisk air, causing her to rub her small arms to keep warm. I'm not surprised she's cold. The woman I took in the heat of the moment, those months ago on her living room floor, no longer stands in front of me. I know by looking at her she hasn't been taking care of herself, but actually watching her, searching past the fake bravado she puts on, I see something else. Something that follows her. It hits me like a freight train, like staring into a mirror and realizing you're no longer looking at yourself.

"Did you bring a jacket?" I ask, watching her warm herself up.

"I'm okay. We're almost there." She points up at the shop only a block ahead.

"Didn't ask if you were okay. Asked if you brought a jacket."

"I didn't ask for you to follow me today, and yet you still did, so I guess we both didn't get what we asked for," she says, still walking. Fuck, her little attitude gives me some hope that she isn't so lost. I don't respond. I just reach up and tuck her under my arm to keep her warm.

"What the hell are you doing?" she asks, trying to move out of my hold.

"You should have brought a jacket," I explain, keeping her in my embrace.

"Let me go, please," she says, trying to duck out, but my hold is too firm.

"Quit moving or I'll throw you over my shoulder," I threaten, meaning every word of it. Her movements still, her fight not that desperate to leave.

"You never used to be this annoying," she huffs after a few beats, probably put out knowing my heat is just what she needed.

"No, you used to be the annoying one," I reply as we walk up to the front of her shop.

"Sy, you don't have to do this." She stops suddenly and turns to face me. I can already see the argument play out over her face.

"Holly, don't even bother. I'm staying. Told you, it's club business," I continue to lie. "You should get inside; you're going to be late." I nod toward the woman opening up the front doors.

"Fine, but you're wasting your time," she adds before disappearing inside.

She might be right, but I still stand there for a few minutes watching her through the glass as she prepares for her day. Her fake smile is plastered on as she laughs her unrecognizable laugh. She looks up a few times, but doesn't acknowledge me. After watching her start on her first client, I walk across the street and get myself a coffee. I look around, searching for a spot where I can watch her for a few hours. I know I'm probably taking this to the extreme, but after the party last week, seeing her lost in her head, I need to do something to pull her out. Everyone back at the clubhouse is worried about her. If only she could see we want to help her. My cell vibrates in my pocket and I fish it out, hoping it's Rue telling me she managed to clear my weekend so I can make the trip back to Brighton. I pushed my visit out this year, slowly starting to distance myself, but guilt has been eating at me the last few days and the need to see her is strong.

"Yeah?" I answer without checking the caller ID.

"Where the fuck you at?" Nix barks down the phone.

"I'm out," I reply, not telling him my business.

"Beau needs a second man on his pickup tonight. You free?"

"No, I'm out all day," I tell him, not prepared to leave Holly alone.

"Where you at?"

"Is it important you know?"

"Quit fuckin' around, Sy. Can you do it?" he asks, sounding pissed I'm fucking with him. I should say yes. This is the first call Beau has gotten through for the underground recovery we voted in months back. I know it's huge for him, but I've come this far with Holly; I'm not going to leave her alone now.

"I'm with Holly today, so no, I can't fucking do it. Send Hunter with him," I say, annoyed I just told him what I was doing.

"You're with Holly, right now?" His tone suggests he doesn't believe me.

"What the fuck, Nix! Yes, I'm with Holly."

"Holly is at work, so quit fuckin' around."

"I know she's at work. I just fucking walked her there."

The line is quiet as he takes in what I just revealed. *Fucking great.*

"You walked her to work?" he asks in his no bullshit way, but I can hear the smile in his voice.

"Is that all you wanted?" I ignore his question.

"You, Sylas Dean, walked Holly to work?"

"Fuck off, Nix. I'm hanging up now," I growl into the phone, not in the mood for his shit.

"Have fun," he chimes down the line before I end the call. *Smartass.*

I know he has a reason to be shocked. I've gone from wanting nothing to do with her, to not being able to keep away, to giving her space. But I'm done. I've given her enough time and I'm tired of waiting for her to pull herself out of her head when I know I can help her. She just has to trust me.

"Are you going to buy anything else today?" the waitress asks after I've been sitting here for the last hour.

"Do I have to?" I snap, enjoying the quietness of watching Holly work.

"Yeah, you have to," she replies in her whiney voice.

I stand, not in the mood to listen or argue with her. Dropping a twenty, I leave and decide to watch Holly from afar. I keep her in my line of sight, and try not to read too much into the familiar feelings which settle inside me every time she searches for me. Instead, I focus on what she doesn't want people to see: the darkness prevailing. It threatens to send her into oblivion, one I know about all too well. I've had years to perfect the façade she's now putting on show for the world to see, but she's so absentminded and lost in her own thoughts she doesn't even realize how obvious it is. I've tried to fight the need to help her through the glooming shadows that lurk around her. But for reasons I don't even understand, this pull she has on me is so strong, walking away is not an option.

16

Holly

"GIRL, I'M TELLING YOU NOW, IF THAT FINE PIECE OF MAN-candy was standing out the front of the shop waiting on me, you'd have to hold me back from mauling him right there on the street," Gabrielle says, standing next to me. "I mean just look at him, all dark and tattooed. Jesus on a cracker, if you don't want him, I'll have a play," she continues her verbal assessment of Sy.

Gabrielle is one of the other stylists who work at Vault Hair. She took me under her wing on my first day and hasn't left me alone.

"Gabrielle," I sigh. She hasn't stopped for a breath, verbally undressing Sy for most of the day. The woman won't give up.

"Holly, look at him," she says, reaching out and lifting my face from the paperwork in front of me. "That man is sex on fire. You damn blind or what?" I pull back and turn toward her. Her long, dark hair is pulled up into some kickass bun on top of her head, braids entwined all through the masterpiece. She peels her eyes off Sy, who's standing across the street, to turn and look at me.

"I'm not blind. I can see," I agree with her assessment. I silently add, *but Sy and I are just complicated*. We may have had a connection once before, but now, things are too messed up.

"He's so mysterious. Maybe I should get a tattoo from him," she smirks, resting her elbow on the desk, her head lost in her personal daydream.

"You do that," I say, going back to my paperwork. I've had a busy day, picking up two new clients plus the few I had booked.

"You wouldn't care?" She sounds shocked.

"Why would I care? I already told you, he is just someone I know. That's it." I try to let the words be true, but I know I'm only lying to myself.

"Holly, the man has stood out there all day keeping an eye on you. I've watched him watch you. He might be someone you know, but that man out there, is feeling something else for you," she says, pointing toward Sy. She shakes her head at me and walks to the back of the salon. I look up and catch Sy's stare; his chin lifts, giving me his signature nod. I awkwardly raise my hand and wave over at him. His lips quirk in a small lift, awarding me with his grin. Dropping my hand, I get back to my work as an unfamiliar sensation flows through me. Excitement? Anticipation? Something settles over me; it slightly outweighs the dread I always feel. For the first time in a long time, I find myself not wanting the sadness to take over and bring me down.

"Looks like Mr. Dark and Dangerous is heading our way," Gabrielle says, walking past me with her bag and coat. "You okay if I head out? I have to pick up Rosie. Derrick's on late nights this week." Rosie is Gabrielle's five-year-old daughter and Derrick is her amazing husband.

"Yeah, it's okay. I'm just finishing up now." I wave her off, my eyes still on Sy as he walks past the glass door.

"See you tomorrow," she laughs, leaving us alone in the empty salon.

"You're still here," I state, packing up the desk, not quite giving him my eyes. "I thought you would have given up." I'm shocked he's hung around all day.

"Nope, told you, I was on watch all day. How was your day?"

"Busy," I answer while reaching for my bag.

"What have you got goin' on now?" he questions quietly, watching my every move.

"Just heading home." I pull my hair up on my head.

"You want to get something to eat?" he asks.

"Eat?"

"Yeah, I'm starved. While we're out, we may as well pick something up," he shrugs, looking around the salon.

"I'm pretty tired. I was planning on a quiet night."

"Okay, I'll order us some takeout," he suggests, completely ignoring my idea of a quiet night. "What do you like?"

"Umm, I was just going to have a glass of wine, a bath and go to bed," I admit, and then cringe internally at the visual of it. Sy doesn't respond. Instead, he stands before me; his dark stare now piercing into mine.

"You need to eat, Holly."

"I'll make something at home." I lie, knowing I don't have an appetite.

"I watched you all day today; you haven't stopped. No arguing. I'll order you some takeout. You ready?" he asks, ending all conversation of dinner and stopping me from replying.

"I'm capable of looking after myself, Sy."

"Really? 'Cause from where I'm standing, you're not doing a good job. So, until you start, I'll take over for you."

"I don't need taking care of. I'm doing an okay job, thank

you," I fight, knowing the words coming from my mouth are a lie. I can even hear it.

"Babe, your clothes are falling off you. As beautiful as you are, you look like shit," he points out, and in that split second, the sadness that lives to bring me down falls over me again. The small reprieve I was feeling not five minutes ago, now feels fragile by his words. Just like me. "Don't even think about it, Holly." He steps forward into my space.

"Don't what?"

"I'm not letting you get lost again. I'm not letting you become me." His hand reaches for my face, but I pull back at his touch. "I've watched you. I've kept my distance, but I can't do it anymore. I told you that night in the hospital. I won't let you push me away."

"Don't push me, Sy," I beg, knowing he's my weakness.

"I'm not pushing. I've given you time for that to settle in. I think your time is up."

"Sy—"

"Your act is not working for me. That smile you hide behind doesn't fool me."

"I don't know what you're talking about." I step out of his space, needing a moment to breathe.

"This perfected act of yours. You think you have everyone fooled." He shakes his head. It's a slow shake, which makes me forget the panic that's rising. Slowly, anger takes its place.

"You have no idea what you're talking about. How dare you!" My voice rises and at the same time heat floods my cheeks.

"Come on, baby. You can do better than that," he smirks, setting my blood on fire in frustration.

"Fuck you!"

"There she is. I'm starting to see her," he whispers, his eyes shining with excitement. "The real you is still in there. I just have to piss you off to convince her to come out." His voice is low and filled with amusement, making me angrier. My hands go to his chest, an impulsive reaction to his accusation.

"I'm here. I've always been here." I push hard, but his hands come to my wrists, trapping them in his grip.

"You might think you've been here, but Holly, you've been missing, and I'm not going to let you do that anymore."

My defenses fall, his hands on my skin unraveling me. "I don't know if I'm ready. I don't want this pressure. I'm not brave enough," I foolishly admit. I don't know why I cave to this man, admitting truths that don't need to be voiced. I've done so well keeping my shit together, yet now he's in my face for one day, I'm giving in.

"You don't need to be brave, Holly."

"Sy," I murmur, trying to pull out of his grasp, but he holds on tighter, forcing me to forfeit.

"Holly, don't say anything. Just trust that I've got you. Let me help you, okay?" His grip on my wrists loosens, but I don't have the strength to fight him anymore. I stand before him exposed, stripped back, my body begging for comfort, for affection, *for the touch of another.* His hands move down mine, and his fingers part my own, locking them between his. The warmth of his touch takes some of the panic away.

"Let's just start with dinner," he says, drawing me closer. The smell of leather, oil, and Sy comforts me. I nod into his embrace, words no longer needed as I selfishly take what he doesn't know he's offering. Would he still be willing to help me if knew the reason I hurt the most? I know it makes me weak, but I'm not ready to find out.

Past

Sy

"Do you know that sharks rarely get cancer?" she asks from the window as she soaks up the morning sun. Her question jolts me, keeping me stuck in the same position for a few minutes as I process her words. I'm not surprised at her random fact about sharks. It's her favorite topic, but the cancer word has my full attention. When we first found out about the cancer, Katie didn't want to label it. In her mind, labeling Keira's disease was giving it power, so we decided to tell Keira she had special blood that needed important medicine to make her better. At the time, it was appropriate. She was five years old and didn't need to know the ugliness of what cancer was. As the years went by and with the cancer returning, we never called it what it was. Always just her special blood that needed more medicine.

"I didn't know that," I answer her question, coming back to the moment.

"It says it has to do with the 'epigonal organ' they have. We don't have *it."* She continues to read from her Shark Dictionary we bought her last month.

"I did not know that either, sweetheart." I keep my voice level and as calm as I can manage.

"Do you think when I see God, I should tell him that people need the epigonal organ?" she asks. Her tone is so serious it takes me a few seconds to figure out how to answer her and not scream in anger. She's been asking questions like this the last week. Innocent to her, but soul-crushing to Katie and me.

"I think that would be a good idea," I reply, the only thing I can say at this moment. I want to get up and put my fist through the wall, scream at the top of my lungs at the injustice, but none of it will take away the fact that my daughter is dying. The special blood that needs more medicine just isn't going to cut it anymore. My daughter has cancer. She's going to die.

17
Holly

"I HAVE A NINE O'CLOCK WITH DR. ELLIOT," I TELL THE young receptionist.

"Take a seat," she smiles and nods over at the quiet waiting room before going back to tapping away on her keyboard. It's the morning after Sy walked me to work, hung around all day and then proceeded to buy me dinner. We didn't discuss what happened those two times five months ago, when we caved in the heat of the moment, or this connection we have. I didn't tell him about the baby or even talk about the shooting, but each time I see him, it gets harder and harder to keep it all inside. I know he has a right to know, but talking about it, hell, just bringing up the possibility of talking about it has me shutting it out.

"Holly," Dr. Elliot calls from her office, breaking me from my thoughts.

"Hi." I stand and make my way into her office. Her room is not what I was expecting when I first walked in last month. I had this vision that I would walk into a stuffy room, lie back on a leather couch and tell her all my worries and have her feel sorry for me.

"Take a seat," she says, motioning to the sofa across from her armchair. Placing my bag down next to me, I sit back into the cream suede sofa. I take a pillow from beside me and place it on my lap, relaxing into the comfort of her room.

"How have you been, Holly?" she inquires, sitting across from me. Her pencil skirt and blouse are so neatly pressed I wonder how she manages to pull off her perfect look. Her blonde hair is blow-waved into a neat bob style, just like every other time I've come, and her perfectly applied lipstick complements her outfit. The woman is so well put together; she makes me look like a hot mess.

"I'm good," I answer as I fold my hands together, stopping myself from fidgeting. I always hate this part. *The niceties of how my week was, before getting into the real reasons of why I come here once a week.* Insecurity eats away at me as the sadness attempts to consume my thoughts. I started seeing Dr. Kendal Elliot when I didn't even want to get out of bed. I didn't understand why I was so upset, why I kept pushing everyone away. My family didn't know what to say, didn't know how to help me grieve. It wasn't until I had a visit from Nix that I realized I wasn't coping. The badass biker telling me I needed to pull my head out of my ass was enough to get me up and moving. I stood there and cried for what I had become. He held me while the waves of emotion washed over me, and then pulled out his phone and made my first appointment.

"Want to start with a page from your book?" Dr. Elliot smiles, returning me to the present moment. She knows how much I hate this part. I've tried all my tricks to get out of it, leaving my notebook at home and begging her to read it out for me. I hate the anticipation of it, of listening to the words pour out of me when I'm feeling most vulnerable.

"Sure," I reply, knowing the quicker this is done, the quicker we can move on. Taking a deep breath, I flip to my most recent entry in the diary I've been keeping for the last few weeks.

"I didn't really get much down," I lie. This journal is filled with so much shit, I just hate repeating it.

"That's okay. Let's hear what you have," she counters. If I weren't about to let her into my darkness, I would smile at her persistence.

"Tuesday the second. Today has been a bad day. I'm sick of feeling so weak. Why can't I just feel peace? Why does it have to be so hard?" I read aloud in a shaky voice, scanning the pages filled with my scrawled handwriting. "I don't want to feel like this, like I'm in a constant state of anguish. Why can't I just pick myself up? I know I'm playing the victim card, but I can't stop. I hate that about me. I hate how this controls me. That I can't just wake up and be okay." I begin to cry through my words, resenting every moment of it. My inner-most thoughts spew out of me, holding me together, but at the same time, they possess the strength to break me.

"Very good, Holly." She smiles her gentle smile. "Can you tell me why you think you have a hard time reading your diary back to me?"

"I don't know. Sometimes, when I start going down the path of feeling sorry for myself, I can't stop. It's like I work so hard trying to feel okay, but then I do this and feel worse." I shrug, not really understanding why I have to relive it over and over.

"Well, that's the purpose of these exercises. You're not playing the victim, Holly. You are a victim. Getting these feelings out is normal. You're not going to break. It's okay to feel those things. They are a normal reaction to what you have experienced."

"But is it? Shouldn't I be over this by now? I feel like I need to just get over it, get over this pain, this loss, but I can't and it's messing with my head." I let out a shaky breath. This panic consumes me. It takes everyday things and makes them impossible to endure. *When will it all be okay?*

"Holly, you experienced something that was life threatening. You were shot. The same bullet killed your child. That is what happened to you. That won't ever leave you, so it's okay to be feeling these emotions. It doesn't make you weak, or helpless. You had something taken from you. You need to stop worrying about how other people expect you to act, or be. There is no shame in feeling like you can't handle the stress of what you went through. There is no shame in wanting to curl up in your bed and feel like you don't want to face the world. What's not okay is hiding these feelings. If you don't talk about what you're trying to bury, then you aren't going to work through this and move forward with your life." I know what she is saying is right, but how do you try to explain to someone who doesn't understand what you are going through? I don't want to bring down my friends or my family.

"I just wish this feeling of dread would go away. That it wasn't so hard to roll out of bed."

"You need more time and you need to let people in. I think you need to tell Sy about the baby," she insists and I know she is right. I know telling Sy is something that needs to be done. How do I even begin to explain my mourning for the loss of someone whose existence was kept secret in the first place?

"I don't think I'm ready for that."

"What are you so afraid of?" she asks, eyeing me carefully. This is something we have discussed many times in the last few weeks, but I don't know what is holding me back from telling him. It's not that I'm afraid of him, but more of what he will say.

"That he will look at it as something that was insignificant and dismiss my loss." I let the truth come out with no hesitation. It frightens me more than anything else.

"Do you honestly believe that?" She sounds shocked, but she doesn't know the situation like I do. He might be in my space now, but before the shooting, the man didn't want anything to do with me.

"I don't know what I believe anymore."

"That's what we have to work on, Holly, getting you to believe again."

"So, he just followed you to work, spent all day at the front of the store, and then followed you home. You both ate in silence, then he left?" Kadence asks, sitting across from me in our favorite coffee shop a week after Sy's weird stalker day. I don't know why I even let on about my strange night with Sy, but he never told me why the club was watching out, so I wanted to know what was going on. I haven't seen anyone else watching me, so what game is he playing?

"Yes, Kadence, he told me it was club business," I tell her, taking a sip of my coffee.

"Well, I have no idea why he would tell you that. Nix hasn't warned me at all, and considering all that's happened, he would have told me, Holly." I know she's right. I knew he wasn't telling the truth. I just don't understand what he's up to.

"Well, looks like I was played."

"Or maybe he is done waiting like he said," she adds. I don't reply. I watch as she tries to work her brain to come up with a way to talk about it. "Are you planning on telling him?" she asks over her mug of coffee.

"I'm getting there," I mumble. I really am. I know I have to tell him, that he deserves to know. I'm just working up to it.

"Well, the sooner the better," she adds, knowing she can't

push me.

"So, how are the wedding plans going?" I ask, hoping to get off this subject.

"We're going dress shopping next week, so make yourself available," she announces, and I fight my need to come up with an excuse not to go. "You know, I'm kind of enjoying this new dynamic to our relationship," she laughs, watching me work through my need to say no. I know she's joking. Hell, it is laughable; there's no denying that. Five months ago, I would have been all over this. Now, I'm fighting my panic at even the thought of going out.

"I didn't mean that," she rushes out, reaching for my hand when I don't laugh at her attempt to joke. I wish I could go back to the way we were before, when she was the one hiding away in our apartment, keeping to herself while I had the carefree attitude.

"But it's true, isn't it?" I squeeze her back. She looks at me with heartache, but I can't get drawn into it. I need to move past this and not get stuck again.

"It was a stupid joke," she whispers, but I won't let her beat herself up about it.

"I'm getting there," I confide. "Slowly but surely. Just give me some more time."

"I love you, Holly. You know that, right?"

"I do and I love you, too," I reply sincerely. "Now, let's talk about this bachelorette party. Can we do Vegas?" I force myself to be happy for her. I'm her maid of honor; this is what I need to do. Besides, keeping my mind busy will help me stop thinking about things that need to be forgotten.

"Oh, Nix will not be down with that," she shakes her head, but her smile tells me she would risk it.

"Okay, leave it with me," I tell her, knowing I'll be limited with that man of hers.

"Just, please, whatever you do, do not make me wear something ridiculous."

"Umm, who are you talking to? I'll make you look good. Don't stress," I say, reaching for my phone when it vibrates. Picking it up, my stomach flutters when I see his name flash on my screen. I hate myself for it, considering I've worked so hard to keep him at arms length the last few weeks. But after the party and now dinner, I can't hide my smile when I see his name on the screen.

Sunshine: Are you busy tonight?

I look at the screen, wondering what alternate universe I'm living in when Sy messages me asking if I'm busy.

Me: No, why?

I quickly type back and place the phone on the table to stop myself from over analyzing my reply. Why did I tell him that?

"So, when do you want to do this? Same weekend as the boys' bachelor party?" I ask, giving Kadence my attention again.

"No, we'll have to do separate dates. We have Z," she says, watching me carefully when my phone beeps again. I pick it up, ignoring her smirk and read his new message.

Sunshine: I'll be over at 5pm

I check the time and see I have a couple of hours.

"You okay?" Kadence finally gives in and asks.

"Yeah," I tell her, not sure why I don't want to fill her in on Sy's message, or him coming over again. Something in me wants to keep it a secret from everyone around us, even her.

"Who are you messaging?" She raises her brow in suspicion when I don't fill her in.

"Just Mom. She just sent me something silly." I somehow come up with a lie and instantly feel like shit. I'm a bad best friend.

"Oh, really? Show me." She smirks and holds her hand out calling my bluff. *Shit.*

"You won't think it's funny," I mumble, placing my phone in my bag.

"You never know, I might think it's really awesome." She shrugs, not fazed with my secrecy. *She knows.*

"Fine, it wasn't Mom. Just leave it, okay?" I spill, feeling the pressure of her stare.

"Didn't think so," she smirks into her coffee. "Just remember, Holly, I have your back, but the longer you keep it all hidden, the harder the fallout will be," she warns, and I know she's right. I just need to tell him when the time is right.

Then again, when is it the right time to tell a man he's lost a child he didn't know he had?

18

Sy

I KNOCK ON HER DOOR, TRYING TO JUGGLE THE BAGS IN both hands before I drop it all. *Fuck. Am I doing the right thing here?*

"Hi," she says, opening the door and looking down at the bags I brought with me. She's wearing some sweater that normally would not be a turn-on, but with her wearing it, she manages to make it look sexy as fuck.

"Hey," I respond, walking past her to the kitchen. "I brought dinner."

"I can see that," she replies, closing the door and following behind me.

"Have you eaten?" I pull out food and set it down in places I'm sure it doesn't belong.

"Sy, it's five o'clock; no one eats this early," she points out, still standing at the threshold of the kitchen and living room.

"I know what time it is, Holly, but I want to know have you eaten today?"

"As a matter of fact, I had lunch with Kadence." She raises her brows, waiting to see if I'll push.

"Well, that's a start," I admit, going back to the groceries.

"What is all this?" she asks, folding her arms over her chest. She looks stuck between shock and annoyance. Shocked that I shopped, annoyance that I'm back here bossing her.

"It's called food, Holly," I joke and watch her fight a smile. I wish she would give it to me whole.

"I know what it is, smartass. Why is it all here?"

"Well you see, last time I was here I didn't notice much in your fridge. Thought I might help you out."

"You went into my fridge?" she chastises me, as if I committed a felony.

"No, I mean yes," I admit, not really sure what the fuck to say. "Shit, is that like a fucking rule you're not supposed to break?" I ask, wondering what the right answer is.

"No, it's just rude."

"You should know by now I'm rude," I tell her what she sure as fuck should already know.

"So, you went into my fridge and thought you would buy me food?" she presses, not agreeing with my rudeness, but still fucking caught up on the damn fridge incident.

"Well, I was concerned for Sam," I offer my first thought when I opened the damn fridge.

"Sam?"

"Yeah, Sam. How the fuck does he survive living here? The dude is a fucking big guy." I remember the first time I met him at the hospital. Tall, broody and didn't even give a fuck he had a group of bikers standing around wanting to know about his sister.

"Sam doesn't live here. He just stays when he needs a break

from whatever screw he has going on that week."

"So Sam isn't living here? You're living by yourself?" I question, my concern going from mild to intense. *How the fuck did I miss this shit?*

"I'm a grown woman, Sy. I can live by myself," she reassures me, but I don't agree with that right now.

"Well, you need to eat more. You've lost weight."

"You say that like it's a bad thing." She gives me one of those fake laughs, pissing me off. When I met Holly almost six months ago, she was already tiny. Now standing across from me, the woman is all fucking bones.

"Believe me, it is." I look her up and down, not at all satisfied with how she thinks she's looking after herself.

"How much do I owe you then?" She clears her throat, obviously done with our argument.

"Nothing, it's on me," I tell her, placing some more food in the pantry. I don't even know what the fuck I bought. I kind of just followed some housewife around copying her shop.

"Sy."

"Holly," I smirk, enjoying playing this little game with her. In the beginning, I fucking hated this shit, but now, the thought of getting a reaction from her just pushes me further to get one.

"Fine, at least let me show you where everything goes," she grumbles as she pushes past me, and starts moving everything I've put away.

"Sounds good," I say, relieved.

"So you didn't work today?" I ask as we silently place all the groceries away.

"No, I only work part-time at the moment," she lets me know as she walks around the kitchen placing everything where it's meant to go. "Why do I get the feeling you already know this?"

"I don't," I lie, not letting on that Kadence fills me in on everything she does.

"Mmmm," she says, not believing me. I don't say anything. I just keep watching her as she pulls down some plates and starts serving up the takeout I bought. "Were you on 'Holly Watch' the other day?" she asks suspiciously. She looks up and catches me watching her.

"We're just keeping an eye on everyone. I had the day off. Wanted to make sure you were okay after the party," I stretch the truth a little. She doesn't need to know the real reasons behind my following her, making sure she was dealing with everything okay.

"And tonight?" she pushes, coming around the counter to sit next to me.

Spinning on the kitchen stool, I face her. "Like I said, you have no food. You need to start looking after yourself, Holly."

"I am looking after myself, Sy, but thank you," she whispers down at her plate. "I might not have a kitchen full of food, but I'm trying hard to get my life back to what it was." She looks up at me; her lost, broken eyes seeking out mine.

There is something about this woman, something that I can't stop myself from wanting. It's the same something that would break me if it were taken from me again, before I even had the chance to claim it.

"Eat," I order, picking up my fork and starting. I don't understand why I have this need to help her, why she's constantly in my head. And what I don't understand even more is why none of this freaks me out?

"When did you get so bossy?" she asks over a mouthful of food.

"Always have been," I tell her, filling my own mouth. She doesn't reply and we spend the rest of dinner in silence.

"Sy, are we going to discuss this strange night of dinner and silence?" she asks, following behind me as I take our plates to the kitchen.

"What do you want to discuss, Holly?"

"Oh, I don't know, Sy. These last few days have been very strange."

"Why?" I turn back to her, watching her bite down on her lip with worry. She doesn't want to ask, but I can see the need to know that flows through her.

"I don't know why. It just has been." She rests her hip against the kitchen counter.

"I already told you, Holly. I'm done with standing back and waiting for you to snap out of this state of denial."

"You think hanging around my place of work, making me eat dinner and cleaning my kitchen is going to snap me out of this denial you seem to think I'm living in?"

"No."

"No?" she fires back with that attitude hidden behind her eyes. We clearly have different views on what is happening here.

"No, the dinner the other night was because I stood outside your shop for six hours keeping watch, and I was fucking hungry. Today, I wanted to see you. Was it to bring you food? Most definitely, but you needed it. I'm cleaning our mess, because that's what you do when you eat at someone's house, not because I think it will get you to open up. That's not what this is about, Holly. I'm not doing any of this hoping you snap out of it; I'm just being here for you and waiting for you do it."

"And what if I can't just snap out of it?"

"You will, Holly, and I'll be here for as long as it takes. Even if that means days of standing outside your work and walking you home so you eat, then so be it. I won't stop, no matter how much you push. I knew when I walked into that hospital room that you needed time, so I walked away, giving you the space you needed, but I can't give you any more."

"But I can't do this," she whispers. Her crystal blue eyes are fighting the tears that I know she won't want to let fall. "It's too hard to pretend when you're so close." Her head whips from side to side. "You make it so hard." She steps back, but I don't let her retreat.

"Make what hard, Holly? It's just you and me here. You don't have to be anything other than you." I step into her space.

"You won't like that person, Sy. I don't even like that person."

"You think I don't see it, Holly? Think I haven't watched you these past few months as you've become someone who slowly falls apart? I don't like this person either. At least the person you're hiding shows some emotion; this person standing here is trying to find a way out." I reach for her hand. Her porcelain fingers, looking so clean, so pure against my inked ones.

"It's okay to not be okay, Holly."

"No, it's not, Sy." She pulls away, turning her back to me.

"What are you so afraid of?"

"I'm afraid of what you'll see," she admits. If she knew what I hid, what I'm so afraid of people seeing, she wouldn't be so afraid.

Darkness has stolen her, and something in me needs to be the person to save her.

"I don't want to fight anymore, Sy," she whispers so faintly I strain to hear her words. But I do hear them, and allow them to give me permission to wrap her in my arms. To hold her and help conquer the demons she fights.

If only I knew what I was battling.

19

Holly

"Oh, my God. Don't look now, but that sex on a fucking bike from last week is about to walk in the shop," Gabrielle says from behind me. Instantly, my hands go to work of their own accord and smooth the front of my blue shift dress. "For all that is holy, you've had sex with him, haven't you?" She elbows my side when she sees my reaction to spotting him.

"What? I have not," I defend myself just as he walks in.

"Hey," he greets me before nodding at Gabrielle.

"Hey," I reply, the sight of him causing me to fumble with the pen I was using to fill out a client card.

"You free?" he asks, looking around the quiet salon.

"She was just about to take a break," Gabrielle answers for me. If Sy wasn't watching me carefully, I'd kick her.

"Don't you have work to do?" I turn and ask her.

"No, I'm good," she smiles.

I don't push it further. Turning back to Sy, I decide my best bet would be to move away from her.

"Guess I'm free," I say, filing the card away for later. "Let me get my bag." I turn, leaving him alone with Gabrielle. Calming my nerves, I hang up my work apron, and fix my hair before heading back out.

"And you have other artists working there?" I hear her ask as I walk up to them.

"Yeah, we just put on another artist. Give the shop a call. They'll fit you in," he tells her, bringing his eyes to me. "You ready?" he asks and I nod. *Am I ready?*

"You don't have anyone in for an hour, so take your time," Gabrielle calls out. Gritting my teeth, I vow to kill her when I get back.

"I'll have her back in time," Sy answers for me. And I hear Gab laugh. *Bitch.*

"So, what's up?" I ask when we walk down the sidewalk. I don't know where we're going, and I don't find myself asking.

"Want to get some lunch?" he suggests, pointing over to one of my favorite diners, 'Happy Chef.'

"Okay," I agree. We walk over and get ourselves a booth toward the back.

"Sy, what's up?" I ask again, wondering if I'll get an actual answer this time. The waitress hands us our menus and leaves us to look them over.

"Not much. What's up with you?" he asks, looking at me over his menu.

"No seriously, what's going on?" I demand when he goes back to studying our meal options. I don't know why he thinks I will just go along with this little charade. I'm not sure what has changed with him, but this new *friend* business is starting to freak me out. What's worse, is every time I see him, he reminds me of the baby, but at the same time, he makes me forget. *How's that for a contradiction?*

"I wanted to see you," he says straight out. No games, no lies.

"Okay, why?"

"I don't know why." He places the menu down. "Fuck, Holly. I don't know what you want me to say. I've tried not to want to see you, tried to go back to ignoring you, but I can't."

"Why?" I find myself asking. "What's changed?"

"I don't know," he repeats like the thought annoys him. I don't know what to say, how to respond. The two times we were together were intense; I'll give him that. But he showed no sign of wanting anything more.

"Sy, I'm not ready for this. I've spent the last few months reliving that nightmare, and I'm getting there. I promise you I am. But this," I gesture between us, "this isn't going to happen," I confirm, and I hate myself for it. I don't know if he thinks he owes me something or what, but the last time we spoke before the shooting, we had no plans to start a relationship.

"Fuck, Holly, I'm not asking for anything. I just…" He takes a breath to gather himself. "I'm not labeling this. I'm not talking about what this is when I don't even understand it myself. But when you walked out of that clubhouse that night of the barbecue, I knew I wanted more. I might not have admitted it, might not have showed you that, but you had gotten under my skin and nothing I did was getting you out. I was so close to following you, but I held off, and I wish I hadn't. Then that shit with Zane went down. I nearly fucking lost you before I ever had you. I can't even tell you what I was feeling then; it fucked with me, Holly. This, right now, is what this is about. I get that this is hard for you, but it's the same for me. Don't make me label it. Don't make me explain it. Just let this be what it is," he says, holding my gaze.

"You guys ready to order?" the waitress addresses us, breaking the moment before I can answer him.

"I'll have a club sandwich and a diet soda, please," I order and wait for Sy to place his.

Just let this be what it is. *Can I do that?*

"So, we're not going to talk about what this is. I'm just going to put up with you randomly showing up at my workplace and being my friend?" I surmise when the waitress finally leaves us.

"Yes, and you're going to do it with a smile," he adds.

"And what happens when—"

"We're not talking about when, why, or how," he points out.

"You know that sounds ridiculous?" I ask.

"Don't give a fuck," he shrugs.

"Okay…" I tentatively agree, still not feeling okay with this situation at all. Whatever is going on between us can go one way, or another. I know that right now I'm not looking for anything more, but I can't help that feeling of knowing that whatever is going on between us could be destroyed with my secret. Part of me is telling myself I should tell him now before it's too late. But then the other part is telling me I'm not ready to get into it. I just wish it wasn't so hard. I wish I didn't have this secret to keep. Maybe things would be a lot easier if I tried to forget about it.

"What the hell are you doing here?" Sy's deep rumble comes from behind me as I check in for my daily workout.

"Wh…what are *you* doing here?" I stammer for a moment wondering why Sy just walked into the gym. *My gym.*

"Working out," he says, checking in using his electronic card. *Shit. Sy works out here?*

"You work out here? I've never seen you here," I accuse, thinking this is one of his setups.

"Been working out here for the last three years, Holly," he informs me as he walks to the locker room. *Well, shit, how did I miss that?* I follow behind hesitantly, not looking forward to working out in front of him. After our two dinners last week and lunch this week, I'm not sure how I feel about what is happening, but at the same time, each moment I see him in this new light makes me want to be better. The whole situation is strange. Before the shooting, he wouldn't give me the time of day. I knew he was struggling with something, and now all I can think about is what has changed. If I weren't so worried it would bring up questions of what happened with us, I would ask.

I go about my business, storing my belongings in a locker and pull my hair up in a small ponytail. I started using the gym two weeks ago when Dr. Elliot suggested it would help with the anxiety. I had never stepped into one before. I've always been one of those people who could eat what I want and never pay the price. When she prescribed it one session, I never thought I would enjoy it as much as I do. I never knew actively going to the gym would help clear my mind and help center me for the day.

I warm up on the rowing machine, not interested in a treadmill or other machines I see the bimbos working out on while they make sure their makeup is perfect. I enjoy the continuous rhythm I can create with each row. I get lost in it. Each stroke pulls me deeper into a place that relaxes me. After twenty minutes of warming up, I move over to the free weights and try not to seek out Sy.

When I first joined, Andy, the gym's trainer, set me up with a beginners program. Light to start off and as I grow strength, we can alter my program. Choosing the twenty-two pound weights, I start with my chest workout. Placing my towel over the bench, I sit down and lower myself back. Bringing the weights above me, I slowly lower them down to my chest and then bring them up again. I repeat the action over and finish out my set.

"You've got some good form there," Sy's voice stirs from above me. I tilt back and find him standing at the head of the bench.

"Uh, thanks." Sitting up, I place my weights down beside me. I look at him reflected in the large mirror in front of me. He stands, arms crossed over his chest. He looks sexy even if the sweat from his own workout shines under the overhead lights. *Jesus, the man sweaty and tattooed is too much.*

"Are you okay?" I question, unsure of what his problem is.

"Do you always wear this?" he swirls his finger at me, looking angry. *Great, cranky Sy is back.*

"Yeah, why?" I look down at my gym outfit, black yoga pants and grey gym top. It's far from revealing, but the way Sy's acting, you would expect to see me wearing what the bimbos over on the treadmills are wearing.

"It's a little slutty, don't you think?" he accuses. I'm so shocked at his words I turn to face him.

"Enlighten me how wearing this outfit, where you can barely see any skin at all, is slutty?" I stand, not comfortable having him looming over me.

"It's so fucking tight, Holly. Every fucker in here can picture your fine ass naked," he growls, looking over at some of the men standing around us. They don't seem too interested in checking me out, more focused on themselves and correcting their form.

"Sy, you've lost it. I can't even respond to that." I turn back around and ignore him. I pick up my weights and begin my next set, pretending he isn't standing over me like a formidable force.

"Go away," I finally breathe when I get through my last set and sit back up.

"No," he simply replies, still watching me.

"Whatever," I mutter, walking past him to move onto the next machine. Setting up the seat, I catch him eyeing off the poor guy at the machine next to mine.

"You know you don't own the gym. You can't just try and scare everyone away," I inform him, placing the rod in the thirty-pound weight slot. Leaning forward, I hold on to the bar and pull back.

"You need to keep your back straighter," he states, stepping forward and placing his palm on the small of my back. "And keep your chin up," he keeps instructing like I need his help. I follow the instructions nonetheless, pressing my chest further out and keeping my chin up.

"Fuck me, don't stick your tits out like that," he growls, stepping in closer.

"Sy," I complain, letting go of the bar and looking up at him. "You're disturbing me," I snap.

"Yeah, well, you're disturbing me with your fucking sexy outfit and now pushing your tits out," he says, frustrated. I try to not let his words affect me—we've been there and done that—but hearing he is still affected by me, moves something in me. *Something I should not be worrying about right now.*

"If I'm disturbing you, Sy, then leave," I suggest, starting up my second set. If he can't handle me working out, then he needs to go. I keep my form solid, ignoring his grunts and growls throughout it. When I finish, I stand, stretching out my chest, ready to move on to the next machine.

"Jesus," he mumbles behind me. Then taking my hand and towel, he pulls me off to the side room.

"What are you doing? I'm not done," I say, beginning to feel like this workout is a bust. He walks over to the built-in storage room and pulls out a set of boxing gloves, and mitts.

"Suit up," he bosses, throwing the gloves at me.

"I'm not boxing with you," I scoff unimpressed. I came here for a workout, not a fight.

"Trust me, it will help both of us. You get to punch me and no fucker will be checking out that tight ass of yours," he says, putting his fingers in the pads.

"Sy, no one was checking out my ass," I argue, but it only falls on deaf ears.

"You get to hit me," he repeats and I give up fighting.

"Fine," I huff, making it sound like a hassle when it's the best thing I'll probably do today. I strap my hands into the padded gloves and get ready to unleash my anger on him.

"Have you ever boxed before?" he asks, moving over to the middle of the room.

"No, never," I confirm, following behind him.

"Plant your feet into the ground and use your upper body with each strike." He demonstrates the fluid movement. His body grace-fully moves from side to side with each hard jab and punch. "Got it?" he asks, coming to stand in front of me.

"Yeah, I think so." I nod and position myself.

"Okay, come at me for fifty jabs," he insists and I nearly fall over.

"Fifty?" I gasp.

"Fifty is nothing. Quit your bitching and let's do this," he says, pumping me up.

I ignore him and adjust my stance before starting. With the first hit of glove to pad, I feel a rush of excitement.

"Harder," he commands. So I do just that, each strike intensifying with more power than the last. My abdomen starts to ache slightly. The power behind each hit is probably not helping the situation, but I can't stop the need to keep going.

"That's it, girl. Keep those feet planted," he continues to instruct. My body takes over; the rush of hitting something hard and fast is like no other, and before I know it he calls, "Fifty."

My arms drop to my sides, heavy from their actions. The familiar burn in my muscles set in.

"Shit, Holly. You've got a good arm on you," he compliments, shaking out his hands.

"Thanks," I grin, feeling lighter than I have in a long time.

"Let's do a combination this time," he suggests, banging the pads together. "Left, right, left. You got it?" He demonstrates, and after the first go, I pick it up easily.

"Left, right, left," he continues to instruct as we build the momentum. My body feels alive with each jab, each hook, and each connection to the pad in front of me. We continue to work out for another thirty minutes, only stopping when someone walks into the room to set up for their class.

"What are you doing now?" I find myself asking after we pack up our equipment and walk out. I'm not sure what that whole session has done to me, but I'm feeling fresh, alive, and for the first time, present in the moment.

"Day off today, so nothing planned," he says, stopping out the front of the female locker rooms. "What about you?"

"Same, but I have to do some planning for Kadence's bachelorette party." I know I wasn't excited about planning it to begin with, but now it's happening, I can't wait to throw her the best party ever. He nods and we both stand there waiting. For what I don't know, but for me, it's the fact that I don't want to leave, which is confusing considering only a few weeks ago I didn't even want to be around him. "I'm going to go and get a Gym Junkie juice after I shower. I always get one after a workout," I mention. "Do you want to come with?" I ask. The invite doesn't even feel awkward; the ease between us grows each time we see each other.

"Sounds good," he agrees. "Give me ten minutes. I'll meet you at the front?" he questions, walking the rest of the way to the male locker rooms.

"Okay," I nod in agreement. I can shower and look half decent in that time. Pushing through the doors, I stop and call out to Sy, "Thanks for today. It helped," I add, not sure if he understands *how* it helped, but just letting him know is enough.

"Anytime." He gives me his signature head nod and leaves me standing like a goof. Gathering my wits, I get through my shower and meet him out the front in less than fifteen minutes.

"You ready?" he asks, looking up from a fitness magazine when I come to stand in front of him.

"Yeah, let's go."

The walk to the juice bar is silent. The quietness is settling, even taking us to a comfortable place again. I don't know what this is with Sy and me. I can't pick the exact moment everything changed, but nonchalance now flows easily between us.

"Have you ordered here before?" I wonder when we walk into the bright green juice shop.

"No, first time." He raises his brows playfully before reading the board above the counter. I'm going to have to get used to this new side of Sy.

After ordering my new favorite, Raspberry Reflex and Sy choosing a post workout smoothie, we sit out in the morning sun.

"We should work out like that again," he mentions, taking a sip of his Bone Crusher. "What the fuck is in this one again?" he queries, his face scrunched up in distaste.

"It can't be that bad?" I smile, picking it up and sipping it. The chocolate and peanut butter smoothie is disgusting. "It's all right." I shrug, hiding my distaste and handing it back to him. "We should do this again. I had a good time. Who knew punching you could be so much fun," I joke and he looks taken back for a moment. "What?" I ask when he keeps looking at me.

"Nothing," he shakes his head. "I'm free tomorrow. Tell me what time and I'll meet you here."

"Okay," I agree. I'm not sure what I'm getting into with him, but I did have a good morning; a good morning *punching him* that is.

"Great," he states, taking another sip of his awful smoothie. I can tell he doesn't like it by the pained expression on his face, but I don't say anything. I just sit quietly, savoring the moment. *Who knew enjoying a juice with Sy would be so relaxing?*

"Oh, and if we're going to work out again, you're going to

need some different clothes," he adds, taking us right back to where we began. I swear the need to punch him again burns strong, but I don't reply like he wants me to. If he thinks this is revealing, wait until tomorrow.

"Holly, I love it," Kadence says from the cream sofa in front of the full-length, mirrored wall. We're shopping for bridesmaid dresses, and I stopped caring what she chose twelve dresses ago. Our quest to find the perfect maid-of-honor dress wasn't planned. Kadence sprang it on me as we were in town looking for bachelorette supplies. She lured me into the shop with promises of wedding gown samples, not bridesmaid's gowns.

"It's okay." I don't even try to fake my annoyance at it.

"You don't like it?" she asks, looking sad again. It's the same dance we've done after each dress I have tried on.

"I like the first one," I tell her again for the eleventh time.

"You know, I think you're right," she says and I can feel my temper slowly rising. Of course I'm right. "Let's try that one on again." She smiles up at me as she takes a sip of her coffee that the sales person fetched for her. I wasn't allowed coffee since I'm the one trying the merchandise on.

I'm going to strangle someone soon.

"Sure," I reply, pasting on my fake maid-of-honor smile, and march my ass back into the changing room to try on the first dress I tried on an hour ago.

"You know, I think the color is all wrong," she calls through the curtain.

"The color is fine," I say, stepping out of the dress, and hanging it back up. Handing it out to the shop assistant, I patiently wait for her to bring me back the first dress I tried on. Looking in the mirror, I take the time to look at myself. The harshness of the changing room lights are in full effect. Thinking back to Sy's comment about my weight loss, I wonder how much my body has changed. The purple, four-inch scar left behind by the bullet, and the two surgeries to save my life has a long way to go before I can accept it. It's not the ugliness of it that affects me. I know with time the scar will be faint and won't mock me. No, now it's just a harsh reminder of what I lost, what was horribly taken from me.

"You okay in there?" Kadence pulls me out of my thoughts and back into the ugliness of my reality.

"Yeah," I wheeze out, not realizing that I was captive in a memory and had pushed myself into a small panic attack. *At least it wasn't a huge* one.

"Holly, are you sure?" Kadence's panicked voice asks again, but I can't focus on her as the all-too-familiar feeling of panic claws up my back. The fear, the pain, all spiraling me out of control. Dropping to the floor, I lift my knees up and bring my head between my legs.

Just breathe through it, Holly. You can do this, I repeat over and over, trying to calm my panic.

"I'm coming in." I hear her words, but they don't register in my mind, falling short at the wall of anxiety currently building inside of me.

Memories and sounds coming at me only keep pushing me deeper into the ugliness of that night. The ugliness of what we experienced.

"Focus on my voice, Holly," she says, kneeling down next to me. "You're safe here," she reassures me carefully. And while I know I'm not going to die, there is no controlling the feeling of fear and loss of control. We sit like this for a few more minutes; it could be longer. I don't know. When I do eventually come back to the dressing room, I feel drained and ready to leave.

"Hey," Kadence says, reaching out to touch my arm.

"Oh, my God," I finally acknowledge her. "I'm sorry," I whisper when she leans forward and embraces me.

"No, I am." She squeezes me tighter. "You scared me," she admits, pulling back and wiping her tears away.

"It just came on. I haven't had one in the last few weeks," I admit, wondering what the hell just happened.

"It's okay," she shushes me, not having any part of my apologies. I don't know what I'm sorry for; the whole thing is embarrassing.

"Is everything okay in there?" the shop assistant queries through the curtain.

"We're good," Kadence calls back and I realize I'm sitting in my underwear on the floor of the changing room with my best friend. I let out a small giggle at how ridiculous we must look, followed by another and before I know it, I'm laughing. I don't know if I'm laughing at the fact that it's funny, or if laughing helps stop the tears. Whatever the reason, I continue and pray I don't stop.

20

Sy

"Catch me."

"Keira?" I call when I hear her high-pitched laugh echoing through the field.

"Daddy, you came," she replies, laughing off into the distance.

"Come back." I reach out, but I can't see her, only hear her.

"Catch me," she whispers again, but no matter how hard I try, I can't find her.

"Look at that sunset, Daddy," she laughs again, the breeze carrying the sweet sound farther and farther away from me.

"Keira," I yell out again, desperate to find her, to touch her, to see her.

"Bye, Daddy," she murmurs, only this time, I see her. She stands silhouetted against all the colors of the universe as the afternoon sun sets.

"Wait, Keira!"

My pleading pulls me from my sleep. *Fuck, not again.*

Reaching over to my nightstand, I pull a photograph of Keira, out of my wallet. One of the only ones I allow myself to have. Her small head, bald from treatment, shines under the brightness of the hospital lights. *Fuck, I miss her.*

Reaching back over, I take out the second photo of a time when I was happy. Katie and Keira both stare back at me, laughing at something I had said. Life back then was worlds different to the one I live now.

Placing my most prized possessions back safely in their place, I climb out of bed and make my way up to the clubhouse. No point in trying to go back to sleep now, especially after that nightmare.

"Yo Sy, you're up early," Jesse calls from the sofa as I walk into the main room.

"Come join me," he smacks the ass of the blonde next to him, to wake her. "Time to go, baby. Get your shit and split," he says, smiling down at her. She obeys, taking her half-naked ass down the hall.

"What's happening?" I question, ignoring the woman and making my way into the kitchen in search of some breakfast.

"Ahh, you know, same fuck, different hole." He follows, laughing at his own joke.

"You're a sick man, Jesse," Beau replies, looking up from his breakfast when we walk into the room.

"Aww, come on, you know it was a good one." I don't reply, not getting into it with either of them. This is what it's like living in the clubhouse.

"What have you got going on this week, Sy?" Beau asks, giving up his argument with Jesse.

"I'm busy with the shop all week. Why?"

"Just had a call from Tiny. We have a girl coming in this week, need some help setting her up," he explains while making coffee.

"Well, if I'm free, then I'll be there," I tell him, drinking from the juice carton.

"Eww, Sy. Use a damn glass," Kadence scolds, walking in behind me.

"You stayed here last night?" I ignore her glass comment, turning to see her in her pajamas.

"Yeah, Nix had to work late and Z is at my parents. Didn't want to sleep alone," she admits, looking down. It makes me realize she must also still be dealing with the shit Zane and fucking Gunner put them through that night. *I wonder if Holly has problems sleeping.*

"Hey, baby. I've told you not to leave the bed, before I wake." Nix comes up behind her, groping her in places that make her bitch him out in front of us.

"So fucking whipped," Beau says under his breath but for all of us to hear.

"Whatever, asshole, you're just jealous," Nix calls him out, but I don't stand around waiting for his reply. Leaving them, I head back to my room to get ready to meet Holly.

I wasn't expecting to run into her yesterday. I did know she had started at the gym a couple of weeks ago. Kadence mentioned it one night that she was working out, but I didn't know it was at my gym. After waking up from a fucked-up sleep yesterday, I needed to release some pent up frustration. Normally, I work out at night when it's less busy, but when I pulled up and saw her getting out of her car, I knew it was meant to be. At first, I was pissed at the outfit she had on. Before she even walked through the door, some beef-head fuckers were checking her out. The skin tight yoga pants and tight-as-fuck top that pushed her tits together were any mans fucking picture of sexy. She has no idea how gorgeous she is. It's not even an attempted sex appeal; it's a natural sexuality that she exudes even when she doesn't realize she's doing it. That's why I had to pull her into the private boxing room, before I started pissing around her to mark my territory. She might not be mine just yet, but she will be and I'll be fucked if I have to watch some juiced-up fucker undress her with his eyes.

Picking up my gym bag, I throw in a change of clothes, hoping to convince her into going for one of the fucking disgusting drinks she says she gets after every workout.

"I'm out," I call to the boys as I walk past them having breakfast.

"You heading to the gym?" Jesse asks around a mouthful of food.

"Yeah, I've got to get an early workout in," I mention, hoping he doesn't invite himself along.

"If you give me twenty, I'll come with," he says. *Fuck*.

"Don't have time to wait around today, Jesse." I knock him back. If there is anyone I don't like working out with, it's Jesse. The man is as bad as the fake bitches who check themselves out in the mirror. No, he's worse.

"Your loss then," he shrugs, going back to his breakfast.

"What gym do you go to again?" Kadence eyes me wearing a sneaky smile.

"Just down on main," I answer, not liking her assessing me.

"Huh, that's where Holly works out." She smiles again, but I don't react. *Never react.*

"Never seen her there," I say, turning and walking out the door. If she thinks she will have me slipping up, she has no idea who she's dealing with.

"Have fun," she laughs, and I wonder just how much she knows. Has Holly told her, or is she as observant as me?

I don't reply as I leave the room.

I pull up at the front of X-Sports Gym and see her instantly. *Je-*

sus. Fucking. Christ. She has on a tiny pair of fucking shorts and a skin tight top. She may as well be wearing her fucking bra and panties. She smiles over at me, and it's one of the real ones. Not the fake shit she likes to put on show for everyone. It takes everything in me not to pick her up, throw her over my fucking shoulder and take her away.

"Hey," she greets me, looking up in my direction. I know she knows I'm pissed. I can see it play out over her face. So instead of giving her the reaction she's hoping for, I act like it doesn't affect me.

"Hey," I say, nodding down at her. "You ready to do this?" I ask, walking past her to swipe my access card. She doesn't reply as she follows.

"I'm gonna go change," I tell her, walking into the locker rooms and leaving her behind. I have to adjust myself in my gym gear and try to control my anger over the little stunt she just pulled. Giving it a few moments, I walk out not knowing how I'm going to be able to get through the morning being so close to her with her dressed the way she is.

"You good to go?" I ask, walking up to her. She's talking to Andy, the fucker douche-bag trainer who has a big mouth and bigger eyes that don't know how to stay above the chin.

"Yeah," she answers, saying goodbye to Andy and following me. I don't know what is happening right now, but this is not how I expected our morning to end up. I look over at her and see her looking unsure as she follows me into the room.

"Wanna tell me what the fuck that was about?" I finally ask when we let ourselves into the private room.

"What are you talking about?" she challenges, walking past me to the storage room, retrieving the gloves and pads.

"You know exactly what I'm talking about."

"No, really I don't," she protests, passing me the pads.

"What the fuck are you wearing?" I finally cave and ask.

"Gym clothes. I picked them up yesterday, do you like?" she sasses, and I'm so fucking close to kissing the sass out of her, but that would just be pushing it. Instead, I drop the pads, rip my shirt over my head and throw it at her.

"Put it on," I demand as she catches it.

"What?" She jerks back, her eyes growing wide.

"Put the shirt on, *now*, Holly." I punch out each word, not in the mood for games. She holds my gaze in anger and my shirt with disdain.

"What's your problem?" she demands, mimicking my pose.

"You are my problem. You have no clothes on for starters. Why do you insist on making this harder on me when I'm already struggling?" I ask her, wanting an answer.

"It was a joke," she huffs, putting the shirt on and covering her half-nakedness. The shirt falls to mid-thigh, and I don't know what's worse, seeing her in tight fitting gym clothes, or seeing her in one of my shirts.

"Fuck," I growl, frustrated.

"What now?" she sighs, looking innocent.

"Nothing. Now get your ass here so we can work out," I boss her, picking up the pads and feeling better that no other fucker can see her. I didn't realize just how hard this shit would be. I know I need to tread carefully, take it easy on her, but the more time we spend together, the easier it is to lose control. I just have to keep doing what I'm doing and pray she finally comes around. 'Cause if she pulls any shit like that again, there will be no controlling my reaction.

21

Holly

"MOM?" I CALL OUT, WALKING INTO MY CHILDHOOD HOME. The smell of her famous chicken wing marinade fills the air.

"In here," she sing-songs from her favorite place in the house: her kitchen.

"Hey." I round the corner to see her preparing lunch for our Saturday grill out.

"Hey doll, how are you?" she questions, looking up from the kitchen island and giving me a huge smile. She looks beautiful today, not that she doesn't normally, but put together. Her pale blouse looks new and her tawny brown hair is blown back away from her face. I can see she's put a light coating of mascara on her eyelashes, making her blue eyes seem bigger.

"I'm good, Mom. How are you?" I come forward around the

large stone-top bench and kiss her cheek as she dries her hands on her apron. Our kitchen is huge and holds so many warm memories of growing up. It's the kitchen where I bonded with my mother. We'd spend our early evenings here when I was a teenager talking about school, friends and boys while she taught me how to cook. If I needed to find my mother, I would walk into this room, and more often than not, she would be here, baking away or preparing something to feed us for our next meal.

"I'll be better when your father sorts out his new grill." She rolls her eyes at my father and his new toys.

"He bought a new one?"

"Don't ask me why. He's only had the last one for barely a year, but he insisted." She smiles, shaking her head at my dad. After thirty years, my parents are still happily married. She loves his annoying ways because he continues to be annoying. I know they adore each other. You can see it in the way they are together. Speaking without saying words. The way they move in sync like they know what the other is going to do. That makes me want what they have.

"How's work?" she asks, moving over to the fridge to retrieve more tomatoes.

"Getting there, slowly building up my clients," I fill her in. We normally talk every other day, but since I've been back at work and spending more time with Sy, I've been neglecting her. I know she's suspecting something is up.

"Well, that's good, honey. I knew you would do well there." She continues to chop away, making her famous salad.

"Where's Sam?" I ask, grabbing a glass down from one of the cupboards and try not to let out a cry of pain. After working out with Sy all week, I feel like a truck has hit me. I've never been so sore from exercise. The first day I woke up, I thought I was sick. It wasn't until I said something to Sy the other day that he told me it was a good thing. After a hot bath every night, I try to stretch out the worst of it.

"Ohh, Sam is bringing a girl. He just called earlier." She sounds excited, like the thought of her boy bringing home a date is something she has been waiting for forever.

"Sam is bringing a girl home?" I ask, shocked, and then realize why she looks so together today. She dressed up to meet her.

"He didn't tell you?"

"No, he didn't tell me."

"Tell you what?" Sam cuts me off as he walks into the kitchen. I'm about to drill him when at the last second I see a small, pretty blonde girl come in behind him.

"Oh, hello." Mom stops her chopping and dries her hands to greet Sam's new girl.

"Mom, this is Claire. Claire, this beautiful woman is my mom, Melinda, and my sister, Holly." He points to both of us.

"Well, look at you." My mom takes her in her arms, and embraces her like a long lost daughter. I try not to groan as she embarrasses the poor girl.

"Mom, let her go. You're scaring her," Sam finally says, trying to pry Claire out of our mom's arms.

"Oh, hush." Mom swats him away while keeping Claire at arm's length. "Let me get a good look at you. Oh, you're such a doll," she says, looking her over. I can already tell my mom is in love. She only calls her favorite people dolls. Claire smiles shyly and a light blush coats her cheeks. I can tell she is perfect for my brother. He is demanding, bossy and too pigheaded to go head to head with a similar match. No, he needs someone soft and sweet; someone who gets under his skin in another way. I have no doubt Claire already has by the way he's looking uneasy for her.

"Hi." I smile and wave over at her, hoping to stop my mom from freaking her out. Sam must like her if he brought her home, and we don't want to scare her away. "Nice to meet you."

"You too." She smiles back and gives an awkward wave.

"Where's Dad?" Sam asks, taking Claire's hand and tucking her back into his side.

"Outside fixing the grill. Go help him. He's been grumbling all afternoon about it."

"Come on, baby, let's go see my dad," he says, leaning down to kiss her forehead. I've never seen my brother this way before, and of all the emotions running through me, the one pulling at my heart the most is happiness—happiness for him and the girl who is clearly brightening his world. I'm silent as I watch them go out to meet Dad. As soon as the back door closes, my mom turns and squeals.

"Oh, my gosh, she is beautiful." Her hands come out in front of her, expressing her excitement. "Who would have thought he would meet someone so soft and beautiful," she sighs, lost in the moment. *Oh, God, Mom.*

"Calm down, Mom. You'll scare her off."

"Oh, please, I wouldn't scare anyone off." She goes back to her salad. She's right. My mom's pretty kickass, and everyone loves her. It would take a lot not to like my mom.

"You're right, but if you don't calm down, you might scare me off." I smile as I fill up a glass with some wine.

She stops and looks up, "How are you feeling?" she asks, taking on a serious tone. She asks me this question every time I see her, and as much as I love her for it, sometimes it's just nice to not have to answer.

"I'm good, Mom," I assure her, knowing it's the best way. I don't want to tell her that this week I had a major panic attack in the middle of the changing room, or that I woke up in a sweat from a nightmare twice. I don't even want to tell her that spending time with Sy has helped me either. I know she is only looking out for me, but I hate seeing the concern fill her eyes when she knows what a crappy week I've had.

"Well, that's good, baby," she smiles, leaving it be for today and going back to making sure lunch will be on time.

"Want me to do something?"

"Where's my baby girl?" My dad's loud voice calls from the back door, cutting off my offer to help.

"Hey, Dad." I smile, place my glass down on the counter top and walk to my favorite man in my life. His salt and pepper hair looks as thick as it did fifteen years ago. The groomed mustache that he's worn since the day I was born has only just started turning sliver-white, but it's his eyes that I love the most. The laugh lines have increased over the years, telling a story of how much he has lived and loved. My dad has always been a handsome man, but when he smiles, he's something else.

"I didn't know you were here," he says, walking up to me, taking me in his strong arms, and squeezing me tightly. I hold in the urge to groan at the pain of his hug over my sore muscles.

"I was about to come find you," I wheeze, watching over his shoulder as Sam walks back in with Claire.

"Well, let's get this started. I'm starved," he exclaims, always ready to eat. "Liddy, you ready, sweetheart?" He turns to look at my mom.

"Yeah, just waiting on you, Jack." She smiles up at him.

"Then let's eat." He leans down, smacking her ass as she walks forward. My mom giggles at his smack.

"Dad," I groan, not wanting to see that. I might love them dearly, but it's too weird for me when they get all touchy feely.

"How's Kadence?" Mom inquires after we've sat down to eat out on the back decking. Sy was right when he said I haven't been eating much. The last few months I've barely been hungry, but the last few weeks my appetite has started to return. I ignore the looks between my mom and dad and continue to pile my plate.

"She's good. Her bachelorette party is coming up."

"Oh, good, and what do you have planned?"

"Oh, you know, strippers, games, drinks, the normal fun

stuff," I inform my mom while watching my brother, and father roll their eyes.

"Sounds like fun," Claire smiles across from me. The more I watch them, I can see how much my brother is taken with Claire by the way he looks at her. I've never seen him so attentive to a woman before.

"You should come," I invite her, just as I see my brother's eyes meet mine.

"Hell, no," he says, shaking his head.

"Sam." Mom scolds him for the use of hell at the dining table.

"Sorry, Mom," he rushes out, like the pansy he is. I smirk and his eyes narrow.

"I'm serious, Claire. If you want to come, you're more than welcome," I tell her, ignoring his glare.

"Umm, thanks. I'll think about it," she says, looking over at Sam. I'm willing to bet that if he weren't sitting there, she would totally be down with it.

"When did you become so caveman-like, Sam?" I question, pissing him off more.

"Stop it you two," Dad says before we get out of hand, but I have no problem taking him on.

"What's the matter? Afraid the strippers might show her what she's missing out on?" I laugh, and he practically growls from his spot next her. The table falls silent, and I look up to see my family staring at me.

"What?" I smile as they continue to watch me.

"It's just… I don't think we've heard that laugh in such a long time." Mom breaks the awkward silence.

"Oh," is all I can say, and my smile falls from my face when I see my dad wipe a stray tear away. "Come on, guys. I haven't been that bad," I try to lighten the moment, but they remain silent, watching me as if I'm a stranger.

"You've been pretty bad, sis," Sam speaks next. I think back over the last three months. Have I not been hiding the pain as well as I thought? Have I not been sheltering my family enough?

"I didn't know," I say, feeling like an asshole for all I've put them through.

"You've been fine, sweetheart." My dad clears his throat. "It's just good to see you happy again."

"Well, I haven't had much to be happy about," I admit for the first time aloud.

"And you feel like you do now?" Mom asks, knowing that something is up.

"I'm not sure," I reply honestly, not ready to share what I'm feeling when I'm not even sure what it is that's happening between Sy and me. I know my newfound confidence and happiness has to do with him; we just haven't defined what we have, and I don't want to push it. Do I want more? Yes. Even if this thing is just a friendship happening between us, then I will be happy with that. I feel a lightness within me whenever he is around. Even if he has the power to turn that light to dark, I find myself wanting to risk it more and more. I look up and catch my family watching me, and I smile at them—an actual genuine smile. I'm not sure if whatever it is that is happening will last, but in this moment right now, I'm happy. I'm going to take that happiness and try not to lose it.

Past

Sy

"I hate you," she spits from the bathroom floor, her drugs lying carefree beside her. She doesn't even try to hide it anymore.

"I hate you, too, but that doesn't mean I'm going to sit here, and watch you kill yourself."

"I wish you were the one who died. She didn't deserve to die," she continues to spit her venom. I'm used to it. I've been blocking it out for two years now, so I'm conditioned to it. I know it's not her talking; it's the drugs. The Katie I knew wouldn't speak like this.

"You don't think I wish for that every day, Katie? I would fucking sacrifice anything to swap places with her." I run my hand over my face in frustration. I don't know why I bother.

"Why are you even here, Sylas? I don't want to see you anymore," she slurs, resting her head back against the bathroom wall. Fuck me, she's a mess.

"I'm taking you into Whitehaven Detox," I tell her, picking up the used syringe she just shot into her arm. She is beyond my help now.

"No, I'm not going back there." She sits up in a panic. "I won't do it."

"You will, Katie. Last month I found you sitting in a pool of your own blood. Now you're shooting up? If you don't come willingly, we are going to admit you for evaluation." I threaten her with what her family and I spoke about earlier.

"Why won't you all just leave me alone?" she screams, hitting her head back in frustration. "Just leave me alone."

I don't know why I don't just walk away, walk away from the train wreck that is my wife, but I promised Keira I wouldn't. I didn't realize it would be so fucking hard.

22

Holly

"SO, WHAT ARE YOU DOING TODAY?" SY ASKS, STRETCHING out his booted feet on my coffee table. I want to tell him to get his feet off my furniture, and that it's rude to wear his shoes in my apartment, but seeing them on my coffee table stirs a different emotion in me instead.

"Nothing much," I answer, sitting back and forcing myself not to say anything about the shoes. Today isn't the first time he's just shown up. It's the third time this week, to be exact, and the tenth time in the last three weeks. I've been counting. Normally he shows up for a reason, dropping in after dinner, or to bring me one of my favorite juices, but this morning he had no reason. 'Just wanted to come by,' he said before walking in and making himself at home. I was only half mortified that I was still in my pajamas; at least I had on a matching pair.

"What have you got going on?" I ask, enjoying these comfortable moments between us where I don't have to pretend. Between the dinners, lunches, gym workouts and the quiet nights between us, a real friendship is forming. One I don't want to lose. I think he feels the same way. I mean, why else would he keep turning up?

"I was thinking of going for a ride." He picks up the remote, flicking through the channels and then settling on some shark show. "Wanna come?"

"Where are you going?" A ride on Sy's bike? That's hardly a chore.

"Babe, you don't ask, you just ride." He shakes his head like I've got no clue. I try not to let the word babe affect me, but for some stupid hormonal reason, the silly female tendencies in me see it as something else.

"Um, Sy?" I ask, unable to stop myself.

"Yeah?" he answers, still looking at the TV.

"What are we doing?" *Shut up, Holly,* my brain is screaming at me.

"Watching TV," he answers.

"I can see that, but what's happening here?" I ask carefully, unsure how to address it. I know we said we wouldn't label it, but things are changing, and I need to know so I can keep up.

"Holly, what are you really asking?" He turns to face me.

"Well, you keep turning up, our dinners, then the gym and now rides? I'm not sure what's happening between us," I rush out, yet at the same time wishing I never said anything in the first place.

"What do you need to know?" He smiles, freaking me out more.

"Well, one, why are you suddenly smiling? And two, what's going on with us?"

"I'm smiling cause you're acting all cute, and I didn't realize how fucking adorable you could look in pajamas with your hair up like that," he says, sitting back still staring. "And to answer your question, what's happening? We're just two friends hanging out on a Sunday morning, so relax," he says, turning back to the television.

"Well, I'm glad we sorted that out," I grumble. His response tells me nothing I don't already know, and at the same time disappoints me.

"Me too, babe," he agrees, still watching the TV screen. Seriously, this man is so strange that I don't know what the hell to do with him.

"And I don't look cute in these pajamas," I add, annoyed he said that. I look anything but cute.

"You're right, you don't look cute." His comment confuses me, before I see the side of his mouth curve into one of his sexy smiles. "You look sexy as fuck." He turns, giving me his eyes. "And if you keep giving me attitude, this friendship will get weird," he adds and I have to physically work through the lump that's formed in my throat. My mouth snaps closed, shocked he just threw that in there. I blink once, twice and still don't know how to respond.

"Breathe, Holly," he instructs, but who needs to breathe when one is having an out of body experience. I finally draw in a sharp breath at his command. "Jesus, girl., if I knew your blush ran that deep, I would have tried to embarrass you sooner," he chuckles, shaking his head.

"What are you talking about?" I finally get past the small shock. *I know I asked, but I wasn't expecting that.*

"Baby, you really want to talk about this today? You ready for it?"

"I don't really know what *it* is," I admit.

"It is this," he says, reaching and slightly touching my hand.

The warmth of his skin against my hand sends tingles up my arm, like a jolt of lust running through my veins. The electricity in the air pulls me into his space. The tip of his tongue peeks out over his lips and his hooded eyes watch my mouth as I stare at him. "You feel that?" he rasps, and I nod, feeling it all the way through me from the tip of my nose to the bottoms of my toes.

"That's what we need to talk about. You ready for that?" he gently asks, while slowly drawing circles over my skin. I nod, not listening to my screaming heart yelling at me that it's not ready. My stomach drops at that all-encompassing encounter of totally surrendering to the feeling, to an emotion, to this man.

"Holly, I'm going to kiss you now," he murmurs, barely above a whisper. The words caress my skin like the heat of a fire on a chilly night, and my eyes close at the heaviness of what is about to happen. The emptiness of my heart is long forgotten as I balance on the edge of what this man can give me. It's like he awakens something in me, and as my body hums in anticipation of feeling his lips, there's no chance I can put it back to sleep.

"Hurry," the word slips from my mouth just as the roughness of his lips touch mine. I'm expecting something more, something as urgent as what I'm feeling, but it's a soft, yet deadly touch. My body moulds into his, like our simple connection gives me permission to relax. Deepening the kiss, my hands move to his chest, gripping the front of his leather cut. The rhythm of my heart beats out of time as I close my eyes and become lost in the taste of him on my tongue, and the feel of the leather between my fingers. I don't think I've ever met a man that tasted so good, and now that I have, I know I'll never be able to forget it. Leaning into me, we fall back, and instead of fighting it, I find myself leading. My hands pull him closer toward me in a desperate move to keep him from pulling away.

"Holly," he whispers against my lips, but I don't stop. My body is disorientated from the feeling of something other than pain.

"Holly," he tries again.

"Hmmmm," I hum against him, but I don't give him a chance

to reply when my mouth takes over the kiss. The taste of this man is like a drug that I've been craving, a drug that will fix a little bit of the broken inside of me.

"Holly," he rasps out, speaking more firmly this time. He pulls back and breaks the connection. My eyes open and I look up at him with hooded lids. *Holy shit, what just came over me?*

"Sweetheart," he sweetly says, sitting back on his haunches.

"Oh, God, I'm so sorry," I whisper, trying to push past him to run and hide my embarrassment.

"Holly, stop," he growls. His tone doesn't stop me, but his hold on my wrist does.

"I didn't mean to do that," I rush out, insecure at being pinned down by his stare.

"Do what?"

"Kiss you like that. I'm sorry. I don't know what came over me."

"I told you I was going to kiss you."

"Well, yes, but then I completely lost control," I admit. He smirks, like the idea of me losing control is funny.

"Babe, that was you losing control?"

"Well, if you hadn't stopped me, I would have probably started humping your leg or something."

"Humping my leg?"

"Most definitely humping. I may have even started panting," I joke, and for the first time in months, I laugh at myself. He doesn't respond and I cringe internally as embarrassment fills me. *Just shut up, Holly.*

"Did you actually laugh?" he finally asks, taking my chin in his hand, forcing my face to look up at him.

"Umm, yeah?" I pull back, but his hold on my face doesn't falter. "I've laughed before, Sy," I comment, not understanding the issue.

"You may have laughed before, but Holly, not one of those pathetic half-assed laughs has been real. Haven't heard the real thing in a long fucking time," he says as a small smile slowly breaks out over his handsome face.

"You missed my laugh?"

"I miss a lot of things, Holly. Some so significant I wouldn't even know where to begin, but your laugh, the sound of your happiness is something that makes all those significant things hurt a little less."

The fact this man could be as broken as I am makes our connection solidify.

"You want to leave for that ride?" he asks, leaning back into my space, the smell of mint on his breath reminding me of his addictive taste.

"Not now," I tell him, letting the pull of his scent drag me in closer.

"Good," he says, crashing his lips to mine, this time harder. I whimper as his tongue demands entrance. Long gone is the gentleness from before. Now taking my mouth is the same man who took me hard and fast on the floor of my apartment months ago. We're immersed in kissing, touching and heavy breathing, and it's the most incredible feeling in the world.

"Holly," Sy breathes, coming up for air as he lightly kisses along my jaw and down to my neck.

"Yeah?" I manage to say, reaching for his shirt as each connection of our lips pulls me further under his spell.

"I'm not going to fuck you. Not now, 'cause this is not what this is about," he says in-between each kiss, "but that doesn't mean I don't want to. Fuck, I want to," he groans, taking my hand and bringing it to his hardness that's covered in denim. "Believe me, I want to strip you out of these sexy-as-fuck pajamas, and worship every inch of this fucking milky skin, but I can't," he growls into my neck when I groan in frustration. "Don't do that, baby. It's only going to make this harder." He pulls back to look at me. "I didn't start this to go there. I just needed to kiss you."

"Okay." A combination of relief and frustration fills me. "So you just want to be friends who kiss?" I ask, trying to get my head around this. I hold back my internal mantra pleading him to say no.

"Fuck no. I want you to be my woman and I want to fuck you so hard that you won't ever want to be anyone else's," he rumbles, making my body yearn for more. "But I also know you've got shit going on and I'm not gonna push you." His thumb traces my bruised lips, his top teeth biting down on his bottom lip when I let my tongue peek out.

"Holly," he warns, resting our foreheads together.

"Okay," I agree, knowing this is what we need, what I need. My body might want to move to the next step, but my heart knows that whatever is happening can't be rushed.

"I don't want to fuck this up, Holly. So for now, dinners, kissing and when I'm not kissing you, I'll take you on a ride. But if you ever tell the boys, shit will get serious," he warns and I can't help the grin that spreads across my face. Sy joking, kissing and teasing me is not what I ever expected from him. It might not be wise to let him give me this light when I'm still holding so much back, but I've been surrounded by darkness for so long that the small glimmer of hope he offers shines so brightly. I can't help but pray I can find a way out.

23

Sy

Sy: I'll be over at 5pm.

I READ MY TEXT AGAIN FOR THE FIFTH TIME BEFORE I DEcide to send it. Fuck it. If it's coming on too strong, she'll just have to deal with it.

After spending the day on the bike with Holly last Sunday, I dropped her home and went back to the clubhouse. I threw a few back with the boys and then crawled into bed, replaying the whole day over in my mind. I had no intention at all to drop in to see her, but before I knew it, I made my way to her place and was knocking on her door. I had no idea that our morning would end up the way it did. I knew going into this with Holly that it would be a slow burn, not something like we had in the beginning and I was okay with that. It's not what I want. I want to sink myself inside of her, but fuck me, after that kiss, I'm willing to do whatever it takes. I don't want to rush her; whatever she decides she needs, I'm ready to do. It's been a long time since I've let a woman affect me like this, or given this much away. I know I'm entering new territory, something I never thought I'd see myself doing again, but there is something about her that makes me want to try again. I know one day, if this continues, I'll need to tell her about my past, let her in on what I live with, but even the thought of letting her in doesn't sound so bad.

"What the fuck are you doing?" Jesse says, looking back over his shoulder to watch me set up my station.

"Shut the fuck up and turn around," I tell him, pocketing my phone, gloving up and trying to get Holly out of my head. The asshole is in for ink and I'll be fucked if I'm going to sit around sharing stories.

"Who the fuck you texting? Never seen you look at your phone so much," he states, turning back around.

"No one," I tell him, cleaning the area I'm about to work on. I'm not about to tell him about Holly. The asshole will be all over that.

"Didn't look like no one."

"Jesse, shut the fuck up."

"Whatever, they'll soon realize what an asshole you are," he laughs, but I don't. Holly already knows I'm an asshole.

"Why the fuck are you in such a good mood this morning?" I ask him, checking the placement and making sure it's even.

"Aww, man. Bagged this chick last night in the back room of Liquid. So freakin' tight," he groans, remembering the moment.

"Jesus, Jesse, I don't want to know about that shit," I scold. Jesse is the biggest fucking whore. I sometimes worry about his manhood. "I hope you're fucking wrapping that shit up."

"Always, brother, always," he laughs, resting back.

"How's that?" I ask, checking the placement on his ribs. This design he's had me working on for the last few weeks will eventually be huge. Starting from the top of his ribs, down his side and around to his back; each and every detail of the drawing is a significant moment to him. I don't ask questions. I just draw up his design. In this case, I tidied up Jesse's design. I didn't expect to learn he had hand-drawn the sketch he handed me a few weeks back himself.

"Fucking A," he says, standing in front of the mirror. "Let's do this," he insists, coming to lie back down on his side.

"You at Liquid tonight?" I ask, settling in for the two-hour job. This is the only place you'll ever find me seeking out pointless conversation. The sound of my ink gun buzzing, and dull, monotonous talk—there is something about it that calms my mind.

"Yeah, girls have their party tomorrow night. Need to sort that shit out," he says, revealing one bit of the puzzle Holly has been hiding.

"They're having it there?"

"Yeah, fucking stripper and all."

What the fuck? Like hell is some fucker gonna swing his dick in Holly's face.

"Does Nix know this?" I look up, pissed he would even be okay with this shit.

"I don't think he does. Was going to talk to him about it tonight," he says, looking down at the needle.

"Can't see him being all right about it," I put out there as I go back to tattooing Jesse's side.

"I'm betting he won't be, but he's whipped so who fucking knows what he's gonna do."

"I say we cancel that shit. Some asshole swinging his dick in his old lady's face… the picture alone will have him coming out of his skin," Jesse laughs, moving too much for me to keep going. I don't know about Nix, but the picture has me seeing fucking red.

"Or we could call in new talent," he grins and I can already tell I'm going to like the idea that's running through his head.

"What sort of new talent?"

"The sort that will piss them off, and make for a good fucking laugh."

"Let's do it," I agree, not needing to think on it. Holly isn't seeing some other guy's cock when she only needs to see mine.

"Wanna run it by the Prez?" Jesse suggests, reaching for his cell.

"Fuck no, just do it," I order. Nix will agree anyway. This way his hands are clean.

"Holly's going to shit a brick," he warns, searching his phone for the contact. She probably will, but I'd rather a pissed off Holly than a turned on one. If anyone is making her wet, it's gonna be me. I don't say that to Jesse, just continue tattooing his ribs while he makes the call. As of tomorrow, I know I'm in deep shit, but I can't help the smile forming from just thinking about it.

"What's happening at this bachelorette party?" I ask her later that day from my position on her sofa. As soon as I arrived at hers, I made myself comfortable and have been firmly fixed on my back while she reads.

"We're just going to Liquid. Why?" she asks suspiciously, looking over her book at me. Her eyes narrow when I don't respond.

"Anything else I need to know about?" I finally ask.

"Nope," she smiles, going back to her book. Even if I didn't know she was lying for sure, the guilt plastered all over her face is a dead-set give away.

"What the fuck are you reading anyway?" I ask, annoyed she isn't giving me her attention.

"Just something Kadence left behind." She goes back to reading. Her lips move as she reads, making her even cuter.

"Is this one of her porn books?" I lean forward and pull it out of her hands. I've heard Nix talk about these smut books she reads. He told us one night it was just pure porn.

"Sy, give it back." She jumps up, trying to pry it out of my hands.

I keep her at arm's distance and read aloud from the book. "*He allowed his molten juices to intermingle with hers,*" I read over her screaming. "What the actual fuck, Holly?" I ask, trying to hold her off as I read some more. She climbs onto me, her ass right in my lap, but I can't even think about that now.

"Give it back, now!" she demands, but I don't; instead, I read aloud, "*Plunging into her glistening moistness.*"

"Sy," she screams, snatching it out of my hands before I can finish.

"What the fuck are you reading that shit for?" I ask, concerned she's being brainwashed. *Molten juices?*

"It was just lying around. I picked it up one day," she tells me, trying to move off me, but I hold her in my lap, enjoying her sitting there. "It's not just about sex," she adds, trying to defend it, but I can see her blush.

"What's it about then?" I ask, running my hands up the back of her dress, loving the feel of her under my hands.

"Umm, it's about this guy who gets run over," she explains, arching her back into the feeling of my hands lazily stroking her soft skin.

"Go on," I encourage, watching her stumble.

"He … umm …" She pauses. "He was—" She breaks again, too lost in my touch. "You're distracting me," she complains, dropping her head to the side. Her soft, pale skin looks delicious. I lean forward and gently kiss her before lightly nipping at the area.

"What are you doing?" She whimpers at my touch.

"Kissing you," I say in-between caresses.

"You are a good kisser," she admits, bringing her hands up to my neck, pushing me into it.

"What have you got planned for tomorrow night?" I ask, trying to distract her.

"I'm not telling you," she breathes out heavily, not falling for my interrogation tactics. My hands move to her strap, as my heartbeat picks up at the anticipation of pushing her to the next step. I want more than anything to strip her naked and feast on her, but I know she's still shaky; the last thing I want to do is scare her. My fingers fumble over the thin strap, releasing it from her shoulder. She looks down at me, but I don't let her look stop me. Following on, I work on the second strap. She pulls back, looking down at me, lust evident in her eyes.

"What are we doing?" she whispers, unsure, but I can't grasp if she's shutting this down, or just needs to understand what it is I'm asking for.

"I want to see you," I admit, knowing I want more, but willing to take whatever I can get. She takes a shaky breath before bringing her hands around her. Releasing the zip, her dress falls to her waist revealing her perfectly round breasts. *Fuck.* I had forgotten how perfect she is. The pink tips of her nipples stand erect, begging me to lick them, take them between my fingers and pull. Even though I'm trying to control this, having them in my face is just too much. My hand comes up, lightly grazing the side of her breast, skimming over the nipple.

"Sy," she breathes, arching once again at my touch. I'm on the edge of control. I don't know how to do slow, or be gentle when it comes to her. The need to claim this woman is strong, but then I succumb to the need to protect her, my brain reminding me of my priorities and Holly's fragile state.

"You're so fucking beautiful," I admit, leaning forward and taking her nipple in my mouth. Her body responds, her nipples sensitive and responsive. My dick strains in its position, begging me to let him free, but this isn't about me. This is about Holly.

"More," she implores, pulling my head to her breast. Her body rolls against mine, her pussy hitting the tip of my cock with each movement. "I need more, Sy," she begs in a crazed state.

"What do you need, baby?" I look up, searching her face for what she needs.

"You," she whispers, peering down at me. Her cheeks flush with arousal, her lips glisten.

"You've got me," I say, kissing her nipple again.

"No, Sy, I need you." She takes my head and forces me to look up at her.

"How bad do you need me? 'Cause, baby, I'm ready as soon as you are, but fuck, once I start, there is no stopping me," I warn. I know right now if she says stop, I'll be able to walk away, but once I get her under me, there will be no stopping.

She looks down at me. Her panic is laced in arousal, telling me this is moving too fast for her.

"Let me take care of you," I say, running my hand down her side then sliding up her dress.

"Just me?" she questions when my finger finds her prize.

"Just you, baby," I confirm, letting her off the hook.

"What about you?" Her question comes out breathy as my finger moves through her wetness.

"I just want to see you come apart," I tell her, meaning every word. As much as I want to take her right now, show her just how much the last few weeks have affected me, I don't want her retreating.

"When I take you, Holly—and I will—there will be no questioning of if you want that. Do you understand me?" I ask as my fingers slide into her tight heat. She doesn't reply, her head now lost in the feelings my fingers are drawing out of her. I forgot how responsive she can be. I feel her tighten around my fingers, her greedy pussy milking my hand for all it's worth.

"Do you understand me?" I ask again, ensuring she's on the same page.

"Yes," she hazily replies.

"Yes, what?" I challenge, hooking my fingers to find her G-spot.

"When you fuck me—which you will—I'm going to want it, Sy." She forces out shallow breaths as her hands come to my shoulders.

"Good, girl. Now, ride my fingers like you would my cock," I command, watching her do as she's told and build herself to the crest.

Fucking A, I don't know how I'm going to survive this shit.

Her hair smells like cinnamon and hot apples. I remember the smell from the first time I met her. Cinnamon, and hot apples; the smell that makes me hungry for warm pie in one moment, and then makes me hungry for her in the next.

"Sy?"

"Yeah, baby," I reply, pushing her hair off her neck to lean in and kiss the soft skin.

"Did you just smell my hair?" she asks, her voice sounding sluggish from sleep. After I made her come with my fingers, her body was spent, so I carried her to her room and told her to rest. I know I'm entering dangerous territory being in her bed. Even having her close when I'm on the edge is not good news, but I know this is what she needs.

"I love the smell of it," I tell her, not caring if I sound like a fucker for it. "I'm liking your hair getting longer, too," I admit. I was fucking pissed when she cut it off. I loved her hair when I first met her.

"What is it with you and my hair?"

"I think you're beautiful any way you wear it, but do you remember that night you walked into my shop? You strode in wearing that short fucking dress, and those fuck-me heels. Any guy in a one-mile radius would have had a hard on for you. Hell, you had me hard, even with all of that attitude you were throwin' around." I laugh when she pinches me. "But it was your long hair shining under those fluorescent lights that had me." I wrap my finger around the now shorter strands.

"I'm growing it again," she whispers, turning to face me.

"Don't do it for me. Have it however you want it. Like I said, you're beautiful no matter what. I just miss having something to hold on to," I joke as I remember when I pulled it at her apartment.

"I needed to feel like I wasn't that person anymore, that scared woman who lost herself in that old barn." She looks at me, her eyes showing the truth to her statement. "It was my way of controlling it. It sounds lame and maybe it is, but cutting it off was therapy for me."

"I get that," I murmur, running a finger along her collarbone.

"You do?" she asks, seeming shocked for a moment before coming up on her elbow.

"Yeah, why do you think my body is covered with these?" I run my hand up my inked arm.

"You're hiding." It's barely a question, more of a statement.

"I've always been hiding, Holly." I admit the cold truth. I've been alone for a long time, unsure if I would ever want to let anyone in. It didn't even occur to me I've spent all this time trying to get her to let me in that I don't know how to do it myself. I know I need to tell her; tell her about Keira, and about the past which has shaped me into the man I am now, but how do you tell something like that to the woman you're falling for? Allowing a person to see the hurt I wear on my skin, or what lives in my heart, is something I don't ever give freely. Miraculously, she has been able to bring something out in me I buried a long time ago. Underneath all the anger and pain that follows me around, I feel something I haven't felt in such a long time: peace.

"You don't have to hide with me, Sy," she says and I believe her. I really do. I just don't know how to tell her.

"I like being in your bed. I should be in it more often," I tell her as I kiss her softly.

"You should stay the night," she says, and even if she hadn't suggested it, I wouldn't have left. Not with the smell of her still on my fingers.

"Your brother's not planning to come in tonight, is he?" I ask, hoping she says no. Even if he doesn't live here, he has a key and calls in frequently. I've managed to avoid him, but knowing our luck, he turns up the night I stay.

"No, he's staying at my parents' house tonight. He and Dad have an early fishing trip. Don't worry. We're safe," she jokes. "My poor mom will be up sending them off with a packed lunch," she laughs, picturing it.

"Your mom and dad seem close," I say, watching her smile.

"They are," she nods. She doesn't need to tell me she likes that a lot. "If I ever get married, I hope after thirty years, I'm still happy like them," she says. "What about you? Are your parents still married?" she asks me. *Jesus, tonight is the night for home truths.*

"My dad died three years ago and my mom walked out on us when I was ten," I tell her. She sits up, shocked at my story.

"Oh, God, Sy, I'm sorry. I didn't know." She looks uncomfortable, but there's no need for it.

"Don't be. My father was a drunk all my life. He was a member of Knights Rebels MC and thought he was a god." I shake my head, remembering what sort of man he was.

"Wow, so your dad was in the club when Red was president?" she asks.

"Yeah, I grew up with Nix and Beau. I was a few years behind them so I didn't go to school with them, but at club get-togethers and family shit, we would hang out," I reply, thinking back to the shit the boys used to get up to.

"Is that how you joined the club?"

"Fuck no. I left the moment I could. Didn't want anything to do with my old man or the club. He didn't care when I left. We never had that relationship and I wasn't interested in trying. I only came back when he was dying. The club had pulled their shit together by then. Nix was Prez, and he took me in. Didn't think I wanted in, but after spending the last few months with my dad, seeing how the club looked out for him in the final days, it just kinda happened." I leave out the part that I really had nothing to go back to and the thought of joining a family when I had just lost mine was more than I could hope for.

"And you don't know where your mom is?"

"I tried searching for her when Pops died, but couldn't find her," I explain. My mom didn't want to be found.

"That sucks, Sy. I'm sorry." She goes back to lying on me.

"Nothing to be sorry about, Holly. I just didn't have the same experience as you." I lean forward and kiss the top of her head.

"I wish you did," she whispers, but I don't reply, because for a while in my life, I did. I slept next to the woman I called my wife for ten years. I planned to grow old with her. Then I found out she wasn't who I thought she was. Far from it.

"Come on, baby. Let's sleep before I take those sexy pajamas off and do things that I know you're not ready for," I tell her, watching her blush.

"I wish I was ready," she says. As do I, but I know deep down the moment she is, it sure will be worth the wait.

24

Holly

"THE NEXT SHOT IS ON ME, GIRLS," KADENCE SAYS, THROW-ing back her head and slamming down the amber liquid before hitting the shot glass on the table in front of her. We're out for Kadence's bachelorette party; the night after Sy and I made it to third base. Sy made me come with his fingers then we went back to kissing like teenagers and hanging out. He wouldn't let things progress any further, only saying it wasn't about that. I don't know how to take it; I do know the more we spend time with each other, brings me slowly out of the place I've been held captive in the last few months. The dull ache that lives in me makes way for something new. With every smile, I surrender a little more of myself and every touch tethers me to him. I knew after the first time we met there was a connection. I just didn't realize how strong it would be and that it would grow into a friendship of all things. I know we are both in some kind of limbo, not sure where this is all going, and the more time we spend together, the harder it is for me to gather up the courage to tell him about the baby. If I'm not careful, I will end up ruining what we have with my lies.

"No, this night is about you. No paying for drinks," Kelly says, throwing her drink back and bringing me back to the room.

"Not to mention we know the owner, ladies," I laugh, looking at her as she sways to the music blaring through Liquid's speakers.

"Aww, guys. I love you all so much." Kadence smiles over at us. She looks adorably ridiculous with her cheap veil messed up on her head.

"So, are Nix and the boys going out tonight?" Mia, Kadence's friend from school, asks, looking out over the crowd below us. Jesse gave us the VIP section of Liquid tonight. It didn't take too much convincing to get him to agree, and surprisingly, he let us bring in some special entertainment. I'm not sure if Nix knows what's happening. Hopefully Jesse kept his word. When I tried to get the club's okay for a Vegas trip, Nix shut it down. He wasn't comfortable with us being out unprotected since their recent dealings with some major hitters in the drug trade. And fair enough. We came to an agreement to keep it in Rushford and Jesse would let us use Liquid. We've had a great day so far; starting it off with a girls' day at the spa where both Kadence's and my mom joined us for facials and lunch. I tried to keep the day about Kadence, but at the mention of Sy's name, our moms would not leave me alone. I was glad when we parted ways to get ready for dinner and drinks with the girls. I don't think I would have handled the questioning looks from mom over dinner.

"The bachelor party is next weekend. We have Z to worry about now." She smiles, looking as happy as ever.

"You didn't tell Nix about the stripper, did you?" I ask, watching her.

"Nooo." She drags the word out, so I know she is lying.

"You told him," I accuse, annoyed she didn't keep it a secret.

"He knows not to bother us," she says, shrugging like it's no big deal.

"Pffft! Nix leave you alone? Jesus, you really are in love," I laugh at her naïvety.

"What? He will—" She stops to think for a moment. "You're so right. He is so going to fuck with us tonight," she huffs, realizing her mistake.

"Don't worry. I'll sort him out," I tell her, not letting her night be ruined by a bunch of sexy bikers.

"I've had the best night, Holly. Thank you for putting all this together."

"The night's far from over," I tell her, knowing the best is yet to come.

"You know I love you?" she says with the biggest smile.

"You only like me 'cause I booked you the hottest stripper I could find," I tease, trying to keep the tone light. The last thing we need is emotional Kadence coming out.

"No, I love you because you are my best friend and I'm so thankful to have you in my life," she starts in on her drunken declaration of love.

"How much have you been drinking?" I laugh, feeling guilty that I'm hiding my friendship with Sy from her.

"You love me too, don't deny it." I do love her, so I don't argue.

"Someone call for a stripper?" Jesse's voice booms from the top of the stairs and he starts moving his hips in perfect rhythm to the music. Damn, the man is sexy. I'll give him that.

"Go away, Jesse," Kelly shouts from the back booth. "We don't want to see it."

"Just keeping an eye on you crazy girls," he winks, walking

forward to where Kadence and I sit.

"Jesse," I warn. "You promised we would be left alone," I accuse, not in the mood for his games.

"Yeah, yeah. I know. Your stripper just turned up. Just making sure everything is okay," he explains.

"Okay, well, we are comfortable as you can see, so buzz off." I swat him away. We don't need a big-brother act tonight.

"Okay, okay. Enjoy your party," he laughs, holding up his hands, and backing away to the stairs. "You girls behave now." He winks before turning and leaving us.

"Let's do another shot," I shout, ready to get the entertainment started. I order another round from our personal waiter and sit back ready for the hot male stripper I booked two weeks back. My phone beeps in front of me on the table and I pick it up, expecting a text from the stripper. Instead, Sy's name flashes on the screen.

> **Sunshine:** Enjoy your stripper.

I look at the words, unsure how to respond. Evidently, the guys have been sharing information.

> **Holly:** How did you know about the stripper?

I type back as a funny feeling settles inside of me. What is he up to?

> **Sunshine:** I have my ways.

I read the text back and know he's up to something, but before I can reply the music in the VIP section stops and a deep voice rumbles from the top of the stairs.

"I'm looking for a Kadence Turner," he shouts, and I nearly fall out of my chair. A large man wearing a worn cop's uniform stalks to where we sit. His outfit hugs his body tightly, the buttons on the pale blue shirt look dangerous; like they could be a hazard and pop off. I don't know if I want to scream or cry, because instead of muscles that go on for days, and a six pack you want to lick, we're stuck looking at a beast of a man who has to weigh at least three hundred pounds. No six pack in fucking sight. I don't know who the fuck he is, but I'm willing to bet the boys have something to do with it. Most probably Sy.

"Fucker," I say, reaching for my phone to call the man in question as the fat guy starts moving to some eighties' porn song.

"Yes?" Sy answers on the second ring.

"What did you do?" I ask, watching the fat man shake his ass and start stripping down to what I think is a thong.

"You got our present?"

"He has bigger boobs than me," I shriek, watching the fat-a-gram pick up his gut to reveal a bright green thong hiding underneath it. I'm half-mortified and half-bursting with laughter.

"He does?" he asks before erupting in laughter. It's the first time I've ever heard him laugh. The raucous sound so deep and thick with emotion you can't help but become addicted to it.

"Are you there?" he asks when I don't reply, too lost in his rumble.

"Yeah, I'm here." I smile, making sure I remember every moment of that sound.

"Are you pissed?"

"Umm, my best friend only gets married once and you just ruined her only stripper experience," I snap down the phone, remembering why I called. *Am I pissed? Is this man for real?*

"You're pissed," he concludes when I don't answer.

"Of course I'm pissed."

"Don't be pissed. It's a joke. Did you honestly think Nix would ever be okay with some fucker flashing his cock in his woman's face?"

"Well, when you put it like that, no," I answer, not denying his point.

"Exactly. Now go enjoy your stripper," he orders before hanging up. I hold back my laugh at the ridiculousness of it, then hold back the need to vomit as the stripper makes Kadence run her hands down his shiny body.

"Holly, I'm going to kill you," she shouts, closing her eyes as her hands rub over his slick skin.

"You have your fiancé to thank for this one." I laugh when her eyes bug out.

"Don't worry, ladies. The real stripper is downstairs," Jesse laughs while cringing as he watches the cop do some weird move with his baton. I give up looking; it's safer that way.

"He is? Send him up, please!" I beg, hoping the fat man runs out of breath soon from his vigorous exercise, or gives up. Either way, I'm happy.

"Sure thing," he says, heading downstairs. Kadence looks like she is going to pass out from laughing, but I'm just relieved that the real guy is downstairs.

Five minutes later, my life isn't any better when a redheaded female wearing a nurse's outfit walks up the stairs looking for an injured Kadence. By this point, Kadence doesn't give a fuck, letting both the guy and woman give her a lap dance. I'm beyond mortified, silently plotting my revenge.

"You do know the boys have a stripper organized for Nix," Kelly says, sitting back and watching the show.

"They do not," I say, not liking that shit at all.

"They do," she confirms, giving them up.

"I'm going to kill them. I'm going to kill them with these very hands," I threaten, shaking my fists.

"I think we need payback," Kadence says, not at all creeped out anymore.

"Payback. Those boys need payback!" Kelly laughs and all the girls cheer in agreement.

"Payback! Let's do this then," I say, eager to screw with their plans. After settling the tab, I tip the outrageously expensive fat-a-gram and the skanky redhead, and then pile everyone into two cabs back to the clubhouse.

"This is war," I tell Kadence, watching her buzzing next to me as we get closer to the Knights Rebels compound.

"It's so on," she agrees and I can't help the giddiness settling inside of me. I haven't felt like this in such a long time. A feeling of awareness settles over me like I've stepped out in the cool brisk air on an autumn morning. And I realize that this moment outweighs the ugliness. It's one of the best feelings in the world.

"What the fuck is she doing here?" Kadence seethes when we walk into a packed clubhouse ten minutes later. My earlier happiness in the cab ride comes crashing down when I realize who she means.

Tina.

The club whore who happens to be sitting so close to Sy, she's practically humping his lap. I don't make eye contact at first, unsure how to play this out. Sy and I haven't given a name to what is going on with us, and we sure as hell haven't told anyone about us. *Us?* Shit, I don't even know if there is an us, or if I should be losing my shit right now because she just put her grubby paws on his chest. What I do know is that I'm drunk, feeling for the first time in a long time that I don't even have to fake happiness, and the thought of dealing with this right now in front of a clubhouse of people I barely know has me wanting to retreat. I know I'm stronger now and letting this whore ruin my night is not on the table. I want to make this feeling last forever. So, instead of staking my claim, I turn and try to ignore Sy and focus on keeping the buzz I've got happening.

"Let's do some shots," I say, trying to keep up the hype. I drag the girls over to the bar.

"What are you ladies doing here?" Nix asks, pulling Kadence to him and claiming her mouth.

"We needed to surround ourselves with some sexy men after the gifts you sent us," I inform them, smiling over at Brooks and Beau, before finally turning my gaze to Sy and glaring. His eyes narrow, watching me carefully, but he doesn't respond. The whore has now moved in close to another guy, but that's beside the point.

"You like the naughty nurse we hired for you?" Nix laughs. "It was Jesse's idea," he adds. Of course, it was fucking Jesse's idea.

"I'm serious, Nix. Why the fuck is Tina here?" Kadence says, becoming more pissed off by the minute. I look over at Tina to catch her glaring at my best friend and decide she needs to be gone.

"If I were you, I would be leaving right now," I call out, getting her attention.

"Well, luckily, you're not me," she sneers back and I take a step forward, ready to show her just how much she wishes she were me.

"Tina, take a hike," Nix says, looking down at Kadence, but ordering it loud enough she gets the hint. Tina stands at Nix's command and walks outside, probably to go and bother some other guy.

"Oh look, she's like a pet, obeying your command," Kadence says when Tina's gone, making us all giggle at her snide remark.

"You're fuckin' hot when you're jealous," I hear Nix tell Kadence and I can already see her caving.

"Oh, no you don't, Kadence. One, he ruined our sexy stripper experience and two, it's still technically your bachelorette party. No Nix-fix for you." I take her hand and drag her away from him.

"But he's so sexy," she complains while I shove a shot her way.

"Don't be swayed by the sexiness. We are still pissy," I remind her, but she has that love look in her eyes, and I know I'm speaking to a brick wall. Payback was a stupid idea.

"Right, we are pissy." She shakes herself out of it, giving me a little hope.

"I'm stepping out on the payback. My man looks sexy as hell over there, and I need me some of that," Kelly says, moving away to go to her husband.

"She's weak. Don't listen to her," I tell Kadence, but even as I say it, I know she's torn. I look over at Nix and see him smirking at her. I know she's a goner when he crooks a finger at her. She holds steady before I let her off the hook.

"Go," I sigh, defeated. She doesn't even skip a beat and goes to her man. *Dammit.*

I look over at Sy and he's still watching me. *Fuck.* Coming here was a bad idea. I should have just gone back to my place. Not wanting to out our friendship tonight, I turn back to the bar and force myself to ignore him.

"Hunter, my main man." I smile at him and take a seat. "So, how is your night going?" I ask, hoping he will play along. I know I'm playing a dangerous game with Sy; ignoring him while he sits there watching me, but what does he expect me to do?

Hunter leans in and whispers so only I can hear, "I'm not fucking dumb. I nearly got my ass beat last time you played this game, Holly." I don't know how to respond at first. Is Sy watching right now? Tilting my head back, I let out a laugh pretending he just said something funny. Hunter simply shakes his head.

"You fucking owe me for that, Holly," he warns before stepping away. *Shit.* Quickly turning back to the room, I see Sy move from the sofa and stalk over to where I sit. I don't have time to run away before he's in my space.

"You better hope you're drunk right now, 'cause if you're fucking playing games sober, you're gonna have a sore ass tomorrow," Sy's voice caresses my ear.

Oh. My. God.

"I don't know what you're talking about," I reply, standing and excusing myself. I can't be around him at the moment, especially when he says things like that in my ear. Walking away is the only option, until he follows me and drags me into the hallway, trapping me against the wall, and bringing my hands above my head.

"How much have you had to drink?" he grills, leaning into me.

"What's it to you?" I fire back.

"I need to know if I can fuck this attitude out of you, or if I should be letting you sleep it off," he growls, pushing his hard cock against me.

I repeat, *Oh. My. God.*

"Why does it matter if I'm drunk or not?" I ask, openly letting the idea of Sy's angry fuck entice me. We've been teetering on the next step all week. I know he wants to; hell, in the heat of our makeouts I want to.

"Oh, it matters, Holly. When I take you, you won't be drunk, and I won't be angry."

"But I like angry sex," I challenge, not understanding why he's angry. I'm the one who should be angry.

"Oh, I do, too. But fuck, baby, I don't want you to be able to blame the alcohol." He dips his head and takes a deep breath of me.

"Why are you always saving me, Sy?" I wonder, probably ruining the moment, but I need to know. How did this man go from not even giving a fuck about me to making sure I'm safe, or that I'm not drunk so he's not taking advantage of me?

"Someone has to, Holly," he says, curling his finger around a stray hair.

"Maybe I don't need saving," I mutter, feeling brave as I push off the wall and walk toward his room. I might be drunk, but we can do other things.

"Don't ever say that, Holly." His harsh grip stops me, spinning me back against the wall. "Someone once told me that and it broke me. Holly, don't break me," he says so quietly that I wonder if I even heard it. "You need time? That's all I'll give you, but don't ever ask me not to save you, 'cause I won't listen. I'm not walking away from this. The sooner you realize that, the better."

Past

5g

"I can't deal with this anymore, Katie," I tell her from the window, trying to find the words that need to be said. "There's only so much I can deal with. I can't make you want to live and I can't keep bringing you back."

"I told you to stop trying," she fires back. "I don't want to fucking live, so stop trying to fucking save me!" she screams while her mother sobs from beside her.

"You don't mean that," her father says, taking her bandaged arm. It's her fifth attempt to end her life, and I don't understand how she keeps failing. No, that's not true; I know why. She's addicted to it. Addicted to the pain.

"Don't fucking touch me. I don't want you all here. I don't even want to be here." She thrashes from side to side, pushing her family away.

"Get the nurse in here," I tell her sister as I come forward to try and calm her.

"I hate you. I fucking hate you all so much. Let me go to her. It's your fault," she spits, thumping into my chest. I don't correct her. I don't stop her; instead, I let her release her anger. I've been where she's at; I've felt that extreme anguish and pain that feels like someone is tearing you open. The only difference is I've moved past that soul breaking feeling. It never leaves you; I've just learnt how to not let it destroy you. She hasn't.

The doctor comes in, the nurse following behind. I don't watch as they fill her line with something that will only bring on darkness. I just hold on to her, knowing that this will be the last time. I can't do this anymore. I can't help her when she won't help herself. She holds on for a moment longer, putting up a substantial fight before the drugs take over and pull her away. Laying her down, I step back from the bed.

"Are you sure you want to do this?" her mom asks, sweeping the hair back off Katie's face.

"If I don't, then she's only going to bring me down with her," I tell them. They might not get it, but they see it. They see the fucked-up situation I'm trying to get through. My child is dead, buried two years ago, a child who wasn't mine by blood. Every day I'm reminded of that while her mother throws her life away. I stayed as a promise, but at what cost? I can't help her. She's like my personal cancer, spreading through me and tearing me apart.

25

Holly

A HEAVY HEAT COVERS ME, BUT IT'S THE SOUND OF SOFT breathing close to my ear that pulls me out of sleep. *What the hell?*

Shifting my body, I groan. The movement awakens an almighty headache.

"You awake?" a deep grumble asks me. *Sy.*

"Yeah," I croak, feeling worse each moment my eyes are open. I don't remember drinking that much last night. "Want to tell me why I'm in your bed?" I ask when I realize I'm wearing only a pair of black lace panties.

"You put yourself in it, wearing what you're wearing, too," he replies. *Oh, shit.*

"You could have put me on the couch, another room perhaps," I say, looking up at the roof, too afraid to turn and face him.

"Would you have preferred Hunter's?" he asks, causing me to turn and look at him.

"What?"

"Yeah, Hunter. The one you were flirting with last night," he says, causing me to cringe. *Shit. How much did I have to drink?*

"Well, maybe if I woke up in Hunter's bed there'd be less talking," I'm not even sure what I'm saying, but I might as well play along.

He moves so fast that before I know it my hands are above my head and his body is over me.

"Is that what you want, Holly? You want me to fuck you when you're so drunk you don't know whose bed you're lying in?" he demands to know, his tone dangerously dark.

"I was joking," I say, trying to calm my racing heart. The fact I'm in Sy's bed alone has my blood running hot. His face drops and for a second I brace, waiting for his mouth to crash to mine. Instead, his mouth moves to my ear.

"Fuck, Holly. I'm fucking struggling here—having you sleep next to me all night. Your tight ass rubbing up against my cock," he murmurs into my ear. The warmth of his breath prickles my skin and the heat of his words awaken me.

"Sy," I swallow, my body aching for something I haven't had in such a long time. I try to get my hands above my head to move, but his grip tightens.

"I don't think my cock has ever been so fucking hard," he tells me, nipping at my neck while his lower body grinds up against me. His hardness hits me right between my legs and my body involuntarily grinds in rhythm with him.

"This is wrong," I moan as he bites down harder. We shouldn't be doing this here. We said we were going to go slow. That we would wait.

"No one said it had to be right, sweetheart," he counters, releasing one hand and moving it down my body. "Besides, that's not what you were saying last night."

The anticipation of his touch has me moaning out his name.

"That's it, baby. You remembered," he growls as he moves my lace panties aside. "Been thinking about sinking my cock into you for the last five months, came so close to it last night," he says, running his fingers through my wetness. I hiss at the touch, his fingers spreading my arousal up to my clit.

"Sy, we can't do this here." I break through my moment of weakness. I want this so much, need it so much, but the thought of having him inside of me leaves me feeling too vulnerable. His fingers stop their sensual assault as his eyes come to mine.

"Is this a game to you, Holly? 'Cause I'm fucking over playing it when I don't know the rules."

"Let go of my hands."

"Answer me," he growls, gripping harder and pushing them into the pillow under my head.

"No," I fight as panic claws at my subconscious, but I don't let it win. *He can't see it.*

"Holly, I control this," he says, leaning down into my space. "You think this is a game? Think you can come into my clubhouse and tease me, over and over?"

"You think I'm teasing you?"

"What else would you call it?" he questions.

"Sy, I don't remember much about last night," I admit sheepishly.

"You don't remember walking in and fucking acting sexy just to piss me off?"

"No!" I protest.

"Don't lie to me." He settles more weight over me and I rack my brain, trying to remember what happened once we arrived back to the club.

We walked in, and I found fucking Tina sitting on the edge of the sofa next to Sy. Bingo.

"Yes, I remember now. The whore, Tina, was all over you," I reply, pissed all over again.

"Whore?"

"Yeah, the trashy whore. I mean if you're hard up for a fuck, you could pick someone with more class," I say, growing more pissed the more I think about it. I'm not sure if I'm allowed to have a claim over him, but the vision of her whore hand on his shoulder just pushes me over.

"You're fucking jealous?"

"Umm, no. I don't get jealous," I scoff at his accusation.

"Wanna try that again?" he replies, smirking.

"You're very handsome when you smile," I say, changing the subject.

"Don't change the subject, or I'll slide your panties aside and sink myself into that tight cunt of yours and fuck you so hard you'll be wishing you just answered me." His words hit me hard and fast as a wave of arousal covers me. *Sweet baby Jesus, did I just come?*

"Holly," he warns when I don't reply.

"Fine," I huff and he just stares me down. "The woman is a whore. Why did you even let her touch you?"

"I didn't let her touch me. If you hadn't jumped to conclusions when you walked in and simply looked away, you would have seen that I nearly pushed her off the side of the sofa."

"I'm sorry," I say, feeling like a moron.

"I'm only going to tell you this one time, Holly. Don't ever play that shit again. I nearly fucking killed Hunter when you were smiling up at him. You walk into my club all sexy and ignore me; it's not going to end well."

"Sy—" I begin, but he cuts me off.

"No, I'm not fucking kidding, Holly. Those smiles are for me, no one else. Do you understand me?" he growls, holding my gaze.

At first I think he's joking, the ridiculousness of his command has the same smile play out over my face.

"Yes, Sy, for you," I play along, giving him my answer.

"Only for me," he replies and then he kisses me. His lips claim mine, hard and brutal. It's everything that represents Sy, so I take it all. Take everything he gives me because that's what I crave, what I need. My hands go around the back of his neck, pulling him further into me. My adrenaline spikes again, only this time, I don't let the panic rise; instead, I get lost in his mouth and how he can manage to make me come undone by just one kiss. The butterfly feeling once again flutters to life, the sensation never getting old. Moments pass, our time lost in the intimate act of our mouths dancing together, and when I think there is no possible way this moment could get any better, he pulls back and holds my gaze.

"Sy?" I gasp out a breath when he doesn't say anything.

"I'm gonna fuck you now, Holly, and I know I said we would take things slowly, but I can't handle slow right now. I need to fuck that smile out of my head and give you a new one. One that only I have put there." He pulls back his hands, going to his boxers, pushing them down his legs and taking his thick length in his hand.

"Okay," I agree, not sure I would be able to deny him. "Condom," I add, needing that protection.

"I'm clean," he says, watching me, still lazily stroking his hardness. Oh, God, what is it with a man pleasuring himself?

"Condom, Sy," I repeat, not letting myself make that mistake again. He holds my gaze for a moment longer before reaching next to his bed and retrieving a condom. Taking himself in his hand again, he strokes it a few times before tearing the condom wrapper apart and sliding it over his angry cock. The veins throb before my eyes and I hold back my panic. I'm about to have him inside of me. Oh, God; Sy inside of me, connecting with me. I know he needs this, because I made him need it this way right now, but if we are going to do it, I need something from him.

"Wait," I rush out, halting what I know is going to be a brutal attack.

"Fuck, Holly," he groans, thinking I'm stopping it again.

"No, I want to see you," I whisper, unsure what I'm asking. "Please?" I don't hold back my plea and wait for him to knock me back. We never had the intimacy the first time. If this is going to be the start of something new, something real, I need something more. He pulls back, slowly and deliberately and for a second I think I've ruined our moment. Instead, his hand goes to the back of his shirt and rips it over his head. I hold in my gasp as I take in every inch of his chest and arms that are decorated in ink. I know I've seen some of him that morning after Kadence's party and the morning at the gym when he ripped his shirt off in anger, but I was too caught up in the moment to really see him. Now, laying under him, I see the art adorning his skin in a different light. *He's so fucking beautiful.*

"You're covered," I reach out, touching the colorful artwork etched into his body.

"Yeah," he responds, taking my hand in his to stop me from touching him.

"Is this okay?" I ask, feeling like his comfort level just dropped. *Does he not want me to touch him?*

"Yeah, just you touching me isn't helping my control," he says, and before I know it, he's sliding my panties aside and filling me with his thick length.

"Sy," I moan as he stretches me slowly.

"This is the only gentle you're gonna feel, baby. So hold onto the headboard, don't let go and whatever you do, don't stop looking at me," he demands, the power behind his words making me clench at the anticipation of what is about to happen.

"Fuck, Holly. Don't fucking grip my cock like that again, or this will be over before you know it," he says, and then slides into me over and over again. It takes less than a minute before he has me building. The impending wave of total submission comes rolling through me and I have no option but to ride it. The power and the dominance all pushing me into the deep end of what I can only describe as a mind blowing orgasm.

"Holly." The deep rumble of his voice jolts me back into reality. "Look at me," he demands, and my eyes spring open. I didn't realize my eyes had closed. The colors behind my eyelids were playing out a euphoric dance before me. "That's it, sweetheart. You wanted this, didn't you, baby?" he growls, slamming into me and making me clench. "Fuck, Holly," he groans, losing himself in the sensation for a moment and my heart sings that I have the power to make this man come undone. "You're not gonna come yet, Holly. Only when I tell you, and when I do, you're gonna squeeze that tight cunt of yours for me and come all over my cock. Do you understand me?" He continues to fuck me verbally with his filthy words. "Tell me, baby, tell me how much you want it."

My reply comes instantly, begging him to fuck me. "I want it so bad, Sy," I moan, ready to explode.

"You want me to make you work for it?" he asks, still slamming into me at a brutal pace.

"Don't make me work for it," I plead, my head thrashing side to side. The last thing I want to do is beg, but I will if I have to.

"Say please," he demands.

"Please, please, please," I beg, not caring if anyone in the clubhouse can hear us. I'm so close, my mind has checked out, leaving my body anticipating the pleasure I know he will deliver.

"That's it, baby. Come, now." His thumb finds my clit and he rolls the bundle of nerves like a pro, throwing me over the edge headfirst.

"FFFUUCCK!" I scream my release before his mouth silences me, drinking in my verbal approval. Every nerve in my body is frantic, the pleasure now becoming my pain as the explosion rips through me. He drags out his orgasm, holding on for a moment longer before biting down on my lip, following me over and releasing himself. The intensity of the rumble that leaves his throat makes me hot all over again.

"Fuck. I'll never get tired of your heat, baby," he moans, slowing his movements.

His vocal performance was more desperate than the first time we had sex; it almost shocks me. There is nothing sexier than a man who likes to express himself and Sy expressing himself was just… "Wow," I say after a moment of heavy breathing. He looks down at me and at my smile, and returns it with his own.

"That's what I wanted," he murmurs, rubbing his jaw along mine, and every time he touches me gently, I fall a little more for him.

"So this is what happens when you take things slow?" I ask after my breathing goes back to normal.

"No, that is what happens when you tease me," he counters, nipping and kissing at my neck.

"I'll make sure I do it more often," I joke, tilting my head back granting him better access along my neck.

"I don't doubt it." He pulls back and smiles down at me. I can feel the after effects of his cock slightly pulsing while still inside of me.

"Does anyone know I'm here?" I ask, realizing what just happened and how loud we were.

"Don't know," he says, slowly sliding out of me.

"Well, does Kadence know I'm here?" I ask, watching him climb out of bed and walk to the bathroom to take care of the condom.

"She went home with Nix, but knows you stayed at the club." He comes back, handing me a glass of water.

"Oh, okay," I say, feeling relieved I won't have to walk out and face her.

"Why? You worried what she might say?" he asks, taking the glass back from me, placing it on the side table and climbing back into bed beside me. Am I afraid of what she'll say about Sy and me, or what she'll say when she learns I've been keeping this from her?

"No," I lie. I know what's she going to say and I'm just not ready to hear it.

"Good, now come here," he says, pulling me close to his naked body. "I'm not done with you."

"What? You're not gonna leave?" I ask, trying not to laugh at my joke, even if a small part of me is worried that now that we've had sex, this is what is going to happen again.

"What the fuck?" he pulls back, his eyes hardening through his stare.

"Sorry, just a joke," I assure him, biting at my bruised lip. *Oh, God, way to go.* He watches the movement and I see his gaze heat up.

"What am I gonna do with you?" he asks, softening when he knows I'm playing. "Seems you've bewitched me with your smile, your pussy and now your humor," he says between kisses.

"Aww, now, now. You've always loved my humor."

"Only when it's not pissing me off, Holly," he says,

"Is there anything that doesn't piss you off?" I ask, holding back my laughter when he narrows his eyes. "Oh, my God. You are such a cranky ass, Sy," I tell him as I roll over and cover him with my weight. I trace the tattoos on his chest, the ink containing so many stories I can't wait to ask him about.

"You smiling at me doesn't make me cranky," he answers, running his fingers through my hair.

"Umm… I'm pretty sure you just fucked me hard because I was smiling," I tease, leaning forward and kissing his lips.

"No, I was pissy 'cause you *weren't* smiling at me, not the other way around," he sets me straight, taking my arms, and rolling me to my back, and covering me again. "Now, I'm gonna eat you out hard for reminding me how pissy you made me," he states, and if that's punishment for making him pissy, I'll take it willingly.

26

Sy

"WHAT ARE YOU DOING HERE, SUNSHINE?" SHE ASKS through the small gap of the old chapel door. It's Nix and Kadence's wedding—exactly two weeks since I woke up with her in my bed and made her mine. She hasn't accepted that fact yet, but she will soon. Preferably tonight.

"I wanted to see you," I answer simply, forgetting why Nix sent me back here. Shit, I became distracted when I saw her standing there looking so fucking beautiful and when she called me Sunshine. She hasn't called me that name in such a long time. I don't know how to react.

"You look handsome," she says quietly, looking back over her shoulder, "but you shouldn't be here. Kadence is getting changed and then I need to fix her hair." She leans forward bringing her lips to mine in a chaste kiss.

"Can't wait to get you out of this dress," I admit, drinking her in.

"Go, before someone comes." She pushes me back, but I don't leave until I sneak one more kiss. She rolls her eyes, closing the door on me before we get caught. I'm so fucking over hiding from everyone; I'm about to shout it out for all the assholes in this chapel to hear. I walk away only to remember what Nix sent me to do. Knocking again, I wait for her to answer.

"What now?" she asks when she sees it's me again. I narrow my eyes and she grins.

"I forgot this. Nix wanted me to give them to Kadence," I say, pulling out a small package.

"How did you forget that?" she asks, shaking her head.

"Well, you opened the door and I was lost in your beauty," I smoothly reply, not even giving a fuck that I sound like fucking Jesse.

"Yeah, yeah... go, before anyone sees you." She takes the package from me and steps back.

"Wait," I say, putting my booted foot in the way to stop the door from closing.

"Sy, we're going to get caught," she pleads, and I know in this moment, I'm not hiding anymore.

"Who cares?" I ask.

"Well...erm, I don't know?" she hesitates.

"Told you I don't want to hide us, Holly," I growl, not understanding what her issues are. We might have started off as friends, but we've been growing closer every moment we spend together. As far as I'm concerned, the moment she let me sink inside of her she became mine.

"Can we talk about this later?" she pleads, looking over her shoulder.

"Oh, we will be doing more than talking," I threaten and watch as a blush spreads across her cheeks. Satisfied, I give her a wink and leave her to get the bride ready. Who knew this wedding would be so much fun. Walking back out, I nod to Nix, letting him know it's done. He nods, and then goes back to talking to his dad, Red. Taking my seat, I wonder how long this is going to take. The thought of sitting in this fucking suit for longer than I have to makes me sweat. The last time I went to a wedding, it was mine. It was nothing the likes of this. I never thought I would get married, but then I met Katie and I was in love. And the rest, they say, is history.

"Brother." Jesse comes to stand next to me, pulling me out of my thoughts. "I think they're ready," he says, nodding as Nix takes his place. The asshole looks as uncomfortable in his suit as I feel standing here.

"Do you think Kadence is still pissed about the party?" Jesse snickers, looking over at Nix and the new eyebrows he's got coming through. We had our bachelor party last weekend. To say it ended well would be a lie. After the shit we pulled on the girls with the stripper the week before, Nix was in the doghouse. We had to find some new fun: no stripper for Kadence, no stripper for Nix. Not that it bothered me. I didn't need to see some whore ride a pole. We just hung out at the club until Nix passed out. Jesse came up with a brilliant plan to strip him, shave him, and drive him into town and leave him. Apparently, it was something they did for hazing when the recruits came through as fire fighters. I knew it was a bad idea. I don't think Jesse was counting on the local police who picked us up halfway through chaining him to the lamp post.

"I wouldn't bring it up to her," I advise, knowing just how pissed all the girls were about not only our party, but theirs. But it was Kadence's eyes when she walked into the station the next morning to pick us up that told me she was beyond annoyed we landed Nix in overnight lockup. Nix was more worried about his balls and who had touched them, than his fuming fiancée. We were lucky; we got a break and charges weren't laid. The Rebels relationship with the police in the past has been strained, but in recent times, it's been a hell of a lot better.

"I didn't know the cops would be there," he defends, but before I can reply, the music fills the chapel and everyone around us stands.

I look back, feeling a little claustrophobic in the small room, but then I see Holly step up to the threshold, and everything stops. *Jesus H. Christ.* Seeing her for a brief second earlier doesn't even compare to seeing her stand before everyone at the foot of the aisle.

"Fuck, Sy. You need to sort that shit out before someone tries to get in on that," Jesse stirs me. I know he knows I'm already in, so I don't comment. I just keep watching her.

I know today is meant to be about Kadence, but fuck, Holly looks so fucking beautiful it hurts. I can tell she's nervous, her eyes never looking up as she passes rows of friends and family.

Six months ago, this woman would have lit up this whole chapel with her smile. Even though she never makes eye contact with me, I can't stop looking at her. Even when Kadence comes down the aisle, my eyes never move from Holly. I'm mesmerized, watching everything she does. She captivates me. Her beautiful pain and her heart-break draw me in. I can see she still fights a small amount of her anxiety, but after everything we've been through, she's slowly coming back.

"You're meant to be watching the bride." Jesse nudges me, making me stumble in my spot.

"Shut the fuck up." I elbow him back, realizing my stumble has caused people to look. *Fucker.* Nix and Kadence continue with their vows, too lost in each other to even care as I go back to watching Holly. Jesse's right. I should be watching the couple we're all here to see, but I don't want to. I can't keep my eyes off her as she stands before me, looking more beautiful than I've ever seen. Her hair is done up in some fancy-shit way that would normally bother me, but it doesn't, because the color is almost back to the blonde that she first had when I met her. She smiles as Nix stutters on his words, and then wipes a stray tear away as she watches them kiss. And when it's all over and done with, she finally looks over at me and gives me the most beautiful smile I've ever seen. Finally, my sunshine has come back.

"We're heading out in an hour, so be ready," Beau says, coming back outside, letting me know we have the go ahead for tonight. He took a phone call fifteen minutes ago letting him know we are needed. We haven't had a call for a couple of weeks, and this one will be my first ride along. Tonight is a transport, stepping in and helping a young girl onto her next stop. It's not ideal since it's Kadence and Nix's wedding, but when you get the call you have to go.

"What do you mean you're heading out?" Kadence asks, coming into the conversation.

"I've got a pickup and I need Sy with me," Beau answers for me. Thank fuck, too. I'm not dealing with Bridezilla. Shit has been tense since the party and I'm trying to stay in her good graces.

"What the hell is a pickup? You do know it's our wedding night? We haven't even had cake," she states, folding her arms across her gown, growing angrier after each question.

"Leave them be, baby. They have shit to do." Nix pulls her chair closer to him and rests his hand on the back of her neck.

"Nix, it's our wedding night."

"And I wouldn't okay it if it wasn't important."

"Fine. There will be no cake for you then." She points to the both of us. Fine by me. I don't even like the shit. I'm more annoyed I finally have Holly relaxed and enjoying herself, and now I have to leave. Today in the chapel when she smiled over at me, I took that as her accepting not hiding us anymore.

"Change of plans. We've got to head now," Beau says, looking up from his phone, pulling me out of my thoughts. He stands, signalling Nix to talk.

"Fuck, babe," I turn to Holly, leaning over to whisper so only she can hear. "I'll explain later, but I want you in my bed tonight."

"Okay," she nods. I don't know why she decided she would stop arguing with me, but I fucking love it.

"Okay," I repeat back to her then lean in further and lightly touch my lips to hers. She hesitates for a moment before she gives in, and softens to my kiss.

"Be back," I promise, ignoring what's sure to be a shocked table, hell, a shocked clubhouse. But I don't give a fuck. It's her smile which has all my attention.

"Hurry," she whispers. If I don't step away now, I'm not going to be able to leave.

"Let's go," Beau demands, so I stand and walk out, leaving my woman in my club. Fuck, that sounds good.

"Be safe," Nix warns, and from his tone, I already know this shit is going to cause a fucking long night, but I can't help the grin on my face knowing that my woman will be waiting for me.

27

Holly

"Sunshine?" I ask as I hear Sy's bedroom door open then close.

"Yeah baby, it's me," he replies, coming forward.

"Are you okay?" I watch him drop his stuff on the bedside table and strip off.

"Yeah. It went longer than we thought it would," he says, climbing into bed with me and taking me in his arms. We were enjoying Kadence and Nix's wedding until he and Beau were called off with club business. "Did I miss anything?" he asks, kissing the side of my neck.

"No, Nix and Kadence left not that long after you," I tell him, remembering the look Kadence threw me before she left. I know I have some explaining to do, but tonight was not the night to talk about it.

"You get any shit after I left?" He smiles when I turn and face him.

"You mean after you kissed me in front of half the club?" I cock my brow.

"Yeah." He laughs when he sees my expression.

"What do you think? I had Kadence and Kelly on me like a bad smell and I couldn't get them to leave me alone," I say, only half-annoyed. I made the decision back in the chapel that I was willing to let him in a little more. I knew keeping it from Kadence was getting harder, but when I looked up and saw Sy watching me, I knew I didn't want him to feel like we were sneaking around.

"Well, I'm glad they all know. Now I don't have to worry about sneaking you out of here tomorrow." He runs his nose along my jaw.

"Are you going to tell me what happens on these pickups?" I ask, wondering what the urgency was.

"It's not what you'd expect," he shrugs, pulling back.

"It's not drugs?" I joke, knowing it would never be that.

"Beau is working with this group of people who help women out of abusive relationships."

"Really?" I ask, shocked for a moment. Okay, not what I was expecting.

"Yeah, it's a big organization, spanning over a few states. Makes it easier to move the women without them getting caught."

"Where do they go?" I ask, still getting my head around the fact the Knights Rebels are a part of this.

"Anywhere, everywhere. Tonight was only my second one. It wasn't a recovery, but a drop off. She's settling here in town and we'll keep an eye on her."

"So what's the difference?"

"Well, this one was easy. She's going to be staying here in town. We'll help her find a place, somewhere to work and we will keep her under our protection and make sure her asshole ex doesn't find her. The other one I've helped with was a transport. She was a young woman. We didn't pick her up from a shelter, or set her up in town. We took her from one pickup point and onto the next. We keep moving them along so the trail gets lost."

"Do you know where she is now, or if her husband has found her?" I ask all at once. I've never heard of any of this before, and it blows my mind that things like this happen.

"No questions, no information is given. The person who sets up the move is the only one who knows full name and details. Everyone else just does their part. Makes it easier if anyone comes looking."

"You're amazing, do you know that?" I smile, loving that they are a part of something like this.

"It's all Beau, baby. It's his gig. We just help out when we can."

"Well, you all are amazing," I tell him before kissing him softly. "The Knights Rebels are amazing."

"Yeah, yeah. Give your man some loving then if you think I'm so amazing." He rolls me over so I'm covering his body.

"My man?" I tease, whispering in his ear.

"Yes, your man wants to fuck his old lady." His hands dig into my flesh as I pull back at his comment.

"Umm, old lady?" I almost choke on the words. Old lady? Jesus, how did we get there?

"What do you think is happening here, Holly? You're with me and I want you there by my side," he says, pulling me back down into his space.

"I knew we were moving things along, Sy, but old lady? That shit is serious." I fight the panic clawing at me. I'm not ready for that.

"I want serious, baby. You're it for me." He looks so sure that I feel bad that I'm questioning it, questioning us.

"I just, I thought we were going to go slowly, with everything happening," I say, remembering his promise not to label it.

"Babe, I know we both have our own issues that might just make us a little fucked up, but sometimes I look at you and I think maybe being fucked up doesn't have to be so bad."

I don't respond, unsure of how we came this far without my untold confession coming to light. I know I should tell him about our baby, but it's like the secret is a virus, a disease spreading through me, taking control of my body from the inside. Now I'm stuck, it holds me hostage and no medication can cure my guilt.

"What are you thinking?" he asks, taking my chin and forcing me to look at him.

"Nothing, just trying to work through it, Sy." I don't want to ruin our moment, so I continue to keep my secret. He looks at me, assessing me in his own way, but I hold his stare, waiting to see where this goes.

"Well, work it out quick. I want to fuck my old lady," he says, rolling us so now he covers my body.

"So everyone thinks I'm your old lady?"

"Yeah," he mumbles, kissing down my neck.

"All of them?" I breathe out.

"Holly, half of them already knew we've been seeing each other," he informs me before latching onto my nipple.

"What? Oh, God, they've known about us," I rush out, getting my words caught as he rolls my nipple between his teeth.

"Don't care," he growls, moving onto the next one.

"Well, I care," I moan, letting my concerns get lost in the sensation of his bite.

"You shouldn't. You never used to." He pulls back, watching me. "You never used to and maybe that's a good thing, maybe it isn't, but this here, Holly, is all that matters with us. Not anyone else. Just us, okay?"

I feel his words and believe them. *I need to tell him.*

"Sy," I say, trying to find the words.

"Shhhh," he whispers, moving down my naked body. "I just want to taste you," he says before running his tongue along my stomach.

"Sy," I try again, but know this isn't the time when his fingers spread me open and he runs the tip of his nose along my center. I know I have to tell him and I will, just maybe not this second.

"I'm so fucking hungry, Holly. I could eat you all fucking night," he groans like a starved man, before lightly skimming my clit.

"Don't tease," I complain, waiting for his touch.

"But I love watching you squirm, baby," he purrs and blows a warm breath over my heat.

"Sy, quit it," I demand when he lightly touches me again. It's nowhere near enough to give me what I'm aching for.

"I'm not going to quit it, Holly. I'm going to slowly bring you apart with my mouth and then fuck you so hard you won't be walking easily tomorrow." He looks up, his eyes dancing with fire at his threat.

"Yes," I eagerly plead, waiting for what he is offering.

"But before I do all that, I think I want to watch you suck me first." He changes his play, crawling up my body and moving to the side.

"Sy, come on. Don't be a tease," I pout, frustrated I'm not getting the attention that I need.

"You know you love it." He smirks as he rests back, his arms folded behind his head. "Knees, now, Holly," he pushes, in his no-bullshit voice. Normally, if a guy talked to me like that I would tell him to fuck off, but the way Sy says it—demanding and unrelenting—makes me want to surrender. Moving down his body, I do as I'm told and reach for his rigid length.

"Spread those sexy legs so I've got a good view." He continues to break me with his words. I should be embarrassed at my willingness to submit, but I'm not. My legs spread of their own accord, straddling his body so my pussy is in his line of sight.

"Fuck me, you have a pretty pussy, baby," he says, running his callused finger through my wetness. I don't know what qualifies as pretty, but whatever it is, I'm glad he approves. "Now, my pretty pussy," he adds as I stroke him in my hand.

Leaning down, I lick the pre-cum beading on the tip of the bulging head. I savor the hiss that leaves his lips, letting it push me forward, taking him to the back of my throat.

"Fuck, baby," he groans as he slides two fingers inside of me, stretching me. "That's it. Suck my cock the way I like it and maybe I'll let you come," he growls, making me work harder.

The dynamics of our relationship is unlike what I've ever had before, but I know what Sy offers is what I need. He gives me permission to not be okay, to struggle and fall, and in return, I surrender. I allow him to take the lead and guide me back because if it weren't for Sy, I'd still be sitting in the dark, exhausted, and fighting alone.

"No, no," he shouts, pulling me from my sleep. Sitting up, it takes me a minute to get my bearings before I realize he's dreaming. "Keira." He continues thrashing next to me. I don't know if I should wake him, or let it run its course, but the louder he gets, the more stressed he becomes.

"Don't leave me, baby," he mumbles and the darkness in his voice confuses me.

Who the hell is he talking about?

"Sy?" I shake him softly, but he's a deep sleeper. This is the second time I've heard him call out in the middle of the night. "Sy," I try again.

"Yeah?" he wakes, sleepy and confused.

"Are you okay?" I ask carefully. I don't want to ask him who

Keira is. The way he said her name has me holding off.

"Yeah, why?" he sits up and looks around the room.

"You were having a nightmare," I tell him, watching him wipe the sweat off his brow.

"I'm fine." Standing, he walks out of my room and to the bathroom. I'm not sure what's happening, if I should follow him or leave him alone. Hearing the shower, I sit up and switch the bedside light on. I fight the need to go to him and the need to let him have a moment. My desire to comfort him wins out in the end.

"Can I get you anything?" I ask, walking in and watching him stand naked under the water.

"I'm good." He looks up and I can see in his eyes something is haunting him, but I don't push.

"Want some company?" I smile, hoping to make him feel better. We've shared a bed every night this week, always at my place, and for the last two nights, he's woken shouting the same name.

"Yeah," he smiles, liking the idea as much as I do. I strip off, and then step into the shower.

"Have I told you how fucking beautiful you are?" Leaning toward me, he kisses me as the warm water trickles over both of us.

"Yes, you have," I reply, bringing my hands around his neck. "Have I told you how incredibly sexy you are?" I ask back. His body is amazing, making me weak just looking at it.

"Not as sexy as you." He pushes me up against the glass.

"You want my mouth or my cock?" he asks presumptuously, running his nose along my jaw.

"What? You're not even going to clean me first, Sunshine?" I smile and he acknowledges with a growl.

"Don't tease me. I need you," he complains. I relent, seeing just how on edge he is.

"You want my mouth or my pussy?" I ask the same question back, trying to give him what he needs.

"Dirty girl, you know I'll take you any way, but right now, I need that tight cunt of yours," he purrs, sending goose bumps to my skin.

"We don't have a condom," I sigh as his hand moves between my legs and trails his finger along the seam of my smooth lips.

"You know I'm clean. Haven't been with anyone since you," he says and as much as I want it to be my only issue, it's not. The last thing I need right now is to get pregnant.

"I'm not on birth control," I admit. When I found out I was pregnant, I stopped immediately and haven't started back up again. He groans, resting his head to mine.

"I thought you were."

"I was and now I'm not," I tell him, hoping he doesn't ask why.

"I wanna fuck you bare, babe. You need to sort that shit out," he tells me, sounding unimpressed.

"I am. I'm getting the shot next month," I laugh, watching him get pissy. I've been doing some research and found the shot would be best suited for me; no worrying about remembering to take a tablet the same time every day. I just have to wait for my next period. "Where's your stash?" I step out and wrap myself in a towel.

"My wallet," he answers, sulking like a little boy who's had his candy stolen.

"Don't pout," I laugh, leaving him alone. I race back to my room to the bedside table and pull out a condom from his wallet. I'm about to close it when my eyes spy the photo hidden in the back. I know I shouldn't look and that going through his things is wrong, but the unknown is calling me to peek. Slowly, I pull it out and take in the family staring back at me. *What the fuck?* Sy has a family?

"What are you doing out there?" Sy calls out from the bathroom, but I'm so lost in the picture staring back at me that I don't reply.

Sy has a wife and daughter and I had no idea. Does he still see them? Why doesn't he talk about them?

"Holly, what the hell are you doing?" I look up and see him standing at the door, a towel wrapped around his waist. I didn't even hear the shower turn off.

"You have a daughter?" I think I whisper the question, but I've never heard a whisper yelled so loud.

"What the fuck? Give that to me," he demands, the earlier playfulness gone. I see the pain behind his eyes. That darkness that I once thought was anger now shows itself as grief.

"You *had* a daughter," I correct myself, and his eyes tell me I guessed it right. He can't hide the pain in his expression. "Keira," I say her name, the same name he's been speaking in his sleep. *It all makes sense, now.*

"How do you know?" His hands go to the doorway like he needs the balance just to stay upright.

"You call out for her at night," I tell him in a soothing voice. The urgency to comfort him overwhelms me, but I know he won't want that right now.

"I don't want to talk about it." His pained look goes back to the hard gaze I've come to know.

"How could you not talk about her?"

He doesn't respond as he still holds my gaze. I can't help the first tear that falls for him, for what he has lost. I don't know what happened to Keira, but the pain in his voice when he calls her name deep in his sleep is raw. I hear it, feel it and standing in front of me right now, I see it. I don't know how to comfort him. I don't know how to get him out of this situation. When his emotions are raw, exposed to me in a way they have never been, I want to take it all back, let him have his space, but I had to push.

He walks past me, grabbing his jeans and shirt. Dropping the towel, he pulls them on without any underwear.

"Sy, talk to me," I plead, watching him pick up his boots and cut.

"You shouldn't have seen that," he says, walking to me.

"Don't leave," I try again, wishing he wouldn't shut me out.

"I've got to go." He snatches his wallet from my hands and leaves me standing here, finally understanding him.

Past

Sy

"Daddy, you need to be strong for Momma. She's not brave like you." Keira's last coherent request plays over in my mind as her frail body loses its life in my arms. When I made that promise two days ago, I didn't know that I would be faced with the realization that maybe I wasn't as brave as my daughter thought I was. Maybe I needed someone to be brave for me.

"Sylas, we should take her in." Katie's broken voice startles me as I come back to the moment.

"No, she would want to be here," I reply as I continue to sway on the wooden porch swing that Keira loves. This was her favorite place in the house, and if my baby girl leaves us tonight, she will be here.

"Sy," Katie tries again, but I don't want to hear what she says. I want to play over every conversation I've had with Keira this week. I want to memorize her beautiful face one last time before it's too late. I want to hear the rattle in *her chest for as long as she allows it, even if I know she's in pain. And even though it kills me to admit it, I want to ask her to fight for just a little longer.*

"Daddy," Keira wheezes. It's barely a whisper and something inside of me knows it's going to be her last word. Her chest rises in a slow inhale as she struggles to drag air into her lungs and the rattle of the mucus that sits on her chest slowly fades.

"Let go, baby girl. I've got you," I whisper, knowing what I want is selfish and not what she needs. It's time. I have to let her go.

"Sylas, I can't watch this. I can't sit here and watch her die," Katie sobs harder next to me as the minutes tick by and the sun goes to bed.

"You can and you will," I tell her, but she doesn't listen. Her body heaving in uncontrollable sobs, she stands and walks back inside, into the arms of her mother and father.

"Momma's okay. She just needs a moment," I whisper, rocking her closer to me as my world slowly tears apart. "I love you, baby girl," I tell her one last time as a sob rips from the bottom of my stomach and roars through my chest as an awareness that I might not survive this settles over me.

In the next breath I take, Keira takes her last, and that soul shattering feeling that has lived with me for the last two years shakes me one final time as I feel her spirit leave her body. I don't let her go. I don't fight the tears. I just hold her to me, kiss her forehead and tell her I love her. It's not until the sun fully sets and darkness surrounds us that I know she's free. Under the light of the stars, in her favorite spot, I say goodbye.

My baby is free.

28

Holly

"HOLLY?" SY'S VOICE HITS THE BACK OF MY NECK, AS HIS arm comes around me, pulling me closer to him. *He came back.*

"Sy?"

"I need you." His voice almost breaks me. I wasn't expecting him to come back tonight. When he left, he looked so lost that I was worried he wouldn't find his way back to me.

"You have me, Sy. You have all of me," I admit, feeling myself getting in deeper with this incredible man. He rolls his body over mine, covering it with his heavy weight as he leans into my space.

"No, I *need* you, Holly." His desolation calls to me. I know we need to talk about a lot of things, but the fact he came back says more than words, so I give him what he needs. *What we both need.*

"Take me." I give him my permission, letting his touch cancel out the ache in my soul. Our connection when we're together leaves the pain behind. His hand trails down my side, taking my thigh and pushing my legs apart, settling between them. His touch is desperate, like the need to lose himself in me is driving him forward.

"I need to bury myself in you and not feel this anymore," he whispers, slowly sliding his hard length into me. I don't argue or fight it. I should tell him that he needs to use protection because we are being unsafe, but I don't, because I'm lost in his need for me. The fear that I'll lose this connection is so strong that I refuse to pull away. All I want is for us to get back to a few hours before, when death and heartache were buried deep.

"You make me forget, Holly. You came and eased the pain, and I don't want to lose this feeling," he admits as my body accepts him. He starts off gently, stroking me to pleasure, but as he sinks further into me, his movements become rough and hard. Each thrust pushing me further into the deep end. My body has never known such pleasure, letting him come apart above me, revealing himself and what he needs.

But my heart has never felt such pain.

How am I going to tell him now?

"Fuck, Holly," he groans, lost in his own bliss while I'm lost in my own lies. "Come, baby." He bites down on the soft flesh of my breast, and like every time he commands it, I obey. Only this time, when I come apart, I'm surrounded in a cloud of unease and guilt—guilt for allowing him to bury his pain, and unease for letting this secret hold me as an emotional prisoner for so long. "That's it, baby," he groans, following me over. He stills his movements staying planted in me.

"Shit, Holly." He shakes his head coming back to himself. "I'm sorry." He moves to pull out, but I wrap my legs around him.

"Hey, it's okay." I reach out, holding his face. "It's okay, Sy," I try to reassure him.

"You're crying. Did I hurt you?" he asks, but the tears aren't from the pain of what we just experienced or what he just unleashed on me, but the fear of what his past means for us now. How can I burden him with something that was so devastatingly painful to me, but could possibly be so insignificant to him after losing a living, breathing piece of his heart?

"No, you didn't," I say as he slowly pulls out of me. Reaching over, he gets me a tissue. Taking it from him, I use it to clean myself up.

"Uhh, sweetheart. That was for your tears." I look up and see him watching me.

"Ohh," I say, holding in my smile. I can't help the giggle that comes when he shakes his head.

"Here," he says, passing me a new one. "I'll get a washcloth." He stands and heads to the bathroom. He returns a few moments later with a wet washcloth and my sweet Sy is back. I don't say anything. I just watch him carefully as he helps me clean up. He then takes the cloth back to my bathroom. I nestle back under the covers, wondering what's going to happen next. He walks back in keeping quiet.

"Come to bed." I reach out for him. I'm not sure if I expect him to take my hand or to reject me. I don't exactly know what's happening here. He walks forward and climbs back into my bed next to me.

"Three words is all it took," he says after a few moments of silence.

"Three words?" I ask, unsure what he means but desperately needing to know.

"Acute Myelogenous Leukemia. She was dying. And she wasn't mine." He says it so casually that the impact of the words doesn't register to begin with. *Wait, Keira wasn't his?*

"I don't understand, Sy?" I sit up, needing to face him. He lies on his back, looking up at the ceiling, his arms folded behind his head. If he hadn't just dropped that bomb, I would say he looked peaceful, lying in the aftermath of an orgasm.

"The day we discovered Keira's cancer had come back was the day I found out I wasn't her biological father." He sounds so distant, lost in the past. "We had just finished chemo and were hoping for good news, but it wasn't, and then I found out she wasn't even mine." He looks to me and I don't feel the anger in his words, but I see it in his eyes. "Not that it made a difference to me. It never has. Keira will always be my daughter, always."

"Jesus Christ, Sy," I say as my heart breaks for him. No wonder he lives with so much animosity pouring out of him.

"It was a feeling of having the whole world at my feet then having it pulled out from beneath me. I can't even begin to explain it."

"What happened next?" I ask, trying to understand this man. Understand how he lives with the ugliness of what happened.

"Nothing. I walked out of the room and went up and sat with my daughter while they tried to find out if her biological father was a match for her next treatment." His answer shocks me for a moment, but then it doesn't. This man is everything I've never known he could be, and at the same time, everything I never knew I needed. Behind the façade, lies a devoted father who is drowning in his own grief.

"So you just went on as normal?"

"I wouldn't have walked away even if she didn't have cancer. Even if he was a match and could save her life, she was my life, Holly. I breathed for her. While she didn't have my blood running through her veins, she was mine." I don't say anything. I let his words tell me what type of father he was. He stops for a minute, lost in his head and I don't know how to comfort him, how to make it easier.

"She was beautiful," I say, remembering her picture.

"She was so goddamn beautiful. And smart. Jesus, she was so

smart. She loved watching the Discovery Channel. She would sit there for hours watching show after show about animals, and everything she learnt, she absorbed." He becomes lost in the memory. The comment makes sense with all those animal shows he watches. *He watches them for her.*

"How old was she?" I ask, unmoving, waiting for him to tell me in his own time. I want to know all about her, but I don't know if I'm pushing his limits.

"Seven. She was meant to start school that week, but instead, she was sitting in a hospital, her small body getting pumped with chemo."

"God, Sy." I lie back to match his position, needing to be closer. "You don't have to tell me," I say, now unsure if I can even handle hearing his pain.

"I should have told you sooner, but I've been holding off." He turns to face me, drawing closer, until we are laying face to face. I don't say anything. No words are needed. Rather, I let him hold me in silence and give the moment the respect it deserves.

"I knew she was dying. I had prepared myself for that. I even thought I was ready for it, but fuck, I was wrong. Nothing prepares you for that, Holly. Nothing conditions you for that nightmare of watching someone you breathe for take their last breath."

I'm not prepared for the sob that tears from my throat at hearing his words. Talking of what he lost only brings more heartache. Knowing I am now keeping something from him like his ex-wife did is going to destroy me.

"I'm so sorry, Sy," I cry against him. He doesn't say anything. He holds me as I cry for a beautiful child named Keira. Crying for the family he lost, I cry wondering how the loss of the baby we shared could ever compare to that.

29

Sy

"YOU READY TO GO?" I ASK THROUGH THE DOOR, MY PAtience wearing thin the longer she stays in there. It's Kadence and Nix's welcome home party, and the longer she takes in there, the longer it is until I can get her back home. We've been laying low the last couple of days. After the other night when I opened up about Keira, things have been different. Not in a fucked-up way, but something has shifted in both of us. I feel like I can move forward with Holly without having this over us. And I feel like she gets why I am the way I am. We still yet to talk about Katie. I put up my walls on that subject. Talking about Keira has been enough for me, but I know it's something we have to talk about. Eventually, I will have to tell her that I walked out on Katie. That I left her after multiple suicide attempts and drug overdoses. That I walked while she was grieving the death of our child, and haven't gone back. One day I will tell her all the things I wish didn't happen. Today just isn't the day.

"Yeah, give me five more minutes," she shouts.

"We're late, Holly," I declare, getting pissed the longer she takes. I don't like waiting at the best of times, but waiting for my woman to leave the bathroom is high on the list of shit that pisses me off.

"Oh, hush. You can leave any time, Sunshine. I'm driving remember?" she replies, reminding me she has an early start tomorrow.

"Why is the door closed anyway?" I ask, opening it without seeking permission to barge in.

"Habit," she answers, looking up at me through the mirror.

"Babe, we're going to a barbecue," I tell her when I see the short number she has on and a pair of fuck-me heels to go with it. Jesus, this woman is a fucking knockout and she's *mine*. Mine. I never thought I would claim another woman again, but after the last few months, it's become more than just a desire to have her. It's a yearning for something more than lust. It torments my every thought. Even as I fought an internal battle of denying myself her touch, I knew she was different. I wanted to let her in past the walls of hard concrete I surrounded myself with. I wanted her to break them down and replace the ice encompassing my heart with her warmth. Looking back to when I saw her lying on the floor of that old shed, my hands covered in her blood, I realize the fear running through my veins that night was a fear that confirmed the feelings I had been denying.

"So what, Sy? I like to dress up," she explains, going back to her makeup. She leans over the counter closer to the mirror and I have to stop myself from taking her there and then as she's bent over in those heels. *Fuck me.*

"Baby, it's a biker clubhouse, not the fucking Ritz." I try to get her to see how pointless this whole exercise is.

"Sunshine…" She turns, ready to give me attitude and I can't help but smile. "Quit smiling for starters, and who really cares if I'm dressing up?" she questions, her hand going to her hip. *Total fucking drama. Total fucking peace.*

"Well, if you keep turning up at the clubhouse like that, Hunter will get the wrong idea. He already thinks you like him," I tease, knowing Hunter became a pawn in Holly's flirty behavior just to piss me off.

"I'm not interested in Hunter, you goof." She rolls her eyes looking cute as fuck.

"He doesn't know that," I add, knowing he does. I just like pushing her.

"Yes, he does, Sy. He knows I love you," she says and I watch her hand still as she applies some sticky shit to her lips.

"You love me?" I ask, not at all freaked out at hearing her say it.

"Well, not *love* love you, more like I love your cock." She replaces the lid to her lip shit and rubs her lips together, trying to hide her slip-up. A classy recovery, I'll give her that.

"So, you just love my cock then?" I move closer to her, wanting her to admit what she just slipped.

"Well, I love you filling up my pantry," she smirks, acting cute again.

"Anything else?" I lean into her space, pushing her lower back into the basin.

"I love it when I get to punch you in our gym workouts," she adds, looking up at me.

"You love me?" I whisper, resting my head to hers.

"Maybe." She looks away, unsure.

"Maybe?"

"Okay, a little, but only this week. If you're not careful, I'll revoke that love right back," she jokes, making me fall a little more.

"You can't take it back," I say before kissing her. Hard. Her hands come to my cut, pulling me closer as I pick her up by her waist and place her on the vanity. I move between her legs to get closer to her.

"Wow," she breathes when I pull back. Her hands come up and wipe my mouth of that sticky shit she left behind.

"You know you don't need that shit, right?" I ask, running the back of my hand on my lips to wipe the last bits.

"Umm, yes, I do." She rolls her eyes at me. "And now you've messed it all up." She turns to look at herself in the mirror. I don't know what she's on about. I've seen her done up, waking up, and sweaty at the gym and it wouldn't matter to me. I still think she's sexy either way.

"You're crazy," I say, kissing her again, not caring if I'm messing with her makeup.

"Sy, we're late," she complains when my hand moves up her thigh.

"Don't give a fuck." I want to make the woman who loves me, come.

"Sy, no," she protests half-heartedly. I hold back my laugh at her pathetic attempt to push me away.

"Shhh, it won't take long," I promise, letting myself out of my jeans.

"Condom, Sy," she says as I pull her to the edge of the sink and move her panties aside.

"No, I need you raw, baby," I make it known as I slide straight into her slick heat. Fuck, whenever she is around me, I feel like I can just get lost in her. I want to live inside of her.

"Sy, no. We aren't safe," she pushes back, breaking our connection, but that doesn't stop me as I try to find my way home again. I know she's not on the pill, but fuck, having her raw right now out-weighs my concern about the consequences.

"I'll pull out, baby," I tell her, meaning it. "I just want to feel you come around my cock, give me that connection," I plead, sinking back into her slick heat. She doesn't argue, letting me in without a fight and I regret my promise when she hugs me so tightly I don't know if I can last getting her there.

"Fuck, baby. You feel so fucking good," I groan, pumping my hips harder into her. Our cries fill the small bathroom, our bodies coming together so perfectly like they always have. "Holly?" I call as I feel her tighten and myself get closer.

"Yeah?" She looks up at me,

"I love you a little bit, too," I profess, kissing her hard as her body falls over the edge of her orgasm.

I haven't said those three words to a woman since Katie, and even though Katie gave me something irreplaceable, Holly has given me something I didn't know I needed: her light. I look at her and I see something more. She makes me forget about the past, the one where I had it all. She takes the constant ache that lives inside of me and turns it into something I don't deserve. And when she looks at me, fuck, when she smiles up at me, everything changes. The old gets lost in the new. Her light shines through my darkness and as I stand here in this moment making love to her against the bathroom counter, I realize my affliction doesn't matter.

She matters.

30

Holly

"YOU SHOULD HAVE SEEN HIM. IT WAS RIDICULOUS," Kadence laughs, replaying one of their adventures of their time away in Mexico. We're back at the clubhouse for a welcome home party for Kadence and Nix. They only left three weeks ago, but so much has happened while they've been gone it feels like a lifetime ago. Sy and I have grown so much in that time. Knowing what he lives with has really shown me what type of man he is. When I slipped up earlier and told him I loved him, I didn't think he would respond. I didn't mean to let it spill, but once I said it, I couldn't take it back. I wasn't expecting him to say it to me. I know our relationship has been a journey, and unconventional, but having that friendship mixed in just makes it seem so easy.

"He had this poor taxi driver pulling over every few miles to throw up. Poor baby," Kadence continues to laugh over her new husband's misfortune of traveling.

"I'm never going there again," Nix grumbles next to her, unimpressed with everyone laughing at his expense.

"Aww, come on. It can't be as bad as when Jesse ate that bad seafood in Vegas," Kelly reminds them.

"That's right. He couldn't even ride his bike home. We were stuck there for a few days." They all laugh at the memory.

"I'm allergic, assholes," Jesse says, walking out and catching the end of the story.

"You're not allergic, idiot. It was food poisoning." Kelly laughs.

"Pretty sure you ended up shitting yourself, too," Brooks adds, causing everyone to laugh again.

"Whatever," Jesse says, reaching for his beer, but I can see the small smile he's fighting.

"Well, what's been happening while we've been away?" Kadence asks once they all calm down.

"Not much," we all answer around the table.

"Nothing as exciting as a vacation in Cancun," I say, eager to know more. She looks at me with a knowing smile, telling me we will be talking later. Everyone now officially knows Sy and I are together since I pulled up behind him earlier. He climbed off his bike and stalked to me before planting a kiss on my mouth that told all who were watching, *she's with me*. I think everyone seems to have accepted it and moved on, except my best friend.

"Beau has been in a feral mood since you've been away. I don't think he liked his role as acting-Prez," Jesse comments.

"Where is Beau?" Kadence asks, realizing he hasn't come in tonight. He's the only one who didn't turn up for the get-together.

"He's out on club business," Jesse answers.

"What sort of club business?" Kadence turns to Jesse.

"Club business that's not your concern, baby," Nix answers for him, his tone letting her know not to ask. I don't know what the big secret is about what they are doing. Sy told me without any problem. This is the second time Nix has shut down talk on these pick-ups, evidently not wanting anyone to know.

"Really, Nix? Club business. Last time I checked, I'm a part of this club, too," she says, and for a moment, I sit shocked at her attitude. Kadence can give it good, but when it comes to club business, she generally keeps tight-lipped, especially in front of everyone.

"Calm down, baby," Nix says, pulling her down to sit on his lap.

"Don't tell me to calm down. Stop telling me to calm down all the time," she growls and I'm not sure what is happening between them but I'm not used to seeing it.

"Kadence, calm down." Nix's tone is darker this time; he means business.

She stops and looks down at him. "Shit, sorry," she shakes her head, catching herself.

"Jeez, the honeymoon really is over," Jesse jokes at their little episode, trying to ease some of the tension swirling around us. *Something isn't right.* I look over at Sy and catch his gaze; he looks just as shocked as me.

"Sorry, I'm just tired." She waves it off, leaning into Nix to kiss him. "The flight took it out of me," she recovers, back to her usual self.

"You sure you're okay?" Nix whispers but we can all hear it.

"It's probably the baby," Z announces across the table, rendering everyone silent.

"What baby?" Kelly's excited voice fills the shocked room.

"Shit," Kadence curses as her panicked eyes come to mine.

"You're having a baby?" I ask on a whisper, trying to keep my voice level and not show the pain I'm suddenly feeling.

"Um, yeah, we only just found out yesterday," she quietly admits. The table erupts in congratulations while I slowly wrap my head around it. I don't know how to respond to her news. The pain I have been feeling has slowly started to fade with time, but at her news, a new ache grows. *Is it jealousy?*

"I'm sorry. I wanted to tell you tonight, alone—"

"I'm so excited," I cut her off. Not wanting this to become something more than what it has to be, especially in front of Sy. This would be the worst time for him if this were to come out.

"I just didn't want you to find out like this." She rises from Nix's lap and comes to stand near me.

"Am I missing something?" Jesse asks and I look around, horrified that everyone has zoned in on my reaction. "Why does it matter so much to Holly if you're having a baby?" he asks the seemingly obvious question. *Why does it matter? It doesn't. I'm fine,* I tell myself.

"Jesse," Nix warns, but I can already see it dawning on Sy's face.

Shit.

"What the hell is going on?" Red calls from the door, not clued in on the tension buzzing in the backcourt of the Rebels Clubhouse.

"Nothing, Dad. Take Z inside for me," he says while I try to get my head around what might possibly be coming out right now. *I just need to get up and walk inside, away from this,* my brain tells me.

"I'm okay, guys. There's nothing to make a big deal about." I stand on shaky legs, finding myself throwing my fake laugh while Red takes Z inside.

"Holly." Kadence's eyes fill with the sweetest sadness I've come to recognize well. I don't want her sadness, but it calls to me, and every time I see it, the torturous past all comes back to me. Full force.

"I'm still lost," Brooks says, sitting next to Kelly.

"Shhh," Kelly whacks him on the shoulder, telling him to be

quiet.

"Congratulations, guys. I'm so excited for you both," I try again, hoping the more I say it, the more I'll feel it. Panic claws up my body, scratching to be released. *I can't do this here.* I pick up my bag and try to come up with something that gets me the hell out of here.

"What's going on?" Sy finally speaks, looking between Kadence and me, and all the fight in my body leaves knowing he won't give this up, not now.

"Nope, all good," I say, not looking at him but focusing on Kadence. "So, I just remembered, I should really go," I fumble out, not even making any sense considering we've been here for less than an hour and haven't even eaten yet.

"Holly?" Sy calls to me, but I'm a coward and I just can't face him.

"I really have to go. I'll call later." I turn and escape inside as Kadence and Sy both yell out for me. *Jesus, that wasn't strange at all, Holly.* I make it to the hallway before Sy catches up with me.

"Stop, Holly," he demands, cornering me into the small space.

"I can't—" I begin to say before he cuts me off.

"Don't even fucking think about it," he warns.

"Sy," I begin, looking up at him, only to wish I didn't. The softness I've come to love these past few weeks is replaced with that hard, menacing look he holds so well.

"Why the fuck were you sitting there with a pained look on your face knowing our best friends are having a baby?" There's no point denying it. I know from the look in his eyes he knows something is seriously up.

"Sy," I reply shakily.

"What is going on?"

"I was pregnant," I rush out in a mess of desperation and regret. Just saying the words aloud has my breath coming out in rapid, painful spurts.

Darkness creeps in, and ugliness flows out.

"What?" he practically chokes. His tattooed fists ball at his sides. The air between us is thick with deceit and accusations and there's nothing I can say that will make it better. *This is what I've brought on myself.*

"Before, when we were together, I fell pregnant," I begin to cry because this is not how I wanted to tell him, not how he deserves to find out. "I lost the baby when I was shot."

"You hid this from me?" he states the truth, but I hate the accusation behind it. I knew this moment was coming, but I didn't expect it to be now, in front of our friends and family.

"This really isn't the time, Sy," I try to reason with him. I can't do this here, do this now with an audience in the other room.

"It's okay, Holly. You don't have to explain anything right now," Kadence follows us into the hallway, arguing for me, saving me.

"Like fuck she doesn't!" Sy's shout has me jumping out of my skin.

"I wanted to tell you so many times before. I tried but I just…" I trail off, shaking my head. "And then finally when I was working up the nerve, I found out about Keira and I couldn't bring myself to add to your pain. I couldn't do that to you." My voice comes out shaky.

"Who's Keira?" I hear someone mutter in the background.

"Don't you fucking dare bring her into this," he roars which causes me to step back into the wall.

"Brother, you're scaring her. Calm down." Jesse now comes into view, ready to come to my rescue.

"Fuck off, Jesse, I've got a right to know." His words a reminder of the harsh truth; he did have the right to know.

"You do, but this isn't the best time," he tries again, stepping up beside me. His presence doesn't calm me, or make me feel safe that he's here because I know I deserve Sy's anger.

"No, you're right. The best time would have been five fucking months ago," Sy spits the reality of it all back at me. He's right, and I've struggled with that every day. I should have told him.

"Sy," is all I muster up. Closing my eyes, I try to draw some strength to give him the answers he needs.

"This is what you've been fighting? This is what has had you so far in your head?" he continues to throw his questions at me. Questions I wish I knew how to answer. I want to try and explain to him how as much as I wanted to crawl out of this fog, I just couldn't. Or that living in this state of heartache has been exhausting, but I can't. I can't give him what he needs. Instead, I just nod. Nod for every accusation he throws at me, every angry comment laced with hurt that he spurts and just hope that when he's done I'll be left unscathed.

"You didn't think I had a right to know? Didn't think I should have known this? Were you ever going to tell me?" he finally whispers so gently that I open my eyes eager to see it.

"Of course I was," I offer that small scrap of hope, hoping he can see my struggle.

"Why didn't you tell me then, when I sat outside your hospital door for two fucking weeks, waiting to see you? Or how about those nights we stayed up talking about everything and nothing?" He looks so broken and angry that I can't process his questions fast enough. It's like everything is coming down around me and I can barely keep myself from falling apart.

"I should have told you, but I didn't know how. Then it became more than just dealing with telling you. I got lost, Sy. I've been trying to cope the best I can, fighting through the pain, fighting what I feel for you. I didn't want you to feel this heartache, this darkness. I couldn't bear to watch you try to live with it, too. Then it didn't matter in the end because the baby was gone," I blurt it all out, knowing that half of it is true, the other half a desperate plea that I think I can trick my mind into believing.

"Didn't matter?" he scoffs, getting angrier the more I try to explain.

"Well, what would you have had me do, Sy? We had sex twice. You barely fucking talked to me. You didn't seem the type to want to play happy fucking families," I snap back, not understanding how one minute I'm begging for mercy for my fuck up, the next fighting him in my defense.

"YOU HAVE NO FUCKING IDEA WHAT I WANTED!" he slams his fist into the wall next to me, shattering the plaster open.

"Right, this is over," Kadence says, stepping into our space, her hand coming between us, but I don't let her pull me away.

"You say it doesn't matter. Then what does matter to you, Holly? 'Cause it sure as fuck matters to me that I made a child with you," Sy continues, ignoring the audience we have gathered. Ignoring that his brothers close in around us, concern and anger painted on their faces.

"I didn't mean it like that," I choke as my chest tightens and my head aches. Frustration that I can't find the words that I need burns me. "It matters to me, Sy. I live with this daily." I stare back at him as the first tear crawls down my face.

"Well, I'm glad you've lived with it every day while I've been kept in the dark." He storms past me leaving me standing there, alone and breaking and surrounded by our friends.

"Honey," Kadence whispers after a few moments in uncomfortable silence. The panic that I had been battling wins out, suffocating me in its grasp. The ache in my heart slowly starts to seep out for the world to see. I haven't felt like this in such a long time that the sensation frightens me. I need to get away before I break in front of everyone. Turning on my heel, I race the rest of the way to the door as my skin prickles with the awareness of what's to come.

"Holly," someone calls for me, but my mind has checked out,

my escape my only concern. Making my way out into the parking lot, I rush to my car and throw myself in before the panic completely takes over. I lock the doors as my body heaves in silent sobs and my perfectly constructed armor comes crashing down. I want to turn it all off, shut everyone out and hide my shame.

"Open the door, Holly." Someone bangs on the window, but all I can see is my tunnel vision and I'm spiraling into it at full speed.

"Holly, open the door or I'll break the window." I hear another voice, this time deeper, but I can't control my actions. My main worry is not letting the darkness take me. A large smash pulls me back, then my front door opens and I'm pulled from the driver's seat by strong arms. I don't know what I was thinking trying to get out. I know I'm not capable of driving, not capable of even talking. I just needed to get away from here.

"She can't drive in this state," I hear Kadence say behind me. My mind doesn't fight the intrusion and my body sighs at the strength.

"I'll take her to my room," Sy's voice rumbles from his chest.

"I don't think that's a good idea," I hear someone argue, maybe Jesse? But the heaviness of my heart makes it too hard to speak.

"I've got her," he says, still moving forward.

"You need to take it easy on her," another voice orders but I don't hear his reply. My body gives up the fight and my eyes become heavy. The only comfort I feel is two strong arms holding me.

31

Sy

I PULL UP AT THE DARK, EMPTY PARKING LOT AND CUT MY bike's engine. I haven't been out here in the last few months, but no matter how long it's been, it never gets easier. In the beginning, I used to come out here every other weekend. It was my way of feeling connected to her. I would sit under the stars and try to picture every part of her face, and I'd talk to her. Tell her about my day and ask how she was doing. Some nights I would fall asleep under these stars, and wake on the dew-covered grass feeling like my world shattered all over again when I realized I wasn't dreaming, but living the nightmare.

"Hey, baby girl," I greet her as I place her favorite daisies down. "Sorry I haven't been back in a while," I tell her, brushing stray leaves off the marble headstone. Fall is here reminding me of another Christmas I have to get through without her. After cleaning up the area, I sit back on the cool grass in front of her. I wasn't sure coming here tonight when I was hurting so much would be wise, but now I'm here, I know I made the right decision.

"I miss you, Keira," I say, looking up at the same stars that have always been here. I sit in silence, running over everything that happened back at the clubhouse earlier tonight. I want to rewind the whole fucking night, go back to earlier in the evening when I was making love to Holly, not tearing her apart.

"I hope you're doing good up there, baby." I close my eyes and breathe in what I imagine her reply would be. Something about how she is having a wonderful time and how much she misses me.

She always had this upbeat attitude, always finding the good in everything. When she lost her hair with the aggressive chemotherapy, she still found a positive to it. Telling her mom and me that now all the pretty hairbands she loved to wear wouldn't get lost under her thick dark curls. She wore those headbands with pride, not caring that her bald head represented a sickness that was going to kill her. Instead, she showed the world that even though her body was failing her, she was still going to do everything a seven-year-old girl wanted to do.

"What did I ever do to deserve this?" I roar up at the sky in anger, reliving those memories. I'm not expecting an answer to my question, no one ever replies. I learnt a long time ago that grief never goes away. I'll always live in two worlds: the world that was with Keira and the world today. And the only way to survive is to find a balance between both. I thought I had been balancing the two well, but now—now I don't even know where my head is.

I just know tonight I want to live in Keira's world, the one that holds no answers or happy endings; just memories of my daughter, some beautiful, some heartbreaking. I know I'll find it hard to come back. I always do. Only now, it's made harder with both worlds filled with loss. Resting back into the cold dew of the late night grass, I let the grief of the past and the grief of the present wash over me. I know I need to go to Holly, see if she's okay, but I can't. Right now isn't about Holly; it's about me. So I lie at the foot of my daughter's grave and mourn the loss of two children. I let the years of pent-up tears fall. I let the anger running through my veins out and punch the soil that houses my child. Hating that this is my life, and knowing that there is nothing I can do about it.

32

Holly

GUILT AND GRIEF ARE MY ONLY FRIENDS. ONE WEIGHS heavy on my heart while the other mocks me from afar.

"Holly, are you okay?" Doctor Elliot asks, pulling me from my inner thoughts.

"Yeah, I'm good." I readjust my hands, looking back up. That's the second time in the last thirty minutes I've drifted off into my head—drifted off remembering Sy's words.

"Want to try that again?" She smiles, seeing past my bullshit.

"I'm getting there," I admit, and it's the truth. Finally having the truth out there isn't as daunting as what I thought it would be.

"So, as I was asking, have you heard from him?" she repeats the dreaded question.

"Not since that night. I'm giving him some time." She gives a simple nod, no compassion in her eyes. It's been a week since that night at the clubhouse. After Sy smashed my window to get me out of the car, he carried me back to his room. The panic attack that hit was one of the worst ones I've experienced. I wouldn't have driven off since I couldn't even keep my eyes open. It was as if my body was shutting down because the whole situation was just too much. He didn't say anything as he held me through the uncontrollable sobs that racked through my body knowing that my secret was out. I wanted to talk, wanted to tell him how sorry I was, but the words wouldn't come. I could sense his anger as he held me from behind on his bed, and I didn't blame him for it, but I didn't understand why he was holding me with tenderness when I knew he didn't want to. He didn't want to hold me in that moment, but he did. He held me until I fell asleep and then I woke up alone in his bed the next day. I didn't know where he was or if he was coming back, so I left, wanting to gather myself together properly before I saw him again.

"Have *you* tried to talk to him?"

"No," I answer, wishing I could talk to him. Each day gets harder not hearing from him.

"Why is that?" she asks, not giving up.

"I don't know. Maybe from fear of rejection?" I shrug, unsure I understand my concerns. I think it's fear, fear of what he will say. Fear he might dismiss what we've lost.

"Fear?" she asks, looking up, her interest piqued.

"Fear of his anger."

"Do you think Sy is angry?" She asks the question that's been weighing me down from the moment I served up the hidden truth.

"I know he is." Of course, he is angry. I kept something from him. Something huge. Even if he held me and let me mourn our child, he is angry.

"Why would he be angry?"

"Why do you ask all these questions?" I deflect, but she expects it, so she waits patiently for me to answer. "Fine. He's angry because I couldn't trust him with the truth when I should have. He's mad because I hid it, pushed him away." She nods, writing more shit down in her stupid book.

"So, are you going to talk to him, Holly?"

I don't reply, unsure of the answer to her question. Can I go to him, open and willing to accept whatever wrath he delivers my way? And then could I walk away if he delivers a blow I'm not ready for, knowing this is my fault?

"Okay, I want you to do some homework this week," she says, letting my non-response slide. "I want you to write yourself a letter giving you permission to let go of your guilt."

"Do I deserve that?" I retort, not feeling very deserving after the shit I've put Sy through this last week.

"Why wouldn't you? You're a human being, Holly; you make mistakes, and you did what was best for you. Yes, you should have told him, but despite the circumstances, I understand why you didn't, and I'm willing to bet Sy understands that." Her words give me a little glimmer of hope. I want to believe this is the case, that Sy's anger and rage was a reflex of the hard man I know he can be, and that maybe now, after a few days to calm down he realizes why I kept it from him.

"I want to see you in three weeks this time." She changes the time frame in between appointments and for once, I don't have the feeling of panic that she just pushed our appointments further apart. "Keep journaling and write that letter," she reminds me as her final demand. I stand, agreeing to her orders, and when I leave her office, I smile because I feel like, just maybe, it's all going to be okay. I just hope Sy is willing to let me talk.

I drive into the compound around eight o'clock that night. I know I should have called instead, but the thought of him hanging up on me made me drive all the way here to make sure he couldn't do just that. The lights are low, and a few bikes line the courtyard. Shutting off my car, I suck in a deep breath and pray I get through this. *Yes, you will. Just walk in there and sort this out.* I talk myself into it.

The short walk to the clubhouse feels like a mile, each step bringing me closer to the man I miss so much.

"He's not here," a voice stops me as I get closer to the door. I spin and see Jesse resting up against the brick wall, taking in the dark sky.

"He's not?" I stammer, losing control of my breathing after being frightened.

"No, he's out," he tells me, not taking his eyes off the stars.

"How is he?" I bravely ask. I know he's a guy and a biker at that, but Jesse is Jesse. He wouldn't be Jesse if he didn't know everything about his brothers.

"Been better," he divulges and I feel defeated. "But still better than what he was before you came along. How are you?"

"Same, been better," I use his words back at him, and he nods but doesn't respond. "Will he be back tonight?" I need to see him.

"No, he's out for the night."

"Okay, thanks, Jesse." I turn and walk away, conflicted that I'm going home without speaking to him but feeling somewhat relieved I'm getting out of it.

"I'll tell him you came by," he calls out, and I almost tell him not to, but then I remember I want him to know that I'm stepping up, and letting him in.

"Thanks, Jesse, I appreciate it." I give him a soft smile and head back to my car.

"Don't fuck him over, Holly," he replies, and I know no response is needed; he's not looking for a discussion, but giving me a warning. If I didn't understand this brotherhood code that they live by, I would have been offended. Instead, I smile, knowing Sy and I might just make it through this, *together*.

33

> **Jesse:** Holly just showed up looking for you.

I LOOK DOWN AT THE TEXT JESSE JUST SENT ME, AND I FEEL something settle in me. *Relief?* If we weren't in the middle of trying to get a young woman out of Redwick, I'd be on the back of my bike riding to her place and knocking her door down. It's been a fucked up week to say the least. After losing my shit and watching her fall apart, I couldn't walk away. I watched her from my bike when she followed me out to the forecourt. I thought she was chasing after me, but when I heard Kadence and Nix call out to her as she climbed into her car, I realized I had unleashed my fury on her in the middle of a panic attack. She'd had the same look in her eyes as she struggled to breathe back at the hospital five months ago. I should have known then when I saw her panic she was hiding something deeper. But that knowledge didn't stop me, didn't stop the anger I imparted on her while she stood in the hall trying to fight the darkness from taking her. After Katie, I never thought that I'd feel enmity like that again, but right before my eyes, that feeling came back full force.

When she got in the car, I couldn't ride off. I was already feeling like an ass for letting that all play out in public, in front of our friends. I wasn't going to let her break like that in front of them. When I walked to her car, smashed the window and took her in my arms, I felt the fight leave her. I knew I had fucked up and pushed her too far, so I held her in silence, unsure where to begin or how we would move past it. I knew she would have struggled with her decision to not tell me, but as the hours ticked by and I held her in my arms, that anger I was feeling turned into sadness, which turned into relief, which then ended with grief. It was a cycle, and every emotion pushed me to a new frame of mind.

So I left her in the middle of the night, driving the two hours to visit Keira. A part of me wishes I hadn't left, hadn't walked away, but I just couldn't face her when I had no idea how I was feeling. Anger, grief, relief?

I never thought I'd become a dad again. After Keira's death, I vowed that I wouldn't allow myself to open my heart up like that again, to endure that love like no other with the risk of it being taken away. But now I don't know how I feel. Having had a week to work through the emotions of Holly's revelation, the thought that I was so close to having that again makes me want to snatch that vow back.

"You wanna get off your fucking phone and watch what you're doing?" Beau grumbles beside me as we sit and wait for a phone call. We're about to move into our second recovery for this month. Jesse was meant to ride along with Beau tonight, but I agreed, needing to get out of the clubhouse.

"Fuck, Beau. Don't get your panties in a twist," I tease him and even I'm shocked for a moment.

"Fuck me, that text was from her?" he guesses, considering my reaction to his moody comment.

"It wasn't."

"Bullshit. One minute you're sulking, the next you're fucking teasing."

"Whatever, asshole. It was Jesse."

"Yeah? What did he want?" he asks, and I pause, not sure what to say; the bastard has me.

"I fucking knew it," he sighs. "First Nix and now you."

"Me what?"

"You, you're fucking pussy whipped, lost in your head over some bitch."

"Watch it," I warn, not liking him call Holly a bitch, no matter what she has done.

"See," he accuses, and he's right. I'm a fucking goner.

"Whatever," I shrug, hoping he lets it go. I don't want to talk about anything with him regarding Holly.

"Yeah, whatever," he murmurs. Only his whatever comes across as disappointment. We sit in silence for a few more minutes both lost in our thoughts. *I wonder why she came now? Tonight?* The desperate need to know eats away at me. Until the phone vibrates on the dash.

"Yep?" Beau answers softly into the phone. "Okay, be there in five," he hangs up and starts the truck. "You ready?" he asks, looking concerned.

"By the look on your face, no," I say as we pull out of the parking lot. I need to prepare myself for what I see tonight; this is my third ride along and each time it gets worse. Seeing these women so beaten and scared fucks with me. I know this is Beau's thing, his passion, and I know what we are doing is the right thing.

I just find it hard to stay calm when I witness what happens here.

"You know my sister died at the hands of men like this?" Beau breaks the silence a few minutes later as we head to the first safe house.

"Yeah," I reply, unsure how to respond. Fuck, what do you say to that? I only found out about Beau's sister last year. Jesse was talking about it one night and I had no fucking idea that's what happened.

"Could have killed the fucker, too. Could have taken him out with my bare hands." His voice becomes harsher with each word he speaks.

"Why didn't you?" I know if I had a sister and her husband killed her with his fists, I wouldn't hesitate to fucking kill him.

"Because I wanted justice for my sister. The fucker would have gotten off easy."

I nod, agreeing to some extent, but in my quest of redemption and letting go, I haven't got to that point yet. "This is why you do this?" I ask, wondering why we slowly seem to be getting in deeper.

"Yeah, these women, if they don't get out, they're dead. I wish my sister had that option, a place to go."

I don't say anything, what is there to say? I wish he didn't have to live with that. Wish we all didn't have to live with some of the ugly shit from our pasts.

After a few more silent minutes, we pull up to an old dirt road and turn down it.

"We need in and out on this one; she's been patched up, but she needs medical attention, fast," he tells me as we come to a stop out the front of an old barn.

"Where are we gonna get that, Beau?" I ask, feeling uneasy again. Fuck, this is going to get out of hand. We've never had a pickup that needed medical attention before.

"Let's just see how bad she is. We need to get her out first."

He reverses the old truck we use for pick-ups, and slowly brings it closer to the entrance.

Leaving the engine running, we exit the truck and Beau heads to the back door, knocking while I make sure no one comes down the drive. The light outside the porch illuminates the inky night and then the back door opens.

"She's not good," a woman's voice says and the fear in it puts me on edge.

"Okay," Beau replies, walking past her into the house. I wait outside making sure we can get out without being seen.

"Door, Sy," Beau whispers, coming into view while carrying a small unmoving woman in his arms. I don't stop to look, just open the back doors for him, and step back as he climbs in and positions her on his lap.

"I'm gonna stay back here with her. You drive," he orders, his stare tense and I know not to argue.

Closing the back doors, I make my way around the front and pray the trip to the Knights' safe house is smooth. Fuck, a woman messed up in the back of the truck would never be classified as a night gone smoothly.

"She can't be moved. That arm needs to be reset and I suspect a few of her ribs are broken," the doc we called up an hour ago tells us as he packs away his medical bag. Once we got her to the safe house, we realized things were about to get tricky. The poor woman was so fucked up we had to call in a marker to get him up here, something the club does not like to do.

"We need to get her out to the next drop off," Beau says from his chair next to the woman's bed.

"She's not going anywhere. Not until that arm is reset and cast," the doc firmly replies.

"And how do we do that?" I ask, concerned this woman's chance of getting away is becoming slim.

"I'm going to have to go back to the clinic and get more supplies," he explains, removing his gloves.

"Is she going to be okay?" Beau asks, coming to stand with us.

"I think the main concern here is who that woman is. That's what I would be worried about, fellas," he replies, looking over at her, "and how you're going to keep her hidden."

"Who is she?" Beau asks, just as confused as I am.

"That woman there is Mackenzie Morre," he informs us.

"Fuck, Mayor Morre's daughter-in-law? Jesus, I didn't see that one coming," Beau says, looking back over at her.

"Yes. Her husband, Chad Morre, is known for his temper, and this isn't her first beating either." He leans in closer so only we can hear. "His father smoothed out the last indiscretion without too much media attention, but this is beyond that." He lets us in on that valuable information while looking concerned.

"Fuck," Beau curses, realizing just how much shit we are in if we don't get her out, and fast.

"Do you know this asshole?" I ask, wondering what's so special about him.

"Yeah, fucker is some punk-ass attorney. Thinks his shit don't stink. But it's his father we have to be worried about. The mayor has more power. You need to get your stuff up here straight away so we can get on the road." Beau turns back to the doc.

"Even if we get it set, she still might need surgery. Her arm is bad. Without x-rays, I won't know the extent of her injuries," the doc delivers the bad news. *Shit, we need to get out of here.*

"We can't take her to the hospital, especially with her husband's connections," Beau bellows back.

"You might not, but I can," the doctor says, writing something on a piece of paper.

"Call this number and ask to speak to a Sydney Patrick. You

need to quote this when you get through and tell her we have a code three coming in and we will need two rooms," he fires off his instructions. "Use your burner cell. We can't have it traced."

"How are we going to get her into the hospital? Can this person be trusted?" Beau questions, not looking confident with the plan.

"I need to collect some more supplies. Once we stabilize her, we'll discuss this. Until then, I suggest you settle in for a stay, boys." He walks to the door. "I'll be back as soon as I can. Call me if anything changes," he adds, leaving us alone with a woman who will more than likely have her husband out looking for her as soon as he realizes she's missing. *Fuck*.

"You might want to call Nix," I tell Beau as I head to the chair ready to sit it out. "Things just got a whole lot more fuckin' complicated."

"You fucking think?" he growls, walking next to her bed.

This is the last thing I needed tonight, especially with Holly coming to me, but I can't leave Beau. Settling in for the night, I try not to let my mind wander to Holly and what she wanted. I'll only worry. All I can do is hope when I get back, we can sit down and sort this out, 'cause I love her. I might be angry she kept her pregnancy from me, but I love her all the same. And knowing what we both lost breaks my heart.

"How bad is it?" Nix asks down the cell when we're about to head out. Beau made the call an hour ago but couldn't get through, leaving me to deal with a pissed-off Prez. We should have been heading back into town, not spending another night out.

"She's pretty messed up. Doc says surgery, but we got bigger problems."

"How so?"

"Mayor Morre."

"Please tell me that fucker is not connected with this."

"Daughter-in-law," I tell him what he doesn't want to know.

"Fuck me! We are fucked if this shit comes out," he sighs, clearly knowing who this asshole is. "When can you get the fuck out of there?"

"We're about to take her in, but depending on what she needs, we might be another day," I tell him and fucking hate it. This is the last place I want to be, but helping this woman is our priority. We can't just leave her.

"Get your asses home as soon as possible. The fucker has bigger connections than anyone in that town. You keep your eyes open. Last thing we need is that fucker onto us."

"Yep, on it," I tell him before hanging up and walking back inside.

"You get on to him?" Beau looks up as I walk back into the room. Mackenzie is awake, sitting propped up by a few pillows.

"Yeah, all good. Says to get back as soon as possible." He nods, looking over to the messed-up woman.

"You need anything?" he asks her. She shakes her head no, her face looking worse as the night moves forward.

"How long until we can move?" she croaks out, her breath choppy as the movement sends pain to her face.

"The doc's on his way back. Should be getting here in about thirty," Beau answers her.

"He's going to find me." Her panic is not unwarranted. The asshole has instilled fear into her, but we will do everything in our power to make sure that won't happen.

"No one is going to find you. This wasn't in the plan, but we're gonna work with what we have," Beau assures her.

"You don't know him like I do. He *will* find me. He did this because he knew I was leaving. I don't know how he knew, but he knew," she whispers.

"Listen, Mackenzie. We will do everything we need to do to get you out of here safely, but we have to get this arm set. It's too badly damaged to move you to the next drop off. We have the connections here. I promise you he won't get to you." I don't like the feeling that settles in me at hearing Beau call her Mackenzie, or his absolute promise that her husband won't find her. I know we will do everything in our power to get her out, but that's not to say we won't run into some problems. We need to prepare ourselves that her husband might find her.

A car pulling up into the gravel drive has me on alert.

"Did the doc call?" Beau asks, standing as I move through the cabin to get the guns.

"No, he said he would call five-minutes out," I tell him as I retrieve my Beretta 92FS.

"Whatever you do, don't make a sound," he whispers to a petrified-looking Mackenzie as I pass him his weapon.

"Get her to the back room," he instructs, moving to the front window.

"It's him. I know it is," she cries, not listening to Beau's command.

"Woman, be quiet," I growl, moving back through the cabin. She nods, silent tears falling down her face.

"I need to move you. It's gonna fucking hurt, but you can't make a sound, you hear me?" I ask, leaning down into her space. She nods, my stare telling her we are not fucking around. We don't know who is coming up the drive, but the doc has been on plenty of call outs to know not to show up unannounced. "Bite down on this." I hand her a clean towel. "Okay. One, two, three," I count and pick her up over my shoulder, careful not to move her arm. I can't help the ribs and I know she must be in some fucked-up pain but she holds in her screams as she bites and moans into the towel. "Good girl," I tell her, placing her down on the bed in the back room. "Hang on," I instruct, moving to the free standing closet and pushing the heavy fucker aside.

"What's going on?" she asks removing the towel from her mouth.

"Whoever is out there is not meant to be here. We have to hide you 'cause if it's the police, they're here for you," I tell her, flicking the lock on the secret door hidden in the wall.

"I can't go in there," she shakes, looking at the dark space.

"It's either in there or back to your husband. What do you want?" I ask, losing my patience, my nerves on edge. I need to get back to Beau. She nods, understanding it's our only way.

"Okay," she agrees, standing shakily from the bed and walks forward slowly, with every step the pain is evident on her face.

"Please don't leave me in here long," she pleads as I go to pull the door closed.

"As soon as we get rid of whoever is out there, we'll be back," I promise, closing the door. Pulling the closet back into place, I flick the switch off and walk back out to the front room.

"We've got two sheriff's cars pull up," Beau says, keeping eyes out the window. "Both about to approach. She secured?" he asks, placing his gun in the back of his jeans.

"Yep." I take a drink from the fridge and pull up a chair around the small kitchen table. The knock comes next, and with a nod of our heads, we know shit is about to go down, and can only pray that they don't find her.

"Sheriff, what brings you out tonight?" Beau asks, opening the door to three officers. I don't know how I feel about this visit. Mackenzie has been out of her husband's clutches for not even three hours and he has the whole county's sheriff's department looking for her. The fucker is dirty or the mayor has something on him.

"Evening, Sir. We have our men out searching for a missing woman, Mackenzie Morre," he says, looking past Beau's shoulder into the cabin. "You haven't seen her around have you?" he asks and I can't get a hold on if he suspects she's here or if he's just doing a routine doorto-door check.

"Nope, haven't seen anyone. We're just dropping in for a rest before heading back to Rushford," Beau plays it cool, letting him know we aren't planning to stay.

"Knights Rebels I see." He nods down at Beau's cut.

"Yep. Just had an out-of-town engagement. Gonna head out of here soon. If we see your woman, we'll let you know."

"You don't mind if we have a look around do you?" he asks. It's not like we can say no without looking like we're hiding something.

"Sure," Beau steps aside, letting the three officers in.

"Evening." The sheriff nods, walking into the kitchen and removing his hat. "Just a routine check," he informs me, looking around the small space.

"No problem," I reply, playing it cool. He stands in the entry as his officers clear the cabin.

"All clear," they say, coming out of the room that Mackenzie is hiding in. Internally, I let out a sigh of relief. *Thank fuck.*

"Okay, well, thank you for your cooperation. You be sure to let us know if you see or hear anything." He nods, replacing his hat and walking back through the door.

"Of course," Beau replies, letting them out.

After a few moments of silence and making sure they have gone, Beau races to the back room to let Mackenzie out.

"She's scared of the dark," I tell him when we find a hysterical woman cowering in the dark.

"Fuck," he curses, helping her out of the small space. Her screams fill the room as he moves her to the bed.

"Go get the meds the doc left," he orders, placing her down on the bed and climbing in behind her. I don't know what's happening, but this shit is not normal. I've never seen Beau so protective of a woman before. Moving back through the cabin, I pick up the pain meds and pray whatever is happening here is just Beau comforting a broken woman and nothing more, 'cause if it's more, the club is about to enter a whole new world of trouble. With the likes of this Morre family, I doubt they're going to stop until the woman is found, and knowing Beau, he won't give up until this woman is safe.

34

Holly

"SO, HOW FAR ALONG ARE YOU?" I ASK KADENCE, TRYING my hardest to hold in the tight feeling putting pressure on my chest. I've been avoiding her the last week, blowing her off every time she has called. I know she's been worried, concerned that her news has sent me backward in my recovery, and while the news came as a shock, hearing she is becoming a mom when I'm not, doesn't hurt as much as she thinks. Yes, a small amount of jealousy has stirred in me the last few days, but I think the panic that came over me after her announcement happened because it reminded me of the secret I was hiding from Sy.

"Twelve weeks," she whispers, unsure.

"Twelve weeks? Wow!"

"Yeah, Nix wanted to try as soon as he put that engagement

ring on my finger," she laughs nervously. "We only found out the day we left for Cancun. I had no time to tell you."

"Kadence, stop." I hate she has to try and explain it to me.

"I wanted to tell you in private. I wasn't sure how you were going to react," she rushes out like she needs to get it off her chest.

"It's okay, Kadence. I'm happy for you," I smile, and I do mean it. It hurts to think that had things been different, I would have been doing this along with her, but I still love her, and knowing she is about to start this journey is amazing.

"Have you spoken to him?" she asks, treading lightly on a subject she knows causes me pain.

"I went to see him yesterday, but Jesse said he was out of town," I tell her and watch her look sad again.

"Yeah, he's been out a few days."

"How has he been?" I torture myself with my need to know.

"About as well as you, but like I said, he hasn't been around much, and Nix won't talk about it with me." I nod, not feeling any better. "I'm so sorry, Holly. I feel like this is all my fault."

"It's my fault. I should have told him sooner. It would have been kinder to him not to have done it in front of everyone, but that's on me. Now, I just wait."

"Well, they went out on club business and something happened. I'm not sure 'cause as you know, my husband won't let me in on these secret pickups." She raises her hands up and air quotes pickups.

"I'm sure he has his reasons, Kadence," I say, not sure what to tell her. I know about what happens. I just don't know if there is a reason Nix won't tell her.

"You know what they're doing, don't you," she accuses, her eyes trying to stare it out of me.

"No," I lie.

"Holly, don't bullshit me. What is it?" She comes forward, sliding closer.

"Kadence, if Nix doesn't want you to know, I'm not going to tell you," I tell her, deciding a pissed-off Nix is worse than a pissed-off Kadence.

"Oh, my God. You bitch. Tell me, now," she growls, making me laugh.

"Oh, you really are hormonal, aren't you?"

"Oh, my God. Am I ever," she agrees. "Nix is in for a rude shock. Now, tell me," she demands.

"I really am happy for you, Kadence." I change the subject, reaching out and taking her hand. "I love you and I can't wait to see you as a mom." She wipes at her face before embracing me in a tight hug.

"I love you, too," she cries into my neck, almost squeezing me to the point of suffocation. I let her hold me, let her comfort fill me. I'm not half the mess I was laying in the hospital, and I know a lot of the reason why is because of her constant love and support.

"I'm going to need some more coffee after these tears," I announce, standing to refill my cup.

"Make me jealous why don't you," she calls out.

"You want anything?"

"Coffee," she begs, but she already told me no to caffeine now that she's pregnant. "No, I'm good," she replies as the doorbell rings. "I'll get it," she calls, getting up and moving to the door.

"Sy? Is everything okay?" I hear her ask, and I feel the world spin around me. *Oh, God. He's here.*

"Is Holly in?" he asks and the sound of his voice centers me. I didn't realize how much I missed hearing it, how much I needed to hear it.

"In the kitchen," I hear her tell him, so I quickly face the sink, trying to busy my hands. I have no idea what I'm going to say. I'm not prepared for this. Yesterday, I was full of answers, full of passion to see him. Now, I'm second guessing that he even wants to see me again after the way we left things.

"Holly, I need to run. I'll call you later," Kadence calls from the door. As I turn, I see him standing before me.

"Okay, bye," I say back, never taking my eyes from his gaze. We stand like this for a moment, leaving Kadence to find her way out.

"Hi," he finally speaks, breaking the silence between us.

"Hi," I reply, feeling like a fool.

"You came to see me." It's not a question but a statement. He folds his arms across his chest as he leans back on the doorframe.

"I did," I admit, wishing the awkwardness wasn't there. Long gone is the easiness between us, and I know it's my doing. I put that between us, but that doesn't make it better.

"I'm so sorry," I break first after a few beats. I've realized I'm not ready for him to shut me out. He walks forward, his arms envelope me, and as much as I don't deserve it, I'm thankful for it.

"I wanted to tell you. I swear it." I cry for the mess we find ourselves in.

"Don't talk," he instructs, picking me up and carrying me down the hall to the bedroom. I don't argue, the tears too heavy and my heart too broken.

"We're going to make it. Tell me we are going to make it, Sy," I plead, feeling painfully disconnected from him. From us.

"We'll talk tomorrow. Just let me hold you." He places me in bed and tucks my back to his front.

"I wish I could take it back." The need to explain myself is too much to hold in; I can't keep the words inside. He doesn't respond, doesn't tell me it's okay, because it's not and I know it won't ever be. He just holds me as I cry for the baby we lost, for the lies that were told and when I'm all cried out, I ponder once again on the thought of whether we can pull through this.

35

Sy

HER BLONDE HAIR SPLAYS OUT OVER THE DARK PILLOW and her white skin glows in the first light of the morning sun coming through the window. *She's so fucking beautiful.* I know she's awake, know she's probably pretending to sleep, like me. Is she too frightened to talk, or does she not know what to say, or how to react? I know I shouldn't have left it this long to connect with her. Hell, leaving her wasn't the best thing, but I just couldn't get a handle on my feelings. I didn't expect to be caught up in Redwick with Mackenzie and waiting for her surgery, but now I've had the time to work through the emotions of the past and the present, I want to shake her and ask why? Why couldn't she trust me with this? Why, when I thought she was coming back to herself, was she just pushing that hurt further down?

"Sy?" she whispers beside me, breaking through our charade.

"Why?" I try and keep my words short and soft, but I know I can't control the harshness in my voice.

"Why?" she repeats back to me.

"Yes, why? Why didn't you tell me?"

"I had only found out two weeks before–" her body shudders when she drags in a large breath. "Before the shooting," she finishes. I force myself not to react. Knowing that fucker Edwards took this from us just fuels my rage. If I could go back and kill the fucker again, I'd make sure it was more painful.

"And after, were you going to tell me?"

"I don't know."

"You don't know?" I pull her shoulder back to watch her face. Her eyes are puffy and red; her tear-streaked cheeks only make it harder for me. *Fuck. She's been dealing with this on her own for that long.*

"Each time I went to tell you it became harder and harder," she cries as her hands come up to cover her face, *still hiding from me. Always fucking hiding.* I pry them down, wanting to see her when I talk to her, but afraid I'm going to push her too far.

"You should have told me, Holly."

"I was going to, but then I found out about Keira and I just didn't know how it would compare with what you already lost," she answers me, but her reasoning just pisses me off. How could she think that?

"You think that makes a difference, Holly? Yes, I lost a daughter, but you had *my* baby inside of you. No matter what you think, that matters to me."

"I'm sorry, Sy," she hiccups as tears drown her face.

"How could you keep this from me?"

"You don't know what it's been like, what I've been through." She wipes at her face, the panic still there, but I can see it's not as strong.

"You're right. I don't know what it must have been like for

you, but you know I know what loss feels like. It wouldn't have made a difference to me, Holly. I could have mourned our child with you. Instead, you took that from me."

"I'm sorry I didn't tell you. I tried to tell you, but I didn't know how. You have every right to be angry, but this was taken from me, too, Sy." She breaks in my arms and the past comes crashing back and the memories bring on a new wave of sadness. "It was taken from me too," she repeats. Her words become lost in the sobs of her grief. I hold her as she finally lets me in, but I don't say anything, my mind and heart still coming to terms with it all.

"I lost the baby," she sobs, turning her anger toward me, her fists hitting at my chest.

"Our baby," I correct her, letting her have this moment. This is what she should have given me, this moment right now. I don't know how I would have responded six months ago if she had told me she was pregnant. I knew I wanted her—knew from the moment I met her she was different, and maybe the news would have pushed me away or brought me closer to her. I don't know. But I do know that in the last few months we've grown closer, I've fallen for this woman, and knowing something we created was taken from us, something that could have grown into someone amazing who can no longer be, makes it hurt so much more.

"I know we were only in it for fun, Sy, but when I heard that heartbeat, it didn't matter. I was going to be a mom." She cries harder, letting her emotions show. There's nothing I can tell her that will make it better, no magic potion to stop the hurt. So I don't say anything. I hold her and let her cry for a baby we shouldn't have lost. A family we could have had. And I do it knowing I feel the same way. A prickly sensation covers my body, confusion clouds my mind and for the second time this week, I feel the painful sting of tears.

★★★

"I thought you'd left," her sleepy voice drifts behind me as I flip the bacon over in the frying pan.

"No. Just got up to make you something to eat." I turn and watch her looking uncomfortable—maybe unsure. She had fallen back to sleep after crying in my arms for over an hour, so I left her to sleep and decided to make breakfast. "Come here." I hold my hand out for her, hating she doesn't know how to act around me now. She falters for a moment before taking the first step.

"Why does this feel awkward?" she asks, burying her head into my neck.

"I think you're the only one who's making it awkward, baby." I pull back, watching her. She's right. There is an air of unease around us.

"I just don't know how to act. I don't know how I feel." She steps back and hikes herself up on the counter. "I don't know how *you* feel." She whispers the last part without looking me in the eye. I want to go to her, tell her everything I'm feeling, not just the pain and the hurt, but that the lies she told were too much, she knows this. She knows how far we had come only for it to be shaken.

"How about I feed you, then we can talk," I suggest, going back to the bacon. "Have you eaten this week?" I ask, looking up when she doesn't answer.

"Not much," she admits, making me feel worse for keeping her at a distance for so long.

"Well, let me feed you." I turn, reaching up to get the plates out.

"Are you still angry?" she asks when I lay the plates out next to her, clearly not ready to wait.

"I don't know. I think I'm just numb," I tell her honestly, because I don't want to lie anymore. I think the anger has gone, and now I've come to the conclusion that we need to move forward. I'm not going to lose her over this, and I don't want to push her away.

"I hate that for you." She looks down again at her hands, which sit on her lap.

"And I hate that for you, too, Holly. But we can't change it now." I walk forward and lift her chin with my finger. "What you did pisses me off more than anything, I can understand on some level why you were afraid to let me in, to let me help you heal. However it doesn't change the way I feel, Holly. It's just a whole lot of shit to deal with." She nods in understanding. "Come on. Let's eat." I step back to let her down. "Coffee?" I ask, moving to the coffee pot.

"Yes, please," she answers, walking around the table while I serve up our breakfast.

We eat in silence, the comfortable peace we've always shared together slowly returning.

"Can I ask you a question?" Her voice pulls us out of the quietness. I nod, knowing whatever she has to ask, I'll answer just to get us back to where we were.

"Would you have wanted me to keep the baby?" Her eyes look so unsure, as if the answer scares her, but the depth of her vulnerability is what scares me.

"What the hell, Holly?" I spin in my chair, reach out and pull her from her seat to sit on me. "I wanted you before I found out about the baby, Holly. I'm not going to lie. I never thought I would want another child after Keira, but knowing our child was in here—" my hands go to her stomach, "—fills me with hope. Hope that my heart can handle that again. I *would* have wanted him or her just as much as you did."

"You say that now." She looks up. "What if I was pregnant again now?"

"Could you already be?" I ask as a small fire lights inside of me. I was not expecting her to say this, but Jesus, could she have my child growing in her?

"I don't think so. I mean it could be possible. We've done it a couple of times without protection, but I think we're safe," she says and a small part of me hopes she's wrong.

"Okay, so we be safe and we'll see how we go," I tell her, not sure how I feel about that.

"Well, if you stop coming in me, we would be safe." She stands from my lap and takes our plates to the sink.

"Now, Holly. Don't be like that. You love it," I tell her, not even caring my heart is leading me now.

"Sy, we need to stop. I'm certain we will be fine with the dates, but no more."

"What if I don't want to stop?" I ask, following her. She turns back, looking at me like I've lost my damn mind and maybe I have, but the thought of us trying for a baby doesn't scare me like I thought it would.

"You have to. We can't keep risking it." She turns back to the sink. She's saying that now, but all I can think about was the haunted look in her eyes when Kadence said she was pregnant.

I move in behind her. "What if I want to fill this belly again?" I ask, bringing my arms around her stomach. I don't know if it's the right thing to say and I don't care. Her words of possibility have sparked a dormant fire I didn't know I had hidden.

"Well, that's not going to happen," she says, pushing my hands away. "Be serious, Sy. We are not ready for that."

"Never been more serious about anything, baby. Knowing you had my child in here…fuck, knowing we created a life together and we could have been parents makes me realize just how much I do want our own little family," I confess. She doesn't say anything, just watches me carefully.

"Sy, I don't know if I'm ready." She turns to dry her hands and faces me again. "Our relationship has been a tumultuous road. I feel like whenever we get to our next destination, something else happens. Can't we just get to the next step without faltering?" I know what she's saying is true. I know we've had a hard time, but that small chance she's carrying my baby is flashing at me like a neon sign and I can't let it go even if I wanted to.

"It was never going to be easy, you and me. We were doomed from the start with what has happened in my past, but look at us here, now. Don't push me away because it scares you," I tell her, knowing what she's doing and refusing to put up with it. "You love me. I love you." I pull her to me, bringing her back to my front, my hands finding her flat stomach. "If we have a baby in here, I know you will be ready," I tell her, confident she will be. She might be able to brush it off as not wanting to know, but for me, more than anything I want to find out if my seed is planted in her. My baby. My woman. *Mine.*

36

Holly

'*I KNOW YOU WILL BE READY.*'

Sy's words echo around my mind the next morning in bed as I try not to give away that I'm awake. Truth is, I've been awake for what feels like hours. Sy woke me earlier, with one of his nightmares again, only this time instead of Keira's name being called out, he was shouting Katie. I don't know what to make of him calling out for his ex-wife. When I first found out about Keira and Katie, Sy only talked about Keira. He refused to talk about Katie, only telling me that they are officially divorced. This new change in him has me concerned. If he doesn't want to talk about it, then I don't know how to help, or if I can help.

I feel him shift behind me, but I don't move, still needing more time. I don't know if I'm pretending like I did yesterday morning when I woke up in his arms after crying all night, or if this morning's act is a result of what Sy suggested over breakfast yesterday. Lying in his arms, reliving our conversation over and over in my head, I know he's right. The thought of having a baby nestled back in my belly would be amazing. I just don't know if I'm ready for it, ready to open myself up to that sort of vulnerability. I know I've ached for what we lost, for something I wasn't sure I even wanted in the first place, but when I told Sy I wasn't ready, I meant it.

"Are you awake?" His deep, thick voice breaks through my thoughts.

"Yeah," I reply, giving up my act and turning over his way.

"How are you feeling?" He smiles down at me as I huddle in against his chest, my hand feeling the beat of his heart.

"Let's not leave here," I say, telling him how I feel in this moment. We both played hooky yesterday and decided to do the same today. We spent the day lost in our own world, away from everything around us, together trying to repair the broken pieces of what we had built. It's what we have to do to move on from the lies of the past, what needs to be done to try to find our balance again.

"We have to go back out. You know this," he says, lifting my chin and forcing me to look up at him. He holds my gaze and I know he can see through my panic.

"What's going on?"

"Nothing, nothing. Just the thought of leaving this apartment is daunting now."

"You've been acting weird since we talked about the baby," he says, calling me out. *Shit.*

"I just don't want to rush into anything. We're still stumbling. Just please don't put that pressure on me. On us," I tell him, feeling in over my head. It's just all too much.

"There's no pressure, baby. Just let it be." He pulls me closer to him. "It's you and me. Whatever happens, we do it together. You got that?" I nod in response, forcing myself to let it go. He's right. There's no point worrying about it until we have to. I need to put it out of my mind.

"You need a haircut," I tell him, taking my hand and running it through his longer hair and noticing the messy strands around his ears.

"Yeah and I have this hot woman who apparently cuts hair for living, but she's always too damn busy," he jokes, taking my wrist and kissing the inside of it.

"I thought you liked cutting it yourself?"

"I did, but now I've got a fine-ass woman like you who does a much better job at it than me, maybe I want you to cut it."

"Okay, I can cut it," I tell him, feeling nervous about the task.

"Naked," he adds as I agree.

"Naked?" I choke out and he growls, no doubt picturing it. "Could you be any more cliché?" His grin tells me he actually finds the idea appealing. The idea of me standing in front of him naked while I cut his hair, would be the best vision ever apparently, if his hard cock pressed against my thigh is anything to go by. I let out an unladylike snort.

"If I cut your hair naked, I would get nothing done," I tell him, seeing the whole thing play out in my mind. "You wouldn't be able to keep your hands to yourself." I speak the truth, knowing more than anything it would end up with me on his lap. *Why am I arguing about this again?*

"I sure as hell will be able to keep my hands to myself, Holly," he scoffs and I almost believe him. *Almost.*

"Wanna bet?" I find myself asking, wanting to prove him wrong.

"You're on," he smirks before kissing me hard.

Five minutes later, Sy sits on my dining room chair, my black cape draped around him while I stand there, naked. *Completely na-*

ked.

"I've never done this before. I can't believe I agreed to this," I say, picking up my clippers. I try not to let his stare break my concentration, but the tension in the room is building by the minute and I don't know if I'm going to last.

"Sweetheart, there have been a lot of things I've done for the first time with you, but this is by far my favorite," he rumbles as his gaze burns through me.

"Keep your hands to yourself, Sy," I demand, my heart rate picking up. Turning the clippers on, I come forward and begin. He doesn't move or talk, the buzzing sound filling the room. The vibrations of the clippers run up my arm and all through my body. The sensation is so intense I don't know if the thick tension in the air is causing it, or if it's from the erotic act as his stare burns through me, but an awareness runs through me that's just as fervid as the buzzing clippers in my hand. I don't ever want it to stop. I try to keep my body away from him, moving around at arm's length so he doesn't touch me, but as I lean over, trying to make sure I get it even, his finger trails along the side of my waist. The feather light graze sends a tingle down my spine, like spurts of electricity jolt through me. *Just from one touch.*

"No touching, Sy." My breath comes out choppy as I warn him. I then lean further over him hoping he does cave because the ache between my legs is becoming desperate.

"I'm struggling, Holly," he growls. The rumble of his frustration goes straight to the throbbing in my core, setting me on fire.

"You're going to lose." I sashay my hips and move to his other side. The throb between my legs has taken on its own pulse and squeezing my thighs together only makes it worse.

"I don't think I can keep that promise," he admits, ripping the cape off then pulling me to his lap.

"Sy," I laugh, twisting to face him.

"Fuck, you're sexy," he says, dropping his mouth to mine.

Flicking the power off on the clippers, I let them drop to the floor.

"Your haircut is going to be uneven now," I tell him as he trails kisses down my neck and his finger spreads me open and slides through my wetness.

"Jesus, woman, I hope you don't treat all your clients like this."

"Only the special ones," I yelp as he nips at my neck, slides two thick fingers into me and then removes them in a slow and deliberate pace. The pleasure and pain that Sy brings me only makes me want him more.

"I am special," he says, taking his finger to his mouth, and slowly sliding it past his lips. "Fuck, you taste so sweet," he groans, closing his eyes and dropping his head back in total satisfaction. I laugh at his reaction. I've never had a man be so vocal and expressive. "Why are you laughing?" His head comes up.

"Because you're sexy, sweet and cute," I tell him and I know he won't like the words I've used to describe my man.

"I'm not fucking cute," he mumbles, making me laugh louder.

"You're amazing," I tell him, this time kissing him hard.

"I ain't that either."

"Sy, you're the most incredible person I've ever known. What you have experienced in your life is what gives you that hard exterior, but deep down in here—" I pat his chest, "—is what I see when we are alone. It all makes you the amazing man you are, and those qualities are why I fell in love with you." I look at him, hoping he sees what I feel.

"This," he places his hand over mine, "is only better when I'm with you, baby." He leans forward and kisses me. He makes me fall in love with him more when he says things like this. Soon, we'll be going back to work, back to the clubhouse and our families, and then this Sy will only come out in the privacy of his room or my apartment. So, I'm going to enjoy every moment of it while we can.

"I think you need to pay me in sexual favors for your haircut," I laugh, bringing us back to the playful side I love most about us.

"I'm on it, baby." He stands, holding me in his arms and walks down the hall, back to my bed. "What's the damage?" he asks, playing along.

"Four orgasms, please." I hold my straight face.

"You greedy minx," he growls, dropping me down on the bed. "I'll give you two with my mouth, and two with my cock," he tells me, dropping to his knees.

"Sunshine," I moan as his tongue slides up my center, and whatever I was going to say is long gone. All that matters is his tongue and a promise of four orgasms.

37

Sy

"LOOK WHO'S COME BACK!" JESSE SHOUTS WHEN HE SEES me walking in through the clubhouse Tuesday morning. I hold in my smile as all the boys start hanging shit on me.

"Did you forget where you lived?" Brooks adds, slapping my back walking past me.

"Fuck off," I grumble my normal morning greeting. It's been a few days since I've been back to the clubhouse. When we came back from the recovery on the weekend, we filled in the boys about Mackenzie, and our visit from the sheriff and then I headed straight for Holly's, determined to sort it out. It wasn't an intentional move, but definitely a necessary one. After the fallout of everything that happened, I needed to get things right with Holly. We spent the last few days excluding ourselves and trying to find our way back to where we were. I did speak to Nix and Beau, keeping up on the Mackenzie drama, but for the most part we stayed locked away, not ready to face anyone or their questions. I didn't think the news of the baby would bring up so many memories of Katie and Keira, but it has. Even letting Holly in about Keira has been hard enough. I know I'm still holding onto some guilt with Katie, guilt that I need to let go, but I'm working up the courage for that. To go see *her*.

"What's going on?" I ignore them and ask the reason why we've all been called in.

"Sheriff's department is on the way in with a warrant," Nix answers, looking more pissed off than normal.

"What the fuck?"

"Jackson just called. Says it's out of his hands and they'll be here within the hour."

"Mayor is dirty as fuck. Who knows who he has under him," Brooks puts in and he's right. I just didn't think anyone would have made us.

"We have anything to hide here?" I ask, knowing we keep it clean and above board, but who fucking knows what might be hidden within these walls.

"Yeah, everything has a permit. We're good. Just pissed this fucker is playing with us."

"I think the asshole has a hard on for you," I say, wondering just how stable this fucker is.

"We sure we got Mackenzie out okay?" Nix questions, running his hands over his face.

"She was dropped off and no one made us," Beau assures him. After waiting for another hour for the doc, we were able to get Mackenzie down to a hospital and get her into surgery. She needed her elbow reset, and plates put in to help with a shattered forearm. I was surprised the woman was still lucid after waiting that long with her arm seriously messed up.

"How the fuck does he know we had a part in it?" I ask, wondering where their information is coming from; first the visit to the safe house and now here.

"Only guess would be someone saw us."

"We were in and out," I state, not understanding how that was possible.

"Some fucker might have made the truck. Registration is in Nix's name," Jesse comes up with a plausible explanation.

"Having the Knights Rebels in their town could have tipped them off."

"How can we be sure that someone in the hospital didn't make us?" I ask, remembering the two males who helped us when we moved Mackenzie from the truck into the secured room at the hospital.

"Everyone who's in on this is legit," Beau insists, still not sold on the idea we were snitched on.

"Boss, they're here." Hunter comes inside letting us know our guests have arrived.

"Everyone keep their mouths shut." Nix stands and walks outside as they pull in.

"Well, if this isn't a pissing contest, I don't know what is," Brooks says as two county sheriff's cruisers and Jackson's truck pulls into the forecourt. Three officers pile out, followed by Jackson, and the fucking asshole, Chad Morre.

"Nix," Jackson greets, walking up and handing over a piece of paper. "We have a warrant. I need you to get the guys out so we can search the premises."

"What the fuck is that fucker doin' here?" Nix ignores the warrant, but looks over to the asshole who's behind all this. It's not normal protocol, but knowing what we've learnt of the fucker, he doesn't go by protocol.

"We're looking for a Mackenzie Morre. We've got reason to believe she might be here, or you might know her whereabouts,"

Jackson replies, ignoring Nix's question.

"Nope, no one here and nothing to hide."

"We'll check around and be gone then," he informs, not looking happy about it. Nix doesn't say anything, just nods and lets the three officers through to do the search.

"You know this is bullshit, right?" I ask, pissed the asshole is in our compound.

"Just keep your mouths shut and they will be gone soon," Jackson says, lowering his voice so only we can hear. We stand around for a moment longer in silence, waiting for them to search for someone who isn't even here.

"You didn't show up to family game night," Jackson says to Jesse, breaking the silence. If you didn't know they were brothers, you wouldn't guess it. Where Jesse is blond and easy going, Jackson is dark and solemn.

"Was busy," Jesse replies, shrugging. I don't know much about their family, but I do know they used to be tight before Jesse joined the club.

"Well, Pops is having a game night next week so you should come," he tries again, but Jesse doesn't respond, just nods.

"Are you going to be checking to see if my wife is in there, Detective, or just chatting about bullshit family game nights?" Chad calls, still leaning against the car.

"Chad, the three officers are on it."

"Jesus, Jackson, you gonna let this fucker speak to you like that?" I ask, growing more annoyed by him. *Who the fuck is this guy?*

"It's better just to let him think he's got me by the balls. I'll enjoy it more when I take him down," Jackson explains, letting us know where he stands. He might be stuck right now but if push came to shove, he would handle the motherfucker.

"All clear, Detective." One of the deputies comes out a few minutes later.

"Impossible," the fucker, Chad, calls out, making his way forward. "Just tell us where she is and this will all be over with," he says, looking smug in his pressed suit, which just pisses me off.

"Even if we knew where your wife was, I wouldn't tell you," Beau fires up, pushing off the wall.

"Beau," Jackson warns, stepping in as the officers walk toward Chad.

"So you do know where she is?"

"Don't know where she is," he shrugs, pissing him off more. I move in, not liking this asshole on our turf showing no fear or respect.

"I know you know where she is. Your truck was seen leaving the last place she was at," he sneers.

"Don't know anything about that. What I want to know is why are you going to all this trouble to get her back? You clearly don't love her with all the bruises she's had in the past," Beau fires back and sits dangerously close to crossing the line. We need to play it cool here. Not give him any idea we know anything.

"Stand down, Beau," Jackson grinds out, stepping in front of him.

"Can't you see these lowlifes have my wife? Who knows what they are doing with her," Chad has the audacity to accuse. Yeah, fixing her up after *he* broke her.

"Couldn't be any worse than what you've done to her, hey, Chad?" Beau goes at him again, not giving a fuck that there are witnesses around.

"Beau, calm down," Nix orders, pushing him back out of the firing range. "Take a breather," he suggests, pointing over to the side of the parking lot.

"Chad, get in the fucking car," Jackson snaps, running his hand over his head.

"I know they have her," he spits, walking back over to the cars.

"Jesus, Jackson. What a fucking mess," Nix says, shaking his head.

"Well, this is what you're up against. This guy is fucking dirty as fuck. He has his eye set on you. I'd watch your steps for the next few weeks. He's not giving up." Well, fuck, this guy is a loose cannon and one we don't want hanging around.

"We've got it," Nix nods, heeding the warning.

"And make sure you turn up next week, Jesse," Jackson adds, turning back to his brother. "I'll let him know you're coming." He smirks before nodding and turning back to the truck.

"No, I'll let you know," Jesse argues.

"Be there, little brother, or we will be having words, words you won't want to have." There's no room for negotiation in his threat.

"Fucker," Jesse mumbles, watching his brother get back into his truck.

"What a clusterfuck," I say, watching them all drive out of the compound knowing it's not the last time we'll probably deal with this shit.

"Tell me about it. I fucking hate games night; always happens on Saturday night, the best night for pussy," Jesse sulks next to me.

"Not that, you dickhead," I say, turning and hitting him over the head. "Jesus, Jesse. Stop thinking about your fucking dick for one second." Following everyone else, I head back inside.

"So, we lay low until this blows over," Nix says when we get back inside.

"You got a contact for Mackenzie?" I ask, wondering if we'll know if she needs help.

"None. That's not how this works. We recovered her. She won't come back now. She's been trying to get out for the last two years. This was her only chance at getting free. She's scared of the fucker."

Fuck.

"Well, let's hope this blows over. Maybe he'll get a new lead and leave us alone," Nix says, getting his shit together to head out.

"We done here?" I ask, needing to head over to Ink Me. After taking the last couple of days off, I need to check in.

"Where you going?" Jesse asks, being a nosey fucker.

"I was planning on going to check on Ink Me. Then if it's okay with you, I was gonna head back to fuck my woman. Need to know anything else?" I ask, walking down the hall to get a bag. I'm staying with her, and if I have it my way, I won't be leaving so I'm gonna need some clean clothes.

"Ha ha ha, fucker. Will you be back for the club meet tonight?" he asks.

"I'll be back with Holly later, don't worry," I tell him. As much as I want to stay in bed with my woman, I need to make sure she's included in the club life.

"I think I preferred it when you weren't getting laid," he calls out, needing to have the last say.

"That's because you're a jealous fucker." I laugh my ass off down the hall.

"Fuck me, he's a goner, Brooks. Look, he's even fucking laughing these days." I hear him having a go, but I don't respond because he's right. I am a goner and there isn't anything I can do about it. The woman has me by my fucking balls and she knows it, too.

God, help me.

"Holly?" I call out, walking through her apartment. I know she's here 'cause her car sits in the same place it was when I left earlier this morning. "Holly?" I call again, setting down the grocery bags on the counter top and going in search of her. I messaged her to let her know I was coming back and knocked when I got here, but when she didn't answer, I tried the door realizing she hadn't locked it. *We'll be talking about that later.*

Walking through the apartment, I hear the shower going and I get excited that I've turned up just in time. Turning the corner, I'm more shocked than I thought I ever would be.

"What are you doing?" I ask, but instantly regret it. I should have kept my mouth shut and stood there watching her.

"Ahhh," she screams, my voice freaking her out. "What are you doing here?" she frantically rushes out, realizing she's been caught in the act.

"Holly—" I drag out her name, smirking at the guilty look on her face.

"Sy, get out of here," she punches out her demand.

"I'm not going anywhere." I admire her body relaxing under the flow of the water. Resting back against the wall, my cock grows against my fly. "What were you doing with the shower head?" I ask again and watch a slight blush grow over her cheeks in embarrassment, but I'm not going to let her off so easy. "Don't stop 'cause I'm here."

"You want to watch me get off?"

"Sweetheart, that's a fucking dumb question."

"Shut up, Sy. Go away."

"No, I'm not going anywhere. Continue what you were doing 'cause it's sure as fuck hot."

She looks hesitant but only for a second as she moves the showerhead down between her thighs. She parts her pussy lips, the soft, pink flesh begging for me to come and take over, but I don't move. I stay rooted in my spot as the hard flow of the water hits her right where she needs it. "Wait…" she pauses and looks up. "If I do this, I want to see you do it, too," she challenges, but she doesn't have to tell me twice. I pop the buttons on my jeans and reach in and grab my throbbing cock. Her eyes go to my hand while I watch her bring herself to an orgasm. "Oh, God, this is so fucking hot," she breathes out, her face flushed and her hair stuck to her forehead. Fuck, she is beautiful. Her lips part, her head falls back, and her hand comes to the glass that separates us, holding her stance as the beginning of her orgasm takes her.

"Look at me," I growl, wanting to admire her face as the pleasure consumes her. I walk forward as her eyes come to mine, and for once, I don't see the pain, don't see panic. I see lust, pure fucking ecstasy.

"Come, now, Holly," I tell her and listen as her release echoes around the room, the sound switching something in me. I pull the glass door open just as my release takes me over. My cum hits her naked, wet body, but her eyes never leave mine. I step into the shower, still fully clothed and take her mouth, catching the last soft moans as her orgasm slows. The taste of her on my lips brings me back to the happiness I crave from her. I bite down on them, reminding her this is how I like it, hard and soft, always hard and soft, but for this woman I'd have it any way.

"That's the last time a shower head is ever that close to your pussy. Do you understand me?"

"Whatever, Sy," she says, stepping back and resting her shoulders against the glass wall, a small smile playing on her lips.

"I'm serious. You only come apart like that again by me," I tell her, stripping my wet clothes from my body and throwing them out onto the bathroom floor. She doesn't look up, still in her post-orgasm state. I take the shower head from her hands and switch the flow to wash away the cum from her stomach. Seeing it stirs my cock again. Leaning down, I take her nipple in my mouth, the temptation too great to ignore.

"You can't order me to not masturbate again," she sasses, but her argument is invalid when she moans as I roll her sweet nipple between my teeth.

"Yeah, I can, sweetheart. You touch your sweet pussy again when I'm not here and you won't be able to sit for a week," I answer back, meaning every word. "What the fuck you doing in here anyway? I only ate your pussy this morning," I wonder while lathering up some soap to wash her back.

"I was horny because I was thinking about this morning," she explains, but that doesn't make me feel any better. "You told me you wouldn't be back till tonight," she says, tilting her neck back as I lay kisses on her body.

"You should have called me, baby. I would have dropped anything to feast on your pussy," I tease, my mouth watering wanting to taste her.

"Yeah, like that's going to happen…um…Hi, Sy, I know I've just had you in my lair for the last few days, but my vagina is throbbing for your tongue. Please drop what you are doing and come and eat me out," she jokes, but there's no telling my cock that. Her words bring him to attention. Even after just emptying myself on her, the need to bury my cock deep inside her is strong.

"You ready for me again?" I ask, moving my hand down to her smooth lips.

"Yes." She spreads her legs, giving me better access.

"Good, cause I'm gonna fuck you raw, fill you with my cum and then wash you clean. You understand me?" I ask, watching her quiver at my words.

"Sy," she breathes, "we're risking it." Her words fight it, but her body is ready to obey me in an instant.

"Good. Now bend over and show me that pretty pussy," I demand, my control slipping when she does as she's told. "Spread them wider," I instruct, watching her feet inch further apart. Her tight little asshole stares back at me and even though we've never talked about it, the thought of taking her there has my balls aching. My hand moves on its own accord, trailing up along the inside of her thigh, and grazing her pussy lips before running a slow and deliberate trail to her back entrance. I see the muscle flexing at my touch.

"You want me to take you there, baby? 'Cause I'm going to," I promise her with the intent to fulfill it soon.

"No," she answers, but I hear the interest behind her words.

"Yes, you do. Don't lie."

"It's going to hurt," she complains, tensing up when I add some pressure.

"Not if I do it right," I tell her as I slide my finger down to her pussy, and drag her wetness up to her ass. *Fuck, what I would do just to fuck her there.*

"Okay," she breathes out, moving her body in motion with my lazy strokes.

"Not now, baby, but soon," I promise, becoming rock hard knowing it will happen soon.

"Okay," she moans when I slide the tip of my finger past the entrance to her ass.

"Fuck, woman, don't tempt me now." I inch my finger further in.

"More," she begs as I slowly slide my finger out. Stepping forward, I line my cock up with her pussy and let her heat take me.

"Fuck, you feel tight," I murmur, letting the tightness of her pussy grip my cock. I don't know what feels better, her tight cunt, or the warmth of her asshole around my finger as I sink further into her.

"Keep still," she instructs, holding onto the shower seat. She spreads a little wider and leans forward, slowly sliding off my dick. I want to follow her, stay planted deeply, but her command stops me. "Sy, let me." She slowly sinks back onto my cock, repeating the process in a deliberate rhythm. She might be riding me at the slowest pace, but it couldn't feel any fucking better.

"Fuck, I can't even begin to describe how fucking awesome that feels," I tell her as she continues to glide along my cock. I want to dig my hands into her side, grab on and just bang the fuck out of her, but the feeling of her slowly milking me is holding me off. I follow her movements with my finger, slowly easing in and out of her ass, at the same pace my cock slides out of her pussy.

"Sy," she murmurs, keeping her rhythm up. I'm not lying; I've never felt anything like it before. The overwhelming need to explode sits at the base of my spine, but the slow movements as she slides forward then back just holds me off.

"I don't know what you're doing with that cunt of yours, but I don't ever want it to stop," I groan as she clenches around me drawing out her own orgasm. "Fuck," I shout as stars burst from behind my eyes when I release one of the most intense orgasms I've ever had. "Woman, you're too much," I admit, fumbling with my feelings. I feel like I've just been taken to the edge and don't ever want to come back. *How the hell did I end up here? Wanting to completely surrender to her.* "You're so fucking amazing, Holly," I tell her when she stands to full height.

"Right back at you." She turns and her eyes light up with her smile. It's a smile that lets me know all is right in our world.

38

Holly

"I'll have the chicken melt, please." I order, handing the menu back to the waitress.

"And for you?" she turns to ask Kadence.

"I'll get a double cheeseburger with bacon and a side of loaded fries. And I'll have a chocolate milkshake and strawberry milkshake," she smiles sweetly.

"Two milkshakes?" the unsuspecting waitress asks.

"Yeah." Kadence shrugs like it's no big deal.

"Okay, I'll be right back," the young waitress says, taking our menus to place our order.

"What?" she asks, catching me looking at her.

"Are we expecting Nix?" I tease.

"Ha-ha! I've been so hungry the last week or so. I can't get enough." She leans back resting her hands over her growing bump.

"How have you been?" I ask, feeling like we haven't had a chance to actually talk. I haven't had a moment alone since that afternoon Sy came to my apartment three weeks ago. It's not that we haven't spoken, but so much has happened. Between mine and Sy's issues, which we've had to work through, we've been living in our own world of work, club life and being together. It's meant my life's been pretty hectic.

"I've had the worst heartburn the last few weeks. I swear to God, I can't wait to have this child vacated," she complains, making me laugh.

"Kadence, you're not even halfway," I laugh at her being over it.

"Don't remind me. Seriously, why did I ever let Nix put a baby inside of me?"

"'Cause you love him and want to have little biker babies," I remind her while laughing at her annoyance.

"Babies? Hell no. Just one, thank you." Her face turns ashen at the thought of doing it all over again.

"So, what do you think you're having?" I ask like I ask every time I see her. I have no idea why she wants to keep the surprise. I hate surprises.

"I don't know. Some days I think it's a girl, and then some days I think it's a little Nix." She smiles as she rubs her belly.

"I think you're having a girl," I surmise, looking forward to seeing Nix cope with a little girl. *The man is screwed.*

"If it's a girl, I'll need to get out of town. Nix will never survive," she jokes. Nix Knight will not cope with a mini Kadence.

"So, what's happening with you and Sy?" She turns the questioning back to me.

"Nothing exciting." I smile at the thought of everything that is amazing with Sy.

"Yeah, sure looks like nothing," she argues, even though she is used to me not sharing gossip about our relationship.

"It's going really well. You know how private he is," I say as a way of explanation for us keeping to ourselves. The others don't know about Sy's past. It's something Sy has decided he will tell them in time, but for now, it's between us. "We're getting there," I admit truthfully. "I feel like we've moved on from the drama and finally getting past it all," I explain as our food is brought over to the table.

"I'm so happy for you, Holly, and you look happy," she notes after a few minutes of eating in silence.

"And you are glowing." I smile back, loving that this is our life at the moment.

"Do you think? I feel so tired and fat," she replies, once again making me laugh.

"Well, you don't look fat. How's your bump coming along?" I ask, concerned about her scarring and what the specialist has told her.

"We're just keeping an eye on it. If it gets too much in the next few weeks, we will look more into it." She doesn't look worried.

"Good, now you just need that husband of yours to lay off the bubble wrap." I laugh at Nix and some of the stupid shit he has done since they found out Kadence was pregnant.

"Oh, God. Don't remind me," she laughs. I know she says it's annoying, says she hates it, but I can see she secretly loves it.

"Excuse me, ladies." A tall, well-dressed man approaches our table.

"Hello." Kadence smiles up at him. His ash-blond, tailored haircut is disheveled and unkempt, like his hands have run continuously through it in frustration.

"You don't mind if I sit, do you?" he asks, pulling a chair from a nearby table. The question is void when he pulls up a seat, but I keep my opinion to myself. Something is off about this guy. I just don't know what.

"Umm, sure," Kadence says, looking at me, trying to gauge if I know him.

"I was just watching you from across the diner," he says, looking smug like he has a secret and is ready to share it.

"Yes?" I prompt him when he stops for some reason.

"And you are absolutely glowing." His lips thin, attempting a smile, but failing miserably. Insincerity oozes out of him.

"Oh, well, thank you," Kadence awkwardly replies.

"Yes, definitely glowing," he repeats, reaching out and stealing a fry from my plate. *Is this man for real?*

"Excuse me, we're enjoying a lunch date here, so if you don't mind…" I try to be diplomatic and not come across as a bitch, but this guy is seriously starting to creep me out.

"I wonder what your husband would do if you just went missing one night? Perhaps not make it home from Rushford Primary," he questions with a high dose of threat.

"I beg your pardon?" I exclaim and go to stand, but I don't get far when his large grip is thrown out, squeezing tight around my upper arm to get my attention.

"Sit down, bitch. I'm not done," he sneers, his grip tightening when I try to kick him under the table.

"Let go of her, asshole," I hear Kadence say, and for some reason, I can't help but get thrown back into a memory.

"Don't fucking touch her, asshole," I yell out to Zane.

"Don't worry, Holly. You can watch. Then you'll be next," Zane taunts and the bile I had been holding down since being thrown in the van, slowly starts to rise.

"Don't," Kadence pleads with him. "You can have me, but please don't touch her," she says, giving herself over to him.

"What the fuck is wrong with her?" I hear someone ask, but it comes from a distance and I feel myself slowing starting to fade into the black. The threat of this man is pushing me back to that day in the shed.

"You're fucking scaring her, asshole," Kadence says, her voice laced in concern. *Breathe, Holly*, my mind tells me, trying to take back control. I shake my thoughts clear, not letting myself get pulled back into the past. My eyes come to Kadence and her body relaxes when she realizes I'm not about to have a meltdown in the middle of the diner.

"I've got a message for your husband, Kadence," the man spits out her name, which concerns me even more. *Who is this man?* His hold on my arm tightens when I try to pull out of his grasp. A whimper leaves my lips, his fingers digging deeper. I should shout out, lash out, but I still feel like I'm in a daze; like I'm watching the moment happen but have no control over it.

"You tell him if he doesn't tell me where my wife is, he'll know what I'm feeling real soon." He releases me, pushing me back with such force my head hits the back of the high booth seat. And as quick as he was there, in our space, he's gone.

"Are you okay?" Kadence reaches for my throbbing arm, her soft touch soothing the dull ache.

"Yeah," I say, still not believing what just happened. "Are you okay?" She doesn't reply, already dialing out on her cell.

"Nix?" she says, looking up at me. "Some asshole just approached and threatened us." She stops to listen to what he says. "We're fine. Yeah, Happy Chef," she confirms before hanging up.

"Are you sure you're okay?" she asks again looking down at my arm.

"I promise. Just give me a moment," I tell her, trying to grasp the reality that I'm sitting in a diner and not back in that awful barn.

"Nix is on his way down," she informs, her hand moving to mine, offering me a tight squeeze.

"Is everything okay here?" The waitress comes up checking on our meal.

"Yes, can we have some cold water?" Kadence asks before dismissing her. "Wanna tell me what's happening?" she asks after a few more minutes of me trying so hard not to be dragged down into the dark part of my mind. I have fought day and night these last few months not to be held hostage in those memories, and with one touch, I've spiraled back into it. Enough is enough.

"I'm good," I finally say, coming out of the moment.

"Okay, good. 'Cause Sy was with Nix and even I know he's going to be pissed with what's happened." She points to the outline of the five-finger death grip the asshole just left me with.

Oh, shit.

"Tell me exactly what he said," Nix asks, sitting next to Kadence, his temper rising by the minute. Three of them walked in thirty seconds ago, exactly ten minutes after Kadence called out the SOS. Sy, Nix and Hunter.

"He said to tell him where his wife is or you'll know what he feels like," she relays the message back but I don't hear his response. I'm too lost in Sy's stare.

"Sy?" I ask, hoping he doesn't lose it. I'm trying to let him work out whatever is going through his mind, but I can see him struggling.

"I'm going to fucking kill him," he growls his first words since walking in to the diner.

"No one is killing anyone. You both need to calm down," Kadence says, trying to be the voice of reason in this cloud of anger.

"I might not kill him, but I'm gonna fucking try."

"Sy, I'm okay. I promise." I reach out to soothe him with my touch.

"You don't look fine." He comes in closer and searches my face. "Did you have a panic attack?" he asks, seeing what I hoped he wouldn't.

"Just a small one, but it's okay, Sy. I'm fine," I try to reassure him. I feel good I was able to bring myself out of it; that I didn't let it take me completely. In the past when I've had them, they drain me, but right now, I'm feeling good. Strong.

"You haven't had one in a couple of weeks." He shakes his head like he's still working it out. "I'm gonna fucking kill him," he says, working himself up again.

"Okay, well, this is getting us nowhere. Nix, talk some sense into him. This guy is the mayor's son, right? You can't kill him." Kadence tries to reason with Nix, giving up on Sy.

"I don't give a fuck if he is Gandhi, Kadence. This fucker has been messing with us for three weeks now. Shutting down the bar with licensing dramas and harassing the boys, we can deal with that, but this is going too far. Threatening something that is mine, my wife, my child, the fucker is going to be in a world of pain." Nix looks to me, then to Sy and I see it in their eyes: this is serious shit.

"Gah, seriously, this is pointless. Come on. Let's just go back to the clubhouse." Kadence looks over at me, trying to get me to convince Sy to calm down. I really don't think that's going to work.

"Good idea. Hunter, follow them back and stay there until we get there." Nix stands, moving out of the booth and letting Hunter sit.

"Nix, no," she tries to argue, but I already know it's not worth it. The boys have made up their minds.

"Baby, stay with Kadence until I get there," Sy tells me and then kisses me gently.

"Sy, please don't go," I try to get him to see reason.

"Holly, this is one of the times where you just have to turn the other way. He put his hands on you, marked you. Don't ask me not to do anything about it." He leans back in and quickly kisses me again, then pulls back.

"Sy," I call, but he's already moving out through the diner to go who knows where to do who knows what.

"Watch her, Hunter," Sy says, holding his gaze, and something passes between them before he pushes through the door out to his bike. Nix follows behind and we look through the glass shop front as they climb on their rides and roll out.

"What the hell just happened?" I ask Hunter, feeling like nothing but a world of trouble is heading our way.

"You fuck with Sy, this is what happens, Holly. Trust them to do what they need to do." He leans forward and eats from Kadence's plate.

"It was kinda hot," Kadence says, lost in the moment.

"Well, let's hope they don't end up in jail," I reply, concerned at what they are about to do.

"God, that would be even hotter," Kadence fans herself, making Hunter groan. "I swear the further along I get in this pregnancy, the hornier I become," she continues, not fazed Hunter is sitting with us. I laugh, but it's forced, because I can't get out of my head that what the boys have gone to do is a mistake. I just hope it doesn't blow back on us.

39
Sy

"You want to do this?" Nix asks me again as we take the elevator up to the fifteenth floor to the office of Barton Associates, Inc. After making a phone call to Jesse, he got us the details we needed to pay the golden child, Chad Morre, a not so friendly visit. The entire ride over to Redwick, I could feel my temper rising. Between the visit from the sheriff's department three weeks ago, the bar being questioned with its licensing last week and being fucked around numerous times with traffic violations, I know this fucker is messing with us.

"The fucker marked my woman, Nix. I'm gonna do this," I declare, not giving a shit who is around when we walk through those doors. When I walked into Happy Chef and saw the finger marks on Holly's arm, I saw red. It took everything in me not to blow my top in the diner. *Who the hell does this asshole think he is?* Knowing she also had a panic attack as a result of it pushed me over the edge. I couldn't even talk to her; couldn't calm myself down enough to comfort her the way she needed.

"Excuse me, do you have an appointment?" The young receptionist behind the desk stands as we walk out of the elevator and straight past her.

"Don't need one. Chad is expecting us."

"He's not taking any visitors at the moment," she calls out but it doesn't stop us.

"Open up, motherfucker," Nix shouts, pounding on the locked door. He doesn't give him a chance to reply before kicking the door in.

"What the fuck," Chad stands from behind his desk. "Kathy, call the police," he orders, looking past us to the woman who followed us in.

"Don't call the police, Kathy," I tell her calmly. "Go sit down there." I point to the sofa along the wall outside the office. "And don't move." She looks between the two of us, then must realize the right decision and obeys without a fuss.

"What the hell do you want, Knight?" he finally asks, knowing he has to deal with us without hiding behind his father or the law.

"Got your message," Nix informs him, walking in and taking a seat in front of his big fancy-ass table. The office is a decent size for someone with Chad's experience. Two deep burgundy leather sofas sit either side of a glass coffee table in the center of the room and the far wall is lined with a glass bookshelf. Chad stays behind his desk, his jaw ticking as he assesses his options. I stay at the door, nowhere near as calm as Nix. I swear if I move a muscle right now, I'll fucking kill him.

"Yes, well, I hope you take it seriously." The asshole swallows, trying to stay composed. *Not so tough now, fucker.*

"The only thing I'm taking seriously right now is you. You and your hands that were on my woman, motherfucker," I say, stepping farther into the room. I want to go to him, smash his face down on his expensive fucking desk but this needs to be played out carefully.

"Listen, your woman has a mouth on her. I can't be held responsible if she doesn't know when to shut it." His smug smile is all it takes to push me over the edge. *So much for staying calm.* I stalk toward him, watching as he retreats back at my approach. I'll teach him how to shut it.

"You touch me and I'll have you locked up." He backs himself into the wall and tries to throw his weight around, but his threats mean nothing to me.

"I don't think he gives a fuck, Chad," Nix says behind me. My hand comes out fast, grabbing him around the throat and pulling him closer.

"You want to put your hands on anyone, you put them on me, asshole," I sneer and smash his head back into the wall. He grabs his head in pain, which opens him up for an attack to the side. My fist connects with his ribs, doubling him over in pain. The hit doesn't make me feel better when my woman's arm is holding his mark, but it slows some of the anger speeding through my veins.

"This is your warning, Chad," Nix says when I pull him up by the neck again, pinning him to the wall. His fist comes out, connecting with my kidney, but not hard enough to have me doubling over. He starts screaming so I shut him up with my forehead down on the bridge of his nose. Blood gushes out everywhere, with what I assume is now a broken nose.

"Let me try again. This is your final warning, Chad. You need to forget about your wife, about the Knights Rebels and you need to forget we were even here. Because if you fuck with us again, fuck with our places of work, or if one hair on my wife or Sy's woman's head is touched, the next visit will end differently. Do you understand?" Nix asks, still sitting casually in the chair, arms crossed and looking like he's enjoying Chad's position.

Chad holds my gaze as his blood pours from his nose.

"I will find my wife. Fuck you both." It's official. The motherfucker is a dumb fuck.

My mind doesn't think. Dragging him forward by the scruff of his shirt, I spin and use all my power, throwing him through the glass bookshelf against the wall.

"Wrong answer, asshole," I spit out as he looks up at me, dazed. My boot comes to his throat and digs in a little bit harder. "Do you fucking understand?" I repeat Nix's question.

"Yes," he spurts out.

"I didn't fucking hear you."

"Yes!" he shouts louder and I release my boot.

"Good, glad we could come to an agreement," Nix says, standing.

"We'll see ourselves out," I state, leaving him in a puddle of his own blood. We walk out, past the poor woman on the sofa.

"Is he dead?" she asks nervously.

"No, he just had a fall. Just clean him up and he'll sort the rest out," I say, leaving her with the mess. I don't know if what we just did was wise, but the fucker touched my woman. I don't give a fuck who he is. He's going to deal with me.

"You okay, Sy?" Nix asks, watching me closely when we get downstairs and mount our rides to head back to the girls. He's never seen me lose my cool before. He missed the day I put a bullet through Zane's head. I might not have been able to stop Zane from hurting my girl, but I'll be damned if I let it happen again. No one is taking my sunshine.

"Never felt better," I reply.

"So, next order of business is we need to vote on patchin' in

Hunter. We keep putting that shit off and he's getting antsy," Nix says the next afternoon in our church meeting. After Nix and I paid Chad a visit, we came back to the girls. Holly was keeping her shit together, and by the time I got back, there was no sign of the earlier panic. That didn't stop me from throwing her over my shoulder and taking her to my room to make sure she was okay. She was more concerned for the club and what Chad would do. So far there has been no retaliation from it. I hope Chad took the warning and realized he was messing with the wrong people, but something tells me he isn't smart enough. I saw it in his eyes when he was looking up at me with my boot pressed into his throat. The man is desperate, and angry men like that are dangerous.

"We knew this was coming, been talking about it for months, but with everything going on we haven't had a chance to vote on it. Does anyone have any objections?" he asks the table.

"As long as he stops fucking feeding my woman alcohol to get her to flirt with him, I have no problem," I joke. *Fuck, again with the jokes.* The boys look at me like I've grown a second head. Whether because I just cracked a joke or that I don't have a problem with Hunter, I don't know. But as much as the fucker pisses me off and I give him shit about it, I like him and trust his commitment to the club. He's been a prospect for the last two years and he's family. The boy grew up in the club. His family still lives and breathes the brotherhood so he knows the score.

"Sy, you might wanna tell your woman to quit with her flirting, then maybe it won't get the runt into so much trouble," Jesse grins, trying to get a reaction out of me. *Fucker.*

"She's just fucking friendly," I defend her like it even matters. They all laugh and I can't help the grin that breaks free. *Assholes.*

"Let's just fuckin' vote. I've got a pregnant woman waiting for me out there. All in favor of Hunter takin' a patch?'" Nix calls out. Going around the table, we all vote unanimously and Nix calls it. Calling Hunter in, he gives him the speech he gave me, and probably the speech his father gave my father. The words hold true meaning to the club. The brotherhood is tight. They're your family who supports you through everything. Loyalty goes a long way and respect is earned.

"You ready to party?" Jesse stands to congratulate our newest brother on his new right to wear the sanctioned jacket patch.

"Hell, yeah," Hunter says, taking all our pats on the back.

"Then let's fucking party," Brooks hollers, draping his arm over Hunter's shoulders and walking him out. Fuck, I remember my patch-in party.

Booze, pussy and more pussy.

Shit is going to get messy.

40

Holly

"WHERE YOU BEEN, BABY? I'VE BEEN WAITING FOR YOU." Sy's bourbon breath hits my nose letting me know he's already started drinking. I just pulled up and found him waiting for me by the entrance. Sy called a couple of hours ago telling me Hunter was patched in so they were throwing a party. Rearranging my workday tomorrow so I could party late, I made my way home and decided to go all out and dress for the occasion. I don't go out as much as I used to, my time all wrapped up in Sy, and the closet full of shoes and dresses were calling to me. Deciding to go with a midnight black, one-shoulder dress that's tight and short in all the right places, I raced around to make sure I would make it here in time.

"I'm here," I say, letting him embrace me.

"You look fucking sexy," he half growls, half moans.

"So do you," I reply, loving the smell of oil and leather on his skin. "Is everyone here?" I ask when he pulls back.

"Yes, everyone and then some. So best behavior, Holly," he warns with a smile.

"Yes, sir," I tease, watching his gaze darken.

"Sir? I think I like it." He leans into my space kissing me deeply. I don't fight it, letting the kiss deepen to the point that we could skip the party and go straight to bed.

"Come on, before I fuck you right out of this dress," he groans, taking my hand and walking me inside.

The clubhouse is full. The music is blaring and the drinks are flowing. We walk past people who I've never met before; some smile, some check me out, but most just nod. Hunter sits at the bar with two whores on his knees, going between kissing one and groping the other.

"Are you sure you want me here?" I ask, looking around at all the women who are barely wearing any clothes.

"Why wouldn't I want you here, Holly?" He turns to face me and I look around the clubhouse feeling out of my element. The women and men are practically fucking each other on the table. *What the fuck? I've never seen it like this before.* "Don't even worry about anyone here. Just you and me, remember?" he asks, coming forward and kissing me.

"Holly!" Kadence moves forward, taking my hand and dragging me away from Sy.

"Hey! Bring my woman back!" he yells, but she doesn't listen. She just drags me out of the main room and back into the kitchen with her.

"What's wrong?" I ask when we're in the privacy of the empty kitchen.

"Just warning you, this is a patch-in party. Kelly told me they've been known to get crazy, like crazy-crazy." She raises her brows, looking concerned.

"Kadence, it's a biker club. Of course, it's going to get crazy." I laugh at her. But she doesn't laugh, just looks panicked.

"Yeah, and I've partied with them before, and they were a little crazy and I couldn't handle it."

"That's because you're not me. Relax. Don't worry about me okay? Come, let's get me a drink. I need one if I'm going to survive." I turn and head back out to the bar. I might feel out of my element but I'm going to have a good time.

"Holly, you're here," Hunter shouts when we walk up to the bar.

"Watch it, Hunter. You cross over the line tonight and I'll lay you out at your patch-in party," Sy warns from his spot on the stool. I roll my eyes.

"Don't roll your eyes at me." Sy grabs my arm and pulls me to his lap.

"Sy, the man has whore one and whore two on his lap. Leave him alone," I say, looking up at Tina and another whore I've yet to meet. "Make sure you wrap it tonight, Hunter. Who knows what you'll be catching." I curl my lip at the nastiness that is Tina. I mean seriously, this is who he chooses to celebrate getting a patch with?

"Um, excuse me." Tina uses her fake whiney voice. I'm sure she thinks it's cute, but it's just plain annoying. "I'm clean. Just ask Sy. He's eaten out plenty of times."

"What the actual fuck?" Sy growls from behind me, and stands. I lose my seat, but I don't let him defend me. I've got this bitch.

"What did you just say?" I step in, pushing her off Hunter's lap and watching her land on the floor in a heap. My heart does this double beat as her words start to penetrate. I know neither Sy nor I were virgins, but I don't need that shit thrown in my face.

"Please tell me your mouth did not eat her?" I turn, throwing my arm out to the bitch and looking at Sy.

"Fuck, no," he says, his face telling me he's disgusted by the thought.

"You fucked me, Sy. Don't lie," the whore says, standing from the floor, making me want to knock her down again.

"Bitch, I fucked you once. One night, ten months ago. Don't fucking spew your fucked-up bullshit to my old lady. I didn't fucking put you in my bed and I sure as fucking hell didn't taste your dirty cooche. You were a hole, a loose one at that, when I was too fucking lazy to pull it off. Don't confuse it for anything else." Sy sounds angrier by the minute as the clubhouse quietens.

"Well, there you have it. She has a loose hole. Who would have thought that?" I joke, breaking the silence.

"Fuck you, Holly," Tina says when the catcalls start up. I don't even care if that was a bitchy thing to say; the woman deserves it.

"Run along, skank," I say, ready for her to be gone. "If you ever speak about my man fucking you again, I will cut you. Do you understand me?" I get right up in her face. I don't know where this crazy fire is coming from, but knowing this two-bit whore had Sy's cock inside of her isn't helping.

"Whoa there, firecracker." Sy pulls me back against him. "You're sexy when you're angry, but you ain't cutting anyone."

"Aww cat fight, Sy. Let them go," Jesse calls out.

"Fuck off, Tina. Get out before I take you out," he demands, not letting me at her.

"I'm out anyway. I don't need this shit," she says, walking to the exit. "Call me when you get tired of this trash," she throws one last insult back at me.

"Are you kidding me?" Sy rumbles, ready to stalk after her but Nix's voice stops him.

"Don't fuckin' come back, Tina. You know the fuckin' rules. You don't disrespect one of our own or his old lady. Get gone," he dismisses her, going back to talking to Kadence, who is watching me carefully.

I know she warned me, but I wasn't expecting the bitch to be so blatant.

"Come here, Holly." Sy pulls me back on his lap, "I'm so fucking hard right now," he whispers over the excitement of the room.

"Yeah, well, sort it out yourself. I don't even want to think about your hard cock after the reminder of where it's been," I reply, pulling out of his hold. Sy doesn't grab for me, just lets me order a whiskey from some other skank behind the bar. I've never seen this one around before, and I can't help but wonder if Sy has fucked her too. Regretting the choice of only one shot, I order a double and hope it kicks in soon.

"You know she doesn't mean anything to me. She was just a fuck." Sy pulls me back onto his lap.

"Oh, I know. I just don't want it thrown in my face. Fucking bitch just caught me off guard." I tell him, forcing myself to calm down. I'm not one to get jealous. I know what women like Tina are around for; just the mental picture she gave me was enough.

"And for the record, not even a good fuck."

"Sy, I don't want to know about it," I protest, growing pissed off again.

"Your pussy is all I ever wanted." He kisses my neck. "Sweetest pussy I've ever tasted," he continues, not even caring who can hear.

"Shut up and drink." I shove his beer in his hands, ignoring the laughter aimed at us. I honestly don't even give a shit who he's fucked, but I don't want to hear about it either. I certainly don't want to look at the bitch knowing she's had what's mine.

"You owe me, Holly. Now I don't get a threesome," Hunter slurs, already off his face.

"Hunter, I doubt you could even get it up tonight. Plus, I'm sure I just saved your dick," I smirk and hear Sy growl behind me.

"What? I'm only warning the young rookie. If my man couldn't be saved, someone's should be." I smirk back at Sy.

"Excuse me?" This comes from whiney whore number two, her voice sounding offended. She shouldn't be. It's the truth.

"Careful," Sy warns, making me laugh, but I don't push it. The last thing we need tonight is more drama. Instead, I sit back on my man's lap and enjoy my first patch-in party. I've already sent a whore packing; I wonder what else will happen.

"Let's play a game," I say a few hours later. The party has quietened down, and the rest of us are sitting around drinking and laughing. Hunter passed out an hour ago; his whore laying drunk next to him, the party too much for the young rookie. The night has progressed uneventfully. No catfights, fistfights, no orgy—nothing.

"What sort of game?" Jesse smiles, his mind no doubt running off with him.

"Pool," I say, nodding over to the table. "But let's make it interesting," I tease, thinking about how far I can push this. Kadence looks at me, a small smile dancing on her features. She knows I play a mean game of pool, something my dad and brother taught me growing up.

"I'm game," Jesse stands, rubbing his hands together. He has no idea what he is getting himself into right now.

"Okay, how about men versus women. For every sunken ball, the opposite team takes a shot," I stand and walk over to the table, my mind ticking over about how we can play this and win. I watch Sy grin; he must be thinking that the men have this.

"I'm in," Kadence agrees.

"Me too," Kelly adds.

"It's hardly a fair game." Sy stands, coming to join us.

"What's the matter, Sy; you don't think we can win?"

"Fuck no. Jesse is the master of the pool table."

"Well, looks like you have nothing to worry about then," I say, keeping my face neutral. "Okay, let's do this."

"Do you want us to break?" Nix chimes in, smirking like they have this in the bag.

"Do you girls know how to break?" I turn to face them.

"No," they say in unison.

"It's not my strong point so you guys can," I say, watching Jesse snigger while he sets up the table. "Oh, is that how you do it?" I continue to play up to it. I might be laying it on thick, but if these men think they have us figured out, they have another thing coming.

Jesse hits first, breaking the balls and sinking the seven ball first.

"Drink up, ladies," he smirks as we pour our first shot. Kadence is on the water, Kelly and me on the tequila.

"Wow, beginner's luck," I claim before I throw back my shot.

"No, sweetheart. You're playing with a pro," he smoothly replies. It takes everything in me not to laugh out loud. "Get ready to throw back another one." He bounces his brows, taunting us. He follows through with his prediction, sinking another one before missing the next.

"Your turn. Need any tips?" he grins before handing me the cue.

"No, I think I understand it," I reply, setting up my shot. I let their taunts wash over me. I don't react, just carry on, seeming like I'm disappointed.

Sy takes the next shot, sinking another ball making us three down. After two more turns, I'm ready to take it to the next level.

"How about we mix things up." I look up at them. "For every shot I sink, a piece of clothing comes off?" I tempt them, knowing I have this shit covered.

"As long as turnabout is fair," Jesse counters and I agree, knowing I won't be the one removing my clothes.

"Game on."

"Wait, we didn't agree to this," Nix comes into the conversation after almost nodding off in the corner.

"Sit down, honey. We did," Kadence soothes him. Nix is so far gone he believes her.

"You better be wearing panties, Holly, 'cause that dress is coming off," Sy threatens but I don't let him shake me. I have my heels to take off first.

I line up my shot, sinking it into the top left corner.

"Oh, my God, did it go in?" I ask, acting it up.

"Fuck," Jesse curses, dropping his cut to the chair. Sy and Nix, with the help of Kadence, follow suit. Lining up my second shot, I sink it in the middle left pocket. The girls cheer and this time Sy curses.

"She knows how to play," Jesse accuses, pulling his shirt off.

"She's playing us," Sy adds, taking his off. *Fuck me, he's gorgeous.*

"Brooks, take yours off, too, baby," Kelly calls out to a sleeping Brooks on the sofa.

"Hot damn, Jesse. I didn't know you were walking around hiding all that," Kadence announces, fanning herself at his impressive abs.

"I'm not liking this game anymore," Sy remarks, crossing his arms over his chest. I swear the man is the sexiest male specimen I've ever seen. His full body tattoos are the biggest turn-on.

"What's the matter, baby? Scared we're going to beat you?" I stop checking him out and start with the taunts.

"You're not going to beat us," Jesse cuts me off. "If you stop drooling over your man here and take your shot, I'll be able to take the next one and beat your ass." His cocky attitude reappears. Jesse, it seems, doesn't like to lose.

"Okay, Jesse," I placate him, holding in my inner eye roll.

"Come on, Holly. You can do it!" Kadence claps to cheer me on.

Assessing my choices, I decide to sink my ball in the top right corner.

"Two ball, top right," I call out letting them know I mean business. I take the shot and watch Jesse's face fall went it rolls in the pocket.

"Ha! Drop 'em, boys." I can't help the smile as it spreads across my face.

"What's happening?" Nix stirs, causing us girls to laugh.

"Drop the pants, Sy," I repeat, watching him. Carefully and slowly, he releases his belt and unbuttons himself, but not looking happy about it.

"You should strip it all off, sexy," I tease. "Give us a taste of what you stopped us from having at Kadence's bachelorette party," I cheekily suggest, but playful Sy doesn't join us. No, he just drops his denims to the floor and steps out of them. *Jesus, the man is a sex god, standing there in his dark boxer briefs, fully inked body and looking every bit pissed.*

"Pay attention, Holly," Kadence demands, throwing Nix's pants at his face when he grabs for her, thinking he's getting some.

"We want them naked," Kelly cheers, clapping her hands while her husband snores on the sofa.

"Too late," Jesse says, dropping his pants, revealing no underwear, his naked ass on display for all.

"What the fuck, Jesse!" Sy stalks straight to me when he gets a look at Jesse's cock. "Game fucking over. You win," he says, picking me up and throwing me over his shoulder.

"But I'm not done," I laugh, watching Jesse smile down at his cock.

"Oh, my God, Jesse. Stop that," Kadence squeals, turning around. I can't get a proper look, but I can see his hands behind his head and him swinging his body around. I can't stop the laughter from erupting; it's easy to imagine what the man-slut is doing.

"This is not funny, Holly. I can't unsee that shit," he growls, throwing his bedroom door open and kicking it shut.

"Oh, relax," I laugh when he throws me down on his bed.

"You need to make me feel better. Make me forget you just got a look at Jesse's cock," he tells me as he loses his boxers and climbs into bed with me.

"Did you see how big he was?" I joke, gasping when Sy bites down on my thigh.

"Don't fucking tease me," he warns, making me laugh harder.

"I love you, do you know that?" I say, enjoying our night together in the clubhouse.

"I do, and I love you. Now strip, climb on and ride my face to make me feel better, like a good fucking girl," he demands in his unique Sy way. Not wasting any time, I slip out of my dress and do as I'm told.

Because I'm Sy's good girl.

41
Sy

"Katie?" I shout. It's the same dream I've had so many times, but instead of Keira walking away from me, it's Katie and she's taking Keira with her. "Katie, don't leave with her. Please don't leave me…"

"SY?" HOLLY'S VOICE BREAKS THROUGH THE FOG OF MY dream. *Dream or Nightmare?* "Are you okay?" She sits up, looking down at me, concern etched all over her face. *Fuck, another one.*

"I'm good." I climb out of bed, leaving her there and walk to the bathroom. Turning on the water, I splash some on my face and look up into the mirror.

"Sy?" Holly's voice asks from the doorway. She's wearing my worn club shirt and her panties. After I had taken her to bed earlier, I tried to get Jesse's nakedness out of my head by making her sit on my face. It worked until she reminded me again, causing me to spank her smart ass.

"I'm fine, Holly," I snap, not meaning to.

"You're not fine. Don't snap at me." Her arms cross over her chest. She looks cute standing there in my clothes, pissed off.

"Holly, just drop it." I hate that this is still coming up. I haven't had dreams of Katie before and now it's freaking me out.

"Do you still love her?"

"What the fuck?" I turn to face her.

"Do you?" she asks again, not giving up. I don't think she's pissed, but it doesn't stop me from trying to shut this down.

"Holly," I begin, not sure if this is the right time to talk to her. My head still feels hazy from my dream. *What the hell was that dream?*

"Because it's okay if you do," she continues, leaning against the doorframe. "I can't be angry at you for that."

"I once had love for the woman who didn't destroy me, the woman who gave me my daughter, but not now, not after everything." And that's the God's honest truth.

"You've called her name out every night for the last few weeks, since you found out about the baby," she replies, concerned.

"Fuck, Holly. Why didn't you tell me?"

"It only started off with a shout, but it's escalated the last few nights."

"Fuck." I rub my hands over my face. What the fuck is wrong with me? Why do I keep dreaming about her?

"Maybe you should talk about it," she whispers, now looking unsure about broaching the subject.

"Come here," I command. Holding out my hand, she moves forward and takes it.

"There's nothing to talk about. It's nothing but a dream," I tell her, knowing it's not true. I've pushed down my guilt for so long I'm concerned it's going to come down all around me.

"It's not nothing, Sy. Don't lie to me. Talk to me. When was the last time you saw her?" She looks up and her hand cups my cheek.

"What does that have to do with anything?"

"Sy…" She holds my stare.

"A little over two years," I admit. I still can't believe it's been over two years since I rode away leaving her behind.

"Do you know where she is? What she is doing?"

"No, never kept in contact with her," I tell her, sounding like an asshole.

"I think you should find her. Go to her and give yourself some peace, Sy." She looks dejected, and for a moment I think she feels that for me. *For Katie and me.*

"First of all, the last real conversation I had with Katie was when I walked away from her when she was finally getting her life on track. She was clean and she came to me needing to talk. I turned and walked away from her for the second time. She won't want to talk to me. I don't even know if I want to talk to her."

"Why did you walk away?" she asks the one question I've never let myself answer. Why did I walk out? Why did I give up in the end?

"I just don't know, Holly," I tell her, too afraid of the truth.

"I know you, Sy. You wouldn't have left her for no reason. You could have walked away sooner, but you fought. Something made you stop fighting," she surmises accurately.

"You're right. I walked away because she gave up." I step back from her. If I'm going to do this now, I can't have her touching me. "She gave up when I was willing to stay, even after Keira died. Even after I had forgiven her. In the beginning, I was angry at her betrayal, but I refused to discuss anything about her cheating or who Keira's biological father was. I had to put all my energy into Keira, caring for her, living and breathing for her. I didn't want to think about it."

I take a breath, needing a moment before I continue. Holly doesn't move. She waits for me to speak. "When Keira died, I didn't want to lose that connection with her. We were a family and I couldn't walk away from them. So I fought with everything I had to make it work. But it wasn't enough for Katie. I wasn't fighting the same demons she was. She had all this guilt, and as much as I had tried to get her to let go of it, she wouldn't give it up. In the end, I couldn't be strong for her when I was barely staying strong for me. All I wanted to do was mourn the loss of my child and deal with the breakdown of my marriage. I fucking tried so hard to pull her back, tried to get her out of it, but I failed." The guilt that eats at me comes back, whispering in my ear that I didn't try hard enough.

"Maybe she didn't need saving, Sy, but needed to heal on her own," Holly interrupts, taking a step toward me. "We all heal and grieve differently; each journey is unique, Sy, and sometimes along the way, we hurt the ones we love—the ones who love us. If you left when you could no longer help her then it doesn't mean you failed. It means you just couldn't hold on anymore. You had to save yourself, too, Sy. You had to heal, too." Her hand reaches out and takes mine, leading me back to my room.

I don't fight it; the comfort of her touch makes it too hard to pull away. She walks me to the bed without a word and sits down on the edge, pulling me to sit down next to her.

She's right. I had to heal, too.

"Sy, someone once told me giving up is self-defeat, while letting go is self-care. There was nothing more you could have done. You did everything you could to help Katie. You can't tell her how to grieve, or how to live. It isn't your decision. She had to decide what her life should look like, and so did you."

"Fuck, I love you, Holly." I pull her to me and fall back, taking her with me. The words she just gave me are the most honest words anyone has spoken to me. "I don't deserve you."

I kiss her, because if I don't, my emotions will overcome me.

"Don't say that, ever." Her hand takes my jaw, making me look at her.

"No, Holly. You are a promise I never thought I would ever get again, a promise that there is goodness and light." I watch as slow tears fall from her eyes. "Don't cry, baby." I turn and cover her body, placing my arms on either side of her head to take my weight.

"Go see her. Let it all go," she encourages, looking up at me with hope and faith. Something I haven't seen in such a long time staring back at me.

"Let me think about it," I tell her, not ready to commit to anything. My heart and my head still arguing with each other in fear of what I may find, but the desperate need to feel free is strong.

"I love you," she whispers, letting it go, giving me her light. If I hadn't already known what unconditional love looked like, I'd be staring at it for the first time.

"I love you, baby."

Shit, can I do this? I look up at the ivory, two-story, brick home.

Two weeks ago when I held Holly in my arms that night and admitted I didn't need to feel guilty for walking away, I made a vow to myself that I would see this out, one way or another. I knew I had to come here, had to talk to Katie, but as I stand at the front of my ex-wife's house, I want to take it all back. It's been a battle, and one I don't know what the outcome will be, but I know Holly is right. I had to save myself, and I can't be held accountable for that. It's just taken me two weeks to see it. When I finally made peace, I made a call to Katie's parents. To say they were shocked to hear from me would be an understatement. I don't think they were ever expecting to hear from me again, and I didn't expect to get through on their old number. After catching up with them for a few minutes, I asked for her address and hung up. I didn't ask how she was or what she was doing. I didn't want to be swayed. I needed to do this regardless of what I would find.

"Sylas?" Katie asks, opening the door before I can knock.

"Hey," I greet her awkwardly, not expecting her to open the door so suddenly. She looks good, really good. Her long, blonde hair now rests on her shoulders, totally throwing me off for a minute.

"Wow, I'm shocked you're here," she says, shaking her head, looking as affected as I feel. "Did you want to come in?" she smiles and I'm thrown head first into the deep end of our past.

"Momma?" A small girl comes running up and attaches herself to her leg. And it's like a sucker punch. Her small face looks up and all time stops. *Keira?* My body recoils. No, it's not Keira. *Fuck.*

"I shouldn't have come." I turn, leaving her standing in the open doorway. I need to get out of here. I don't know what I was expecting when I came here, but seeing Katie with a daughter was not one of them.

"Sylas, wait," she calls after me. "Wait," she pleads again, so I stop. I stop and wait to see if the shock of seeing that little girl leaves me. It doesn't.

"I really shouldn't have come," I say again.

"Well, why did you?" she asks.

"I needed to see how you were doing. To let go maybe?" I admit.

"You haven't let go?" she asks, shocked.

"I thought I had, but I think this was my final step."

She nods, watching me carefully. "Please come in. We can talk," she offers gently.

"I don't know if I can. She…" I point back to the house, back to her daughter.

"She looks like her, doesn't she?"

"Jesus, I thought I was dreaming it." I let out a shaky breath.

"Try living with it." She smiles but it's not a sad smile. "Some days it's hard. Other days it's amazing."

I nod, not understanding it, but I don't tell her that. "So, you're married?" I ask, spying the wedding band on her left ring finger.

"Yeah, last year," she smiles. "He's inside. I know he'd like to meet you."

"He knows about me?" I think I almost choke.

"Of course. He knows everything, Sy," she replies. "Please come in. I'll ask Derrick to take Sienna to the park." She waits for me to confirm, but I can't.

"Maybe we could go to Keira?" I suggest, not feeling so sure about meeting Katie's family, sitting in her home.

"Sure, let me get my keys and I'll meet you there?"

"Yep," I say, turning to get on my bike. I think I can handle this talk if I'm away from here, away from the family she's moved on with.

"Sylas?"

"Yeah?" I turn back when she calls my name.

"Thank you for coming."

"So, what have you been doing with yourself?" Katie asks fifteen minutes later as we sit at our daughter's grave.

"Still tattooing. I have my own shop back in Rushford."

"So, you did end up going back home?" she smiles, no doubt remembering my vow that I would never go back.

"Yeah, when Pops got sick, I went back and didn't leave."

"I'm sorry I wasn't there for you."

"It's okay," I say, not wanting to talk about it.

"So why are we here, Sy?" She asks the million-dollar question.

"I don't know, just trying to deal with a few things that have come up." I fill her in, without telling her about Holly or the baby.

"I get it. It's been a tough road to recovery, at least for me anyway." She sits back, looking up at the sky. This woman sitting across from me is not the woman I left two years ago and if I'm being honest, not even the same woman I fell in love with. There's something about her that wasn't there before. I just don't know what.

"I'm sorry, Katie, but I have to say I wasn't expecting this, all of this," I admit, scanning her up and down, blown away with how well she's doing.

"You have nothing to apologize for, Sy. I understand. Things were bad. Really bad, and I fucked up. I know that. I pushed everyone away in my suffering and for that I'm eternally sorry. What I did to you, to us…" She shakes her head. "I remember the day you rode off, leaving me standing over there." She points to where my bike now sits. "I knew I lost you forever that day; even when I was desperately trying to push you away. I don't know why you walking away from me made me realize how fucked-up I was, but it did. You should have hated me, but you still loved me even when I deserved your anger."

"I wanted to hate you. All those years, fuck, it would have been easier, but I couldn't because you gave me Kiera," I admit.

"Then I took her away," she whispers, looking up at me carefully.

"I never needed a piece of paper to tell me she was mine, Katie."

"Are you ready to know who he is?" she asks, thinking it's the reason why I'm here.

"No, I don't want to know," I assure her, hoping I never find out. "Keira will always be mine, even if she wasn't biologically mine."

"But we never talked about it. Do you know how hard that was? To have this between us? You never asked. You never showed anger. You just acted like nothing had happened." She's right. I never wanted to talk about it. At the end of the day, we had bigger things to work through. My energy and focus was always Keira.

"I didn't want to believe it, Katie. I didn't want Keira to see it, and I didn't want it to determine my love for her. It didn't change anything for me. We raised her and that's all that mattered."

"And that is why you're a good man, Sy," she says quietly.

"Not good enough to stay, to see you overcome everything. I hate myself for that. Hate that I left you when you were at your lowest," I finally admit the guilt that's had its hold on me the last couple of years.

"I'm glad you did, Sy. If you didn't, I don't know where I would be, or if I even would be?" She runs her hand along the grass I've laid on so many times in the last five years. "Someone had to walk away, and I'm glad it was you. I was self-destructing and no one was going to save me, except me. I had given up, and that's the thing about giving up, you don't realize until it's too late. It took you leaving for me to see it. Any guilt you feel for that, let it go, because I did. I let go a long time ago and you should, too." I don't reply. I allow the truth of her words to speak for themselves. We sit in the entirety of the past, in the words that have hurt us and broken us, knowing we've come full circle.

"Do you think she's happy?" I finally ask, looking up at the clear blue sky, a stark difference to the inky darkness I look up at when I normally visit.

"I know she is." She answers with such conviction, I can't argue. I have to believe it.

"I hope you found what you came for, Sylas. I'll never let go of our family, and I know you won't, but you need to move on, allow yourself to let go." She stands and smiles down at me.

"I'm trying," I answer, feeling lighter than I have in a long time. The guilt weighing so heavily on my heart slowly starts to deplete.

"Take care and be happy, Sy." She breaks the moment of silence and walks away.

"I am," I softly reply, knowing that now, I can let it all go.

42

Holly

"Yes, Sy," I moan as my body spirals out of control.

"That's it, baby. Take it. It's all yours. Milk my cock with that sweet cunt of yours," he rumbles, driving me into complete ecstasy just like every other time he talks filthy to me. I let the feelings of bliss and excitement flow through me when his calloused fingers find my sweet spot.

"I wanna hear you, Holly." His husky demand isn't lost on me. I know what he wants, what he always wants, and if I *want* what I know he can deliver, then I have to give it to him.

"Fuck me, Sy," I shout as I hit the first peak at his command.

"Tell me how much you want my cum," he rumbles as his strokes become more uncontrollable the longer this goes on.

"I want it, Sy," I moan, giving him what he needs, what I need.

"Beg," he urges, leaning down and hovering over my mouth. He knows he's got me right where he wants; on the edge of supreme ecstasy and I can't go back. I'm too close. He knows it and I know it. I need him to finish. I need him to take me home.

"Fucking give it to me, Holly," he shouts, sending me into a tailspin.

"I need it. Yes, give it to me," I scream, surrendering to him as his teeth sink into my bottom lip setting off a spectacular kaleidoscope of colors and emotions.

"Fuck!" he drags out as his orgasm takes over and he loses all of himself inside of me.

"Oh. My. God," I breathe, coming down from yet another uninhibited and explosive orgasm.

"What did I tell you about God?" Sy asks, resting his sweaty forehead to mine.

"Oh. My. Sy," I correct, still feeling his cock pulse in the aftermath of his release.

"Don't forget it," he warns with a glint in his eye.

"Like you forgot we were trying to be safe?" I cock my brow at him. I might have just begged for it, but that was under duress. Sy smirks as he watches me like a cat that ate the canary. He knows what he's doing, and I've given up arguing with him about it. It may be stupid, but Sy has it set in his mind that we are making a baby whether I want to or not. Luckily, the idea doesn't freak me out as much as I thought it would. I know a part of me wants to reach out and try to fill the void left over losing our child, but I know deep down even if it was to be filled entirely with a new baby, it still would remain as something else. Something I wouldn't want to lose because I wouldn't ever want to relinquish the knowledge that we had suffered a loss which was part of us. I wouldn't want to replace one child for another, but the thought of carrying again makes me feel like it could help stitch the hole in my heart that feels so empty.

"Fuck, I love you," he says, dropping his weight on me. I love it when he gets like this; when even just holding himself up after making love is too much for him.

"I love you, too," I wheeze out. "Now get off me, you heavy ass. I can't breathe," I complain, breaking our moment.

"It's okay, baby. You stop breathing, I'll breathe life right back into you." He kisses me again, only this time taking a real breath out of me.

"I love you, Sy. I love you more than anything." I hold his face and mean every single ounce of it. In the last few weeks, something has changed in him. Ever since he went back to visit Katie, there has been a peace to him. The anger and fear he kept hidden seems to have lifted. He still hasn't opened up to the club about his past, but I respect his decision, and when the time is right, he will tell them.

"You want a shower, or you want me to clean you up?" he asks slowly, letting himself fall from me.

"Shower." If we don't get up, we'll end up staying in bed all day, and I need to get ready for Jesse's party soon.

"Okay," he says, moving over me and kissing me until my phone ringing interrupts him. "Fuck." He reaches over to answer it.

"Just leave it," I say, wanting to get in the shower, but it's too late. He's already answering it.

"What?" he shouts out in the way of answering. I hold back my smile knowing Sy is hard and almost always harsh, yet when we are alone, he's anything but. "Now?" he barks, pulling away from me and sitting back. "She's busy right now," he growls, rubbing his face in frustration.

"What's going on?" I ask, trying to get my phone off him.

"I'll let her know," he says before hanging up.

"You can't just answer my phone, Sy. Who was it?"

"Kadence," he growls, resting his weight back on me.

"Well, what did she want?" I ask, waiting for a response when he starts kissing me instead of telling me.

"She said the cake is ready and needs to be picked up."

"Ahh, shit," I curse, completely forgetting about it.

"I'll go and pick it up for you," he offers, knowing I have heaps to do today. It's Jesse's surprise party and I'm the sucker who agreed to help organize it.

"No shower then?" I ask disappointed.

"We'll have one later, when I make you dirty again," he promises, climbing off me to run my errand.

"Can't you do that now? Quickly?" I ask innocently, wishing that the damn party hadn't taken up all my time the last few weeks. It was Kadence's idea to throw the damn party in the first place. As soon as she heard it was Jesse's birthday, she wanted to do something for him, but in the last week she hasn't felt well, so I was stuck with the hard work.

"Baby, I just fucked you and made you dirty, and you wanna go again?" he asks, moving back to the bed.

"Mmmm," I moan when his hand trails between my legs. "Please?" I whimper, feeling his finger drag through our combined cum that's slowly starting to leak out.

"My cum is still dripping out of you and you want to go again. You have a greedy pussy, Holly," he accuses, sinking his finger back into me.

"Oh, my God. Don't say that. You make me sound like a dirty whore when I just want you," I cry, bringing the covers over my head.

"Don't act cute. You'll make it harder for me to leave." He crawls over me, pulls the covers off and kisses me. I don't let the kiss drag me in, only letting it give me just enough to keep me sated until I see him again.

"Go," I push him away when I feel my composure slip. He huffs when he climbs back out of bed and walks away. "Miss me."

I grin as he opens the door.

"Already do," he calls back. And if the smile on my face is anything to go by, I know all is right in our world.

"Come on, Holly," Sy pleads, trying to pull me back to bed.

"Sy, I'm going to be late." I push him back, trying to get away from him.

"I don't know why we can't just have a fucking party at the clubhouse," Sy complains, sitting up and watching me. After going to get the cake for me and dropping it off at Liquid for the party, he came back and decided he would complain about everything that's happening tonight.

"'Cause it seems fitting that we have it at Jesse's favorite place. Besides, Jesse's family is coming and they thought it would be better if we had it at Liquid."

"Fuck, are they all going to be there?" he questions, making me stop and look up.

"I think so, why?" I panic when I see the look on his face.

"I'm just surprised," he says, looking floored. I don't tell him that I spoke to Jesse's dad, who was adamant he wouldn't come if the party were at the clubhouse. I didn't want to argue with him, or any of his family, who all voiced the same demands.

"Don't be. It's Jesse we're talking about here. Everyone loves him. It's going to be great, but I have to go," I advise him, almost tripping over one of his boots. "Sy," I whine, recovering and kicking it out of my way.

"What?"

"Your shit is on the floor," I groan, pointing down to his riding boots and the clothes scattered all over the floor.

"Yeah, so?" he shrugs.

"Well, it's annoying and I keep tripping over it," I simplify what I think is pretty self-explanatory. I don't have time for this right now, but I need to get this out.

"Well, give me somewhere to put my shit and I'll put them away," he replies, sitting up.

"You want like…a drawer?"

"Yeah, or half your closet. Either way is good."

"You mean move in?"

"Sure, thanks for asking," he jokes, making me laugh.

"Is that what you want, Sunshine?" I walk over to the bed. We haven't discussed this subject, but since that night when he held me as we cried over the baby we lost, he hasn't left my side. Either we sleep here or we're at the clubhouse, but we've never talked about moving all our stuff into one place.

"Seriously, woman. You can be so clueless." He leans forward and pulls me to him. "Of course I want us to live together," he declares like I'm simple.

"What, here?" I eye him, unsure I want to live here anymore.

"Here, or we can get a place of our own. Doesn't bother me. Either way, I want to wake up with you every day, in *our* bed."

"We could get a new place," I surmise, thinking of where we could move to.

"Whatever you want. On one condition," he bargains, then nips at my neck.

"What?" I ask, pushing him away.

"You can't bitch me out for my clothes on the floor." He grabs me and pins me to the bed.

"You're going to mess my hair up," I complain as he climbs over me.

"Tell me we are moving in together and you won't ever bitch me out for my clothes and shit bein' around the place, and then you can go," he challenges, being a smartass.

"What if we stay together for fifty years? That's a lot of years not to bitch you out."

"What do you mean if?" he questions. "There are no ifs baby, only whens." He kisses me hard, letting me know just how serious he is.

"I don't know if I agree with those terms." I hold my ground and look at the clock before freaking out. "I need to go, now," I repeat once again, rolling to the left to get out of Sy's clutches. I was meant to be meeting Kadence in five minutes, and I have a fifteen minute drive. *Shit*.

"You're not going anywhere until you tell me you want me to move in with you." He stops me by my wrists and pulls me back. *Typical Sy; no asking, just telling.*

"Yes, baby. I want you to move in with me." I look up and smile at him sweetly.

"Good answer," he smirks, kissing me again.

"Now I feel like we unquestionably just became exclusive," I tease, expecting a reaction.

"What the fuck, Holly?" he grunts, giving me what I want.

"Ha ha ha. You're too easy, Sunshine. So gullible," I laugh, bringing my arms around him.

"But I have to go. I love you." I push him back so I can move out from under him. "And I'll see you later." I turn and kiss him one last time before heading out.

"You better be ready for me. 'Cause I want you in our bed tonight." I don't miss the *our* or his tone. I can't even freak out because this just seems *right*.

Everything with Sy has always felt right.

43

Sy

"**Trust Jesse to know he has a surprise party waiting** up here, then not show up," Kadence exclaims over the loud and annoying music of Liquid. I still don't know why we had to come here. Fuck Jesse's family. If they don't want to come to the clubhouse, then too fucking bad.

"He knows this is going on?" I ask, watching the stairs for Holly to make her entrance.

"Didn't you know?" she laughs, leaning back and rubbing her small belly. She's only just showing, but each week it slowly grows bigger. It makes it hard for Holly and me watching it. I know Holly doesn't let it get her down, and I know I'm trying to get her pregnant again, but sometimes I see Holly looking at Kadence's belly and the look in her eyes just breaks me.

"Well, if he knows, what the hell is Holly doing with him?" I ask, annoyed he's pulling this shit. Holly was dragged into organizing this party two weeks ago, and it's bullshit. I want her all to myself, but everyone keeps stealing her from me.

"It's not his fault. His family said something to him, but we shouldn't ruin the surprise because of it." She shrugs like it's no big deal. *Fuck, Jesse's family are a pain in the ass.*

"She's down there when she doesn't have to be?" I ask, growing uneasy.

"Calm down, Sy. She's with Jesse, which means she will text before they come up," she says when she sees me watching the stairs.

"Knowing Jesse, he found a quick lay and pissed off on her." I turn back to the table, trying not to worry. Since Chad and his father had the clubhouse searched and paid the girls a visit, we've all been laying low. I haven't let Holly out of my sight. I know I'm probably overreacting, but between the asshole who took her and Chad who hurt her, I'm not taking any chances.

"Looks like your woman is fine down there." Beau points down to the bottom dance floor where Holly and Jesse are dancing away, together. *Are you fucking kidding me?*

I try to control my anger at seeing her sexy-as-fuck body sway to the music while a bunch of men look on. She always was a tease, something that attracted me to her in the first place. And I know she's only doing it to get a reaction, but every time I see it, it not only makes me see red, but feel it.

"HOLLY!" I shout over the music, but she doesn't hear. "HOLLY!" I shout again, the anger in me growing each moment she looks at the motherfucker who should be up here, but is instead down there dancing with my woman. I give up the shouting. Even if she did hear me, the fucking minx probably wouldn't stop.

"Sy, you can't go down there." Kadence tries to stop me but I don't listen. Storming down the wooden staircase two stairs at a time, I whistle and finally get her attention. She falters for a moment, reading my anger and assessing what she's going to do with it.

"Come here, now," I mouth over the music. She doesn't respond at first, her eyes moving up to the balcony of the VIP party, and then finding mine again. *Yes, sweetheart. You're meant to be up there with me.* Slowly, a small smile plays on her lips, her grin growing the moment she sees just how pissed off I am.

"Now," I mouth again, but this time my command doesn't stop her. Lifting her hands she goes back to dancing next to a fucking clueless Jesse. Done with this game, I finish taking the stairs and push my way through the crowd.

She doesn't see me; her back is to me as she continues to move her ass to the music, but I know she knows I'm there. Without skipping a beat, I take her hand and spin her around. I don't watch for her reaction, just bend at the waist and pull her over my shoulder,

"Sy! What the hell are you doing?" she shrieks, hitting my back while I smack her tight ass. I keep my hand there making sure her dress doesn't come up to flash any fucker her panties.

"Put me down, motherfucker," she curses, trying to get out of my hold.

"Have I told you that your dirty mouth turns me on?" I taunt, ushering her through the crowd and ignoring all the looks.

"Sunshine, you're going to ruin Jesse's surprise." She tries to wiggle out of my grasp, but I hold her tighter.

"He knows we're up there, and if you don't stop hitting me, I'm gonna slip my hand up this dress and slide my finger into your panties and every fucker in this club will see me finger fuck you. Do you want that?" I ask her. My cock wakes from its slumber at hearing my threat.

"You wouldn't dare," she seethes.

"Try me, baby," I sneer, taking the steps two at a time.

"You're embarrassing me, Sy," she finally says when we get to the top of the stairs. Sliding her down my body, I bring her to a standing position and hold her in front of me.

"No, Holly. You're embarrassing me," I explain to her. "You want me to mark you to let every fucker in this club know you are mine?" I ask, feeling my temper rise.

"You know me, Sy. I like to dance. It doesn't mean anything." She tries to pass it off as nothing.

"I don't give a fuck what you think is nothing. You fuckin' dance like that again, we are gonna have problems."

"There is nothing wrong with my dancing," she fights back, but I know she fucking knows that's a lie.

"You want me to tell you what the fuck is wrong with your moves?" I ask, watching her.

"Oh, please. Enlighten me," she starts throwing her attitude around. Taking her hand, I yank her to me, making her feel the hardness of my cock.

"Every fucker down there watching that little fucking show is hiding one of these," I say, grabbing my cock for added effect. "The only time you dance like that is for me, in our bedroom, naked," I threaten, waiting for her to mentally picture it.

"Whatever, Sy, you're not the dancing police." She pulls her hand back. Fuck me, she is a fucking pain in my ass.

"No, but I'm your fucking man and if I tell you to quit dancing or I'll spank you, you should listen." She holds my gaze, anger dancing behind her beautiful blue eyes, but I can't let her see me cave. I can't let her know that I fucking love it when she argues, when she pushes me to the point of this reaction.

"Can I go back and get Jesse now?" she queries, ignoring my command, and I fucking love it.

"Not until you tell me you love me." I pull her close to me.

"I don't love you, you big bully," she lies, but I can see the truth behind her lies.

"You want to try that answer again?" I pinch her tight ass, nudging her further into me.

"Fine. I love you, but hate your bossy, sexy ass."

"You love my ass," I tell her, knowing that for a fact.

"I do not love your ass. It's too tight," she says, turning and leaving me standing there with an annoyed cock.

"Not as tight as yours, baby," I call back and watch as a mortified expression fills her features. "If you don't be careful, your ass will be mine," I call out, watching her race down the stairs to retrieve Jesse.

"You're so pussy whipped," Beau accuses behind me.

"Fuck off. I am not." I sit down, trying to hide my semi-hard cock.

"I don't know. I think he might be worse than Nix," Brooks chimes in, sliding into the booth across from me. I don't reply. Ignoring them is the best way to go in these situations.

"Everyone, he's coming," Kadence announces, standing from the chair and getting down low. I know this is meant to be a surprise party, but if the fucker already knows we're all here then I'm not fucking hiding. "Sy, get down," Kadence orders, but I don't fucking listen. The asshole owes me an afternoon with my girl, and I plan to make him pay up.

After waiting another few minutes for him to make it upstairs, he finally makes his grand entrance, acting shocked when they all yell surprise. *Fucker played it good, too.* His family approach him first, so I hang back waiting for them to have their time together.

"You still pissy?" Holly asks, coming straight to me and sitting on my lap.

"I don't know. You gonna suck my cock to apologize for making it angry?" I ask, hoping she says yes.

"You wish." She wiggles her ass into my cock.

"Quit it," I tell her, trying to control the urge to leave and fuck her senseless.

"You're no fun," she pouts, acting all fucking cute again.

"When we get home I'm gonna make you pay for that," I warn. She doesn't say anything, just slowly moves her ass against my hardness. I let her, relishing the feeling of it.

"I'm going to get a drink," she says when Beau and Brooks start talking about some new bike. "Do you want anything?" She turns to face me.

"Bourbon, baby," I order and then watch her walk her ass down the stairs.

"You know there's a bar up here?" Brooks laughs, watching her descend down the stairs.

"She's probably going to dance." I shake my head, letting her be. Who am I to stop her from fucking dancing?

"Boys." Jackson walks up, sliding into the seat across from me.

"Jackson." I nod.

"You guys been staying out of trouble?" he asks, looking at us. If he's talking about any of the recoveries or pickups, we haven't had any since Mackenzie. The club decided that until we know for sure Chad has given up, then we keep our hands clean, let it all blow over.

"You heard any more from the Morres?" I ask, wanting to know if we've got the all clear.

"I haven't personally. He stopped coming in riding my ass about finding Mackenzie. I've seen him around, heard some talk. Looks like someone had a go at him a few weeks back, messed him up." He continues to watch me carefully.

"Really? Looks like Mr. Morre pissed off the wrong person then," Beau says, not giving a fuck if anyone knows it was us who messed him up.

"Either way he seems to have backed off. Though last I heard he lost his job, and his father is losing his pull. Chad has gone off the rails. Seems like losing his wife pushed him over the edge," he adds when Holly comes back with our drinks.

"Well, maybe he should have treated her right," I say, letting Holly sit on my lap.

"Now that is something I agree with." Jackson raises his glass. "Great party, Holly. Sorry about my parents." He changes the Chad subject. Thank fuck, too. Just thinking about him gets me worked up.

"Thanks," she smiles, looking over at Jesse and his dad in a heated conversation by the far wall.

"What's that about?" I nod over at them. I know Jesse has a close family, but something isn't right there.

"Long fucking story." Jackson shakes his head at his father and younger brother. Jesse's eyes narrow at something his father says before he replies and stalks off.

"Maybe I should go and intervene." Holly goes to stand but I hold her in my lap.

"Leave it," I warn, not wanting my woman going off to console anyone.

"No, I'll go. They always get like this." Jackson stands and follows Jesse to the bar.

"I wonder what their problem is." Holly turns to look at me. "They refused to come to the party if it was at the clubhouse and now they're on his back."

"That's why we're not having it there?" I ask, finally understanding why this party is here.

"Yeah, they were adamant," she shrugs.

"I think his dad has issues with Jesse's way of life," Brooks observes, putting two and two together.

"Well, don't we all? I think the only one who doesn't have an issue with Jesse's way of life is his cock," Holly claims, silencing everyone for a moment before the boys erupt into laughter.

"Fuck, you're funny, Holly," Beau says, shaking his head.

"That was a good one, wasn't it?" She smiles at the table, but it lights up the whole room. I fucking love her like this, happy and free.

"I love you," I whisper so the boys don't hear me, but I don't give a fuck if they do anyway. They already give me shit like I used to give to Nix.

"I love you, too." She leans in, kissing me softly.

"Get a room," Beau groans from next to me. I ignore him, groaning into her mouth louder just to piss him off.

"Want to go dance?" Kadence comes up with Kelly, looking like they're up to no good.

"Hell, yeah." She stands, turning back to give me a wink. I give her my warning look but she just smirks, sashaying her ass down the stairs.

"You need to put a ring on that one," Brooks chuckles, watching the girls walk down the stairs.

"I'm going to," I admit, not checking for his or Beau's reaction. Wouldn't give a fuck what they thought anyway; this woman is it for me. The sooner she wears my ring, the better.

"Fucking hell, him too?" Beau grumbles, giving his opinion anyway.

"Fuck yeah," Brooks laughs, no doubt loving he called it all those months ago.

"Well, I'm not wearing a fucking suit again," Beau continues to grumble.

"Shut the fuck up, Beau. I'm not fucking whipped like Nix," I tell him, knowing there is no way I'm fucking getting married wearing one either.

"Yeah, we'll see, asshole," he argues, not believing me.

"She has to say yes first," Brooks jokes but I'm not worried. The woman is so far gone, she wouldn't be able to say no to me. Even if she did, I wouldn't accept it. She's mine and that's the end of it.

"She's crazy and doesn't stop. I'm telling you," Kelly says, sitting in the booth next to Brooks. She came back after dancing with Holly for thirty minutes, leaving her when Holly said she wasn't near ready to leave the dance floor. I'd go down and find her, but I know she'll just get me worked up, and I'll end up dragging her out of here before the cake is even served.

"You learn just to sit and watch," Kadence says, sitting on Nix's lap. I can't help the smile that forms on my face. Four months ago this Holly was lost; she walked into the Knights Rebels clubhouse, and I knew I had to help her. Now she's back to her crazy-ass self, and I couldn't be happier. Standing, I decide I need to find her and see this crazy woman of mine.

"Where is my wife?" I hear from a familiar voice over the lull of the crowd.

"Oh, fuck." Nix stands quickly, moving Kadence behind him. I turn and follow his gaze and my stomach drops. *Chad fucking Morre.* You've got to be fucking kidding me. "Answer me, you thugs," he sneers, walking forward. His hair is disheveled, and the dirty clothes hanging off him look like they haven't had a decent clean in the last week, but most importantly and terrifying, he has Holly in his grasp. The man is bordering on a mental breakdown and there he stands, holding my woman, his forearm against her throat. I'm going to fucking kill him.

"I know one of you assholes took her. I fucking know it. Just tell me where she is and no one gets hurt." He snatches an empty beer bottle and smashes it down on the railing, breaking the end of it open, glass shards now covering the surrounding area. Holly screams as the jagged glass nears her throat. I step forward, but Beau and Brooks hold me back.

"Let me fucking go." I try to pull out of their clutches while I search for Jackson. *Where the fuck is that asshole?*

"Just cool it. Think clearly here," Brooks warns, nodding over to where Jesse's closing in.

"You need to calm down," Nix says, stepping forward, but the crazy fucker slashes out in front of him. "Kadence, get to the back of the room now," he warns, keeping his wife out of harm's way.

"I'm not fucking kidding," Chad threatens, stepping forward and taking a swipe at Nix again. I step up, ready to bring him down, right before I see the tip of the glass pierce Holly's perfect skin.

"Ahh!" she screams out, her hands going to the fucker's forearm as blood weeps from the cut.

"Hey, fucker. You better put the glass down before I fucking take you down," I growl, watching Holly's expression move into panic mode. Catching Jesse's attention, we both shift carefully, trying to get Holly out of his hold.

"Come at me, fucker," Jesse says, taking one step closer and getting his attention off me.

"Stay back," he warns again. But if he thinks for a second I'm gonna let him hold my woman with glass to her throat, he has another thing coming.

"Look at me, baby," I call to Holly, trying to keep her here in the moment. Her eyes come to mine, and the panic behind them threatens to ruin me.

"If you fucking hurt her, I swear I'll reach down your throat and rip your fucking heart out of your chest."

"I don't give a fuck what you think you're going to do. You don't know who the fuck I am. You don't know who my father is. This fucking club could be shut down in the next hour. Now, tell me where the fuck my fucking wife is," he barks, taking a step back as I move closer.

I see Jackson come up the stairs, slowly and unaware of what he's about to walk into. Gaining his attention, I quietly signal for him to stop. I'm not sure how, but his eyes lock with mine and something passes between us—a knowledge that shit is about to go down, but we need to play it cool.

"Holly." I search her face, watching fear dance over her features. "Look at me, Holly," I instruct, the authority of my voice calling her back from the darkness. "Just keep looking at me, baby," I say, watching Jesse inch in closer. I want more than anything to just go forward, but one slip by that crazed asshole could have him slicing that glass through her neck. And that's something I will not let happen.

"Don't listen to him." Chad pulls her back, digging the glass further into her flesh. "You fucking took my wife. Tell me where she is," he repeats, pulling her harder against him. But I don't respond. I keep my gaze only on Holly. I know this is coming to an end, but I can't control my rage at not being able to help when she is less than ten feet from me.

"Sy," Holly says. I know she is slipping, but I can't go to her yet.

"Hold on, baby," I calm her, and then I see him falter. Next, I see Nix, Beau and Brooks come forward and right as Jesse walks up to him, I give Jackson the go ahead.

"Now," I shout, instructing Jesse to lunge in from the side, the attack taking him unawares. Spinning around to lash out at Jesse, he loses his hold on Holly. It feels like it happens in slow motion; the broken bottle comes out swinging between Holly and Jesse—Jesse pushing her out of the way and taking a cut to the neck. Then the opposite happens, everything moves fast. The boys jump on Chad while I try to reach for Holly as she loses her footing on the top step. Her hand comes out, reaching for me, but I miss her by an inch as she collides with Jackson and she falls backward down the wooden stairs. Running down after her, I'm left helpless as I watch her fall, tumble and land in a heap at the bottom.

Crashing down to her side, my heart beats dangerously out of rhythm when I realize she's out cold.

"Call an ambulance!" I shout to the people standing around as I feel for her pulse.

"Is she okay?" Beau collapses down next to me, checking her neck where blood seeps out.

"It's okay, baby. You're going to be fine," I promise, not knowing if it's a promise I can keep, but I make it nonetheless, praying to God he doesn't play another shitty trick on me.

44

Holly

"I WANT TO KNOW WHY MY FUCKING WIFE ISN'T WAKING up?" I hear a familiar voice pull me from a dream; a dream of meadows and sunsets and a little girl with dark curly hair running off into the distance.

"Mr. Dean, you need to calm down. Throwing your weight around isn't going to wake her up. Like I told you, her vitals are fine. She just needs some time to wake up," a woman's voice I've never heard before tries her best to calm Sy from his raging outburst.

"Sy?" I croak out, letting the small bits of light filter under my lids. *Oh, God. My head hurts.*

"Holly?" he turns, rushing forward to where I lie and takes my hand.

"Where am I?" I ask, confused for a second as I try to remember the last thing that happened.

"You're in the hospital. You fell," he clues me in while running his finger along my brow. I can tell he has been stressing by the scowl he's wearing.

"I did?" I try to remember what happened.

"You don't remember?"

"No." I strain to think, trying hard to recall how I ended up here.

"What's the last thing you remember?" he asks, searching my face.

"I don't know?" I try to figure out why my brain won't focus on the lost memories.

"What the hell is going on?" Sy turns back to the nurse, demanding an answer.

"I've already asked you to calm down. I will escort you out of the room if need be," she

scolds him and moves next to the bed.

"I'm not going anywhere." Sy stands, looking down at the small nurse.

"Can you tell me what happened?" she asks, picking up my wrist and finding my pulse point.

"She fell. I already told you this," Sy answers for me. I don't know what's happened, but things feel tense in here.

"I'm not asking you, Mr. Dean. I'm asking your wife."

"Wife?" I ask, starting to freak out. How much has happened that I don't remember?

"Do you know what day it is?" She places my arm back down and fills out something on her clipboard.

"Saturday," I answer, knowing today is Jesse's party.

"Okay, dear. The doctor will be in shortly. Everything looks fine. Sit tight," she states, smiling gently before turning a hard stare in Sy's direction.

"Thank God, you're okay, baby. I was so fucking worried." He leans toward me and kisses my forehead.

"We're married?" I ask, freaking out that I don't remember.

"No, baby. I just said that to get back here." He looks down at me sheepishly.

"I'm confused. So we're not married?"

"No, but by the sound of your disappointment, it makes me question if I should just ask you now, and not later when I can have you under me," he says, shocking me for a moment.

"Sy, don't joke around like that." I ignore my rapidly beating heart.

"No one's joking right now." He leans down in my face again. "When I saw you fall, fuck, baby, I swear to God, I felt my heart stop in my chest. You're not allowed to do that again," he says, kissing me softly.

"Oh, my gosh, I remember that guy," I explain as the memories wash over me. My hand goes to my neck, and I feel the small bandage covering my injury.

"Just a small cut, no stiches," Sy grumbles, watching me process it all.

"What happened to the guy?" My first question comes out, needing to know if everyone is safe.

"He's been taken in. The fucker screwed up big time, and after that stunt, Jackson has something to pin on him.

"Jesse?" I ask, hoping he is okay. I remember just before I fell he had stepped in on the side as the mayor's son pushed me.

"He's in the room down the hall. Just some stitches, nothing serious, but he hurt his foot in the fall. I didn't see it, too busy trying to catch you, but I heard it. Fucker screamed so loud."

"Oh, God." My hands go to my mouth.

"It's an old injury so he'll be fine. I think they're just waiting to get a scan of it to rule out any damage." I knew Jesse had an old injury which stopped him from going back to work as a firefighter, but I don't know exactly what happened.

"Am I interrupting?" a female voice asks.

"What's the verdict, Doc?" Sy asks, getting straight to the point.

"Now first thing's first; I need to ask you, Holly, are you okay if Mr. Dean stays in the room while we chat?" she inquires.

"Of course," I answer, wondering what is going on.

"Good. Okay, the CT scan came back negative for any internal bleeding, which is good, but you do have a nasty concussion and we'd like to keep you in for the night," she goes on, explaining the process of a concussion.

"Whatever you need," Sy answers for me. I have to hold in a laugh at his good boy act.

"Now, I'm not sure if the next bit of news will come as a shock, but your blood work came back positive for pregnancy," she enlightens us, watching carefully for a response.

"What?" Sy and I say at the same time.

"We'd like to do an ultrasound to determine how far along gestation is and check on the baby of course, considering your fall down the stairs," she offers, but my mind still can't get around what she's saying.

"Are you sure?" I ask, shock running through me. I knew it was always a possibility that I would fall pregnant again when we weren't using protection, but hearing it still comes as a shock.

"We'd like to confirm with an ultrasound, but by the HCG levels, then yes, I'm sure."

"Do you think the baby has been hurt from the fall?" Sy asks the question that I don't want to think about.

"Oh, God." I begin to freak out. What if something has happened? I can't handle more loss. Not again.

"Let's not get ahead of ourselves. We will get you in for a scan and then we can see what is going on in there," she tries to reassure us, but my panic rises as I think back to the last hospital visit

I had.

"Holly, it's going to be fine." Sy comes to me, taking my hand in his.

"I'm so sorry. I had no idea," I rush out, hoping he doesn't lose it. Not sure why he would, but my heart and my mind are somewhat unstable at this moment, making it hard to connect with reality.

"Nothing to be sorry about, baby." He kisses me again.

"Okay, let's get this gown up so we can see what's happening," she says as the nurse wheels in a machine, ready to start.

"Now? Here?" Sy asks, watching them get the ultrasound machine going.

"Yes, it's very easy and simple these days," she smiles, coming to stand next to us. "Now, Holly, when was your last menstrual cycle?"

"Umm…" I try to count in my head when the last time I had a period was but can't think of one. "I'm not sure. I've been all over the place the last few months." The doctor nods, picking up the wand and smearing gel all over it.

"Okay, let's see if we can pick anything up this way first, and if not, we'll do an internal." She moves to my belly. Lifting up my hospital gown, she squirts the cold gel onto my stomach. This all seems so surreal that we are here right now. I know we've been having unprotected sex, so it shouldn't come as a shock. I just didn't think we would find out like this. She moves the small rounded wand around on my belly and starts flicking buttons on the machine, letting it light up with a picture. I struggle to see the dark screen, but then she presses a button and the room fills with the soft sound of a beating heart.

"That's the baby's—"

"Heartbeat," I finish for her. She smiles down at me. "Looks like you're about nine weeks along and everything looks fine," she confirms, chasing my fear away.

"Are you sure?"

"We will monitor you for the next twenty-four hours, but everything looks good." She grabs a tissue to wipe away the sticky gel.

"I'm going to be a mom," I whisper, watching the screen and seeing the small image of our child. A healthy child. I look up at Sy, afraid this is going to ruin whatever it is we have, but instead of fear or rejection, I'm met with a look of pure joy.

"You're going to be a daddy," I announce through happy tears.

"Marry me?" he asks as a way of replying to the news.

"W-what?" I stammer, looking between Sy and the smiling doctor.

"You heard me. Marry me." He looks down at me, his expression full of hope and excitement.

"Yes," I rush out, not needing to give it a second thought. "Yes," I cry as he kisses me.

"Yes?" he asks again, obviously unsure he heard me correctly.

"Yeah, Sunshine. I'll marry you." I kiss him fiercely this time, knowing I wouldn't want it any other way.

"I love you, baby," he whispers softly.

"I love you, too," I reply, resting my hand over my belly.

"I promise you, Holly, I'm going to be the best dad there is," he assures me, covering my hand with his.

"I know you will, Sy," I agree, and he will. From just listening to the way he speaks about Keira, I know what sort of father he will be.

"I'm going to be a mom." I smile again at the unexpected news.

"We're going to be a family," he states, filling me with hope. Our journey has come full circle. There have been moments filling me with despair and heartbreak. Some days, I thought I could never move past it, but then a small moment of hope appears. It's so magical, so life-affirming that it makes it all worthwhile.

This is one of those moments.

★★★

"Thank God, you're okay," Kadence says, sitting on the end of my bed at the hospital. She came in five minutes ago, and Sy still hasn't let go of my hand to let me embrace her. I understand he's worried about me, but I'm beginning to wonder if he's going to be worse than Nix.

"I'm fine. Promise," I reassure her, trying not to come across too excited. After the doctor left us with the news, I decided I wanted to keep the pregnancy under wraps for a couple more weeks; just until I'm out of the first trimester. Sy didn't agree, but is going along with it. I'm sure he thinks I'm going to cave and let it slip, but I need to let it settle in before I share the news with anyone.

"Do you want me to call your mom?" Kadence asks, probably wondering why she isn't here.

"God, no," I rush out, thinking that would be the worst thing to do. "She will freak out and come all the way down here for no reason. I promise I'm fine." She nods, taking my word for it.

"How's Jesse?" Sy asks, letting go of my hand to come and climb into the bed with me.

"Oh, he's okay. He's been keeping the nurses on their toes." She smiles, shaking her head.

"I feel my ears burning," Jesse's voice comes from the door. *What timing.*

"Jesse, what the hell are you doing out of your bed?" Kadence rushes over to him, helping him hobble to the chair.

"Had to see this pretty girl." He reaches out to take my hand. "How you feeling?" he asks, concern filling his face and ignoring Sy's growl at his *pretty girl* comment.

"I'm good," I smile, but then remember I'm not meant to be too happy. "How are you?"

"Aww, you know, making the pretty nurses fall for me," he

smirks.

"You shouldn't be on that foot, Jesse," I scold him when I see him wince in pain.

"Please, don't you start," he complains, rolling his eyes. "I've had my father and mother on at me about it," he says, shaking his head.

"What did they say? You going in for another surgery?" Sy asks.

"Let's not talk about the foot for a moment, okay?" he asks, making me wonder if it's worse than he's letting on.

"What are you doing in here?" A small brunette in a nurse's uniform comes into the room, scolding Jesse for leaving his bed.

"Ahhh, the one nurse who is immune to my charms. Isn't that right, Nurse Bell?" He wiggles his brows at the poor woman.

"You need to go back to your room. Your mother and father are looking for you," she replies as a light blush coats her cheeks.

"I will marry you if you tell them I left," he says, which makes me laugh.

"Mr. Carter, stop asking me to marry you if I get rid of them. You're a grown man. You tell them to leave," Nurse Bell says, shaking her head at Jesse's immaturity.

"I remember you," Kadence says, coming into the conversation. "You were on when I was in here," she observes.

"That's where I know you from." Jesse slaps his hand down onto his knee, like it all comes back to him. "I swear with the attitude you've been throwing around I thought I had fucked you once and forgot about it," he responds, sending the poor girl's blush to a deep red.

"Mr. Carter, I won't say this again, you need to go back to your room." She ignores his last remark and crosses her arms. I look at her closely and watch as she tries to hide her frustration.

"Will you take me back to my room and give me a sponge bath?" he teases, knowing she's affected by him and trying even harder for a satisfying reaction.

"No, let's go," she insists, coming forward and helping him out of the chair. "You shouldn't be on your leg. You need to use the crutches," she scolds him as they walk off back to his room.

"Bye, Holly." He looks over his shoulder giving me a wink.

"Thanks for helping me, Jesse," I answer back as he leaves.

"I should go, too," Kadence says, coming to kiss my cheek. "I'm so glad you're okay. I was so worried about you." She pulls back.

"I'm good, Kadence. Thank you for coming and staying with me," I say, knowing she has Nix waiting for her outside.

"I'll come by tomorrow once you're discharged."

"She's going to be at the clubhouse," Sy adds, bossing me around again, only this time making the decisions himself. I don't comment, just let him have his say, but make a mental note to talk with him later. If he thinks he is going to wrap me in bubble wrap like Nix has done with Kadence, then he better think again.

"Yes, we will be talking later," he whispers so only I can hear. Gah, he even orders me around when I think I'm bossing him in my head.

Seriously, the man is a headache.

"Okay, say thanks to Nix," I ignore Sy as Kadence leans forward to kiss my cheek.

"Are you sure you're okay?" she asks again.

"I'm fine," I reassure her again. It's not like I don't want to tell her. I do. I want to scream it out for people to know, but something is holding me back. I need it to be just Sy and me for a small moment. I want us to get used to the news before everyone else knows.

"Okay, I'll talk to you tomorrow." She smiles and steps back. "I love you, girl." She waves before walking out the door.

"Love you," I reply and then turn to Sy.

"You wanted to tell her," he accuses, coming to sit on the side of my hospital bed.

"She's my best friend," I defend myself.

"You're the one who wanted to keep it to us. I don't mind," he shrugs.

"Well, I would like to tell my parents first," I admit, knowing if we tell anyone straight away, it will be them.

"Baby, like I said, I don't mind. Now lay back. You need your rest. I don't want anything to happen to you," he says, already fussing.

I lean back, the day catching up with me. "Sunshine," I whisper, letting my heavy eyes blink once. Twice.

"Yeah, baby?"

"You're going to be a daddy," I tell him just as sleep comes. I'm searching for a girl in my dreams. Something about her reminds me of someone and her laugh is so infectious I want to hear her again. As sleep takes me, the sunset comes into view and then I see her.

Keira.

45

Sy

"YOU HEAR BACK FROM JACKSON?" I ASK, PACKING UP THE shop after my last client for the day. I just finished my first day back after Jesse's party and I'm eager to get home to see Holly.

"Yeah, they dropped the charges," Beau says, watching me carefully.

"What the fuck?" I stop what I'm doing and look up at him and Nix.

"Nothing Jackson could do. It was out of his hands." Nix nods but I still can't get my head around it. The asshole attacked Holly in front of Jackson. In front of fifty witnesses.

"Don't fuck with me," I tell them, growing more pissed by the second.

"I'm not fuckin' with you. Why do you think I'm here?" Nix

says, resting his hip against the counter.

"The fucker almost killed my woman. Tell me how they aren't pressing charges?"

"He pleaded out, so lesser charges were laid and he walks away with a misdemeanor and community service." My blood is boiling in rage as I realize the asshole just got off for endangering my woman, my unborn child. My body moves on its own accord, dropping my shit and walking through the shop to the exit.

"Hold on, fucker," Nix says, pulling me back from my exit.

"Fuck off, Nix. The fucker is getting off. Tell me you wouldn't be fucking pissed," I say, pulling out of his grasp.

"I am fuckin' pissed, Sy. But going off half-cocked when he's just been released is fuckin' dumb. Think about it."

"All I'm thinking about is seeing that crazy fucker hold a broken bottle up to my woman's throat. Who's to say he won't give up? He's hiding behind his family's money, getting away with fucking everything while we have to fucking worry about the safety of our women." I know it's not Nix's fault, but I can't stop the pissed-off rant coming from my lips. Holly and I have just come back to a good space. Her dealing with the worry that this fucker could come back and mess with us is just too much.

"We keep our eyes open. We don't leave our women alone, and if the fucker comes at us again, we do somethin' about it. We don't go lookin' for trouble, Sy. We wait. If the fucker is dumb enough to make a play again, we'll be ready and will take him down," he says and I don't miss his hidden promise. If Chad fucking Morre comes at us again, it doesn't matter how above the law he is, we will take the fucker down.

"Holly and Kadence both have their restraining orders out on him. As far as I'm concerned, he fucks with us one more time, we take him. Until then, don't get fucked up over the fucker. He *will* get his time," he finishes as I start to calm down.

I don't like it. I'd much rather head over to him and fuck him up, but that won't get us anywhere. We need to play this out safe and make sure that if he does come for us again, we're prepared.

"Fine, but if the time comes where this goes to the next step, it's me who takes him. I don't give a fuck what's happening, I end it. You feel me?" I ask, looking at both Beau and Nix.

"We feel ya," Nix nods.

"Good, now get the fuck out. I gotta go see my woman," I tell them, looking at the clock on the wall.

"Fuck, always thinking with your cock," Beau laughs, shaking his head. "Careful, you're beginning to sound like Jesse."

"How is he anyway?" I ask, my rage calming.

"He's doing okay. Still refusing surgery," Nix answers.

"Why?"

"Fucked if I know. He says he ain't goin' through it again. Some fucked up bullshit. But we'll see how he goes. Can't even ride at the moment and his parents are on his ass, naggin' him. Anyone would think he was a teenager again."

"You know anything about that?" I ask, remembering how his parents were riding his ass the night of his birthday.

"Won't talk about it. Some bullshit about family loyalty; they don't like the club life and have no problem tellin' him."

"Well, as far as I'm concerned, the fucker is a hero. They need to back the fuck up," Beau says, flicking through one of the Ink Me tattoo books.

"You tell that to his dad," Nix says, shaking his head, knowing more than I do.

"I'll have a word with Jesse, get him to think straight. Besides he can't ride; the fucker will be going mad," I say, but knowing Jesse, he'd probably still try to fucking ride.

"We have a family dinner Kadence is putting on next week. We want you there," Nix says, pushing off the counter.

"I'll talk with Holly," I tell him, walking around flicking off the lights.

"Wasn't a suggestion. You be there. Kadence is worried about her and you keeping her locked up isn't makin' her feel better."

"Like I said, I'll talk to her. My main concern is Holly, not your woman," I warn back.

"Look at you two, so fucking pussy whipped it makes me sick," Beau accuses, coming up behind us.

"Fuck off, Beau," we both warn while still holding each other's gaze.

"You talk to your woman and I'll talk to mine," Nix compromises and I agree.

"Glad we sorted that out. Now can we quit fucking acting like pussies," Beau adds, slapping us on the back.

"Yeah, yeah, asshole, it'll be you one day," Nix accuses as we follow him out.

"Never. The day you see me handing my balls to a woman is the day hell freezes over."

"Never say never, fucker," I tell him as I lock up the shop, realizing just how far my life has changed in the last year. Never in my wildest dreams would I see myself settling down with a woman again, my child growing in her belly. Fuck me, I didn't even think I would let anyone in. Holly changed all that for me, changed the direction of my course, and if that had to happen with an exchange of my balls, I don't even give a fuck. I couldn't be happier.

"I'll remember this day, Beau," Nix warns, mounting his bike. "And when you start walkin' around ball-less, we'll all remind you how fuckin' pussy whipped you really are," he laughs and I join him. The fucker has no idea, and the day it comes, I can't wait to give him shit over it.

"So, Mom and Dad are having a family dinner next weekend," Holly says, resting against the counter watching me make pancakes the next morning. It's been ten days since her concussion and finding out about the baby.

"What sort of dinner?" I turn to look over at her. I love waking up in her place, walking around her kitchen, making her pancakes while she sits on the counter chatting.

"I was hoping it could be a 'we're getting married, Mom and Dad, oh and you're going to be grandparents too' dinner. Do you think you would like to come?" she asks, looking nervous. We've held off telling her parents for the last week, with Holly wanting to wait until she was twelve weeks along. 'The safe period,' she tells me.

"Are you asking me on a date?" I smirk, walking up and standing between her legs.

"Ha-ha, smartass," she says, squeezing my nipple. I repay the action by pinching hers back.

"You want to come out to your mom and dad at a family dinner?" I question, starting to freak out a little. *Fuck, I didn't think this through.*

"Yeah, I need them to know about my baby daddy." She smiles big at me.

"You want to feed me to your parents," I tease her softly.

"And my brother," she adds.

"Oh, shit. That bullhead brother of yours?"

"Oh, he thinks that about you, too," she smiles with a guilty smirk on her face.

"Fucking great," I sigh, not looking forward to that meeting.

"Don't worry. He's found himself a new girl. He's totally pussy whipped," she laughs, hooking my neck in her grasp as she pulls me toward her. "Kind of like you," she murmurs against my lips. I don't respond to her little bite, just take the kiss deeper and pull her closer to me. She wraps her legs around my waist, her hot pussy rubbing against me.

"You think I'm pussy whipped?" I finally ask. Her eyes are

glazed over, and her lips are red from our rough kiss. It's the second time I've been accused in the last twenty-four hours.

"Not at all," she sweetly replies.

"Holly, I'm not whipped," I tell her, stepping back out of her grasp to finish breakfast.

"No, I believe you," she says, sliding off the counter.

"What are you doing?" I ask, watching her lift her dress. She hooks her thumbs into the sides of her panties and seductively drags them down her thighs.

"Oh, nothing much, I just want to see how *not* pussy whipped you are." She kicks her panties up at me and jumps back up on the kitchen counter.

"Removing your panties isn't going to make me cave," I tell her, catching them and bringing them to my nose to breathe in her scent.

"Did you just sniff my panties?" she laughs, watching me pocket them in the back of my pants. I shrug, going back to watching her.

"Of course you didn't, 'cause you're not pussy whipped, baby," she purrs. Her voice sexy as fuck, while her fingers trail up her pale soft thigh. *Jesus.*

Her legs spread giving me the perfect view of her bare pussy. She's a temptation; I'll give her that.

"You don't play fair," I admit, forcing myself not to give in. I've got this. She won't win.

"You know, baby. If you were pussy whipped, you wouldn't be able to handle this right now." She continues to tease me as her fingers dance over her lips, spreading them to show me just how wet she is. *Fuck me.*

A growl erupts from my throat at seeing her spread out for me.

"Are you hungry, baby?" Her raspy voice all but breaks me.

"So fucking hungry," I reply, watching her fingers slide into where I desperately ache to sink myself.

"Then come and get something to eat, Sy," she all but begs. She doesn't have to ask twice. I step forward, drop to my knees, and bury my face in her sweet cunt.

Her scent invades me, intoxicating me. Her moans fill her kitchen, the cries of passion only spurring me forward. Her hands come to my head, her short nails rake along my scalp.

"Fuck, I love your tongue," she moans, her hips riding my face. Thrust and whimper, thrust and whimper. I flick, suck and nip harder, focusing on her tiny ball of nerves.

"Yes…yes…yes," she chants as her orgasm runs through her. I don't relent, pushing her further into the bliss she's living right now.

Her cries fade and her movements slow as I lazily slide my tongue up and down through her wetness.

"Again," she demands, her voice hoarse from her screams.

"You've got a greedy pussy, you know that?" I voice, looking up at her sexy-as-fuck just-orgasmed look.

"Only for you," she smirks, still in her post-euphoric state. I kiss the inside of her thigh, adjusting myself so my cock doesn't feel like it's straining in my jeans.

"I think you're totally whipped over my greedy pussy," she sasses.

"Is that what you think?"

"It's what I know," she shrugs.

"You know, I think you're right. This greedy cunt is my kryptonite."

"Well, what are we going to do about that, Superman?"

"Superman?" I laugh at her joke. "How about SuperSy," I say and I hold back my snort as I take her naked ass and throw her over my shoulder.

Fuck me, I am pussy whipped.

"Are you scared?" her voice breaks through the darkness of our room later that night.

"I'm scared of your dad," I joke, knowing she's asking about being a father, but trying to make light of it.

"You should be. He will so take you on," she giggles, but I hear the concern in her voice.

"I'm a little nervous," I answer truthfully. As much as I wanted this, now that I've had time to let it sink in, my stress levels are getting a workout.

"Me too," she admits, running her hand along her flat stomach. "I don't know what it's like for you, Sy, and I don't ever want to know, but this fear that something is going to go wrong is eating me up." She turns her head to look at me and even if I can't see her expression against the inky night, I know what I would be looking at.

"You don't need to be afraid, Holly." I try my best to calm her nerves.

"How can you say that? After everything you and I have been through?"

"I can say that because I have faith. I trust we are going to be okay. That nothing is going to happen to our child, and I have to believe that. I have to believe in the good."

"It's just hard when it has been taken away from us before," she admits and I know what she's saying. I understand it, but we can't live through this pregnancy worrying about what ifs. If we have a second chance at it, we need to take it. We shouldn't be getting lost in something we can't control. I know it's easier said than done, but we have to try, for our baby's sake.

"Sweetheart, everything good in life involves some level of risk. You have to be prepared to take a risk to achieve an amazing end. I can't promise you nothing bad is going to happen, Holly. I can't do that, but I can promise you right now if something does happen, I will do everything in my power to fight to make it right, but have some faith, baby. Have faith that we have a healthy little person growing inside of you. Know, when she arrives, she is going to be more than perfect; and believe you are going to be an incredible mother." I kiss her and run my hand over her belly.

"She?" she asks.

"Or he. I'd like to think Keira would like a little sister," I say, but I have no problem either way, as long as our baby is healthy.

"That would be nice," she smiles. "I love you, Sy." Her hand comes over mine, connecting us as a family.

"I love you, too, baby."

"Catch me."

"Keira?" I call when I hear her high-pitched laugh echoing through the field.

"Daddy, you came," she replies like every time she has come to me, but something is different this time.

"You're here?" I whisper, looking into her dark brown eyes.

"Look at that sunset, Daddy," she smiles, the breeze carrying the sweet sound of her voice all around me.

"I miss you," I say, wishing this moment was real. "Don't leave me again," I plead, hoping I can hold her again, hold her forever.

"You have to look after my baby brother, Daddy," she laughs, shaking her head, swaying her dark curls from side to side.

"Brother?" I ask as she slowly walks away from me.

"Wait, Keira. Wait for me," I panic when I can't get to her. Why can't I ever reach her?

"Bye, Daddy," she murmurs. Only this time I know it's the last time she'll visit me. She stands silhouetted against all the colors of the universe as the afternoon sun sets behind her. Her favorite place.

"Bye, baby."

Epilogue

Holly

"WHY DO WE EVEN HAVE TO BE HERE?" JESSE ASKS, COMING through the kitchen still limping on his bad leg. It's been four months since his birthday and his foot is still not back to full movement. After holding off for four weeks, the boys were able to convince him to have the surgery to try and repair some of the damage done when he fell. He did say earlier he's looking at another surgery to fix some scar tissue that could be messing around with it. Regardless, he's been cranky, moody and not the Jesse we all know and adore.

"'Cause you're gonna be an uncle, dickhead," Sy laughs at his expense.

"Where are all the chicks?" he sulks, looking out over the back decking where the current party is being held.

"Out the back," I say, pointing to all the women who have turned up for Kadence's baby shower.

"No, where are all the sexy single women? Not the Stepford moms, or the pregnant women." He looks out, trying to find someone he can flirt with.

"Keep it in your pants, Jesse," Nix scolds from his spot on the sofa. Even though it's Kadence's baby shower, all the guys are here watching the game. Being so close to her due date and the doctor putting her on bed rest due to her scarring, Nix refused to leave her alone for the event. They've been told to stay inside and not to bother the festivities happening outside. So far they've behaved, the game keeping their attention.

"This blows," Jesse groans as he gets another beer from the fridge and hobbles back to the living area.

"You okay, baby?" Sy asks, coming up behind me as I finish the final touches to the baby shower cake I made for Kadence.

"I am." I tilt my head back, smiling up at him. This is the Sy I have been living with the last few months; attentive, protective and horny. Something about my pregnant body has turned Sy into a crazed sex-maniac. Not that I'm complaining. It's a hell of a lot better than the protective Sy. Since finding out Chad got off with a warning and community service, Sy has not let me out of his sight. Even to the point of assigning one of the boys on me when I need to go to work. We haven't had any problems, but the further I get along in my pregnancy, the more Sy worries. I think Chad has given up. Finding his wife now is like finding a needle in a haystack. Even the Knights Rebels don't know where she has gone, but that hasn't stopped Sy from being vigilant. It's been crazy and maybe a little over the top, but that's the man I fell in love with. Broody, protective, loving Sy.

"You look so fucking sexy standing there, barefoot in the kitchen making a cake, with my baby in your swollen belly," he murmurs softly as his hands come over my small bump, cradling it protectively.

"You are weird, Mr. Dean," I say.

"Not weird, baby. Just in love." He kisses my neck, letting another swarm of butterflies free.

"Leave your baby momma alone, Sy," Kadence says, waddling in carrying a large gift-wrapped box. We came out about the engagement and baby right after we told my parents that we were getting married and expecting. After the shock that I was going to be a mom wore off, my dad and brother started their stupid protective routine, but Sy survived with flying colors and even won my father over. Sy's family, the Knights Rebels and Co, took it a lot better. Kadence cried in joy over the fact we're both going to be moms together and the boys were all shocked that Sy had asked me.

"Kadence, what the fuck?" Nix growls, standing to take it out of her hands. "You fuckin' know that you're not meant to be lifting shit."

"Oh, relax, Nix," she laughs, waddling to the fridge.

"Will you go fuckin' sit down?" He comes up behind her and reaches in, taking out what she needs.

"Nix, I'm fine." She shakes her head, not letting her bossy husband order her around.

"If I could pick you up and throw you over my shoulder without hurting you, I would. Instead, I'm going to take your hand and walk you back to your chair, and you're gonna plant your ass on it for the rest of the party. Do you understand me?" he growls. I can't even tell Nix off with his badass baby-daddy routine because he's right. She is so close to popping that baby out she needs to take it easy.

"Nix, quit it. I'm fin—" Her last word breaks off as her body doubles over.

"What is it, Kadence?" Nix shouts, throwing the tray of sandwiches to the table, sending them flying everywhere. At first, I think she's playing, just teasing Nix, but when I see the water leaking down her legs, I know she's not joking around.

"Ohhh, I think my waters just broke," she pants, still bent over.

"Fuck, how do we fix it?" Nix says, looking around at all of us.

"You can't fix it, you ass. It means the baby is coming," she manages to say, still struggling with some pain.

"The baby's coming? Right now?" Nix asks again, looking at us for answers. If I weren't concerned for Kadence still breathing through her first contraction, I would laugh at the big bad biker freaking out.

"Kadence, has it stopped yet?" I ask, coming forward, getting down low and looking up at her pained face.

"Nooo," she squirms. "Oh, God, is this normal?" she asks. I don't reply. Instead, I let her try to breathe through it, but counting as I go. After another thirty seconds, I look up at Sy, trying to relay that something isn't right.

"Oh, my God!" she shouts again.

"Call an ambulance," I finally say, making the decision to voice my concerns. Kadence is still leaning over and Nix stands frozen, being absolutely no help at all.

"Ambulance?" Nix finally registers what's happening.

"I don't think she can move far between the contractions. We won't get her to the car," I explain walking to the sofa and pulling off the cushions.

"She can't fuckin' have it here," he bellows out, finally realizing his biker baby is ready to make an appearance.

"Kadence, can you walk?" I ignore his freak out, zoning in on only her.

"I don't think I can." Her voice is filled with strain and panic. "Something is wrong, Holly," she cries in between moaning.

"Nix, pick her up and bring her here," I instruct, watching her struggle. I look to Sy and watch as he places the call to 911.

"Arrghh!" Kadence screams as Nix picks her up, bringing her to the floor in their living room.

"Fuckin' hell, what is going on? We need to get her to the fuckin' hospital, now," he says, placing her down on the sofa cushions.

"I'm serious, guys; this isn't normal," Kadence moans. "Something is wrong." She looks up with a pained expression and I know this isn't a drill. I can see it in her eyes.

"I don't think she's going to make it there, Nix," I tell him, moving around to help pull her panties down her legs.

"The baby's coming," she says, freaking out.

"What the fuck, Holly?" Nix asks, trying to stop me.

"Nix, I need to check her. See if she's right." I look to him hoping he understands my meaning. If the baby is coming now, we need to prepare. He must see the seriousness in my statement or see the urgency in my eyes as his expression turns from panic to fear.

"Everyone, get the fuck out," he yells, letting me continue to slide her panties down.

"Nix, get me some towels. Lots of them," I instruct when I see the blood. "Sy, how far away are they?" I ask, looking back over to where he stands.

"Ten minutes," he says from behind me.

"Oh, my God, Holly. Don't judge my hairy vajayjay. I can't see over my belly," Kadence rushes out, explaining her unkempt lady parts.

"Girl, all I can see is your baby's head. Trust me, it's the least of our worries," I assure her before looking up to Sy wondering how the hell we are going to deliver a baby.

"The head is there already?" Nix races back in, his arms carrying blankets and towels. "Sy get the fuck out of here. I don't want you to see my woman," he says, noticing Sy is still in the room.

"Nix, he can help us," I suggest, holding onto her hand to help her breathe through another contraction.

"Yeah, I've seen a delivery before," Sy says into the phone, ignoring us and focusing on what the operator says to him. I can see Nix and Kadence both look at each other before looking to me for some kind of answer to their unspoken question.

"Oh, God, I want to push," Kadence screams as another contraction tears through her.

"Yeah, she feels like she needs to," Sy replies. "Okay," he says, looking up at Nix "Nix, I'm gonna have to do this brother, unless you want to do it?" he asks, but I can see the struggle on Nix's face. It's something between fear and confusion. The poor man is a hot mess.

"Nix, come here. Get behind her," I order, trying to help him get his head around the fact that his child is about to be born on the living room floor with one of his brother's hands between his wife's legs. He moves around, sitting in behind her and links his hands with hers.

"Oh, God! It's coming," Kadence pants before letting out an almighty scream.

"Kadence, you need to stop pushing. Hold it there," Sy pauses, listening to more instructions.

"I need to push. I need to push." Kadence's voice sounds desperate as she fights off what her body is trying to tell her.

"Breathe through it, Kadence. Like you were taught in our classes," Nix says, finally coming into the moment.

"I don't give a shit what they say, Nix. This feels like someone is ripping my vagina apart." She screams as the next contraction comes on.

"Paramedics are here," Jesse calls through the front door. I can see the guests, gathering around the door, but I don't have time to worry about them right now.

"Bring them through, quickly," I say, watching as she bears down.

"Okay, Kadence. Push just a little, okay?" Sy repeats so calmly that even I find myself relaxing at his composure. She follows his instructions, slowly pushing and breathing.

"That's it, Kadence," I say, watching as the top of the head can be seen.

"Fuck, babe, you're doin' so good," Nix says, wiping away tears and kissing her head. The gesture hits me right then and there. Sy and I are witnessing our best friends deliver their child, an amazing experience and beautiful moment right here on their living room floor.

"Hello," a female and male EMT rush in right on time. "We can take it from here," she interrupts, coming in to replace Sy.

"She's almost there," Sy says, stepping back letting them have room.

"That's it, keep going, Kadence," Nix encourages, holding onto her hands as she squeezes through her final push.

"Okay, Kadence. My name is Jenny and we are about to meet this sweet little baby of yours. Give me one more push and we can get you off to the hospital," she says, spreading Kadence's legs wider.

"Oh, God. Oh, Goddd!" she screams, making me feel terrible and excited all in the space of a second.

"That's it. You're doing great. Now catch your baby, Kadence," the EMT says as she helps to pull the baby out. The sound of a baby taking its first breath of life is something I know I'll never forget.

"Holy shit," I breathe, watching her cradle her baby up on to her chest. It's one of those serene moments, like seeing love at first sight in slow motion. Tears fall from my eyes watching Nix and Kadence meet their baby for the first time.

"Are you okay, baby?" Sy turns to face me as we step back, letting them have their space.

"Yeah," I say, shocked at what we just witnessed. "I love you,

Sy. You did amazing," I say through tears, listening to the sound of their baby's crying.

"It's a girl," Kadence exclaims. "We have a baby girl, Nix."

"Fuck me," Nix curses, causing us all to laugh.

"You freaked the fuck out, Nix." I hear Jesse accuse as we walk into the hospital room. After the EMTs took Kadence and Nix to the hospital, we stayed back, cleaned up and saw everyone off. I don't know what Holly's thinking; we've both been lost in our own thoughts, but after an experience like that, I know I'm sure as fuck ready to hold our child in my arms and watch him take his first breath.

"You're here." Kadence notices us first. She sits up in her hospital bed a little taller.

"Hey," Holly greets her from next to me. "We had to clean up," she says, leaning down to kiss her. "How are you?" Holly pulls back.

"Good, feeling great," Kadence smiles and then turns her gaze to me. "Hey," she looks nervous for a second, and I realize I just delivered her baby. She might be feeling uncomfortable. I look up at Jesse and Beau, nodding at them to give us a minute.

"Come on, Z. Let's go get something to eat." They take him out, leaving us alone.

"You saved me again," she says when they leave us, and it almost chokes me up. *Who knew these people would become my family?*

"No big deal," I say, trying to shrug it off when in reality, it feels fucking good.

"It is a big deal to me," she whispers, looking down at her daughter. "Would you like to hold Harlow?" she asks, smiling. Their little girl's name is sweet and beautiful. She draws me in closer to the bed.

"Harlow?" Holly asks, smiling down at her.

"Yeah," Kadence softly replies. Lifting the small baby up, she hands her over to me, and for a minute I panic, not remembering how to hold a baby.

"You can't hurt her," Kadence says, placing her in my arms then moving away. Taking a step back, I look down at the little girl, her milky soft skin and dark hair reminding me a little of Keira.

"She's beautiful," I say truthfully, looking at Holly and seeing the same sort of emotions flick over her face. We've both seen so much pain and loss in our past; it makes today even more emotional.

"Just like her momma," Nix says, leaning down to kiss Kadence's forehead.

"You want to hold her?" I look up and watch Holly wipe a stray tear away. I want to comfort her, help her through this, but the perfect little baby in my arms makes it difficult.

"Yeah," she sniffs, sitting on the end of the bed and holding out her arms. Carefully, I place baby Harlow in her arms and step back, letting her have their own special moment.

"We wanted to ask you something," Kadence says, sitting up and reaching out, running a finger along her daughter's brow. "We would be honored if you and Sy would be Harlow's godparents," she asks, momentarily shocking me.

"Oh, my God. Yes, of course," Holly squeals in delight, stirring Harlow for a second. "Oh, sorry, sweet girl," she coos her back to sleep with a soft rock, while I watch on in awe of her.

"Sy?" Kadence asks when I don't respond.

I smile at the thought, the poor girl not only has a badass daddy, but she has me and a whole clubhouse full of men ready to protect her.

"As long as you guys return the honor for our boy," I say, giving our own secret away. I don't care if they know. It's Holly who wanted to ask them later, but now seems like a good enough time.

"You're having a boy?" Kadence squeals this time, then starts crying all over the place.

"Yeah," Holly replies, giving me a stare. "We were keeping it under wraps, but looks like Harlow already has Sy wrapped around her little finger." She looks at me accusingly.

"Not as much as you do," I tell her, leaning down to give her a light kiss.

"Smooth," Holly whispers, pulling back.

"Congrats, brother." Nix comes forward and embraces me.

"You, too." I slap his back twice before moving away.

"We would love to, guys," Kadence says, wiping at her face.

"Okay, now, get the fuck out of here. My wife and baby girl need sleep." He takes Harlow out of Holly's arms and orders us out.

"Nix." Kadence scowls but we can see how exhausted she looks. Taking Holly's hand, we say our goodbyes and leave them with promises to celebrate when Kadence and Harlow are released.

"You did good in there," I tell Holly when we walk out hand in hand down the hospital corridor and back to the car.

"So did you," she replies.

"This will be us in a couple more months. Are you ready?" She asks the big question that weighs on my mind. Am I ready? I want to say yes, that I handled holding Harlow and didn't freak out, but the truth is, I know it's going to be a whole lot different when our own baby comes.

"More than fucking ready." I pull her against me, lean down, and kiss her.

"I love you, Sy. Love you more than anything."

And I believe her because I feel the same way. She chased away my darkness allowing me to absorb her special kind of sunshine. Without her love, I wouldn't have been able to step out of the dark and see the possibility of a future. A future where the sun only shines brightly.

Coming Early 2015

Jesse's Story

Acknowledgments

Can you believe this is the second acknowledgements page? Crazytown.

Alissa Evanson-Smith: Whore… Yes, I just called you are a whore in my book. What can I say that you don't already know? It's been twelve months of friendship, and what a twelve months it has been. I wish more than anything I could just jump on a plane and bring you home with me. Why do you have to be so awesome? You are amazing, beautiful, kind, smart, funny, an amazing mom and an unreal friend. Please know my journey has been made amazing just by you alone. I owe you more than you know. Thank you for your hard work. I'd be lost without you. Love you.

Bel Burgess: Wow, you saved me, saved me something huge, Bel. You are talented. You are humble and you know your shit. I love you. I love your passion, your words, and your help. I can't begin to imagine where this book would be without you. I love working with you.

Cassia Brightmore: Lady you are so amazing. Thank you from the bottom of my heart for helping me out in my time of need. Bring on Cleveland my friend.

Gillian Grybas: Gilly Gilly Gilly. I SOLO love you so much! You make me smile. Thank you for loving Sy and Holly SOLO much. Bring on the next one, yeah?

My C.O.W.s - Alissa, Ash, Jess and Bel: this journey has been crazy this time around, now that I'm a real author. But I have always come back to our group. I'll never stop. I DUCKING love you all… **Quack!**

This Group Needs A Fucking Name: When I started this group, I had no idea how important it would be for me to finish this book. You have all embraced each other, helped each other, laughed at each other and encouraged each other. When I think about my author friends, I think of you all. I'm so happy I have you on my side and think the world of you all.

Thank you to my lovely beta readers: Cassia, Gilly, Melinda, Tammie, Jennifer, Tammy and Stephanie. Your enthusiasm for Sy and Holly really helped me finish this book.

It's been a crazy ride. Thank you for loving their story, and get ready for Jesse. I hope he is kinder to me.

Max Henry: Dude… Formatting and blurb shout out to you. You are so talented and so amazing. I love you, lady, hard. I'm inspired by you, by your words and I love your loyalty. Never change.

Nina Levine: Dude, I stopped messaging you, but now I just ask the group… hahahaa! I still think you are all class and nothing less. Thank you for being awesome.

Louisa from LM Creations: My friend, Louisa, okay, so I promised with the last book that Sy's book will be less painful… hahahaha, that was a promise I didn't follow through with, so therefore I dedicate Sy to you. Now, I know you are awesome and disgustingly talented; however, you truly are so humble, so friendly and just a good person. You love hard, laugh lots and I can feel your passion through the screen. You know I would do anything for you. I can't wait till March so I can squish you and try to make you blush. LOTS.

Becky Johnson: You are… a genius, pure genius, you take my words and you do something that only someone amazing can do. I love working with you. Your patience, your opinion and talking me down will never be forgotten. You've made this journey so smooth and I can't wait to continue working with you.

To my Rebels: WOW, we have come so far! So far. Wow, so how do you tell a group of women that you owe them? You have made this journey beyond anything I could have imagined. You are my friends, the kind you never get rid of. You make me smile daily, laugh constantly and most of all you make me happy. I love you all! #CockOn

To ALL the Bloggers: Thank you for your support. I wouldn't have been able to get my name out without you guys pimping *Incandescent*. Reviewing and loving the Knights Rebels boys just as much as I do has been so surreal to see. The whole journey has been crazy.

My Mr. Savage: We survived another one. Maybe barely and maybe with less hair, but we did it. You know, I know this wouldn't have been possible without you. You really are one of the good ones. Up there with all our favorite men we love to read about. You love me without questions. You love me at my worst and have never faltered. You own my heart and don't ever give it back. With the release of *Affliction,* I promise you to do this whole author business thing better. Thank you for being you: for getting me, for loving me. And most importantly, never leaving me. **I love you.**

An avid reader of romance and erotic novels, River's love for books and reading fueled her passion for writing. Reading no longer sated her addiction, so she started writing in secret. She never imagined her dream of publishing a novel would ever be achievable. With a soft spot for an alpha male and a snarky, sassy woman, Kadence and Nix were born.

River would love to hear from you. You can contact and/or follow her via…

Email: riversavageauthor@gmail.com
Facebook: https://www.facebook.com/riversavageauthor
Follow River on Twitter: @RiverS_Author

Want to keep up to date with all the newest news?

Come hang out with River's Rebels
https://www.facebook.com/groups/1513339432229460/

Printed in Great Britain
by Amazon.co.uk, Ltd.,
Marston Gate.